Nyifie Brothers Publishing

WINTER BREAK

JOHNNY B. TRUANT

For Sydney, who makes her father proud.

WINTER BREAK

PART I

Chapter One
MIRANDA

THURSDAY AFTERNOON

My phone dings with a new text just as I hit my first patch of black ice. The sound is like a warning: a scream announcing danger.

The little car's wheels spin for half a second — not even long enough for my heart to beat twice. By the time my pulse is racing, everything feels safe again. This is how I live, Aubrey says: always just a little bit in the past, always responding to threats only after the threat is gone.

My eyes go to my phone, nestled in the cupholder. The brightened screen tells me that I've received a photo, not a message. I wish I could be surprised. I'm not.

My pulse, which was preparing to return to normal, quickens again.

I consider ignoring it. I tell myself the photo's from Mom; she managed to get a bar or two of service up there and sent me a postcard-worthy snap of the view from the sunroom. I tell myself I'll look at it later. It's just for fun, no big deal. Nothing I *need* to deal with now. Why would I need to deal with it now?

But of course I need to deal with it now. My heart knows every-thing isn't *really* back to normal.

I check the rearview, seeing no one. I haven't passed another car in twenty minutes. And so after another quick glance at the road ahead, I slow a little and peek at the phone just like my Driver's Ed teacher told us never to do. The screen unlocks. The new image comes up, part of the same message thread from the same unknown number as all the others.

This time, my mystery correspondent has sent me a snap of what might be a gray concrete floor with table legs in the distance. Like all the other pictures they've sent me, this one is low-quality and full of grain, askew and ill-framed, as if the photographer is a surrealist or drunk. There's not much light. I'm seeing a shoddy camera — an *unusually* shoddy camera, as if the phone is ancient — do the best it can from somewhere dark and dank.

I spy a gas station ahead. It's presumably the one my parents told me to keep an eye out for, because the turnoff to the cabin beyond is easy to miss. I pull in, pretending it's because the last thing I want this far from everything is to run out of gas — *not* because these photos are giving me the creeps and I need a moment to collect myself.

I stop at a pump and take in my surroundings. The place is surrounded by trees, as if humanity here is making a desperate last stand against nature. The small building across the lot is one of those stations that's half country store. Probably where the hermits and Unabomber types who live around here do their grocery shop-ping if they don't want to make the hour-long trek into Leightonville.

I'm about to pick up the phone to look at the new image prop-erly when it rings. I jump, but it's only Aubrey. I put on a smile before answering, because Aubrey can hear facial expressions. It's weird, but true.

"So you're still communicado," she says before I can manage *Hello.*

"What?"

"The opposite of 'incommunicado.' It's a word." She pauses. "Why are you agitated?"

I feel naked, the way she can see right through me even from over five hours away. "I'm not agitated," I say.

"Of course you're agitated. I can hear it in your breath."

"You can't hear anything in my breath."

"You wanna test me, bro?" she chides. "I could tell you what you had for lunch."

There's laughter in her voice, but Aubrey never really plays around. She can pretend she just wanted to say hi, but I guarantee there's a purpose to this call. It's almost certainly to meddle — or, more likely, to try and save me from myself. Aubrey acts like she's my mother sometimes, if my mother picked secrets apart like a detective. She's assessing me right now. She's fishing for something — probably trying to see if I'm as emotionally prepared for this trip as she keeps telling me I need to be.

The pause has gone on too long. Aubrey's tone is almost guarded when she says, "What's going on? Are you mad at me?"

"Why would I be mad at you?"

"I just ... Never mind." But she sounds relieved. "You act like I'm butting in."

"You *are* butting in. You *always* butt in."

"Yeah, but it seemed for a second like you were sick of it."

"I *am* sick of it, Aubrey."

"Well, I know. But I'm so lovable that it all cancels out. Right?"

I sigh. "Why are you calling?"

"Mostly to see if I still could. Where are you?"

My eyes make a visual lap of the land. Right now, the scenery is beautiful. Some colorful leaves are still on the trees, which are tall enough to arch above the road in a micro-canopy. The snowstorm they're forecasting will be the first big blow of the year, sure to finally drop those leaves to the ground. After that ... well ... after that, it'll probably *still* be beautiful. And nerve-wracking, because I'm told the first storm in New England tends to be a bastard.

In the moment, my solitude is almost complete. There's only

one other vehicle at the station. Probably the clerk's. It's a rusty pickup truck, with chains on the tires. *Chains.* For serious snow. In my fuel-efficient import, I'm starting to feel the weather version of underdressed.

"Almost there," I tell her.

"You're already there? Jesus, when did you leave? Six? Seven?"

"We don't all sleep in until noon, A. But no, I'm not there yet. I said 'almost.' I think I've got … what? Another half hour before I'm at the cabin?"

This brings my eyes to the passenger seat, where I've turned Google's directions into a hand-drawn map. Mom warned me to do that. She says there's usually no cell service in the foothills, although with clear skies like we have right now, texts sometimes go through. Counting on GPS, though? That would be a mistake.

"How's the drive?"

"Like an Ansel Adams photo essay. Or a Bob Ross painting."

"Wait. What?"

"A Bob Ross painting," I repeat.

"Oh." She chuckles uncomfortably. "Sorry. I thought …"

It takes me a moment to understand. She didn't hear *Bob* the first time. She only heard *Ross.*

"No." I make myself laugh. "I'm talking about happy little trees."

"Oh."

There's weight in that simple *Oh* — more than usually comes with pity. The thing with me and Ross, Aubrey's made herself part of it. Recently *she's* as averse to talking about him as I'm supposed to be, as if what happened is her fault. And you know what? Maybe she *should* feel guilty. She hated when we started dating this summer, always explaining what an ass he was and how I could do better. She even invoked my parents, saying that any boyfriend I'm scared to tell Mom and Dad I've moved out of the Friend Zone is a boyfriend I shouldn't have. From Go, she's been rooting for our breakup … for my own good, of course.

"It's beautiful here, Aub," I say, trying to turn our moods around. "Mom said she was going to set an easel up in the sunroom and just sketch the entire time. I thought she was exaggerating, but now I sort of want to do the same thing."

"Maybe you should. Give you something to avoid all the awkwardness."

"I've tried. My 'happy little trees' always end up looking like blobs. Not 'happy' at all. I did not inherit the artist gene. I got all of Dad, not so much of Mom."

I shouldn't have said that. It was supposed to be a joke, but "what I got from Dad" invokes one trait in particular. They say alcoholism is heritable. It's why I almost never drink. Why one of the biggest bones of contention between my folks and me back in high school was my social life: their worries about parties, or anywhere I might be tempted. The terrible thing that lives inside my father might, for all I know, live inside me as well.

"How are you doing?" Her voice is more earnest. "For serious."

"Oh, now we're into 'for serious'?"

"For serious," she repeats.

The false smile melts from my lips. I don't really want to talk about any of this.

Not about the strange way Dad has chosen to celebrate the one-year anniversary of his sobriety — all of us hoping this time it'll stick, and that his third try will be the charm.

Not about Ross, who's stopped returning my calls and texts just like Aubrey predicted he eventually would — not that she thought it'd happen so soon, or that she'd be uncool enough to rub it in my face.

Not about the happy sticker this trip is trying to slap over my always-tumultuous relationship with my parents, or the fact that two weeks alone with them after a semester of college will be either wonderful (because they'll honor the ways I've grown up these past few months) or a powder keg (if they keep treating me like a little girl).

Lastly, I don't want to talk about the snowstorm the news has been predicting. Aubrey doesn't know about that one. When we talked all of this out before winter break began, she said I should go on my parents' weird little mountain adventure and try to make nice, but should consider her my safety valve. When Mom gets to henpecking (like she always does), I'm supposed to drive to somewhere with a cell signal and call Aubrey. When Dad starts questioning all my decisions, I should give Aubrey a ring.

It sounded like a good system while I was back at college. It still sounded good while I was at our empty family home these past few days, ostensibly packing extra gear but really procrastinating on our weeks in the woods. Now that I'm in the foothills, though, I'm noticing the system's flaws. I can see how dense the trees are up ahead, and how convoluted the land is with rolling hills and valleys. There are a few cellular repeaters on the gas station roof, but my guess is they're the only ones for miles.

Maybe the skies will clear and I'll be able to call Aubrey from the cabin, but it's more likely I'll need an hour-long round-trip drive to this place if I want to vent without being heard on the landline. And if snow comes? If it's bad enough to block us in? In that case, I won't be able to drive anywhere. It'll be the landline or nothing ... assuming the landline doesn't fail, which it might. If *that* happens, I don't know what I'll do. Just have to sit there with my parents, I suppose. With the mother who arranged every minute of my teen life and the father still fighting his demons.

The thought chills me: *Demons*.

Dad's hope is that spending his one-year AA anniversary isolated will remove the element of temptation, seeing as he blew two previous anniversaries due to social triggers. If he's away from home and his old drinking buddies, hopefully he won't be tempted ... especially since they won't bring booze with them and AirBnbs aren't supposed to stock liquor. And if we end up snowed in? Why, then it'll be even *harder* for him to get alcohol. Maybe that'll be enough to keep him from drinking.

I told Dad it's a good idea, but secretly I keep wondering if either of them has seen *The Shining*.

"Miranda?" Aubrey prompts.

"I'm all right. *For serious*."

"Just 'all right'?"

"I could lie and say I'm great, but you never like it when I insult your intelligence. Or, you know, when I insult that nosy detective thing you do."

"So ... still nothing from Ross?" She sounds like she's afraid of setting off a bomb. "He *still* hasn't called or texted you back? Not about anything?"

"What 'anything' is there? I just want a response."

The doom leaves her voice, turning her back toward the happy side of low-grade bipolar. "I thought maybe he'd have an excuse for not returning your texts. Like he got in a car crash or something." Then: "No? I'll just have to keep hoping."

"It's probably nothing," I say.

"You know. *Hoping* he gets in a car crash."

"I get it."

"But if I could be serious for a second—"

"You? Serious?"

"It's just that Ross isn't who you think he is. He's a liar. In fact, I found out just yesterday that—"

"AUBREY."

She stops.

"We've been through this," I say, stopping short of adding ... *and I'm tired of it.* I've been hearing since we started dating that Ross was an asshole, but that wasn't news. In high school, I always sort of liked him *because* he's a scoundrel. Aubrey doesn't like that answer, though. She's doubled down on her protective, anti-Ross trash talk over the past week, probably to push me quickly into hatred in case he comes crawling back.

"Miranda ..." Aubrey says.

"He's just been too busy to get back to me. That's all this is."

"He's been too busy to *text his girlfriend back?* For *three days?*"

"Hey. Life happens."

"Honey," Aubrey says. "I love you, but take the hint already. Some people are just emotionally immature. This is how immature people break up. They just stop engaging and wait for you to assume it's over."

I rub my forehead. I can't believe that's the answer. Ross and I are too new to end like this. We get along great, having spent years as acquaintances before we started dating. Before all the ghosting, I'd privately begun to think he might be the Love of my Life.

"He can't just leave me hanging. He wouldn't. Maybe he lost his phone."

"Mmm-hmm. So why did he answer *me* when *I* texted him this morning?"

"He answered you?" No, wrong question. "Why were *you* texting Ross?"

"For you," she says.

"You were meddling."

"Of course I was meddling."

"Well, what did you say?"

"I don't know. *Stuff.*"

"And he answered you?"

"In like two seconds. But it's not just me. Carla, Doug, Cassie, Ambrosia ... He's texted all of them since he stopped texting you."

It feels like someone stepped on my heart. The skies, already dim, seem to darken. I don't want to think about this right now — not with two weeks of crazytown parenting ahead of me. Not with Dad puttering around restlessly the whole time, trying to forget the way alcohol stills his torments before stirring up new ones.

"*Just ...*" I trail off, unsure how to justify my way out of this but badly needing to. I need *something* to hold onto as I go into the next two weeks. *Anything.*

Aubrey must hear the desperation in my voice — the need for some hope, or good news. "*Just* what? What is it?"

"I need you to do me a favor."

"Anything. You know that."

"I need you to let me pretend there's an explanation for what's going on with Ross. Let me pretend I'm just being silly, worrying about the way he's ghosting me. Let me believe he'll text me back any minute now. I can't ..." I stop again, unable to say it aloud: *I can't face the fact that it's really over. Not now. Not yet.*

Aubrey almost rebuts me, then half-sighs. "Sure, believe whatever you want. He probably got too busy to call you back. For three days now. That could happen."

"Or he lost his phone."

"Or he lost his phone," Aubrey repeats, even though she just told me he texted her back this morning.

I know I'm deceiving myself. I know Aubrey doesn't believe what she's saying — not for a second. She's never liked Ross. The first time I looked into his eyes and he stared back into mine, I glanced over at Aubrey, and she was already wrinkling her nose like she smelled a rat. She hasn't tried to break us up. That would be crossing a line. What she's done is tried hard to talk me out of him. Ross is like smoking to Aubrey: a bad habit her best friend picked up and needs to kick ASAP for her own good.

"But Miranda? If we're going to play pretend, you need to do something, too."

"What?"

"Stop trying to call him. Stop texting him. You've already left messages. Anything more is just embarrassing yourself."

"But what if he wants to explain?"

"Then he'll be the one to get in touch. Not you. In fact ..." She trails off, thinking.

"In fact what?"

"Well, I sort of think you shouldn't answer if he *does* call."

"But ..."

"Seriously. You're too reactive. Can *we* just talk a few more times before you talk to Ross?"

"We're talking right now."

"*Talk* talk," she emphasizes. "Me and you. For real. I'm not saying don't talk to him *at all*. I'm just saying don't talk to him *yet*."

"But—"

"If he gets back to you and says he wants to talk, call me first."

"Why?"

"Just promise, okay?"

I sigh. I suppose it's better to have helicopter friends than friends who don't care, but at some point, Aubrey and I will need to chat about this overprotective thing. I'm a big girl. I appreciate that she has my back, but I can stand on my own two feet.

"Fine," I say. "I promise I'll talk to you before I talk to him."

She exhales as if she's just scored a deceptively important victory — one that almost tipped the other way. "Okay. Thanks."

I kill the car's engine, sending Aubrey from the car's system to the phone. I pick it up, tell her to hang on, then start fueling. When I come back, my phone's Messages icon — reminding me about that newest strange photo — catches my eye. It makes me cold.

"Aub," I say, lowering my voice as if anyone could overhear in all this wilderness. "Have you ever had someone send random pictures to you?"

"What, like dick pics?"

"No. More like ... I don't know ... totally random stuff."

"I'm going to need some help here, Miranda."

"I keep getting pictures from someone I don't know. They're of, like, a dark building somewhere."

"Someone you don't know is sending you pictures of a building somewhere," she says in her *I-just-want-to-make-sure-I've-got-this-straight* voice.

"Well ... just ... *Ugh*, hang on."

I pull the phone away from my face, then forward her the photos. There are five of them now, sent over the past few days. The number is visible, but a reverse search told me nothing about who it might belong to.

One photo shows a dark red toolbox under a bench in the distance, covered in cobwebs. One shows nothing but different shades of gray — the kind of thing you get when you accidentally take a picture inside your pocket. Two seem to show the legs of furniture, maybe a table and maybe a chair, with the ends of frayed blue rope visible nearby. The last shows the most: wooden walls and a window to the outside that's either boarded over or shuttered.

"Why would anyone send these to me?" I ask.

"Hang on. I didn't get whatever you're sending yet. It says you're typing."

At the top of my screen, a progress bar indicates the photos are still being sent. My gas tank is full, the transaction is completed, and I'm back on car audio by the time Aubrey finally receives what I sent her. That's what I have to expect for the next few weeks:

glacially slow communication with the outside world ... if there's communication at all.

"Okay," she says three minutes later. "I got them. So ...?"

"Well, isn't it strange?"

"Text whoever-it-is back. Tell them they're sending to the wrong number."

"You think it's a wrong number?"

"Of course it's a wrong number. Happened to me. Some lady thought I was a man named Clarence. She kept texting me about an upcoming visit, so I texted back the word 'Obama' over and over until she went away."

"I thought you were supposed to tell her she had the wrong number."

"That's the boring way to do it. The way *you'd* do it."

"I already texted whoever-it-is back," I say. "A few times."

"And?"

"No answer. Just more pictures."

"So it's someone stupid. Ignore them."

"Don't you think these pictures are ... I don't know ... *weird?*"

"Weird how?"

I don't answer, thinking instead. Truth is, I'm not actually sure *how* they're weird — just that they are.

With the engine running and our call on speakers again, the phone is free for me to fiddle with. I look through each of the pictures, disquieted in a way I'd never be able to explain. They just feel *strange* to me: so quiet and lonely. They're like those pictures you find online of so-called "liminal spaces": abandoned malls from the 1980s, playgrounds without children where everything's rusted into a still-life.

I can't explain why the pictures I've been sent feel vaguely ominous, but they do. As if they weren't sent to me by accident, but are instead an odd, unspoken taunt. Or a threat.

"If they're weirding you out, block the sender," Aubrey says.

"I could." But I haven't. And *that's* something I can't explain, either: Despite the way the photos bother me, I can't bring myself to shut them off.

"Look, hey, I've gotta run," Aubrey tells me. "I just wanted to check on you before I went to work."

"Thanks. Consider me checked."

"Call if you need me, M. *Whenever* you need me. Call if your parents are being stupid, or the boredom's getting to you, or ..." She trails off, but the last condition hangs in the air anyway: ... *or if it finally dawns on you that Ross dumped your ass, and the sadness starts to crush you.*

"Sure."

"And remember: If Ross tries to call, call me first."

I try not to roll my eyes. "I remember."

We say goodbyes and hang up. After that it's just me again, all by myself in the car. With Aubrey's voice gone, I'm suddenly more than lonely.

Alone in the world, maybe.

Aubrey's my best friend, but I keep a small circle. Truth be told I've never really been able to count on my parents — not in the same way most kids can. Ross was supposed to be the tiebreaker: proof that as self-reliant as I've had to be most of my life, at least *one* person beyond Aubrey would always love me, always have my back.

I sigh and look ahead. Somewhere up there I'll turn down a dirt road, and after a handful of turns and switchbacks, I'll reach the cabin my parents rented for us to spend winter break together. To reconnect, while Dad does his very best to heal — for good this time.

I'm expecting the visit to be terrible, but maybe that's unfair. I'm an adult now, same as them. Maybe we'll start new, the way Mom keeps hinting. Maybe it'll be great, and I'm wary for nothing.

I put the shifter in drive, but before I pull my foot from the brake, my phone chirps again. It's another photo from my strange, anonymous correspondent ... and unlike the pictures before it, this one chills me for a reason I can easily explain.

It's the first shot with a person in it — a partial person, because I can only see what might be part of a leg. Maybe a foot. It's hard to tell because the camera is poor, there's not much light, and the photographer's perspective is strange. It's almost like they're lying on a floor made of rough wooden planks.

There's something dark, gnarled, and disgusting — like a steak that was shredded by an animal, then burnt black on the stove — in one corner of the foreground.

And the floorboards are covered in blood.

Chapter Two

I consider calling Aubrey back after getting the latest picture. *And* alerting authorities of some sort, although way up here in the hills I'll bet "authorities" means two drunk rednecks.

But then logic descends. It's just a photo. From someone who refuses to even identify themselves. If this is a cry for help, why not say so instead of ignoring my questions and continuing to send pictures? That tells me this could be anything: maybe a joke, maybe proof-of-concept snaps from a low-budget horror film. In either of those cases, the police won't care. They'll tell me to call back when something happens in the real world.

And Aubrey? Aubrey's an overprotective bloodhound. Alarming her won't just make her worry; she'll also skip work to begin a Sherlock-Holmes-worthy investigation that will totally consume her. She's already too preoccupied with pestering Ross on my behalf — not that I asked or even want her to. I can't add some random weirdo's idea of hilarity to her plate.

I delete the thread instead: Out of sight, out of mind. My iPhone asks if I want to block the caller, but I decline. Blocking would be putting my head all the way in the sand, whereas deleting only puts my head in the sand partway. On the off chance this *is* somehow cop-worthy, I've closed my eyes instead of cutting the lines.

I wait after I'm finished, somehow expecting a text protesting what I've done. Of course nothing happens.

A light breeze rustles the thinning leaves. The sound is hollow. It strikes me again how isolated I am — how completely and totally alone. I almost don't want to leave the gas station. There's at least someone in there: a fellow human being who knows enough about these parts to have chains on their tires.

"Right," I say for nobody to hear. "Let's go, then."

But I can't. I won't. Something about the drive so far has filled me with nerves and negative anticipation. I felt so brave when I left, but now my bravery is in shambles. I can't stop thinking of how estranged my family has seemed this past semester. It makes me unable to face them. Why did I leave the house so early this morning? I was trying to get ahead of the weather, but now I'm here with hours of daylight remaining. I'm already arriving a full day ahead of schedule. Do I really need to arrive in time for lunch, too?

I go into the station. There are tables, so I sit at one. I have my laptop, and although there's no wifi, I can still write. I do. I get ahead on a post-break paper. I add to my journal. Anything to pass the time and delay my arrival.

Hours later, I find myself 45 minutes from sunset with no excuses remaining. I need to leave if I want to get there before dark. The clerk has been watching me forever despite my constant buying of coffee, wondering why the hell I've stayed so long in the middle of nowhere. So I return to my car, consult my hand-drawn map, and pull back onto the tiny highway.

The turn ahead isn't as difficult to find as I figured, though the name of the road feels like an omen: *Hard Luck Lane.* It's the last turn I'll make, and yet Mom said there's still a half-hour to go.

The driveway to our rental is past an oversized black mailbox with *2412 - THE GIBSONS* written on it. Even after the mailbox, the driveway forks twice, making me wonder if this is still an actual road. But then I remember that the property is like a little estate: lots of land and a few outbuildings. The first jut terminates at a small barn we've been told is temporarily devoid of animals. In summer months, the owner keeps goats and donkeys there. The second split leads to the main cabin on the left and a smaller utility building to the right. Dedicated power and phone lines are the only blight to otherwise pristine natural splendor.

And it *is* splendid. I'll give the place that.

The areas around the buildings and the small, internal roads on the property are the only places where nothing grows. Deciduous and evergreen trees carpet the undulating slopes in equal number, leaving a mix of acorns and pinecones to crunch beneath my tires. There are even syrup taps in some of the maple trees, stretching out from the driveway in an almost perfect straight line. In most places the trees interlace overhead, creating a fairy-tale landscape beneath. Evening sunlight — the last of it, with sunset mounting in the southwestern sky — streams through the gaps like yellow daggers, each made solid by the dust my car has churned from the road.

There's a massive valley ahead, past the main cabin. From photos, it seems we're perched above a river. The view is a punched hole in front of me, where tree cover gives way to a broad expanse of gold sunlight against the darkening blues of evening.

I'm lost in thought — spellbound by the view, maybe — when something shoots across the driveway in front of me.

It comes out of nowhere, making me scream. It's past in a blur: something brown and large, angular up front and solid and round at the rear. Only once it's past — in the split second before the next thing happens — does my brain pattern-match and tell me it was a deer. It came very close. *Very* close to my bumper.

But before I can exhale, a second thing crosses my path, smaller but still large, upright instead of low like the deer. I can't pattern-match this one right away because everything is happening too fast. Adrenaline pours into my blood, cranking all my senses. I'm amped up, the scream from when I nearly hit the deer still on my lips. This second scare is a low blow, startling me after I'm already startled.

Dad, says something inside me, but the word is just a blip: a squirt of thought disconnected from everything like a song stuck in my head. There's no logic or cognizance. I feel fear and my mind chatters. Nonsense comes in a flood.

Dad. Mom. Ross. Drunk? Deer. Death.

And then my brain shows me a flash — an image, not a word — of a rough wooden floor soaked with blood.

I slam the brakes. Whatever-it-is hits my bumper, the whole of it seeming to lurch toward me on impact. I'm sure I've annihilated it. That forward motion I've just seen is the large-body version of a bug's splat on my windshield.

Then time returns to normal. I realize only a second has passed, or maybe less than a second. Adrenaline haze, always a short-lived phenomenon, begins to wane ... and then I can see again. I can think again. My brain reaches back, analyzing the last handful of seconds.

I saw a deer. And then I saw ...

"Dad?"

Because it's my father I've hit with my car, though only lightly. My brain exaggerated the impact while it was amplifying everything else. I didn't slam into him with my front bumper, and he didn't splat against my hood. It was more like a love tap — a quick two-handed shove to the midsection.

He looks to my left, stopping in his tracks. I follow his gaze and see the white tail of the deer I almost hit disappearing into the undergrowth. There's a flash of color, as if it's got something tangled in its antlers. Then, just as quickly, it's gone.

I put the car in park, open the door, and rush to my father.

It takes a beat for him to truly see me. Until then his head is still mired in whatever strange chase I've just interrupted: Dad running after the deer, a big plumber's wrench in his hand.

Then his head turns, and he smiles as if this is entirely normal.

"Miranda!"

He hugs me, but my arms don't raise at all. His hug is like something one person does to restrain another. I feel the heavy steel of the wrench he's holding tap my back. Then he pulls away and must finally see the WTF all over my face.

"You okay?" He's heaving with breath.

"Of course I'm okay. Are *you* okay?"

"I'm great. Peachy." His eyes dart back the way he came, furtively, as if there's something there I shouldn't see. "Did Mom tell you I started running? Best shape of my life."

I stare at him for a long time. Then I say, "This is where we acknowledge that I just hit you with my car."

He shakes himself off, still trying to recover his breath. I think I broke up an all-out sprint. "Did you? I think maybe I just slapped the hood. You surprised me, was all."

"I surprised you?"

"Well, yeah. I didn't think you were coming until tomorrow." Again he looks forward, where the deer went, then backward, from whence he came. "But that's okay. I think we're ... uh ..."

He stalls out, looking for words.

"I didn't want to fight traffic coming out of New York on a Friday," I tell him. "I sent you both a text. Didn't you get it?"

Dad, still out of breath and holding that big wrench, keeps acting like all of this is everyday. "Not much service up here, sweet-heart. Didn't Mom give you the landline number? The landline's still working. For now."

"Are we going to talk about why you were out here chasing a deer? I could have killed you!"

"Oh, I saw you. I just thought I could get by in time. No harm done."

"Dad!"

"I'm fine. What, do you want a doctor's note?"

"And the deer?"

"It ran through the clothesline. Caught one of your mother's sundresses on its antlers. I thought I could catch it, but I guess not."

I turn my head, but of course the deer is long gone. "You thought you could catch a deer."

"Yeah." Still short on breath. "I've been getting in shape since you left. Turns out having kids in the house makes you fat."

He says it with a smile, but it's a strange smile — as if he's not telling the whole truth. He just keeps standing in front of my car's idling engine the way I used to stand in front of the cookie jar I'd raided, hoping nobody would ask what I had behind my back.

For the first time in years, I really look my father over from head to toe, seeing all of him. I spent so much time as a kid trying to see only the good parts. When Dad's sober, he's the sweetest man in the world. Good to his wife, his daughter, and the people around him. Those were the parts I allowed myself to see, but there were bad parts, too. Those parts I turned away from, when I could.

He's thinner now than when I left for college. I can see some of the muscles in his forearms — even some of the veins. But it doesn't strike me as healthy, the way Dad looks. Instead, he's lean and wiry. Tough, like beef jerky. It's an uncomfortable look, like he's dehydrated and sleep deprived. The usually water-fat flesh of his face has receded, bringing prominence to his eyes. They sit too deeply in their sockets, weary and red.

"Come over here, little girl. Give your old man a *real* hug."

So we hug properly this time — in front of the car, his chest still heaving. When we separate, I sniff the air around him. I don't know why I'm doing it until I realize it's instinct. I'm seeing if I can smell liquor on his breath. *Out here chasing wildlife like Tarzan? Obviously, he's drunk.*

But he's not. The air is clear. All I smell is pine. In the background, so constant I didn't hear it until now, is a brown-noise drone that can only be river rapids or a waterfall in the valley below.

Dad smiles at me, looking me over to see if I've changed as well. I suppose I have. I haven't gained the Freshman Fifteen, but I've definitely gained the Freshman Ten. It's weight I now feel I should have had all along. I used to try so hard to be perfect ... by someone else's definition. Ever since starting school at Fordham, I've tried instead to simply be me.

"Park by the fence rail," he says, pointing up the driveway. "But before you come inside, do yourself a favor and look out over the bluff. The view will take your breath away."

"Okay," I say. "Hop in, stranger. My dad told me never to pick up hitchhikers, but you strike me as an upstanding gentleman."

"I'm not done with my run, Miranda. I'll ... uh ... meet you inside."

He's on a run. Because *that's* what this is, chasing deer through the woods.

Instead of lingering, Dad sprints ahead of me: full tilt toward the cabin. The whole time, he yells for my mother as if to alert her, shouting *Willa, Willa, Miranda's here already; we'd better clean up our messes and get ready for dinner.*

Chapter Three

As I watch Dad run toward the cabin, I decide he's up to something. Or more accurately, *they're* up to something. It doesn't explain why Dad was chasing a wild animal, but it does explain the way he ran ahead of me so he'd reach the cabin first, shouting to Mom.

I drive slowly, obeying my instincts. Dad was right; I'm a day early, and because of it, I'm catching them by surprise. I already saw Dad playing Wilderness Man, and I'd rather not see Mom doing whatever it is she might be doing up ahead: the reason Dad's in such a hurry to get to her fast, so she has time to hide whatever she wants to hide.

Maybe Mom's busting loose, dancing like nobody's around ... because up until now, nobody was.

Maybe she walks around the house naked when they're alone. Maybe it's a sex thing. The idea's a little gross, and if that's what it is, I'd rather not find out.

So I drive slowly, catching my parents' silhouettes through the windows as my tires crunch gravel on the driveway. At first, they seem to be talking animatedly — maybe even having an argument. Then I see Mom rushing around, as if to clean something up. Dad disappears and then quickly reappears outside: a flash of hair visible for a second before he vanishes behind the shed. I want to shout out when I arrive, to tell them to take their time. Whatever it is they're so eager to keep me from seeing? Believe me, I'm in no hurry to see it.

Most of the commotion is either over or invisible by the time I park and open my door, but I still take my time and circle around the cabin to see the view as Dad suggested. Better safe than sorry.

Just beyond the parking area is a short path leading down to a rock-built fire pit with the remains of a recent fire at the bottom. Adirondack chairs circle the pit, while a low split-rail fence guards the whole of it. Beyond the fence is a steep, verdant hill leading to a drop-off.

Dad wasn't just spouting cliches. The view almost literally takes my breath away. Far below is a winding river. The soporific sound of rushing water fills the air. Most of it seems to be coming from my left, around the other side of the cabin. I'd bet anything it's a waterfall.

For a while I just stand there and breathe. *In* with the stillness and *out* with the tense, toxic city air clogging my lungs. The tension in my jaw and shoulders relaxes as the grandeur of the place seeps into me. I'm already having trouble remembering my worries.

The boyfriend who seems to have broken up with me.

The weight of just-completed college exams, grades still unknown.

The pressure to perform, to maintain my scholarships.

Dad's sober anniversary. Mom's constant meddling.

Isolation. The sense of being cut off and alone — helpless.

Unspoken expectations, even now.

Photos sent by an unknown sender, ominous in nature.

The wind gusts. I pull my sweater tighter around me, wondering if I should have brought warmer clothes. It's been temperate in New York throughout early December, throwing off my sense of which wardrobe is appropriate. The unseasonable weather was supposed to end today, though, and now that I'm outside, it's clear it has.

My mind returns to the black ice I hit on the way up — just before the gas station, then again a few times on Hard Luck Lane. I suppose it's below freezing, but the way the sun shone most of the day fooled me. My mind goes to the coming snowstorm. Of course it'll snow, and of course I'm not ready. I drove six hours north today. Just the latitude dropped temperatures twenty degrees.

The sun is almost down, but the chill is coming fast as darkness arrives. I'd normally sit down and watch the sunset, but I'm too damn cold.

I look to the cabin. As the sky outside dims, the light inside seems brighter and brighter. I'm lower than floor level down by the fire pit, so my view is all ceilings. Sometimes I see the top of a head pass by, but now those movements have lost the urgency of before. Now, they're almost casual.

I can go inside, I think. Whatever they wanted to hide should be hidden by now.

I enter to find my parents standing in the middle of the cabin's main room with their hands clasped in front of their waists, weird smiles on their faces. They look like a welcoming committee. And I think: *Yep. They were up to some shenanigans.* Mom's hair is all loose ends, as if she's just gathered it from sexy waves into a maternal bun. Instead of making them look nonchalant, the deliberate casualness of this little scene makes them look guilty.

"So you're early!" says Mom. She hitches, then moves forward. Our hug is awkward.

"Yeah. I nearly hit Dad with my car."

"You did?"

Dad takes over. "You remember — that buck got your dress hooked on its antlers?"

Mom is worse at this than Dad. She's not hiding her discomfort well at all. It's clear I messed up a romantic evening. She's embarrassed, trying to write it off like nothing. Her eyes keep darting all over the place. She wrings her hands. She stutters when she talks, as confused as someone with early-stage dementia. I feel sorry for her, so I pretend none of this is happening enough for both of us.

"This place is beautiful, Mom. Amazing."

"It is? Oh, yes. Of course. You saw the view?"

"I did. Dad told me not to miss it. How about a tour?"

Relieved, Mom smiles and takes my hand while Dad heads back outside — maybe to have another crack at the supposed deer-thief, or maybe for something else.

Mom shows me the sunroom, where her easel and sketching supplies are set up facing a picture-window view of the valley. She shows me the porch, which is all breadth and splendor. The place was built log-cabin style, or at least to appear that way. The inside is rough-cut logs around an open, two-story living room. One bedroom and bath flank the space, while two other bedrooms are up a narrow flight of stairs.

Back in the open kitchen, Mom asks if I'd like anything to drink. It's testament to the disorderly state of my mind right now that I assume at first she means a cocktail. I'm nineteen. Is this how progressive they've become — willing to see me not just as capable, but old enough to offer alcohol?

But of course she means water, Coke, or iced tea. Given Dad's anniversary, there's not a drop of liquor in the house.

We sit across from each other at the kitchen table. The few incandescent lights are probably meant to create a cozy atmosphere, but I wish everything was brighter. Outside, it's nearly dark. I'm already feeling the creep of claustrophobia, as if the roof is too low, the walls too close, the box of old home life already binding me like a straitjacket.

We sit and we sip. Outside, I see the swing of a flashlight as Dad putters in a big thermal coat, doing God knows what.

"How long have you been up here?" I ask.

Her eyes are on the window. On Dad's flashlight outside. It takes a beat before she snaps her head toward me, realizing my question was for her.

"What? Oh. Four days?"

"The place really is amazing," I say. "In the morning, you guys will have to show me around."

"I just showed you around."

"I mean the grounds. I saw there's a barn?"

"Yes, but nothing's in it. I'd prefer we didn't disturb the barn."

"I don't want to disturb it, Mom. I just want to peek."

"Still," Mom says.

"I thought I heard a waterfall."

"Oh. Yes. There's a stand-alone porch that overlooks it. You'd like it out there, if it's not too cold."

"Has it been? Cold?"

She shakes her head. She's still distracted. I wish she'd just let it go. *I'm here now, Mom. And believe it or not, I can actually handle things these days. I'm not a little kid anymore.*

"Not until today. Today it got cold."

"Maybe we can take a walk in the morning."

"Maybe," says Mom.

"Looks like a lot of land. I saw a shed out there, too?"

"Well, yes, but everything other than the cabin is all locked up. Owners' places."

This makes me look at what must be a pantry beside the garbage can in the kitchen. It has a code lock, bearing a sign: *Owner's Closet.*

"This must have been expensive, Mom."

"Oh, it's not too bad."

"And for three weeks. I could have just come home, you know."

Mom waves a hand. "It came highly recommended."

That's not really an answer. My eyes flick around the room, including a glimpse through the window where pole-mounted lights mark the far-off barn and the equipment shed to one side. I'm confident of my assessment that this place is too expensive. Growing up, money was always tight. *Always.* I managed a few academic scholarships, but tuition is steep.

Mom must see the questions on my face, because something melts on hers: one line of defense finally dropping.

"The truth is, your father's drinking took a heavier toll on our finances than you'd think. Two times he drank away all of our disposable income. It even took a chunk out of retirement. We got used to living that way. We had to budget for all his drinking because otherwise we'd fall behind on the mortgage."

I feel my heart sink, both with sympathy and because she's saying this to me at all. My parents were always closed books about anything they saw as "personal matters." Her honesty now is disarming. Maybe she's actually seeing me as an adult. Maybe things really have changed.

Mom's dour face snaps into a smile. "But now it's better. Now he's on the wagon, and all that budget's freed up. I didn't let it get reabsorbed. I started a savings account. I set it aside. A lot of it went to pay your tuition..."

"Oh, Mom, I really don't like the idea that—"

She waves it away. "*Stop*. We have the money, even if it's tight. You're our shining light. Our biggest and best investment."

My smile is two sizes too small. She's trying to flatter me, but I hear only pressure. I used to work for perfection back home, to please them. I thought I'd gotten away from that, able to finally loosen up a little and be someone other than just Willa and Mark's daughter. She's just reminded me, though, that nothing's changed. They're scraping the bottom of the barrel to pay my tuition ... so I'd for damn sure better get A's and fly straight.

I look over my shoulder to assure myself Dad's still outside. I don't see his flashlight anymore, but he hasn't come through the front door.

"How's Dad doing, Mom? Really."

"He's fine, hon. He's your dad, like always."

I sit up a little straighter. I'm used to demurring to my parents, but I told myself that if I was going to spend two weeks with them this winter, I'd stop biting my tongue. So I push just a little bit.

"He was always Dad. But ... *Mom*. 'Dad' wasn't always himself."

"He did his best."

Guilt. Passive aggressiveness. I dodge and weave all of my mother's best tricks like Neo dodging bullets in *The Matrix*. "Of course he did. But he was sick. I'm just asking if he's actually better."

Another of those micro-resets happens on her face. It's satisfying to see. This is like unlocking a series of barricades one at a time.

"I think so," she says. "You know he's always struggled. Two times before now, he made it almost to a year."

I nod. Officially, I was oblivious about all of this. Officially, I never even knew my father was an alcoholic. But in truth, I understood everything. These were the secrets we carried.

"You know how he is about ceremony. He has to mark every milestone. I think that when it came to his condition, those milestones worked against him. He'd want to celebrate by drinking. Maybe it was self-sabotage. But." And here, I see another layer unlock: my mother preparing to be more real with me than ever. "But he's been going to therapy this time, Miranda. *Therapy. Your father.*"

I'm as shocked as she seems to think I'll be. "For how long?"

"Since the first day of his sobriety. It was a package deal. I..." She struggles for just a second, wipes her eyes, then continues. "I told him I'd been burned twice. I didn't believe him when he said he was committed this time. That this time was somehow different. I told him I couldn't take it anymore. I told him I had to make a hard choice this time. I ... I was going to leave him."

Now I'm the one to blink back shock. I keep surprising tears at bay, and nod for her to continue.

"He begged me, Miranda. It was hard to see. So we made a deal. I said he had to see someone. Not just AA, though he had to do that, too. I wanted someone to help him understand the thing that keeps making him sabotage himself. The thing that's actually making him do this, other than the disease."

The way she put that is strange. It makes me think that "the thing that keeps making him sabotage himself" is something specific, not a general concept. I want to ask, but I don't. Whatever terrible secret my father's hiding is his business alone.

"And he's actually been *going* to the therapist?" I ask instead.

She nods. "Every week at first, then every other week. He's *still* going. This is actually the first appointment he'll miss, because we're here."

"So you think it'll stick this time?"

She gives me a wan, broken smile. "We'll see, won't we? Sunday's his anniversary. Three more days. There aren't any meetings up here, but he talked to his therapist and they both agreed that for Dad, this was even better. I'm not taking him at his word, though. I did that for too long. He gave his doctor permission to talk to me, so I did. And the doc told me that yes, this *was* a good idea for Mark. Get him away from his usual stressors. Get some fresh air. It's better than a meeting. The way your father is about anniversaries, making a big deal about his one-year anniversary *while at an AA meeting* might actually have worked against him."

"But things look good?"

Now her smile becomes genuine. "Better than good. *Great.* That's a new man out here. I think he's always been a woodsman — just without the woods. He's been running the trails every day since we got here. And then—"

Suddenly Mom hits a wall. She stops smiling and her face changes, as if she's just remembered there's more to this story. To me, her new expression puts what she just said into past tense: *He WAS better than good. He WAS great. I WAS confident he was a new man ... until something came along to ruin it all.*

"Then *what?*" I ask. "Did something happen?"

"No, no," she says. Her smile returns, but it's fake this time. "He's sober. That's what matters."

I consider prying, but I've done enough of that for now. This is clearly a sore spot. She's just twice burned, like she said. I don't blame her for feeling uncertain no matter how much self-work Dad has done.

"Well, there's no booze up here, right?"

My sorta-joke drops the worst of the worry from her face.

"True," she says. "He won't drink before January whether he likes it or not."

We half-laugh, but what she said strikes me as far from certain. Even if it snows, the father I know wouldn't let vehicular peril stand between him and liquid salvation. He's certainly never let it stand in his way before, having celebrated the failure of his first sober attempt in the emergency room — not because he got hurt, but because his drunken fists did the hurting.

The cabin door opens behind us. Dad enters wearing a big coat and a stocking cap, announcing just how damn shitting cold it is outside. Despite myself — despite the darkness and the claustrophobia and Ross and my strange texts and all this discussion about the fragile balance of sobriety — I laugh.

And Mom, though hers still sounds on-edge, manages a laugh as well.

This will all be okay. My parents are better now. The tension I felt? It's already easing.

"That chili ready yet, Willa?" Dad asks. "I'm starving!"

Chapter Four

I somehow forget I've got my phone tucked into my leggings. I only realize once I'm in the bathroom, when I have to pull it out and set it on the sink. Once I'm washed up, it seems the perfect time to sit on the edge of the tub and check in with the outer world. I have friends waiting for updates, after all.

Aubrey's last text is still on the lock screen. I saw it come in while I was talking to Mom, sneaking a peak while she dabbed her eyes with a tissue. Maybe it wasn't fair, dragging that much out of her about Dad's drinking. I know it was hard for her to tell me all she did.

I don't think her hope is misplaced, for what it's worth. Yes, Dad's fallen off the wagon a couple of times, but he's never done therapy before. The mere idea that my father would open up about the demons that drive him to drink is shocking to me ... and, I'd guess, a good sign. I know very little about his childhood, and I'm his only kid. Who doesn't talk about their childhood *at all,* if that time was full of sunshine and gumdrops? It must've been rough. I'm glad he's talking to someone — that he's serious enough about his sobriety to step out of his comfort zone and give psychiatry a try.

Aubrey's text says, *Okay so how much do you want to murder them already?*

I crack a smile. Thanks, Aubrey. I needed that. I've only been here for an hour, and I'm already exhausted from all this scattered emotion.

I text her back: *You need to delete that. It's evidence they'll use against me when I finally snap. I give myself two days before I turn psycho.*

A moment later, my phone buzzes with an automated message: *Your message failed to send. Retry?*

The top corner of the screen shows one bar, then none, then one again. This lack of connectivity will take some getting used to. It's like entering a room when you know the power's dead, but you still flick the light switch. The brain knows, but hands have minds of their own.

"Miranda?" Mom calls from the kitchen. "Dinner's on the table!"

"Just a second!"

A moment later she's outside the door, yelling again. *"Miranda? Are you in the bathroom?"*

"JUST A SECOND!"

She knocks on the door. I wash my hands quickly and open up instead of shouting again. She looks from my face to my waist, where the still-lit screen of my phone glows through leggings and shirt like a radiant stomach tumor.

"Were you on your phone?" Mom asks.

"I was in the bathroom."

"Using your phone?"

There's no correct response. Yes, I was using my phone, but I can't just say that. The real question is why the hell she cares. What the hell business it is of hers. The question is judgmental, so answering it at all means answering to my mother.

It makes me think of Aubrey's text, and how it made me laugh: *So how much do you want to murder them already?*

Mom's still in front of me, waiting for an answer. My lack of response says it's none of her business. She's got a weird look: not her usual overbearing expression, but instead something more like concern. It's like *I'm* the alcoholic, and phones are my liquor. What's even more ridiculous is that Dad's at the table behind her, listening for my answer and pretending he can't hear us.

"Yes, Mom. I sometimes check my phone in the bathroom. I'm a heathen. Can we please move on?"

"You don't have to be defensive. I was just wondering if you had service."

"I have a bar. Sometimes."

"Oh. Well. Have you been able to use it since you've been here? Sending texts and stuff?"

She's trying to act like it's a casual question with an obvious reason behind it (assessing general connectivity in the foothills, maybe), but this feels like more than curiosity. Meanwhile Dad's still watching, still listening. I get the feeling they were talking about me while I was in here. Comparing notes. Trying to decide how to deal with something. This interrogation is part of it. Somehow.

"I got a text from Aubrey. I can't text her back, though."

"Oh, so you're still hanging out with Aubrey?"

"She's my best friend. So yeah."

"Cassie doing okay, too?" Dad asks.

I hesitate before answering. My eyes flicking to my father. He's suddenly abashed, looking down and away. Cassie lived next door when I was little and was my best friend before Aubrey. She moved away, but we got back in touch when she ended up at Fordham with me, Aubrey, and Ross. I haven't mentioned Cassie to my parents for almost a decade. I'm pretty sure I know what's reminded Dad to ask about her now, but I'd rather not dig up old bones by pointing it out.

"Cassie's good, Dad," I say softly.

Mom bustles into the silence that follows, grabbing a basket of cornbread from the counter. "Well, I didn't *know* if you still got on with Aubrey. People sometimes drift apart when they go off to college."

"We went off *together*, though. To the *same* college."

Mom makes an indistinct noise.

I'm still standing, so it's easy to cross my arms. "What? Why do you care?"

Mom puts her hands up in an overly dramatic display of surrender. "Okay, okay, you win! I'll butt out." She pivots in place and retreats toward the kitchen. "I just wanted to hear a little about your life, was all."

No, no, that's some bullshit right there. That's not what she was doing at all, and I'm trying to decide if I should call her on it.

I spent most of my long drive here psyching myself up for the times when my parents and I would inevitably butt heads, knowing that some amount of nipping-in-the-bud would be necessary. If I'm to survive two weeks back under Mom and Dad's roof, I need to grow a spine and cut their trespasses off at the knees. But is this phone-and-Aubrey thing a hill worth dying on? Should I get into it with Mom over her first passive-aggressive jab, or should I save my protests for something bigger?

I walk to the table and sit without a word. For a handful of seconds, we eat in silence. After another handful, I realize that our ordinary silence will turn tense if nothing changes, so I decide to be the bigger person. It takes inertia to break the quiet.

"So what's there to do around here?" I ask brightly. Maybe too brightly. There are no blinds on the windows. They're black rectangles around us, like someone's idea of somber art: the same dark portrait framed on every wall.

Neither of them answers. I look to Mom, but she's fixed on her food, dissecting a piece of cornbread and arranging the small, identical squares of it atop her chili. It doesn't look like something she plans to eat. More like something she plans to display in an *avant garde* gallery.

Dad's head is turned, looking out one of the windows. There's nothing to see there — just a single pole-mounted light above the storage shed.

"That much, huh?" I say.

Dad looks at me. "What?"

"I asked what there was to do."

"To do?"

"Yes. *To do.* What have you guys been up to since you got here?"

"Nothing," Mom says, like someone poked her.

"Nothing?"

"A good kind of nothing," Dad clarifies.

"There are different kinds of nothing?"

"Head-clearing nothing. Up here, your only choice is to unplug from the world. It's good, to not always be distracted like everyone is these days."

"Distracted by phones? Like I was doing in the bathroom?" I ask. "Because I can't help myself, right? Because I'm addicted to it?"

"Nobody said that," Dad replies.

I eat my chili. I force myself not to slurp at it, like I do with soup. They always hated that. Just like they hated when I chewed with my mouth open. Or refused to fold my laundry, which lived in a pile in my closet, clean but untidy.

"How's school?" Mom asks.

"Good."

"Just good?"

"Okay. *Superior.*"

"You don't have to be sarcastic."

"I'm not trying to be sarcastic."

"You're making me pull information out of you," she says. "Sorry — I thought you might be up for conversation."

"I'm up for conversation. You're the ones who are acting weird."

"How is this weird?" Dad asks. "What have we done that's weird?"

Oh, I don't know. Maybe it was the deer-chasing. Maybe it's this stilted conversation we're having right now, with both of them sitting so upright, it's like they have rods in their spines. I feel like I'm living a parody of something. Possibly a British film, where everyone has problems with everyone else but they're all too polite to air their grievances.

Let it go, Miranda, I tell myself. *There will be enough to deal with on this trip without you picking fights.*

"School is going well," I say, feeling how hard it is, here and now, to say more than the minimum. "I got all A's, except for a B in Calculus."

"Calculus is important." Of course he'd say that. Dad's an engineer. "Was it the tests that got you, or did you forget to turn in some homework?"

"It's a lecture course, Dad. There's no homework. Just a midterm and an exam."

"Just two grades?"

"Just two grades."

"Shame. I wonder if there's an opportunity for some sort of extra credit," Mom says.

I inhale. Exhale. *Let it go. Just keep talking.*

"Aubrey is having a harder time adjusting," I say. "Most people do. I read in the college paper that almost everyone has a rough first semester as they figure the whole 'college thing' out."

Dad nods. "That, and gain weight."

"I never understood that," Mom says, shaking her head. "The whole 'finding yourself' thing. Sometimes people say you have to 'figure out who you are.' What's that mean? *Finding yourself?* You're right here. And *who are you?* You're the same person you've always been."

I set my napkin in my lap. *"Actually*, Mom, psychologists say one of the biggest struggles people have is balancing their internal compass against what the environment tells them. There's one force *inside* us, but a whole other force *outside*."

"Peer pressure," Dad says, nodding with a mouthful of chili.

"Peers, parents, values they grew up believing ... People 'find themselves' when they leave their families and go out on their own, because that's when the outside force changes."

Mom looks up. "So, what, we've been keeping you down? Forcing you to do things our way?"

Yes.

"I'm not saying that. You change your surroundings and sometimes hidden aspects of the person you've always been end up being nurtured while other parts die off. That's all I'm saying."

"Is that why you changed your hair?" Mom asks.

Ah. There it is. I cut my hair short and dyed a swatch of it blue last month. I was shocked nobody's mentioned it before now, but Mom was saving it up, like chambering a round in a gun.

"And the extra earrings," Dad mentions.

"It's deeper than that," I tell them. "I'm talking about internal change."

"But also on the surface."

"Some people change politics. They try new things."

"New things like blue hair."

"Dad."

"What?"

"Can we not talk about my hair?"

"Or your earrings," Mom adds.

"Right. Let's not talk about either."

"It seems performative, is all," Dad says in his *I'm-just-being-logical* voice. "If a person's been repressed, like held-down by their parents, then I guess in that case I understand why they'd throw off the shackles once they're able and finally break free, but—"

"DAD."

"—but if it's truly their 'internal compass' that's making them change—" It sounds like he finds the concept both suspect and annoying. "—then you'd think the change would be *internal*. Not out on display, like waving a flag, like trying to prove something to the world."

"Dad, I'm not—"

"If you ask me," he interrupts, "*that* feels like conformity. All these kids trying to be 'individuals,' but all of them doing the exact same things."

I inhale big. Exhale big. I don't try to hide it.

Mom puts a hand on my shoulder. "I like it." She takes a lock of blue between her fingers, eyes fixed as if studying it. "The hair."

"So have there been many parties?" Dad asks.

"Not really."

"No parties? In *college?* I don't believe it."

"I'm not drinking, Dad." I almost add — just because I know how effective a jab it would be — ... *are YOU?*

"I didn't ask about drinking. I asked about parties."

"You know I'm not much of a party girl."

"I *did* know that," he says. "But, you know ... 'internal compass' versus being repressed back home and all."

Mom eyes Dad, who for some reason keeps looking at the locked owner's pantry. A glance passes between them when Dad's eyes return to center. I can't help but wonder what it's about — these little signals they keep sending each other.

Then his eyes go to the window. Mine follow. When I return my gaze to the table, I see Mom's lips moving. She seems to have used my moment of inattention to mouth something to my father — something they probably discussed in advance, her reminding him to bring it up now.

God. They're about to henpeck the *shit* out of me.

I decide a preemptive strike is in order, and there's only one topic I know will bother them as badly as I want them bothered right now: *Ross*. I haven't told them I moved him from *friend* to *boyfriend* yet, but that's never stopped them from going out of their way to tell me how much he sucks. It's annoying, the way they bring him up when his topic isn't remotely on the table, just to crap on his reputation. Maybe it's time I do the same, turning their own weapon against them.

"You know," I say. "You asked about Aubrey and Cassie, but you didn't ask about Ross."

Mom is so taken-off-guard that she spins toward me and knocks a glass to the ground. It shatters on the tile like a grenade.

"Ross?" she asks.

"Yeah. He's at Fordham, too. You remember Ross from high school? Every time I hung out in a group and Ross was in the group, you couldn't stop telling me to stay away from him."

I'm not sure what strategy I have in mind here. The goal will eventually be to tell them we're dating, but that feels like too big a bomb to drop on Day One. To prepare, I should be easing my parents into the idea — maybe bringing up stories of Ross's soft side and how he's changed. Instead, I'm doing the exact opposite. I'm poking them, reminding them how much they hate him. Even though Ross and I weren't that close in high school, Mom and Dad still warned me against him. It's as if they thought I'd catch douchebag just by passing him in the hallway. As if his shittiness could corrupt others through proximity, like a contact high.

"What about him?" Mom asks.

"I just thought you might like to know how he's doing," I say with an evil smirk. "He visits my dorm all the time."

Mom tries to hide her squirming and fails. "What? Why?"

"Dunno. Maybe he likes me."

Mom looks like she might explode. Dad's on his feet, his back to me as if uninterested in what should be a bombshell revelation. He goes first to the locked owner's closet, then seems to realize his mistake and reaches into the pantry instead. He comes out with a dustpan and hand broom.

"Mark?" Mom says as Dad squats down to deal with the glass. "She says Ross Erlicher likes her."

"*Maybe* likes me," I clarify. "You know ... I always thought he wasn't so bad."

"*MARK?*"

"I heard her."

"*She* is right here, you know," I say.

"Why are you mentioning this?" Mom asks.

"I don't know. Just telling about my life?"

"You aren't sure?"

"Feet up." Dad's on his hands and knees below me, scuttling like a servant and excusing himself from the conversation.

"I'm actually kind of glad Ross has started coming around," I tell Mom. "Does that make you happy?"

"Why would *that* make us happy?"

I shrug. "Maybe you're glad I'm following my *inner compass*. Internally, you know? Not so *performative*."

"Let's move on." Dad is entirely under the table now.

"Or maybe not," I counter. "You always thought Ross was a piece of shit, right?"

"*Miranda!*" Mom hisses. "Watch your language!"

Dad yelps in pain. I look down to see that he's cut himself on one of the glass pieces. When he tries to extricate himself, he slams his head on the underside of the table.

"*Shit!*" he blurts.

"Hey, Mom — Dad said 'shit,' too.' Better tell him to watch his language."

She ignores me this time, leaning down to inspect a copiously bleeding wound on the heel of my father's palm. Red droplets fall from his knuckles, making perfect little splatters on the floor. The shape of the splatters reminds me of the icon Rotten Tomatoes uses for bad movies. It's as if Dad's wound disapproves of the floor. *One out of ten; would not stand on again.*

Mom moves chairs, then helps Dad back to his feet in a totally unnecessary way. They move to the sink. Mom coos at and babies the wound. Her behavior is so bizarre, I keep thinking she'll offer to kiss it and make it better.

"So nobody wants to shit-talk Ross?" I ask from behind them. "I'm shocked."

"Stop saying 'shit'!"

"Shit shit shit! What the hell's wrong with you two?"

"Get over yourself," Mom snaps. "Your father's injured."

Yeah, and she's making it worse, squeezing his slashed hand as if milking it. I roll my eyes, subsume my by-now-enormous irritation, and shoulder her out of the way.

"Let me do it," I say.

"I'm fine," Dad argues.

"No, you're not fine. You probably need stitches." I look more intently. Now that a stream of sink water has washed away most of the blood, I can see the cut. It's deep. "You *definitely* need stitches."

I roll the hand to get a better look, and Dad flinches. The place I was touching was nowhere near the cut. It makes me look more closely.

"Dad? What happened to your hand?"

"I cut it on one of the glass pieces."

"No. Not that. The rest of it."

Because his hand looks like he stuck it into a box of needles. It's covered in tiny scratches, many scabbed with dried blood. A few of his fingers look bruised. He's somehow taken a bunch of skin off of the back. Two of his fingernails are broken and the quick below is sore-looking. The wince he just gave me? I think it came because there's something wrong with his wrist.

"It's nothing," he says.

"It's not *nothing*." I go to turn it again for a better look, but he pulls away. Immediately the blood flow resumes, turning the floor by the sink into a crime scene. "We should take you to the hospital."

"No."

"No?"

"No," he repeats. "It's superficial. Nothing to worry about."

"But how did it happen?"

"I told him to go into town and have it looked at," Mom says from behind us. "Mark, show her your ribs."

"What about your ribs?" I ask.

"I said it's nothing!"

"Mark! You're hurt!" Mom blurts. "I keep telling you!"

I reach for my father's shirt, to lift it and see this rib thing, but he pushes it back down and glares at me for trying.

"I'm fine." This while his wounded hand and the hand holding it cover entirely in blood.

"I told you we should go to the hospital," Mom says.

"And I told you we can't!" he snaps.

"You *can't?*" I say. "Why not?"

He glares at Mom, angry that she brought me in on an issue he thought he'd already won. Something happened before I got here, and Dad didn't want me to know. He's always been proud. Doesn't like asking for help. Once, he passed out while trimming trees. We dragged him to the ER after he fell off his ladder. Turned out he had an ulcer so bad, it'd made him as anemic as a vampire on feeding day. By the time he was treated, they said he only had enough blood left in him to fill a 2-liter bottle. He knew it — knew something was terribly wrong — but the proud, doctor-fearing part of my father kept insisting that if he ignored it, the problem would go away.

Of course, he'd been drinking then. He's not drinking now. *Right?*

"Dad? How did you get hurt?"

"Log splitter," he says.

"You were splitting logs?"

"I wanted something to do."

I turn his hand over again, careful to protect the wrist. "How did you do this on a *log splitter?*"

"I don't know, Miranda," he says with the old edge back in his voice — the one that's usually dormant, but watch out when he sets it free. "Who cares? It did."

"And your ribs?"

"Something broke loose. The piston snapped. The motor housing flew off and hit me in the side."

I look at Mom. "What *really* happened, Mom?"

"THAT'S WHAT HAPPENED!"

"That's what happened," Mom echoes. "I was at the window. I saw it."

"Dad? Let me see."

Reluctantly, he does. I actually know a thing or two about the human body thanks to pre-med, as unwilling as my parents are to give me credit.

I gently touch my father's midsection. I think he's just bruised, nothing broken. The housing that hit him must have flown off with a ton of force, though. He looks like he repeatedly shoved his hand through close-growing thorns, then was hit with a shovel.

"I think it's superficial," I decide. "The other injuries are probably okay, but this new cut's another issue."

"We're not going to the hospital, Miranda."

"Dad ..."

"It's more than an hour away. By the time we get there, everything but the ER will be closed. I don't really want to waste my night and God knows how much money because I got a little scratch."

"How's your pain?"

"Fine," he says.

"Tell the truth. I'm not a hundred percent about this injury on your side."

I look him in the eyes. Finally he says, "Three out of ten."

"Really?"

"Maybe four."

I consider. He's letting me tend to him, and that's something. The biggest surprise is that there's something more pressing to my parents than complaining about Ross.

"You need stitches," I say again.

He shakes his head. "I'm not going to the hospital, Miranda."

"Mark ..."

"No," he tells Mom. "Not now, of all times. You know that."

We trade looks. Then I say, "Okay. Mom: Wash Dad's hand really well with water, then hydrogen peroxide. If you have iodine or Merthiolate, that's even better. I'll be right back."

"Where are you going?" she asks me.

"To get the first aid kit."

Mom reaches for one in the pantry, but I stop her. *"My* first aid kit. The one I keep in my rock-climbing bag, where hand injuries sometimes demand unorthodox solutions."

They wait for me to say more.

"Superglue," I explain.

"You want to *glue* your father's hand?"

"Trust me," I tell them. "I'm not yet a doctor."

Chapter Five

3:13 a.m. I haven't slept, bothered by noise and silence.

On one hand, it's too quiet here. I've spent four months getting used to the hubbub of New York City, and it's turned everything backwards. These days, stillness distracts me. I need traffic to relax. I need the overhead sounds of planes and helicopters and the banging of doors, even if they do sound like gunshots. I'm used to the grumble of car engines, the squeal of under-inflated tires when drivers turn too quickly. I need the pump and hiss of buses as they stop, clank open, and kneel.

Up here, there's nothing. Nobody. We're alone, serene behind the sigh of the wind.

But atop the stillness there are new sounds, like the cracking of branches outside the window behind my headboard that have, so far, made me look three times just to make sure nobody's out there watching. Owls call. Coyotes sing their lonely song to one another across the valley. I hear they get hungry this time of year, able to make a deer carcass vanish in an hour or two. If a human died in the woods, the body might never be found. It's an unsettling thought, hearing them now.

The breeze rattles limbs. It sounds like the eternal rolling of hundreds of dice.

Atop it all is a strange mechanical noise that can't be natural, banging somewhere. It's coming from a manmade thing, I'm sure: on and off, on and off. Sometimes there's rhythm to it. Other times, the clangs and beats seem almost random. Is it a loose gutter, slapping the facing? A rusting tractor accessory like those I saw tucked between trees when I arrived, one part unbolted and swinging? Or is it an intermittent engine, cutting on and off?

It's happening right now. It sounds like something metal being struck lightly with a pipe, over and over again.

I remove the bedclothes and get to my knees, again turning to face the window. Superstitious, childlike fear grips me. Every time I've looked outside, I can first see only my face in the glare on the window, lit by a nightlight I can't turn off. Every time, it takes a moment before my brain pattern-recognizes my own features and deletes them so I can see what's beyond. I'm somehow certain — thanks to the lonely quiet of the mountain night — that when I finally focus beyond my own reflection, I'll see a dark face inches from mine. The face of a stalker. Or a monster.

Ridiculous. Get a grip, Miranda. You're almost twenty years old.

But we aren't really adults when fear grips us, are we? Fear isn't rational. Terror comes from the oldest, most animal parts of the brain, brought forth by instinctual triggers and memories too buried to see. Fear isn't something we think about. It's something that just *is,* rational or not.

Thinking this, an old fear returns like a tap on my shoulder.

When I was eight, I was woken suddenly one night by the sound of smashing metal. It wasn't a huge thing, maybe twice the volume of stomping on an aluminum can. Other sounds followed that had no right echoing so late: a slam, a shout, a pile of noisy objects being knocked over.

On that night, I got to my knees in bed as I am now, turning to face a window exactly where this one is. I saw the back of our driveway, spotlit by the light on the front of the garage. Streetlights cast a sickly yellow glow behind it. The mailbox at the corner, still in shadow, looked black instead of blue.

There was someone at the mailbox. Hugging it. Today, with an adult's perspective, I would have said he was humping it: an unsteady man trying to stay upright. He was wailing in pain; perhaps the thing I'd heard fall earlier had fallen on him.

As I watched, Frank McCafferty came from the house behind the corner mailbox — the house beside ours; Cassie's house — still fastening the tie on his robe. He approached the man, who came suddenly back to life, separating himself from the box as if he wasn't hurt at all. There was no pause after Frank, muted by my window, seemed to ask what was wrong. There was no pause before the mailbox man leapt forward and started pummeling Cassie's dad with his fists. The ferocity of the attack was shocking and inexplicable. Frank never had a chance. He was beaten ... and beaten ... *and beaten.*

I remember ducking down and hiding that night. I closed my eyes and counted to ten. Then I got back up, slowly ... and after I did, I had to wait for the same pattern-deletion at the window as now. First, I saw my face. Only after adjustment could I see beyond.

That's when I realized the monster was *right there*, directly outside my window, not ten inches from my face. His eyes were wide, looking in at me with an unknowable expression.

It — the monster — was my father.

I don't know if he lingered or went quickly away. I don't know why he looked through my window at all — maybe a father's sense of duty; maybe in his drunken state, he thought he'd just protected me. I don't remember falling back to sleep. Somehow, though, I did.

I only know that when I woke up, the sunlight through my window was disarmingly bright. Habit made me go about my morning business as usual, last night's fears less pressing in the daytime. I walked into the kitchen, which was just as bright, and there at the table was my father, hand bandaged and head down over a bowl of cereal. He ate mechanically. Said nothing. Rose from the table with a limp. Went out to the car, parked almost sideways inside a garage littered with spilled tools and paint cans, the metal track for the garage door bent into permanent failure.

What's wrong with Daddy's hand?

My mother, speaking without looking at me: *Daddy had an accident.*

That's all she would say. She stayed home from work that day, canceling my usual sitter. She called a handyman, who fixed the garage door. She cleaned up the pile of scrap that had fallen.

Two weeks later there was a realtor sign in the McCafferty's yard, and a month after that they were gone, even though the house hadn't sold yet. I was too young to wonder if charges were pressed. I knew only that my best friend Cassie went to a whole new home away from us. It was a decade before I spoke to her again.

As I stare into the blackness now ten years later, the memory of the monster at my window reasserts itself. Some primal part of me is sure the metal banging outside is only a prelude. Soon I'll see the Hyde to my father's Jekyll again: sobriety and sanity gone, the monster returned.

What happened to Dad's hand?

That was me last night, after Dad left the main room to putter and Mom and I were alone. In my mind's eye now, I see him beating the neighbor badly enough to put him in the hospital. Was there a lawsuit? Was that when the worst of their financial woes began?

Forget it, I tell myself. *Dad was drunk when he beat up the neighbor — the first of his two failed attempts to climb onto the wagon. He's sober now. He never hit Mom. Never hit you.*

In the morning after that long-ago night, he was repentant. Full of guilt, or full of something my eight-year-old self couldn't understand. That was the cycle: *Anger, guilt. Violence, regret. Terrible actions followed by repentance.*

Every morning he'd promise it was over. He'd turn away from alcohol; he'd get help; he knew better now than to lose control again. But morning became afternoon. Became evening. Became night. And at night, his demons came. He'd rationalize one drink. Two. *Ten.* I always wondered which father I'd find when I left my room. The sweetheart? Or the beast?

What happened to Dad's hand?

And last night Mom told me, *He was trying to fix the water pump. It was an accident.*

Outside now, a breeze stirs and sends leaves cavorting across my field of view. I can see better now that a few lumens from the light above the equipment shed — just like the light at the top of our garage all those years ago — have begun registering on my dark-adjusted eyes. The bulb itself is around a corner, but the illumination it casts gives features to the darkness. I'm not sure it freaks me out less just because I can see some of what's out there.

The noise repeats: light metal banging like pipe on pipe. Is that what Dad was trying to fix when he hurt his hand? This is a rental. Why is he fixing anything?

We're out in the middle of nowhere, Miranda, Mom said when I asked my questions. She sounded exasperated, as if the answer should be obvious. *We didn't have water, the owners live out of state, and the property manager wasn't getting back to us —they're two hours away. What were we supposed to do if Dad didn't fix the water pump? Die of thirst? You should count yourself lucky that your father is the kind of man who does whatever it takes to protect his family.*

I look toward the light. On the shed. From which the noise is once again intermittently coming. The shed hangs halfway over a gradual and enormous downslope that runs all the way to the river below. I'm guessing that like many off-grid homes, this place pumps its drinking water all the way up from there, running it through a few filters before sending it to the faucets. The pump must be inside the shed: the source of my father's injuries. That, plus a log splitter ... despite how many split logs I saw piled under the cabin already. Maybe the pump was worth fixing. But the log splitter? He shouldn't even have had to use it.

My mind shows me Dad clinging to that mailbox ten years ago, then falling on Frank McCafferty as if he was a villain.

Splitting logs that didn't need splitting sounds to me like drunk logic. But he's not drunk now, correct? Mom wouldn't be so teary about his dedication to recovery if he was drinking again, would she? She'd know if it was happening, and she's not that good of an actor ... is she?

Go to sleep, I think. *You're paranoid.*

But that's no help at all. I've been trying to sleep since midnight. The silence and the noise distract me, but that's not truly what's kept me awake. My mind has done that.

Paranoia. Worry. Ross.

I texted Ross again last night, unable to help myself. It's the very last thing Aubrey would have wanted me to do. The text went right through with no hesitation, almost as if it wanted to make sure I had no way to change my mind. No way to take it back.

Just text me back, my message to Ross said. *You can't be this big of an asshole.*

I finally got a response an hour later. It was the emoji wearing sunglasses. Nothing more. Nothing else.

Is he playing with me? Or being a fucker? Is something wrong with Ross all of a sudden: a grown man unsure how to act in society? Who gets a text like mine and sends back an emoji that seems to imply he's too cool for school?

I tried to reply — with vigor, this time — but my bars died. Nothing I sent would go through. Service here is so capricious. One moment it's okay, the next it's garbage.

It took me a minute of staring angrily at my phone before I noticed that another message had arrived during the window that allowed Ross's bullshit reply. It was yet another photo from my mystery correspondent. This one was entirely dark, as if taken inside a bag of black velvet. The only features I could make out were photo grain from the picture itself.

Earlier, after dinner, I tried to poke the Ross issue with Mom. I wouldn't normally want to, but Dad's glass-cutting had interrupted the first time he came up and I felt strangely incomplete. Returning to the topic felt like rubbernecking at an accident. Why would I ever *want* to discuss Ross with my parents, if not to argue for the relationship they don't yet know about? Why would I go out of my way to bring him up, unless the goal was to make them like him in advance of my announcement?

I still don't know the answer to those questions. It felt like obeying instinct — the same instinct that keeps turning me around in bed, looking out the window, certain that someone will be out there, peeking in with hollow eyes.

I only knew that something was amiss. Something, about all of this, feels wrong.

Mom had been reading a magazine. I kept catching her glancing at me over the top of it.

"What?" I finally asked.

"I'm sorry?"

"Do you think I'm going to run off? Do a little dance?"

She laid the magazine flat on her lap, feet up. She was the picture of false calm, acting like the night was going exactly as planned.

"What are you talking about?" she asked.

"You keep looking at me."

"You're my daughter."

"Are you waiting for something? For me to do something?"

"What would you do?"

"I don't know. What don't you *want* me to do?"

She squinted at me, and that's when I thought: *Maybe she* IS *a good actor*. She pretended in that moment that I was the crazy one, but I know I'm not. The entire visit by then had been marred by weirdness. It would have been more out-of-character for me to play normal than to react as I had to my mother's suspicious glances, and yet she squinted and frowned at me, acting like she was trying to understand.

"Are you mad at us?" she asked me. "You've had an edge since dinner."

"You mean since you picked apart every choice I made after leaving home?"

"We're your parents, Miranda."

"Yes. And I'm your daughter. We've established that."

"What's with you?"

I shook my head, frustrated by this gaslighting. "I brought up Ross as an example of all the things you micromanage for me that you don't have any reason to micromanage. It was half a joke, but now I'd really like to know. I want to know why it pisses you off so much, the idea of me being anywhere near him."

This question, of all things, seemed to embarrass her. She acted like I'd just asked about her bathroom habits.

"Oh, we don't have to talk about that."

"We don't? You just want to smear and run?"

"Miranda."

"Mom."

After a handful of seconds, she folded her arms and said, "You sure have come up here with a big chip on your shoulder."

But: *No.* I refused to let her turn it around, making me the crazy one. So rather than answer her accusation, I held my own.

"Is it Dad's anniversary? Is *that* why the two of you are acting so weird? It's the tension, isn't it? The stress of wondering if he'll make it?"

"Yes," she says.

"All of that?"

"Yes," she repeats.

"I didn't demand you pay for college, you know. I could have gotten loans. Or a job."

"What? Why are you bringing *that* up?"

"Because clearly the financial strain is stressing you out. You guys usually won't shut up about money, but now it's like a secret. Why? Let's talk about it. I know it was a stretch to send me to New York. *More* than a stretch. Do you have enough? I don't want to be the reason you can't retire."

"Miranda, we haven't brought it up once."

"I know! Why not?"

"You *want* us to?"

"I don't know, Mom!"

That discussion, before bed, was so strange. I don't know why I tried to pick a fight. At the time, I didn't even understand the way I felt — not that it's become clear in the hours since. Was I angry? Looking back now from 3 a.m., I can't even say. Why would I be angry?

Maybe it's because *I'm* the stressed-out one. *School. Ross. This weirdo sending me photos.* I keep wondering if I should say something about that last one, but to whom and to what end? Maybe I'll have to, soon, if just to unburden myself of this pent-up feeling.

"You aren't complaining about tuition," I said to my mother hours ago. "For you, that's weird."

"Honey, you were pretty upset with the few things we *did* have an opinion on. I thought you were trying to be independent. But if you *want* me to complain about tuition ..."

"I want to know why you hate Ross so much," I blurted.

She perked up at that — at my oh-so-pointed mention. I suppose this was my plan to bring it up slowly: not by trying to improve Ross's image before telling Mom and Dad the truth, but by getting the worst of his image out of the way. It's a bulldozer's approach to arguing, but that's how I felt at the time.

"Why?"

"Because."

"Is he really coming around your dorm? Do you really think he might like you?"

"What if he is? What if he does?"

I saw my mother fighting to keep control. We were very close to the truth in that moment, and Mom did her best not to see it. To not even *imagine* the idea of me and Ross together.

"Miranda," she said very seriously. "We both know that boy's a drug dealer."

Instead of balking, I laughed. I threw my hands toward the ceiling. I stood up and walked in a circle, as if I was restless and didn't know what else to do.

"He was!" Mom said.

"We've talked about this. He had a lot of weed one time, so he sold some of it to—"

"—to *the principal's son,*" Mom finished.

I shake my head. It's just not fair. Over and over again, throughout the entire time I've known him, the tiniest failures on Ross's part somehow happened at exactly the wrong times in exactly the wrong places. He was *phenomenally* unlucky. Yes, he sold weed. *Once.* To Tom Choy, who then turned around and shared it with the principal's son Adeel. The principal found it when she put Adeel's lunch in his backpack the next day. So *of course* there was a minor witch hunt. And *of course* it traced back from Adeel to Tom to Ross. And *of course* my parents just so happened to pick me up from school *the exact day* it all went down, with the final stage of that witch hunt playing out just as they pulled up.

They think the worst of Ross because the universe is an asshole. Ross is 98% good and 2% mischievous, but somehow my parents managed to see only the 2%.

"Miranda," she said, eyeing me in lecture mode, "when you get older, you'll learn that a person's reputation—"

"What, like *you've* never smoked weed? I know you have, Mom!"

"It's not just that!" she snapped, and it's like I hit a nerve I hadn't known was there. It wasn't casual dislike I saw in her eyes. It was white-hot hatred.

"What, then? What other 'reputation' did Ross have?" I honestly thought about it, trying to imagine her answer. He'd had a few girlfriends, but so what? Other than that one time, drugs never even entered the picture.

Mom bustled and shook her head. Either she didn't want to tell me what she was holding against Ross, or (more likely) she didn't have anything.

"Let's just say I'll be happy if I don't ever have to hear about him again," Mom told me in her *and-that's-all-there-is-to-it* voice. She eyed me long and hard after that, telling me without words that if my hints about being with Ross were real, we'd have a very big problem.

I was furious. Mostly with myself, for dragging those words out of her. What's wrong with me lately? Is it possible Mom was telling the truth — that they're doing their best and it's *me* who's got a problem? Why did I goad her? She was quiet before I started provoking her. All would have been well between us, if I'd just kept my mouth shut. What's this vein of self-sabotage inside me lately?

To purge myself, I went for a hard run after our argument. It'd been dark for hours by then, so I did it wearing a headlamp and carrying a flashlight in each hand. Dad, who was dabbing at the untreated parts of his macerated hand with hydrogen peroxide by the time I was laced up and ready, told me not to go out at night. If I absolutely had to run *right now,* he said, I should run up and down the driveway rather than going into the woods, even on trails. He told me how easy it is to get lost out here, and GPS almost never works. Getting lost is dangerous even during the day. Running after dark, though? That's a nightmare waiting to happen.

Plus the cliff's edge, so easy to stumble off of. Plus the coyotes, ready to make me vanish if I fell.

But I was angry and unsettled, so I ignored him. *Wholesale* ignored him. Looking back, I wonder now if I was *trying* to get lost or killed. I paid zero attention to where I went. The trail was rough and technical, all the way down to the river and across a bridge I couldn't find again if my life depended on it. I could barely see. I could have run across a den of bears. Snakes. Evil people, wanting to do me harm.

I just ran, trying to clear it all away. But nothing cleared.

My mind spun the entire time with that thing Aubrey says about me, about how I'm always reacting too late to things that are already over. I tend to reopen wounds after they're already closing. This anger I feel? It might be at Old Mom and Old Dad. Maybe they really *are* trying to make amends up here in the woods. That's the reason Dad told me they got the cabin in the first place, after all: so we could spend some quiet time together away from the world and start over.

My parents aren't stupid. They know our little family was on a fast track to estrangement. Dad with his drinking. Mom with her judgments. Isn't it possible that I'm being unfair here — that I'm picking fights with them because I'm still nursing old wounds ... and all the while, they're trying to move on?

No. They judged every bit of me at dinner.

That's what I told myself as I ran hard enough to collapse. Never mind that it's *all* they did. The rest of what's bothering me has nothing to do with Mom and Dad.

I felt better when my run was over. I somehow found my way back to the cabin, collapsing into one of the chairs around the fire pit with its astonishing view. My breath came heavy for a long time. The moon peeked in and out. I heard that clanking sound but didn't know from where it came. It ended by the time I finally went inside, and I forgot all about it.

Then bedtime. I avoided my parents, sneaking into my room

and making enough noise so they'd know I'd safely returned, but doing nothing to seek them out and say goodnight. I didn't know how I felt. Was I still mad? If so, was there any justification, or was I overreacting?

I kept thinking about Dad when he was drunk, but I know he isn't now. I've saddled this trip with so much old baggage. So maybe the emotion I felt was more embarrassment than anger.

Shower.

Sleep.

Or at least a parody of sleep.

And now here I am hours later, staring either out the window or at the ceiling for hours and hours.

Strangely, despite how late it is, I suddenly notice the sound of two people talking. It's coming from my parents' room, then the living room. They've gotten up in the late-night and are moving around, both of them speaking in whispers and trying to be quiet. I can't make out any of their words. Dad seems to rattle around for a while. I think I hear the outside door open and close.

Dad used to smoke when he was drinking. Is that what he's doing now — heading out for a smoke? What other reason would a person go outside after 3 a.m.?

Stop it. Stop punishing them for the past. Now is now. Have a little bit of trust in them, Miranda.

I close my eyes and try to breathe slowly. Ten or twenty minutes pass, all sounds from my up-late parents diminished again. The clanging from outside resumes, though, and this time it's like a woodpecker against my skull. I can ignore the sounds of New York, but for some reason this single noise won't let me rest here.

Pillow over my head.

A quick and fruitless search for earplugs.

Finally I throw the covers aside, determined to stop whatever's out there from banging. I storm quietly through the living room and out the front door, half expecting a motion-activated bulb on the porch to shine my way forward, but there's no light. Nothing at all unless you count the wan yellow glow from the shed, blocked almost entirely from here. It's dark as hell. Whenever the dinging pauses, all I hear is wind and crickets.

The cold bites into me. I'm in slides, shorts, and a tank top, arms crossed across my chest, breath billowing in plumes.

Make it quick, I tell myself.

I no longer hear the sound, but I have a rough idea of its direction from earlier. It was coming from near the shed. I'll just have to go over there and wait, hoping the sound resumes so I can pinpoint its location.

But then I stop.

Because I can see the apron of light cast by the shed-mounted spotlight now that I'm around the cabin's outside corner, and there's someone standing in its middle. Motionless. A man, maybe twenty feet from the shed door, staring at it.

He turns his head. It's my father. A voice comes from my left side, making me jump.

"It's late. Go back to bed."

I startle, then focus. Mom is over there, wearing a big gray coat and looking right at me. Until I approached, she was just standing where she still is, quiet and still like Dad.

Feeling disoriented, I mutter, "There's a noise out here."

"*Shh,*" Mom says. "It's starting to rain."

It's true. Either I didn't notice before or it's just started. It's more drizzle than rain, plenty cold enough to freeze. If this keeps up for a few hours, we'll have an ice rink by morning.

I stand where I am for a while, feeling cold rain like pinpricks. I walk back inside when neither of them says another word. They just keep idling on the hard-packed dirt, watching the shed. What's happening isn't right, but I don't know what else to do.

My two weeks in this place began today.

And God help me ... tomorrow is only Friday.

Chapter Six

I wake to a knock on my door. It's a gentle, polite knock — the kind a person uses when they only want the attention of the person inside if they're already awake ... or in my case, *almost* awake.

It takes a second to orient myself. I'm in a strange bed, and at first, I'm too tired to understand why. The light and sounds of this place are unfamiliar. It's insanely cold outside my covers — much, *much* colder than I recall.

Then last night comes back to me.

The argument.

My irritation.

The suicidal run I made through the darkness, just to show my parents how few shits I gave about their judgments.

And most of all, the weirdness by the shed in the middle of the night.

I try to summon last night's eerie feeling, but for some reason the whole thing doesn't seem as weird to me now. In the light of day, it strikes me as a lot more normal. Mom and Dad surprised me, but really, they were just standing by the shed, same as I'd gone outside to do. They were probably waiting for the banging noise to start up again so they could stop it, same as I'd intended.

No. It was more than that. They're being strange, and you know it. Something's going on here.

I try to hold onto the thought because it justifies everything. If Mom and Dad are the problem, then I'm right and they're wrong. Unfortunately, though, I'm starting to wonder if that's true. Maybe *I'm* the problem. I was the one who brought up Ross — not once, but twice. I was the one who sat down for dinner not for civil conversation, but to give the snippiest, most defensive answers I could.

It's dawning on me that I may have over-prepared for this time with my parents. I told myself I'd stand up to them if they started picking on me, and I have. I stood up *so* far, in fact, that I pushed them over. Maybe my prejudices are the answer to the question of *what's going on here.*

"Miranda? Are you awake, sweetie?"

I find myself embarrassed. This must be what Dad used to feel like, the morning after a bender.

"Yeah. Yeah, Mom."

"You have a phone call."

My eyes go to my phone. It's right where I left it, plugged in on the nightstand. When I touch it, I see that another photo has arrived. I'm not ready to look at it yet.

Instead, I slide a leg out and put one foot down. I wince, irrationally sure I'll stick to the ice-cold floor like a tongue to a flagpole. When I push away the covers and stand, the feeling intensifies. My breath forms a white cloud every time I exhale. I open the door, then peek through the gap with my reclaimed blanket wrapped around me.

My mother is wearing a coat and stocking cap even though we're inside. I can't meet her eyes. Yep, I'm pretty sure I was the asshole last night.

"It's Aubrey."

I look down. In Mom's outstretched hand is the landline phone. Its cord is so long and distended, she was able to stretch it all the way from the kitchen.

"Oh, and breakfast is ready whenever you want it."

I squint at an assault of sunlight. My room has western exposure, but morning is full blast from the living room's big, east-facing
windows.

"What time is it?" I ask.

"Nine. I saved you some pancakes."

I take the phone. She gives me a small, press-lipped smile and
turns to go.

"Mom?"

She looks back. But I can't say it. I can't apologize for speaking
my mind, even if I spoke too much of it. Even if it turns out I was
the out-of-line one yesterday, it's been them too many times in the
past.

"Why's it so cold?" I ask instead.

"A big front came through last night. The temperature dropped
to something like two degrees and now everything's covered in a
quarter inch of ice. Weather's saying the snow is going to start later
today instead of tomorrow like we figured. And so of course the
furnace went out. Your father thinks the lines aren't insulated properly and something froze up. He's working on it right now."

"The log splitter, the water pump, and now the furnace? What's
with this place?"

Mom shrugs. "We wanted something off the beaten path. Something tells me folks up here aren't too concerned about doing things
the way the inspectors want them to."

After I mutter a nothing response, she turns away again. I start
to close the door, but then I call to her one more time.

"Mom?"

"Mm?"

"Thanks for doing this. The whole thing."

I get a small smile. "You're welcome, Miranda."

With the door closed, I put the phone to my ear. Aubrey's voice
comes at me like a klaxon. Even though I usually wake up early and
she usually wakes up late, she still starts every day at one hundred
and ten percent. Sometimes I hate her for how chipper she can be
when the sun is still so low in the sky.

"No heat?" she says. "You're kidding me."

I lay back down. Bury myself in covers. "I'm going to die up here."

"Isn't it an Airbnb? Why is your dad fixing things?"

I lift my head enough to look out the window and spy my father in a big puffy coat, tiptoeing carefully around the shed. At first, I don't understand the careful way he's walking, but then I remember Mom's mention of ice and look up to see every tree glistening, every branch looking like it's made of glass. It all sags with added weight, cracking like it might give way.

I squint. Why's Dad all the way out by the shed? The heat doesn't come from the *shed*, does it? It's a furnace. It'd have to be inside the house.

"Miranda?" Aubrey says. "You still there? I asked why your dad is fixing things."

She sounds funny. Again, I get the sense that she's sniffing around, trying to gauge my mood before launching into whatever-this-is.

"Who knows." I rub my face, yawning. "I just got up. You woke me up, asshole."

"It's nine."

"So my mom tells me."

"Has Ross tried to call?"

I think of the single emoji he sent me. "No."

"Okay. Good."

"Why's that good?"

"No reason."

"Aubrey..." She was weird about this before. I hate it when she doesn't just tell me the truth, and instead makes me dig it out of her.

"Seriously, no reason," she says.

I sigh, giving up.

Aubrey takes a beat, then says, "So hey. Listen."

I sigh again, keeping myself wrapped in the comforter.

"Obviously you're wondering how I got this number."

"Obviously," I say. "It's not like I'm still half-asleep and oblivious or anything."

"I couldn't get you on your cell and my texts kept bouncing. I figured I'd just have to wait to talk until you called me, but then I remembered you forwarded everyone the Airbnb reservation email like a good little girl. I noticed when you first sent it that there was a landline number in the property notes."

"Okay."

"So I woke up, remembered, and decided I'd call. Give you a break from your parents so you can keep your sanity up there."

"How thoughtful." I'm just trying to keep up. Aubrey's mile-a-minute and hard to catch. Pretty sure she's got ADHD. I've seen her take meds for it.

"Unfortunately, I temporarily lost my phone sometime around breakfast."

"Like always."

"But then I ran into Cassie in the commons and figured you probably forwarded the Airbnb email to her, too."

"I did." I also sent it to Ross, but we won't talk about that one.

"She pulled the email up and handed her phone to me so I could write down the number. I backed out of the email I'd had open when I was done, just out of habit, before I handed her phone back. So basically, I ended up looking at her full inbox. Y'know?"

"This is fascinating." I yawn again.

"No. Listen." Aubrey's voice lowers. "Cass was swiping her dining card, so I had to keep holding her phone. I kept glancing at the screen, because something was bugging me."

"Something was bugging you about Cassie's inbox."

"*Pictures,*" she explains. "Sent from a phone number instead of an email address. So of course I memorized the number."

I sit up in bed, shoving a pillow between my back and the cold wall. "You memorized the number? *Pictures?*" They're just words, but if these weren't *relevant* pictures, Sherlock Aubrey wouldn't be bringing them up. "What was the phone number?"

Aubrey reads it to me. I sag when she's finished, although I don't know what I expected. It's not the same phone number that's been texting *me* strange photos. This is a big ol' bag of nothing.

"That's not the same number as I'm getting stuff from," I tell her.

Aubrey's voice lifts again. I can practically imagine her waving a hand between us, dismissing me because I'm so silly. "Oh, of course it's not. Why would the same person text pictures to you and email them to Cassie?"

"I don't know! I didn't even know you could text pictures to an email address!"

"You can. You just have to—"

"I'm not asking!" I say, interrupting. "Not to be rude, but what the hell? Why did you build me up like that if you knew it wasn't the same sender?"

"Because it gave me an idea."

That's not news. Aubrey is an idea factory. Getting the mail gives her ideas. Eating dinosaur-shaped chicken nuggets gives her ideas.

"What idea?"

"Skor."

"Indeed," I say. "*Score.* Good job, Aubrey." I don't know what I'm saying. I'm still half asleep.

"No no. *Skor.* S-K-O-R."

"The candy bar?"

"The cell phone. You haven't heard of it?"

"No."

"Skor is a brand of disposable phone. A burner. Skors are different from most phones because they use a sending protocol that—"

"I'm way too tired for technical stuff, Aubrey."

She resets. "Okay. Short version. *Certain technical things that you're too tired to think about right now* lead me to believe that the sender of your photos is using a Skor phone. That's why the photos are getting through."

I wait for the punchline. When it doesn't come, I say, "Okay."

"Well? Ask yourself: Who uses Skor phones?"

"I give up."

"The Mafia, for one."

"So the Mafia is sending me pictures?"

"It's not *just* the Mafia, you know." She sounds frustrated, like I should know better despite her giving me the information.

"Let's cut to the chase, Aub. Do Cassie's pictures have anything to do with mine?"

"No. It's just a clue. Whoever's sending you pictures is using a Skor."

"Okay. You just asked me who uses Skor phones like it meant something. Who *does* use them, other than the Mafia?"

"Well, criminals in general."

"*Which* criminals? Obviously, you've narrowed it down to a certain group of criminals or you wouldn't be bothering to tell me any of this."

"Oh, not yet." She says it like the idea is preposterous, even though she started this. "I just know it's criminals."

"And that's it? That's the whole clue? *Criminals* are texting me?"

"That's it."

I don't know how she's sure, but I'm sure it's technical and I simply don't care. This clue is a non-event.

"You aren't interested in any of this?" Aubrey says when I don't respond.

"No."

"Well, it's just that only *very specific types of people* use Skor phones. I've only ever met one person who has one."

"Maybe that's who's texting me, then."

"No, I'm sure it's not them."

I sigh. Big, heavy sigh. "Okay. Then tell me who sent *Cassie* the pictures so we can be done with whatever the hell this is. Maybe they're in cahoots."

"Oh, I didn't ask her."

"You said this is some big-ass clue! Why didn't you ask?"

"Um ... because snooping someone's email is an invasion of privacy?"

"*Aubrey!*" I'm aghast; she's stumbled on a clue but for the first time ever isn't chasing it like a bloodhound. "You could have made something up! Played it off!"

"Well..." I hear discomfort enter her voice. "She had other personal stuff in her inbox. I didn't want her knowing I saw it."

"But—!"

"She had emails about financial shit, like that orphan aid she's on. You know how embarrassed she is about that."

"Aubrey..."

"She even had an email from the med center. About her ... you know..."

"We're all girls here."

"I'm just saying I didn't want to be up in her shit!"

"You're up in *my* shit all the time! What makes Cassie such a princess?"

I rearrange myself with a feeling of high annoyance. I'm convinced none of this is remotely relevant, but for some reason I've become very, very interested in all the information Aubrey can't give me. The less I try to think about my creepy-photo correspondent, the more the pictures freak me out. Thoughts of them just keep circling in the back of my head like a computer's background processing. The smart part of me understands that Cassie's pictures are totally independent of mine, but this "Skor" thing is the closest I've heard so far to an answer ... and given that there's nothing I can do about the sender, I suddenly want to cling to this tiny little clue even if it means nothing. Which, obviously, it does.

"Come on, Aubrey. You're used to butting your way into things. Just tell her you saw a notification pop up and need to know where the pictures came from."

"I doubt she knows anyway!" Aubrey says. "Besides, she's got her notification previews set to maximum! I didn't even have to *open* the other emails to see stuff she wouldn't want me seeing! She had some argument going on with her aunt, grades stuff from the college, something from Ross ..."

That stops me, so I stop her. "Hang on. From *Ross?*"

"What?"

Oooh, no. Aubrey is *not* seriously trying to *What* me right now. My antenna went up the second she said the R word, and we're not going to pretend she didn't say it now.

"Don't bullshit me. *Ross is emailing Cassie?*"

"Um..."

"Ross is emailing Cassie," I repeat. This time it's a statement, because her badly faked ignorance counts as confirmation.

"Once," Aubrey answers.

"Once *that you saw.*"

"Well..."

"At the top of her inbox. Otherwise, you wouldn't have seen it," I say. Despite the cold, heat is flushing my neck and cheeks. "So he's not just emailing her in general; he emailed her *recently.*"

"No, no, it was days ago!" Aubrey stutters. "Monday, maybe Saturday or Sunday..."

"Monday?" I repeat.

"Yeah."

"You think Ross emailed Cassie on *Monday.*"

"Sure?"

"Monday, as in the day Ross started ghosting me."

"Miranda..."

My jaw clenches. I grip the phone tighter and hear its casing shift as if preparing to crack.

"It doesn't mean anything!" Aubrey says. "Let's focus on the pictures. That's why I called you."

Oh, is she talking about the pictures that mean nothing to me? Her distraction game is terrible. "I thought you called to distract me from my parents."

I hear her backpedaling. Aubrey thinks and talks so quickly, she constantly ends up putting a foot in her mouth. She didn't mean to tell me about Ross's email to Cassie, but of course she did anyway. Aubrey could never get away with a crime. If she killed someone, she'd call the victim's friends the next day to see if they suspected her. She'd make it awkward and weird, incriminating herself because she's too hyperactive to simply step back, admit nothing, and stay out of the way.

"I *did* want to distract you," she tells me, "but I couldn't find your number so mostly it was like whatever. Once I saw the pictures, though, I knew I *had* to call you. It wasn't optional anymore. And—"

"He's cheating on me with Cassie," I interrupt. "That's why he stopped texting."

"What? No!"

I can't let it go. Something about the Ross/Cassie thing feels like vindication I've been waiting for all along — a way to explain so many little things that didn't fit before. Truth is, Ross has *always* been attracted to Cassie, and she's always been attracted to him. I think they got up to shenanigans while Cassie and I were estranged, too, seeing as Cassie and Ross never really lost contact. Change the timelines a little and we were almost a love triangle. Cassie says it's nothing and I told myself it was nothing, but truth be told, my Spidey sense never stopped tingling. I even asked Ross about it once. He brushed it off, but I swore I saw something in his eyes.

"They're hooking up, Aubrey. I knew it. Goddammit, I'm so stupid!"

"No, they're not!"

"Yes. It all makes sense now."

"And you're deciding this based on an *email?* An email I didn't even have time to *read?* No. No way. Who hooks up over *email?*"

"You need to get that phone back," I say. "Find out what Ross sent her."

"If I'm getting her phone back to look at anything," Aubrey says, "it'll be to find out where those pictures came from."

"Okay. Do that. Get her phone back and look at the pictures." But my tone is colder than the ice outside. She knows I mean more than I've said.

There's a long pause. Aubrey laughs nervously. I'm stone-faced; she'd fear me if she saw me.

"I'm serious. Do it, Aubrey. Get that bitch's phone."

"You're jumping to conclusions."

"Yeah. I'm jumping to conclusions. I'm jumping to the conclusion that on the same day my boyfriend stopped talking to me, he renewed acquaintances with the girl he's so hot for, he couldn't stop staring at her when we were at the pool even though I was right beside him."

"Oh, come on. That email could be anything."

"Yeah," I say. *"Anything."*

There's a very long pause. Then Aubrey says, "Look. I don't really know what to do here. Should I keep talking, or just hang up?"

I grunt.

"All I know is that he sent her something. I don't know what it was. Or even if she replied."

I grunt again.

"She's your friend, M. Don't you think she deserves some benefit of the doubt? Are you really going to be *this* pissed off without having *any idea whatsoever* about her side of the story? If there even *is* a story? I mean, Ross is stupid. He could just be chasing her while she runs away. Hell, even if something *did* happen between them..."

"So now you think it did?"

"I'm just saying that *even if* it did — which no, I *don't* think it did — people make mistakes."

"Oh. Okay. Let me take some notes here," I say, still fuming. "So Cassie and Ross probably *are* hooking up and cheating on me, but—"

"No, they're not! I didn't say that!"

"—but even so, I shouldn't react. Because maybe there's a logical explanation. A mistake. Maybe she just tripped and fell into his bed."

"Or was so drunk, she didn't realize what was happening until it was too late."

I want to slap her, aghast. "You're not making me feel better, Aubrey! For fuck's sake, Cassie doesn't even drink!"

I hear her reset. In person, she'd be holding up both hands, asking for a pause and some peace. This is all classic Aubrey hole-digging. When she gets flustered, she tends to make bad things worse by accident. Interestingly, I'm usually the one who finally pulls her back from the cliff's edge.

Regardless, I force myself to take a few long, slow breaths. She's right; I'm way, *way* overreacting. I've gone from a tiny tickle of suspicion to Cassie sleeping with Ross due to mistakes and poor judgment. If only Aubrey wasn't so good at accidentally encouraging my paranoia.

It's this thing with my folks that's making me flip out. Between parental stress, last night's oddity, sleeplessness, and cold, I've become a powder keg. I'm keyed up so fully, I'm snapping at absolutely everyone: Mom, Dad, Aubrey ... and apparently Cassie, even though she's nowhere around.

I breathe. Slowly.

"It's okay. I'm done. I'm calm," I say.

"You didn't sound calm."

"I'm calm *now.*"

Aubrey says, *"O-kaaay..."*

I force myself to take a few more breaths. "It's honestly okay. I just need to think about it, is all. You're probably right. I'm kind of on edge. It's not your fault. So seriously, go on. I'll process the Ross-and-Cassie question later."

"You really want to 'process' something like that all by yourself? Alone, while you're going stir crazy? That doesn't sound like a good idea. Maybe we should keep talking it out. Maybe I can make you see there's another side to this."

"There might be. But even if I'm right and they *are* cheating, no big deal. I've basically come to grips with the fact that my boyfriend is a son of a bitch. If he's not screwing Cassie, then okay, sorry for the misunderstanding. And if she *is* screwing him, she's dead to me. That's all."

"You'd do that to Cassie? Just cut her off without a word? After all you've been through?"

"I don't take kindly to betrayal, Aub."

There's another long silence after that. I don't normally get this worked up, and I can tell Aubrey doesn't know what to do with it. She's a little scared of me right now; that's the way it feels.

More breaths. I close my eyes and try to clear my head. Then I say, very evenly, "Everything's fine. Are we done talking about the pictures? It sounds like nothing helpful to me."

It takes Aubrey a moment. In the pause that follows, I hear my parents talking in the kitchen. They're half-whispering, trying to be quiet. I can't make out their words, but very quickly their volume and intensity grow, becoming an argument. I hear my name twice. Dad seems to want one thing, while Mom's arguing for another.

"I only know that Cassie got pics from a Skor phone and there's not many Skors out there," Aubrey says, breaking my concentration. "It's probably nothing at all. But just in case you're going to start yelling at me again, I'd like to see if I can figure anything out *before* going back to her to ask where they came from. I don't want to embarrass her, or admit to snooping."

"I'm not going to yell at you." I check my temper and find myself calmer now — even embarrassed for my outburst. "I'm sorry. It's been strange around here. I guess I'm pretty keyed up."

"Strange how?"

I give her a quick recap, softening the edges of the weirdness simply because I'm no longer sure if any of it was truly weird. Aubrey's fiercely loyal. If I express an opinion, she'll immediately take my side, and woe be it to anyone who opposes her. In the past, she's always gotten along with my parents, though, so until I'm sure whether or not I'm the jerk, I'd rather not turn her against them.

"What about the pictures? Have you gotten any more of them?"

"I got one last night. It's pitch black. Nothing recognizable at all. Plus a ... well, a kind-of-creepy one that arrived right after I talked to you yesterday."

"Send them to me. If you can."

I try, remembering the newest one. That makes three pictures Aubrey hasn't seen, so I attempt to send them all. Of course I've got nothing. Service around here is so in and out.

"Send them to me as soon as you get bars, then," Aubrey says, sounding more like her usual self. "In the meantime: I didn't get anything from Cassie's pics, but it did make me think to look more closely at yours."

"'Look at them' how?"

"Pixel data. Stuff you wouldn't care about."

Or understand, I'll bet. "And?" I ask.

"Well, let's step back a second first. I wasn't done telling you about the Skor yet."

"What haven't you told me?"

"What makes them special. I just get the feeling this is important, even though I can't say why. You're right; the pictures are weird. Kind of disturbing for a reason I can't put my finger on. And coming from a Skor, knowing Skor's kind of customers? Let's just say I'm not taking it lightly."

I laugh — not because it's funny, but because it's my defense mechanism. The pictures have bothered me since I got the first one. Now, my detective-minded friend is implying trouble ... and she hasn't even seen the one that's all leg, mangled black meat, and blood.

"iPhones use Apple's protocol when it's iPhone to iPhone. Try to send big files through iMessage, though, and it'll time out if the network isn't strong enough. Other phones, including burners, use SMS messaging. Some use an even older technology, revamped for the modern age. A lot of the last kind are persistent."

"'Persistent'?"

"Instead of giving up, they'll keep trying to send until enough signal opens up. They'll eventually send unless you're inside a cave, if you give them long enough."

That explains why I'm getting the photos. Here and there, I'm getting bars. When that happens, my mysterious sender's phone is already right there, knocking on the door. I can't always send texts, but I do occasionally receive them.

"I like this whole thing less and less the longer I look at it," Aubrey says. It's clear this has been on her mind overnight. "It feels like something a stalker would do. At the very least, block them. If you were here, I'd suggest going to campus police just in case."

"Oh, come on." I put on a smile that I don't actually feel. "It's probably just someone messing around." Because that makes sense, given the horror image I received.

"That's what I thought, too," Aubrey says. "But then I noticed something. It might be nothing. *Probably* is nothing. But you know my instincts. And I don't like it, just the same."

I feel cold. Colder than even the cold room allows. "What?" I ask.

"The photo that shows the boarded-up window. If you look closely, it almost looks like—"

Before she finishes, a world-ending cacophony comes from outside. It sounds like an avalanche happening all at once: the letting go of something held back too long. At first, I can only brace, unsure what's about to happen. I go still, poised, my body tense, waiting for an enormous hammer to fall.

The sound crescendos outside my window, ending in a boom. At the same time I see a wash of rushing brown as a titanic, ice-covered tree limb thunders to the ground, shattering into a million pieces. Tiny sticks pelt the window. I find myself curled tight, my fists clenched. But it's over now.

As my heart resumes beating, I realize the receiver in my hand is dead.

Outside, the phone line disappears under the fallen branch, severed and useless.

Chapter Seven

When I leave my room to hang the stretched-out phone up at its source, I find my parents standing in front of the long row of windows — the ones that look out on the little parking area. They stop talking as soon as they see me, the way someone snaps their laptop shut when prying eyes walk by.

"What?" I don't know why, but they look guilty. Their faces pretend normality instead of just being normal.

"Miranda," says Dad. "You're awake."

I walk to stand beside them, Dad unsettled as I do so. We look out at the branch that broke the phone line. In the back of my mind, I hear Aubrey's last words: *The photo that shows the boarded-up window — if you look closely, it almost looks like—*

Like what? It was just some random window to me.

"Lucky it wasn't the power line," Dad says. "I think there's a generator. I should check."

He rushes outside without waiting, skirting the big branch like it's not even there. Mom watches him go. Movement closer by catches my eye. I look down to see Mom working her hands against one another, unsure what to do with them.

"It's actually not that bad out there," she says without me

asking. "The driveway's pretty icy, but that's because it's in the shade. Look." She points. "See where there's sun?"

I follow her finger. This is one of those two-faced winter days: bright but cold. Where the sun's been bathing the ice-covered branches for a few hours, the trees are dripping. There's a big round thermometer mounted outside the window that shows the temperature as thirty, but blazing sun trumps those two little degrees below freezing.

"The roads will be fine in an hour or two," she says, but it's like she's talking to herself. "The high today is supposed to be almost forty. We'll have the afternoon, before the storm comes."

I look at my phone. I have a single bar, flickering on and off. I also have one unread text message. It's the new photo. The one from my mystery correspondent — the one sending me unsettling snaps from a phone specifically made to be untraceable. But I don't want to think about that now. I'll think about it later.

If you look closely, it almost looks like—

"I'll bet I can get service if I go out into the front field," I say. I saw it on my way in: open land with huge spools of hay still baled up from autumn.

"Who do we need to call?" Mom asks.

"Maintenance. For the limb?"

Mom is still watching Dad. He's scrambling out by the shed again. Didn't they tell me the shed was locked, like the owner's closet off the kitchen? The damaged water pump was in there. Maybe the log splitter. And maybe the furnace, though that doesn't make any sense. I kept hearing heat kick on and off last night and it sounded like it was in a utility closet by the mud room at the cabin's rear.

"Mom? *Maintenance.* Do you want me to try and call them?"

"No. Nobody."

"Mom?" I almost want to snap my fingers to get her attention. Her eyes have four or five bags beneath them. She looks like she's been up all night. "Mom, this is above and beyond for Dad. Airbnb has protection for this kind of thing. It's not our responsibility."

Outside, Dad is visible again. He's not wheeling a generator, though. He's holding a chainsaw. He fires it up in two pulls, then begins disassembling the enormous, ice-covered branch. The sound through the window is the drone of a million wasps in unison. When the chain touches wood, it's like a monster chewing.

I put my hand on the door.

"Miranda, stay inside."

I push out. Open. The cold assaults me and I pull my blanket-wrap tighter.

Mom grabs my arm. "Miranda. No."

"Oh for Christ's sake, Mom."

I push past her, slipping my bare feet into an anonymous pair of muddy shoes left sitting on the stoop. I assume they're Dad's. Owners wouldn't just leave their shoes around for guests to use.

I'm beside my father quickly enough, surprising him when he sees me. He kills the chainsaw. Mom's instantly behind me, crossing the icy driveway in slippers.

"You're going to give yourself a heart attack, Dad. This is someone else's job. Let it be."

"Go back inside," he says. "It's freezing out here."

"Frozen," I correct. "Past tense." I look up, where the gentle swish of the breeze has become an ominous cracking. It's like we're at the foot of a Jenga tower, just waiting for it to fall. "This isn't safe."

"It's fine."

"It's not fine, Dad. The water goes out, then the heat ... and now the phone? With a snowstorm coming?"

"I took care of the water yesterday. The furnace is already fixed."

"It didn't seem fixed to me. You weren't anywhere near it. I saw you out by the shed. What's in the shed, Dad?"

"The junction box, if you can believe it," he mutters. "Power comes in from the street. That line right up there; see it?"

I look. Almost hidden by the trees is a huge electrical trans-former mounted on a pole. A black line runs from it to the shed. There's no line direct to the cabin — only secondary lines coming from the shed.

"It's all the same issue, Miranda. I've got it under control. One of the pipes coming up from the river plugged yesterday when it got too cold. The pipes run all over the place in there. One dripped on the circuit box this morning. Shorted it out. The cabin's not winterized properly. I patched it up. Added some insulation I found lying around in there."

I take a step toward the shed, to see this building code fiasco, but Dad says, "Don't. It's dangerous."

"Is that what the banging sound was? I heard banging last night."

"Yes," Mom says. "It's a mess, those pipes."

I look at the shed again, then at my parents. "Well, then, we should leave before the weather gets any worse. It's supposed to get *worse*, you guys. We can't stay here if it's falling apart."

"It's minor," Dad says. "It gets cold up here every winter. We were just the unlucky ones to be here when something finally snapped. It's handled. I promise."

I walk toward the shed again.

"Miranda, seriously. It's not safe."

I ignore him. I pull on the shed doors, but they won't budge. I can hear something rattling inside — a loose end my father hasn't dealt with, no matter how competent he pretends to be. He's always been like this. Always feigned confidence even when he wasn't remotely competent. Right now he and Mom are shouting at me to *get back, get back* ... as if I'm inches from a live wire.

"What's the combination?" I ask, noting a number lock above the handle.

"Miranda!"

"What's the combination," I repeat, firmer now.

Dad's got his hands up, palms toward me. Does he think I have a gun? Does he think I'm defusing a bomb? "I don't have the combination," he says. "The owners locked it for a reason."

"But you were *just* in there. To fix the pipes. Or the junction box, or whatever."

"I had to go in through the crawlspace. I won't have you going under there. It's full of spiders."

"The chainsaw, too? The chainsaw was in the crawlspace?"

"They left a closet of tools around the back. If you'd read the property description, you would've seen the note about it. They know things break here sometimes. I didn't want to have to say it, but honestly that's the only reason we could afford the place."

His statement lets all the air out of me: the ultimate parental-guilt death blow. Finances were always a sore spot. Especially with Dad, who's wrapped an outmoded sense of masculine pride into what he sees as failure to support his family. They've been self-conscious about it forever: neighbors in our affluent neighborhood taking spring breaks in Ibiza while we watched Netflix at home. And of course when I went off to a college with diamond-studded tuition? That only made the issue — and my role in causing it — so much worse.

"Look, Dad..." I'm pussyfooting now, not wanting to hurt him. "I just don't think it's safe to stay here with a storm coming. What if one of those big branches out there comes down next? Takes out the power?"

"That's why I wanted to check the generator."

"And?"

"It's fine."

"*It's fine?*" My head turns side to side, scoping the grounds. "What, you mean you already checked it?"

"Yeah."

"You've been out here ten minutes."

"Long enough to check the generator."

I don't understand. He had to have gone to the tool cabinet too because he came back with a chainsaw. Even setting required time aside, I didn't hear any motors start to be tested. What, did he just make a visual inspection? Or did I somehow miss the noise while Mom was inside acting catatonic?

"The genny'll work if we need it, and there's a ton of fresh gas," Dad goes on. "The furnace runs on fuel oil. There's a big tank behind the house and it's almost full. Heat comes from the oil, not the electricity. The furnace just needs enough electricity to run the fan. That's easy enough for the generator to handle."

"Where *is* the generator? Can I at least go and get it?"

"It's not on wheels. It's a big one. But there are lots of extension cords."

I inhale. Exhale. I guess a low-key fight for winter-storm survival will at least keep us from arguing about my hair, grades, and dating life. "Okay. What can I do?"

"Go into town," Mom says.

I turn. *"Town?"*

"Yes." Her eyes dart to Dad, to the shed, to the branches covered in ice, and finally back to me. She's still wringing an invisible dishrag. "You need to get supplies."

"Supplies."

"Groceries. Maybe a lantern or two. For the storm."

"This is ridiculous. Look. I'll spring for a hotel. Just for one night. If the roads are clear, we'll come back here tomorrow."

"No," Dad says. "Forget it. You're not paying for us, for a hotel room."

"Dad..."

"I said no. We're fine here."

"But *you* have to run out," Mom says. "For supplies."

"Water?" I ask.

She nods.

"We have lots of water," I say. "I saw like ten skids of bottles. *Not* in the owner's closet. *Not* off-limits."

"It doesn't belong to us," Dad says. "Give me an hour to get this branch out of the way. The roads should be okay by then. Your mother and I were already talking. This is what you can do for us. You can run for supplies."

But that doesn't make any sense. I did see the water, but that's atop the crapload of water my parents brought with them. Untrusting of tap water, they always vacation with lots of bottles — I know because we always fight about it, because it's hell on the environment. The fridge is so stuffed from their original grocery trip a few days ago, I could barely fit the half-and-half back in there after prepping my coffee. They bought six or seven boxes of cereal. Cans of vegetables, fruit, and soup. There's a chest freezer in the utility room with not one but *two* big Costco bags of chicken breasts. Bread. Enough lunchmeat that Mom's frozen half of that, too. None of this is shocking. A grocery run out here would take several hours. Mom and Dad always come prepared.

"I think my time's better spent helping you with the branch, if you insist on staying," I tell my father.

"I'm not kidding, Miranda," Dad says, making no move to extend me the chainsaw — an implement that, thanks to growing up with him, I can wield as well as anyone. "You said it yourself. A storm is coming."

"And going out on icy roads is more of a problem than making sure we have six months of food instead of just two months," I counter.

"The roads will be fine."

"Dad. Really. Is there a second chainsaw?"

"No," Mom snaps.

"No," Dad says more evenly.

I stroll toward the shed's corner.

"Where are you going?"

"To the tool closet."

"Why?"

"To check out the wide selection of hand saws at my disposal. Or limb shears."

"There's none of that," Dad says.

"You should get dressed," Mom says. "With the snow coming, you'll want to head out as soon as you can."

"Okay. Explain something to me. If the storm's coming, why—?"

I'm interrupted by a huge cracking sound — enough that I look up, sure we're about to be crushed by another ice-covered branch. But it came from the cabin, not the sky: a single hard snap, and now a sound like gushing.

Dad rushes ahead, and then I see: a river of blue-white water is spraying from beneath the cabin's foundation in a river.

"SHIT!"

Dad's on his stomach in a second, scooting into the crawlspace. He works to avoid the water, but some of it still splashes him, fogging like warm breath in all this chill. He'll freeze if much of it gets on him, down there in the deep-freeze.

He vanishes one inch at a time. His profanity dwindles with him.

"SHITSHITSHITshitshit*shitshit*!"

Soon I can only see his feet while he works on something beneath the joists, water and mud absolutely everywhere. Mom's beside me, hands clasped on her chest. Her head steams as if she's hot from the sauna.

"Get me a wrench! A big one! A channel lock!"

Mom looks dumbfounded. She doesn't know tools. I do, though. A channel lock is a plumbing wrench. This isn't good. That plus all the water probably means a pipe has burst from the cold.

I run toward the tool closet, but Dad calls after me. *"Inside! There's a big toolbox at the foot of the coat closet!"*

I start to go, but then I stop.

"Dad? Where's the shutoff?"

"What?"

"The water shutoff!" I have to yell for him to hear me, especially with all the water noise. *"Where do you shut the water off?"*

I'm looking around frantically, searching for the only telltale I know to find buried things: a too-warm spot on the ground where ice and snow melts first. But things here wouldn't be done that way, would they? There's no lid-covered water meter out here, where a master shutoff valve would be. Water comes from the river. The shutoff, if the builders followed their own rules in making this place, could be anywhere. Or nowhere.

But Dad has the answer. "It's in the closet by the pantry!"

"The *owner's* closet?"

Oh. That's not good. That's not good at all. We'll need an axe to get in there. If we don't want to turn the lot into an ice rink, we might have to—

"Yes!"

"But it's locked!"

And in response, he says, *"2412!"*

"That's the address, not the—"

"Miranda! Hurry, will you?"

I rush inside. I'll grab the wrench like he wants, but my next stop after dropping it off won't be the closet; it'll be the shed. Dad's not thinking straight. This is a rental, and in rentals the owners always lock up their stuff. We don't have the owner's closet code, and the door is no joke — clearly solid wood, with hinges concealed so we can't pop them open. The shed door, on the other hand, is flimsy. If I can't get inside through the crawlspace like Dad did, I'm pretty confident I can use a big hammer or wrench to break down the door. What I need to do is turn off the pump: the *ultimate* shut-off, killing the flow at its source.

That wouldn't be smart, though, I think. *Dad already worked on the pump, but he had to half-ass it because I don't think he went out for supplies. That means there are probably leaks in the system, and* that *means that when the pump goes off, the water filling the supply pipe hanging down the cliff will empty back into the river. We won't be able to re-prime it after the broken pipe's fixed. Turning off the pump means turning off our water for good.*

There's no choice. But then I stop at the owner's closet after all, and I think:

2412.

That's the building address, not the code to anything. Dad's confused. We don't have the code. Why would we have the code?

I step toward the closet anyway. Lots of people use *password* as their password. For numerical codes, more folks than you'd think use *1234.* Is it really so crazy to think the owners of this place might use the address? Especially if the place is managed by a manager — someone juggling multiple properties, many easily-forgettable codes?

I tap it in: 2. 4. 1. 2.

The lock glows green. The handle turns without friction and the door opens. I'll be damned.

Inside, installed against the back wall and big as life, is a vertical pipe with a big yellow valve in its middle. I turn the valve perpendicular to the pipe, and the sound of rushing water dies in an instant.

"Thank God," I hear Dad say, muffled, from beneath the floor.

With my heart still pounding, I step back. I can rest now. There's replacement PVC in here and pipe dope in the toolbox. Dad knows perfectly well how to use them. He shouldn't be the one to fix his rental, but he can and will, if it's all he can afford.

I step back, about to close the door again. But then I wonder: Did the owners give Dad the code just in case it was needed, realizing their error in locking up the shutoff when a freeze was due? Somehow, I doubt that's what happened. The code wasn't hard to crack, but difficulty wasn't the question. *Effort* was the question. Dad didn't deduce that code on the spot for me to use. No, he'd figured it out already.

Why would Dad crack the code to the owner's closet? What would even possess him to try?

I open the door again. There's nothing particularly valuable inside at first glance: mostly row upon row of travel-size shampoo, travel-size conditioner, and itty-bitty bars of soap. In the corner is a vacuum and a mop bucket: stuff for the cleaning crew to use between guests. There are a few personal items shoved in with all the necessities, but it's mostly garbage: stuff concealed from guests not because it's valuable, but because it just needed to be out of the way.

Or a liability.

Or because it's against the Airbnb host rules, locked up for safety and insurance reasons.

It's okay to leave power tools out ... but not the small but fully stocked wet bar tucked into an elbow of the shelf.

There's a bottle of vodka.

A bottle of rum.

A bottle of gin.

Brandy. Schnapps. Bitters and other mixers. Even some weird sort of coffee liqueur I've never heard of. None of them are sealed.

While I'm gawking at all the booze, a zippered black case catches my attention. Thinking it might be siphons and funnels — a whole little kit for making cocktails — I reach for it. It's too heavy, though. I unzip it, startle at what's inside, then put it immediately back.

It's a gun. The owners left a gun in the closet, along with the liquor.

I step back, feeling my stomach drop. It's interesting that I'm more bothered by the alcohol — and the fact that Dad knows the combo — than the pistol.

This was all right here. All in plain sight. I don't know why Dad tried the obvious combination to go into the cabinet the first time. I just know that at any time thereafter, he's been able to return.

I shut the closet door, feeling hollow.

"Miranda?" Dad's voice comes from under the floorboards. "The wrench?"

I look down at the toolbox and think: *Maybe he went into the closet to find the shutoff valve just in case we needed to get at it. The liquor bottles weren't front and center. Maybe he didn't even see them. Maybe, despite going to some length to break in where the owners wouldn't want him, he doesn't know all that booze is there.*

But I'm more than Ross's fool if I believe that.

You've smelled his breath, I tell myself. *He's not drinking. He's not drinking. Miranda? Listen to me: YOUR FATHER ISN'T DRINKING...*

I pick up the toolbox as one last word to the sentence begins to spin in my mind:

... yet.

Chapter Eight

Dad works on fixing the burst pipe. Mom paces restlessly for a while, as if something unknown is bothering her, then eventually retires to the drawing room to sketch. Mom sketches whenever she's happy. Or whenever she's stressed-out and needs to relax.

I tell myself it's all the commotion that's troubling her. A limb fell, a pipe burst, and a storm is coming — a storm they won't hear of leaving the cabin to avoid. I tell myself that Dad was just thinking ahead: knowing the property wasn't entirely reliable, knowing his ability to fix things, and wondering about pipes bursting long before one actually did. He didn't break into the closet because he knew owner's closets are where a lot of part-time Airbnb renters stash their booze. He did it because that's where the shutoff had to be. And good thing he did, right? We'd be up a creek if he hadn't had that intel at his fingertips.

For a while, I listen to Dad work under the shed. I didn't mention the liquor bottles to him, and he hasn't so much as looked at me sideways — the way he might if he knew that I know. We're either both pretending there's no shameful secret in play, or there honestly *is* no shameful secret.

I suppose it's possible he never saw the bottles hiding in all that shampoo and soap — or that he saw them but was strong enough to resist. I should take his no-big-deal attitude right now, about my entering the owner's closet, as a good sign. It either means he's hiding nothing or he's so solid in his sobriety that he finds the bottles not worth mentioning. After all, why would he bother proactively defending himself to me if we both know how committed he is to staying clean?

Two voices fight inside my head: an argument only I can hear.

Two more days, says the first voice. *Two more days until Dad's one-year anniversary. He wouldn't throw his sobriety away this close to a big landmark.*

But then another voice says, *Except that he's done it twice before.*

No. Not this time. Not with Mom's ultimatum on the table. He wouldn't. He won't.

He would if he's as stressed-out as Mom is ... if something's bothering both of them as much as you know it is.

I try to laugh at my paranoia. Everything is fine here. Nothing is bothering my parents that they aren't telling me. Nothing is stressing them out. What I've seen since arriving is totally and completely normal.

And the wiseass voice inside me says, *Uh-huh. Sure it is.*

It's an impossible situation. I want to trust them. They've sacrificed so much for me. Finances are just the tip of it. They raised me imperfectly, but when things were said and done, they still raised me well. The ghosts in our past, we've all quietly agreed to dispose of.

We had our dysfunctions when I was in high school, but a lot of that was Dad's drinking, which I keep reminding myself is a disease: not his choice, not his doing. I know how hard they're trying this time. Mom reining in her henpecking and judgments. Dad holding tight to sobriety, tempted by the bar in the closet or not.

But although I want to trust them, I can't ignore my gut ... or this suffocating feeling of unease I can't fully describe. It's not just Mom and Dad that have me on-edge; it's also Aubrey's call and Ross's sudden cruelty. It's the pressure of school and the need to rip out Cassie's throat for hooking up with my boyfriend, if I still believe that, which I'm not sure whether I do. It's the sense of *something's-not-right-here-but-I-have-no-clue-what-it-is.*

It's also the photos I keep getting. Can't forget about those. What do they mean? Who's sending them? Why do they bother me so?

They bother you because one looked like a horror movie, idiot.

But the other photos have been nothing. And when I try to talk to the sender, I get no response — just photos without explanation. Isn't it logical to think it's a prank?

Or a threat.

I hear Aubrey's voice in my head: *I think those pictures are coming from a burner phone — the kind that can't be traced. Criminals use them.*

I look out the window. The trees are dripping now, the air warmed in the past two hours. The sun's been beating down this whole time, surely thawing out the open roads. It's almost noon. Supposedly the storm will begin to hit us 6ish. If I do what my parents want, my errand to the store and back will take at least two hours. I'd like to allow three. I could leave right now, be back in plenty of time.

But why do I even *need* to go to the store? Now that I know that's the plan, I've inventoried what we already have — and what we have is plenty. *More* than plenty. Dad packed like we were going camping. He's got a few tools of his own, some firestarter logs, and a little solar generator should we need it. There's even a small tent with the gear, in case the heat does go out and we have to huddle up for warmth. We have enough food to supply a hotel banquet.

I told them all of this. They don't care. Mom's refrain is, *You can never be too prepared.*

It's ridiculous. Given our current level of preparation, the next paranoid step would be to leave this broken place and wait until the storm passes. The next step would be to keep their 19-year-old daughter near the preparation they already have, not send her out where there still may be ice. You don't make three-hour errands when snow threatens. You don't, my friends, *even leave the house.* But they won't hear me. Their minds are set. The sooner I go, the better.

As if they're trying to get rid of me.

My eyes go to my phone. I still haven't looked at the photo the anonymous sender sent to me this morning. I'm delaying because thinking on it gives me strange dread. I've ignored it so far, hoping it goes away. But why? It came from a whole other world. I have no bars here. I couldn't reply even if I wanted — to the latest photo that, according to Aubrey, patiently waited for tiny oases of cell reception to send me these pics one pixel at a time.

I open it and see a wooden floor. The macro focus has engaged this time, showing a close-to-the-lens nail head that's not entirely hammered down. The camera itself is poor, unable to throw much light on the surroundings, so I can't get any real idea of the bigger picture. Am I looking at the floor of an outhouse? A tar-paper shack somewhere in the slums? We live in a global world. The pics could be coming from the other side of the Earth for all I know.

A cowboy bar in Detroit.

Behind the scenes at Disney, in Orlando.

A hostel in Warsaw.

A hovel in Shanghai.

But why? Why is someone sending me anonymous garbage?

If you look closely, it almost looks like—

In my bedroom, I pull my laptop from my school bag, then transfer the photos from my phone by cable. Now on the bigger screen, I enlarge the picture Aubrey mentioned: the one showing a boarded-up window. Seeing nothing of interest, I open it in Photoshop and adjust the levels. *Brightness up. Contrast down.* I don't understand the histogram tool at all, but I use it anyway. Nothing shows me squat.

The only thing notable in the image is the window itself. The board-up job is imperfect, leaving a gap at one edge through which the camera can see outside. The only problem is the brightness. With the photo's exposure set by the dark room, the sky through the gap is brighter-than-bright white. I zoom in, but it's still almost featureless, showing only vague shapes: slightly less-white whites than the white all around it. So I zoom more, crop, then return to the image controls. I lower the brightness, raise the contrast, and play around with the Levels panel to emphasize shadows and de-emphasize highlights and midtones. This turns the dark areas pitch black, but the grays start to take on shape.

After enough fiddling, I see a perfect arc through the window gap. It's not natural, so it must be a man-made structure. Radiating vertically down from the arc are straight lines, also man-made. So it's ... a building of some kind? Or at least the steel frame of one? I scrunch my face and defocus my eyes, but what's there still makes no sense to me.

"Miranda? Are you about ready to go?"

It's my mother, at the door of my room. Dad's still working in the crawlspace. He's got a little space heater blowing on him down there now. Nice and comfy, in with the spiders.

I shut my laptop, unable to see whatever Aubrey "almost saw" in my photo.

"I can be," I reply. "But Mom. Seriously. I looked again at how much food and water we have, and—"

"You can never be too prepared."

"It might not be safe. Driving."

She seems to consider that. For a half-second, I see maternal concern in her eyes. Then it vanishes and she goes back to the same weird look she keeps giving me. It's the blank stare of a Stepford wife. Or a zombie.

"Oh, you'll be fine," she says. "You've always been a good driver. Won't we all feel better, knowing we're prepared for the storm?"

"Even though we're *already* pretty prepared," I say.

"*Pretty* prepared."

"Even though it makes more sense, if you're this worried, to spend a few nights at the Holiday Inn Express in Leightonville."

"But that would break the spell, wouldn't it? *Us. Here.* Away from the world together." Her gaze softens. It creeps me out a little, the way she looks at me next. "This trip was supposed to be magical. I insist that it is."

I nod mechanically, still waiting for her to come to her senses and take it back. She doesn't. She just keeps nodding at me like someone in shock.

"Are you okay, Mom?"

"Why wouldn't I be okay?"

Oh, just blurt it out. "Is Dad drinking? Are you covering for him? Is that what's going on here?"

Now I get a smile. It's the kind of smile that makes me feel worse, not better. "Oh, no. It's nothing like that."

"Then what is it?"

"Nothing. We're here. We're a family. That's all that matters."

"There's booze here. In the closet. Dad knows the combination."

The creepy gaze snaps, and here again is the hard-edged mother I've always known. "He's not drinking, Miranda."

"But—"

"I said he's not. It's insulting to keep asking. You have no idea how hard your father has worked. You can't know everything he's done to protect you over the years. Through thick and thin, we always only ever thought of *you,* Miranda."

We lock eyes. I decide not to say more, knowing it's the only real choice I have.

So I gather my purse. My keys. My phone, plus a charger for when I have GPS reception and don't want to drain the battery. There's a credit card on the kitchen table — Dad's — with a Post-It stuck to it that says, *Use this.* I grab that too, putting it in my pocket with the supply list they gave me.

They're standing in front of my car like a receiving committee when I walk outside.

"Drive safe," says Mom.

Then Dad: "It's an easy drive. It's almost forty degrees now. Shouldn't be ice. You have the map I drew? The credit card? The list?"

I pat my coat pocket.

"There and back," Mom says. "Two and a half hours. Max."

"And the snow won't be here until six. At the earliest."

"Hurry back," Mom says. "But take your time."

More confused than ever, I walk past my pair of waiting sentinels, noting the way they watch me until I'm seated with the engine running. Dad has something in his hand. Two things, presumably for his fix-it job. One's a hammer. The other is rope. They're halfway behind his back, like bottles of whiskey he's trying to hide.

My parents wave at me. Like robots.

I pull away, soon enough headed down the tree-lined, canopy-covered driveway.

When I glance in the rearview mirror, I see them running back toward the buildings — sprinting in some unknown rush, as if they'd been dying for me to leave.

Chapter Nine

I pause at the end of the driveway to remove Dad's map from my pocket and flatten it on the console. My phone still shows no bars. No new texts. No incoming photos full of curved beams and empty sky.

"Two and a half hours," I say aloud, watching that same sky and thinking of snow. *"Max."*

Gravel crunches as I pull onto the main road. I remember the first parts of this, seeing as I drove them yesterday. The driveway reverse-forks before it meets the road, so the first turn doesn't count; it'd just take me somewhere else on the property. Then it's left at the oversized mailbox, past the big spools of hay that pock the front field, and right at the stop sign. A quarter mile down, the road winds back on itself to cross the valley.

There's nobody in sight as I roll over the rusty tied-arch bridge. My eyes drop to the river below. *Our* river. I'm surprised to discover that I can see the cabin from here, perched on the valley's lip. There's the big picture window. There's the shed. I try to spot my parents — to catch a glimpse of whatever they ran off to do the second I pulled away — but I'm too far for that.

Move along. Nothing to see here.

For a long time, there's only one unchanging road. I'm

descending mountain foothills, so the terrain rolls and the road wraps around it, confusing my sense of direction. I grew up in flat-lands and live now on a city grid, so I'm used to order. In New York, if you miss a left turn, you can just take the next one. On *these* roads, though, you might need to turn right to make up for a missed left. Or go south to go north because there's something — a lake, a peak — in the way. Driving up here gives me vertigo. I have to trust the map more than I'd like. It's an act of faith because Dad drew it roughly, with little thought to scale.

Did I see the red farmhouse with the blue door yesterday? You'd think I'd remember a house like that, but I don't. Is this the right way? Or have I gotten turned around?

The sense of being lost begins small, then grows. Ten minutes in, I'm wondering at distinctive landmarks I should remember from yesterday but don't. The thought that I've made a wrong turn and am headed in the wrong direction boils slowly from there: first an idea, then a consideration, then a worry. Worry finds its own momentum.

If I actually *am* lost, I start to wonder how I'll ever fix it. I don't have a real map — only Dad's scribbles on a literal napkin. GPS remains MIA. Should I turn around? Try to find the place this trip went wrong? Or will that make things worse ... because what if I make a second wrong turn while I'm trying to find my first? If that happens, I won't be anywhere near Dad's map. I'll have to stop at some random house and ask for directions, and horror movies have taught me how bad that idea can be.

Time is running out. Snow is coming. The sky is darkening.

I decide not to turn back just yet, but then snow starts to fall, and I wonder if I'm just compounding the mistake I'm increasingly sure I made.

I should turn back. Retrace my steps. Because I'm pretending at cool, sure ... but deep down I'm starting to panic. Getting snow-bound is bad, but doing it with nobody around and no cell service would be a nightmare. I saw this documentary segment once, about a man trapped off the road by an avalanche. His car kept him from being crushed, and the fact that he was overweight kept him from freezing. He drank melted snow to stay alive. In the end he didn't, though. It took weeks for him to die. His phone was full of recorded farewells: the final signoffs of a man who, from the time he went off the road, knew he was dead.

I gasp with relief when the road makes a T and I recognize the intersection. I turn left, and thirty seconds later I'm pulling into the last gas station before the cabin. This is where I pulled off yesterday, to check in with Aubrey.

I park next to a pump and begin filling my tank even though it's still nearly full. Only after I take a moment to collect myself do I realize how scared I actually was.

Once the nozzle is in my tank and pumping, I look across the trees and ask myself if this is the hill I want to die on. That's usually just an expression, but right now I mean it literally.

I tilt my face to the sky and close my eyes. The flakes are falling more steadily now. For the last quarter hour, I've had the windshield wipers on to keep them at bay. The sun's gone, ducked back behind the clouds almost as soon as I left the cabin's driveway. Its absence makes the air feel twenty degrees colder, though my car's thermometer says it's only three or four degrees. Bright sun will do that. Sun and forty degrees can feel like springtime. Overcast skies, even at the same temperature, are far more frigid.

That's how things feel now, as clouds build and shadows come. It's ... what? 12:45? Close enough to noon, and yet the world feels like twilight, with the sun setting. As before, there are no other cars at the station and the clerk is barely visible inside. I feel incredibly alone. I'm in some strange and remote place where no human should be, like the dark side of the moon.

The nozzle clicks when the tank is full. I've only added three gallons. After, I sit in my car, turn on the engine, and drive to the station's edge, because courtesy tells me unnecessarily not to block the pump. I don't take to the road, though. Even though I know where I am now — maybe even in the big picture, and with GPS back online — I'm reluctant to continue. I've given myself the creeps thinking about that guy in the avalanche, taking lonely weeks to perish under the snow.

With my phone working again like a lifeline, I pull up the weather. Radar is slow to fill in, but with time it does. I can see the big winter storm. The forecast waffles, still not quite sure which way the thing will turn over the next few hours. It's close now, but its arrival time remains TBD.

Do we still have until 6ish?

Maybe.

Probably.

But no guarantees.

"Oh *fuck this*," I say.

I'm going back to the cabin. No shopping trip for me — not as scared as I got when I thought I was lost, and not the way it's starting to snow. Mom and Dad can just deal with it if they think we're undersupplied for the storm. We're not. *Objectively* not. We've got weeks' worth of stuff up there, and assuming Dad's right about the generator (he usually is about mechanical things), we won't run out of heat.

I never should have gone on this errand. They never should have sent me. The temperature must've dropped below freezing again, seeing as snow — not rain or sleet — is coming down. That means there could be ice on the road again like there was on my drive up. Why did they insist I do this? I'm their only child, alone with a blizzard on the way.

I turn the car around, inverting Dad's map, and head back toward the turnoff. Since I've made the drive in this direction before, I'm more confident. I'm not quite as afraid of getting lost this time — and feeling good, because now my errand is over instead of just beginning.

The snow falls faster. I turn the wipers up to high and flick on the headlights to combat the dim. The lights help — but the view, once they're on, gives me vertigo. As the wind builds, snow whirls across the road ahead. My headlights show me each individual flake, swirling and churning like the inside of a washing machine.

I almost laugh with relief when I reach the bridge over the valley again. Snow is sticking to the road now as the storm does what the weather thought it might: obeying a north wind and arriving early.

The bridge means I'm minutes away from the cabin. The sight couldn't be more welcome: a straight roadbed, its single arch a gentle arc in the sky.

My eyebrows draw together. My lips form a straight line. I'm not sure why, but a sudden ominous feeling just shivered up my spine. I can feel the hairs on the back of my neck wanting to stand up as I cross the bridge. It's a gut-deep sense — some symbolic pattern rattling my brain's fear center, the way a driver startles when red and blue lights start flashing behind them.

What is it? Why do I suddenly feel so besieged? I can't put my finger on it. Something about the bridge. About the dark bulk of its massive arch rising above me, girders rising like spokes to meet it. It reminds me of a spider. Of a large metal insect, looking down on me like prey.

Once I'm over the bridge I pause and look back, but the intensity of whatever-the-hell-that-was is mostly gone now.

I shake the strange feeling off. Find the stop sign, then the driveway. The fork doesn't fool me this time; I stay to one side and am soon under the canopy again. Because of it, the snow stops. My windshield clears. My hood is covered with white stuff, though — half an inch at least, and that's on a car that's never stopped moving.

I pause again. Frown again. What's different here? That's when I notice a fresh set of tire tracks in the new snow. Did Mom or Dad leave while I was gone? Why would they do that? Where would they go? Were they worried about me, thinking maybe they could drive to somewhere with bars and call? Because they damn well *should* be worried. This unnecessary errand was dangerous as hell, and it's only because I turned back early that it's not a whole lot worse.

I'm more convinced than ever that Mom and Dad were wrong in insisting we tough it out. We should have gone to a hotel, then come back when the roads were open, when we were safe, when there was once again a way out. But right or wrong, the decision's been made and can't be unmade. Now the storm is here. Now, there's no leaving. No turning back.

The wind is whooping when I park and kill the engine. Across the open valley, the peril of it all feels so much worse. Air whooshes through the trees, rattling them like old bones. Around the eaves, the wail of wind is a sound like screaming.

I pull my coat tight and march toward the cabin, but a noise from the shed catches my attention. From here, I can see the wide-open door. I guess Dad figured out the combination. Or deduced it, same as he did for the code to the booze-filled owner's closet.

The wind screeches with a knife's edge, cutting through the gaps in my coat. I don't have a hat; my ears feel frostbite. I chug toward the shed, retroactively scared and needing the comfort of seeing my father at work. He's great with machines. If the generator has anything to it at all, Dad will make it run.

My shuffling feet cut long channels — not distinct footprints — in the building snow. It scares me how redline all of this is. I turned back early, but almost didn't decide to turn back at all. What if I'd gone even ten miles farther toward the grocery store? How close did I come to being trapped out there? How much danger did Mom's paranoid storm-prep nearly put me in ... and *oh*, the irony of that?

I shuffle faster, but before I reach the square of light thrown by the open shed doors, something stops me cold. It's the exact same feeling I had while crossing the bridge: that sense of some primitive trigger yanking my most terrified strings.

From here, I have a view of that same bridge: the gentle arc, sweeping into the sky. Girders radiating up to that arch, like spokes on a wheel. Just as I could see the cabin from the bridge, so can I see the bridge from here. And then, unbidden, I hear Aubrey's cut-off voice in my head:

The photo that shows the boarded-up window. If you look closely, it almost looks like—

I feel cold. Colder than I am already.

It almost looks like—

And that's when I know. That's when I'm certain. My mind flies back to the photo Aubrey was talking about when she said that, to the image-enhancement I did to see its details. All I was able to see, through gaps around the photo's boarded-up window, was an arch like that. Spokes like that. Aubrey hasn't been here, so she was probably just going to say she saw *a bridge*. But I don't just see *a* bridge when I think about it now. I see *that* bridge.

The picture sent by my mystery texter could have come from anywhere, but it didn't. It came from *right here*. From inside the shed just around the corner from me now, looking through its boarded-up window at this very same bridge.

I jog into the light, to where the thrown-open doors of the shed give me a view of everything. Inside I find my parents, who thought they had hours before my return.

They've backed Dad's truck up to the shed as if preparing to load it. A tarp's been laid flat in the bed. Blue ropes are fastened to the truck's cargo ties — four at the corners of the bed, ready to hold something down. But the truck's not what draws my attention. What does that are my parents, both of whom are crouched beneath a tool bench made of plywood and metal pipe. Dad's right hand is smeared with something red, as is half of Mom's coat. Behind them are a few tools: a hammer, a saw, and more blue rope.

Between them is someone else: a third person whose face is bruised and bleeding.

It's Ross.

He's tied tight to the pipes supporting the tool bench, his mouth covered with a gag. Based on the stains below where he's tethered, he's been here for a while. Something's wrong with one of his arms. I can't see all of the left one, but it doesn't seem tied down. It's ... *wrong* somehow.

"Mom? Dad?"

They both spin as if stuck by a cattle prod. Their expressions are slack and horrified, seeing me where I am.

"M-Miranda!" Dad stammers. "This isn't what it looks like!"

PART II

Chapter Ten
AUBREY

"—Steel girders," I say. "Like a building. Or a bridge."

I wait for Miranda to comment on what I see in the most interesting of her uninteresting pictures, even though it's not much to go on. But she doesn't respond.

"Miranda?" I say. *"A bridge'?"*

She says nothing.

I pull the phone from my face to see our call's been disconnected. I try to call her back, but all I get is one of those old-fashioned recorded messages saying the number is out of service. So I try her cell, but it goes right to voicemail — no surprise, considering weather up there's only getting worse. I've got an iPhone. She's got an iPhone. Chances aren't great that we'll even be able to send texts until the storm is over.

I text her anyway: *Your landline cut off and now it won't go through. Let me know if you get this.*

But after a bit of spinning, my phone tells me the message can't be delivered and asks if I'd like to try again. I decline. There's no point. That's the problem with the new-school phones. They try for a few seconds, then surrender. Unlike Skors, which never give up.

"Are you headed out?" asks my roommate, Suni.

I'm still stuck in my conversation with Miranda, wondering what just happened. For a moment I can't respond because I'm not in New York anymore. My mind is up in New Hampshire, dodging snowflakes with my best friend.

"Earth to Aubrey," Suni says.

"What?"

"I asked if you were heading out."

"Why?"

"Because *I'm* heading out." She cocks a thumb over her shoulder. "Remy's double parked. I'm thinking maybe I leave him there just for fun. But I'm torn, because I also want to get the fuck out of this place. How would you handle the situation?"

"Don't manipulate your brother into getting a ticket for double-parking," I say.

Suni looks disappointed. Usually I encourage her to do bad things.

"But do listen to 'Never Gonna Give You Up' on repeat all the way home to drive him crazy."

"His stereo doesn't work."

"But your phone's speakers do. That's why it's brilliant."

She tips her head at me, wondering about something. At the exact same moment, a car honks from outside. I'm a big fan of Suni's family. They're always fighting, but in playful ways. It's like they want to hilariously destroy each other. I've never had so much fun encouraging people to disagree.

"You okay?" Suni asks. "You look weird. I mean, like, weirder than you normally look."

"I was talking to Miranda and the call just dropped. No warning."

"And?"

I frown and shake my head slowly, one time to each side. So what if the call dropped? It happens all the time. I should let it go and move on, but for some reason it sticks to me.

"I just get a strange feeling."

"About a call dropping?"

"I'm not sure what it's about."

"Uh-huh. Okay. Well, you have fun with that." Suni leans over where I'm sitting on the bed to give me a halfway hug. "I'm out. See you in the new year."

After saying goodbye to me, Suni bends at the waist and pets my dog, Abby. Technically we're not supposed to have pets in the dorms, but technically I keep bribing the RA with my vast stash of frozen Girl Scout Cookies and technically everyone loves Abby anyway. She doesn't make noise, gets along with everyone, and has long, free-dangling strands hanging from her ears and eyebrows that for some reason we call "personality hair." Somehow this is reason enough to keep a 50-pound dog in a place where even hotplates and toasters are forbidden. But then again, that's me. I've always been good at understanding the people around me and using what I know about them to get what I want.

"And you," Suni tells Abby. "You just stay cool."

"Gravel," Abby replies. She doesn't make normal dog noises, just these weird ones that sound like human words. One more reason to keep her around, from what I hear.

Suni exits. I hear her through the window a minute later, yelling at her brother that his car is a polluting piece of shit. Remy shouts back that if she has a problem with it, she can take a bus home. I watch as Suni gives him the finger. Remy returns the compliment. Then Suni throws her stuff in the back and they drive off, and I'm left alone with this odd feeling in my gut.

Why do I feel this way? What's bugging me that I can't let go? There's weather up where Miranda is, and I'd called her landline. Phones go out sometimes in bad weather. It's nothing unusual. Nothing to worry about.

"Burlap," Abby grumbles.

I pet her furry black head and say, "Exactly."

Chapter Eleven

With Suni gone, I pack my bags with halfhearted effort. It's been a half hour since she asked if I was about to head home for the holidays, but Suni's only known me for a semester. If she knew me better, she'd understand the answer without me having to give it: *It's complicated.*

Arguments or not, Suni actually likes her family. Me? I blossomed when I left for college, and going home means pruning myself back to the tidy little stump I was in high school. Miranda and I met by bonding over our bad parents. She got lucky in the years between then and now; her dad got sober, and her mom seems to have realized she can't helicopter-parent Miranda forever. My mom has had no such revelation. And my dad? I'm not even sure where he is right now. Our other friend Cassie recently lost her mother and now has no parents at all. I'm not sure if I prefer her situation or mine.

Suni went home to good food and good times. I'll be going home to a constantly annoyed stepfather and a bootcamp designed by my mother. She'll have me studying nonstop for classes I don't even have yet. If we had any money, she'd hire a tutor and a personal trainer so I could work off the college weight — which, by the way, *Mom's* been gaining for decades without college as an excuse. She isn't big on self-improvement for herself. She only goes all-in when it's about improving me.

I look at my open duffel. I've packed one pair of socks and the little fingerboard I use when I want to practice guitar but don't want anyone to actually hear me play. Which, for now, is never. I'm terrible, but I love it. I'll have to guard my little fidget toy carefully. If Mom finds out I'm trying to pick up an instrument, she'll start intruding on that, too. I'll come home hating guitar as much as I hate flute, piano, and the old-timey literature Mom used to make me read.

Socks. The board. Yeah, I'm really doing a great job of packing for this trip right now.

My phone lights up with a new text message. My mom is psychic. She knows when I'm trying to avoid her, or when I most don't want to hear from her. Which, now that I've tasted freedom at college, is all the time.

But the text isn't from my mother. It's from Del, my boss at the student information office.

i know your going home but any chance you can work today, james is sick

Dammit, Del. You know how hard it is for me to respect you when you can't capitalize, punctuate, or spell properly.

I look at my bag with its inadequate cargo, thinking about how little I want to go home. I tell Del that yes, of course, I can take that shift and any more you care to give me.

Then I text my mother: *Was all ready to come home today but my stupid boss says I have to work or he'll fire me. Might have to wait until tomorrow.*

Mom texts back: *Bring your textbooks.*

On my way out the door, Matt the RA grabs me by the shoulder.

"You're harassing me," I say, looking at his hand.

"Tell me you got the note I slipped under your door."

I nod. "Yes. I just said, 'You're harassing me.'"

Matt ignores my sarcasm. "Vacuum. Lint roller. Sometimes they do dorm-room spot checks over the break, and if anyone finds out you have a dog, it's going to be on me. You have to clean up all the pet hair, Aubrey. You promised."

I nod, resetting myself to earnestness. "You're right. I did. I will." Then an idea dawns on me. "If I stay, they won't do a spot check, will they?"

"You mean stay *over the break?* Why would you want to stay over the break?"

"Lots of people stay."

Matt shakes his head. "*Three* people are staying and every one of them is international. You don't want to spend Christmas in an empty dorm if you can help it, Aubrey. It's too sad. Believe me."

I look at him silently. We've had this conversation before. The deal-breaker, and I know it, is that Abby is my dog, not my parents', and that means she stays with me. It's not like I can hand her off and stay in the dorm on my own, and I know perfectly well that my chances of her being seen by the wrong people increases when nobody else is around as camouflage. I can't get out of going home no matter how much I may want to. All I can do is put it off for as long as possible.

"Clean up all the dog hair before you go," Matt says, correctly interpreting my non-response as surrender. "Remember, I put my neck on the line for you."

"And for Abby. You love Abby." I look back toward my room, as if we might be able to see her sleeping inside.

"Of course I love Abby. But just do it, okay?"

My head bobs. "Thanks, Matt. Seriously." Then I look up and down the emptied-out hall. "How long are *you* staying? Need any help with the rest of the cleanup? I happen to know that one of the boys' rooms put an opened can of tuna in the vents just because. It's going to stink like nobody's business by the time we come back."

"Go home, Aubrey."

"I'm actually going to work."

"Go home anyway, Aubrey."

. . .

WORK IS SLOW. IT SHOULD BE; THE SCHOOL HAS MOSTLY EMPTIED. Really, Del just needs a warm body behind the information desk, and honestly, he probably doesn't even need that. I'm here out of institutional habit. Maybe Del even knows my situation and tossed me James's shift out of pity.

I wish it was longer, but the shift I've picked up is what Del calls a "patch" for some reason: just two hours long. Having burned half of it already, I've only got an hour left until it ends. One hour, and then I have to go back to the dorm and pretend to pack all over again. Maybe I can stretch departure until morning, seeing as I already seeded it with my mother. But that's the longest I can delay: *tomorrow.* By noon at the latest, I'll be on the road, queued up for two weeks of maternal deprogramming.

I'd rather eat live scorpions. There has to be a way out of it.

Although I've been through my options a few times already, I pull out a slip of paper and brainstorm legit reasons to spend the holidays anywhere but home. Unfortunately, there really aren't any. I don't need to keep my dorm room warm. I don't have work; after today, the information office will be closed. There was maybe a time when I could have sought out an over-break job that would require me to stay, but now it's too late.

I pick up my phone and text Miranda again: *Ugh. I'm really going to have to go home, aren't I?*

My phone replies with a little red icon and a message: *Your message failed to send. Retry?*

I retry, knowing I'll get the same result. And of course I do.

I set the phone face-down on the desk. I tap my fingers on the wood beside it, then devolve into a rhythm something like a military march. The room is dead quiet. *Too* quiet. The rhythm doesn't fill the silence; it draws my attention.

I make a chain of paperclips. I fold a sheet of printer paper into an airplane, then throw it across the room to land in one of the big, fake plants. This, too, emphasizes the building's desolation rather than distracting me from it.

I must be going crazy, finally broken by thoughts of too much mothering and broken fathering. If I'm going crazy, can't I be admitted to a psych ward or something? Even shock therapy sounds like more fun than enduring my childhood home.

Maybe I should put on some music.

I flip my phone back over and wake it. It's still on my text thread with Miranda. Distracted, I forget about music and scroll back through our messages instead. I see the fisheye-lens pictures of Abby I've sent to Miranda and the memes she sends back. Miranda's current favorite? That would be "broccollie" — a collie with broccoli for a head. I still don't get it.

I stop at the photos she forwarded me, opening each one. That unsettled sense I had earlier returns as I look through them. The feeling is different from my desperate, *who-am-I-kidding-by-trying* thoughts of staying at college over break. This is more like intuition. This is my sharp, puzzle-solving side coming to life — the side Miranda usually calls "meddling."

People say I'm flighty, and I guess I am ... but not when it comes to questions and mysteries. Miranda says I should major in whatever cops major in, seeing as I came in undecided. I actually looked into it, guardedly optimistic that with the right grades and grit, I might even make the FBI. I just have a way of knowing when something's amiss. I'm a human lie detector. That's how I knew Ross was bad news long before Miranda saw it coming.

Yeah. *Ross.* That's a topic I'd rather not think about right now either.

Frowning, I reach down and pull my laptop out of my bag. The photos are on here, too, already run through a few manipulations and filters.

First, I open the one that shows the scaffolding through the boarded window — the thing that might be a building or bridge. That's the only one that gives a clue about location, because it's the only one where you can see outside. It's not helpful, though. Girders could be anywhere. I already checked the metadata on the photos, but there's no location info. I shouldn't be surprised: in the interest of "professional privacy," Skor phones proudly advertise that they don't have GPS.

Again I drum my fingertips on the table. My brain is obnoxious when it gets like this. It knows something's wrong, and that knowing could only come because it observed something and drew a conclusion. So why won't my brain just *tell* me what it saw that it finds bothersome? It's like this weird guessing game, where half of me already knows the answer and the other half has to figure it out.

It's not this picture that's bugging me, I think. *Bridge or no bridge, this photo feels clean.*

I glance at the picture that look like an accident just to get it out of the way — the one that seems to have been taken inside someone's pocket by mistake, showing only indistinct grays. After, I check the most interesting and potentially clue-filled photos: the ones that show chair legs and the frayed end of a blue rope.

But after scanning the entire frame of both like a game of Where's Waldo, I confirm what my gut told me right away: nothing hair-raising in either of them.

The final photo, however, gives me a tiny jolt. It's the slightest bit of feeling, but definitely there. And I think: *Maybe this is it. Maybe something in* this *picture doesn't sit right. Maybe it's the reason I can't quite connect the dots — why all this innocence bothers me so much.*

There's a sound in the office. I lift my head, scanning what's beyond the back of my laptop. Still, nobody's here. Still, the entire building sounds like a tomb. Still, I'm all alone.

I return my attention to the screen, adjusting the photo to make it brighter, darker, more and less contrasty. I zoom and scroll. At first, I see nothing more than is immediately apparent: the underside of a workbench of some kind, the whole thing draped in dust-heavy spiderwebs, with a toolbox way back in the distance. The floor is worn-down wood. The grain of its planks has turned it into a relief map after many years of wear: overly deep peaks and valleys that follow the whorls of the tree it was cut from.

I frown. Then I adjust the contrast again and close in on a part of the floor that doesn't quite fit the pattern. And that's when I see it.

Barely there — as if carved by something soft like a fingernail rather than something hard like a tool — are a pair of initials with a plus sign between them. It's the kind of thing lovers might carve into a tree, but not as deep and without a heart scribed around it:

RE

+

MW

It could mean just about anything.

But whatever else those four letters could be, they also happen to be Ross and Miranda's initials.

Chapter Twelve

Ross's roommate Dion has long white dreadlocks and smells perpetually of weed. His face is covered with blond stubble that never grows — more like failure to shave than an actual beard.

"Yo," he says, peering out when I knock on his door.

"Um, hi. Is Ross home?"

Dion leans against the doorframe, then takes his time looking me up and down. "No, but I am."

"That's great. But I'm actually looking for *Ross.*"

He takes a beat, then says, "You're Aubrey, aren't you?"

"Yeah."

"I saw you the other night. Last week. In the lobby."

"What lobby?"

"The one in this building."

"Why would I be in this building?"

"Dunno. Looking for Ross?"

"Why would I be looking for Ross?"

"You're looking for him right now, aren't you?"

"Yeah, for my friend. *I* don't give a shit about Ross."

Dion's head bobs at my profanity, which came out a little too easily. It's important that he understand I have no interest in Ross or anything Ross does, ever. I never would. Never had. Not even recently.

"It's just that I'm observant. I'm interested in people." He points at me in a knowing way. "You don't like Ross, do you? That's why it was strange to see you in our lobby last week, if you hate Ross so much."

"I wasn't here last week. I told you already."

"And maybe a few other times. Ross knows a lot of people, but I swear I remember *you.*"

"I've seen Ross as little as I can since high school. You're thinking of someone else."

Dion shrugs and nods again, as if he doesn't believe me. The nod says, *Whatever you say.*

I think of beer. Of late nights. Of urgent errands made for things I needed. Then I shake those thoughts away, along with guilt, and re-focus on why I came here. I've got a curiosity to solve.

"Look," I tell Dion. "I just want to know where Ross is. It's not really any of my business, but—"

"Yeah, you're right about that," Dion interrupts. "It's *not* really any of your business. But that doesn't stop you from being all up in it, does it? Seems I'm always hearing about *Aubrey* around here. 'Aubrey this. Aubrey that.' Funny, since you've seen Ross as little as you can since high school. There's only two reasons I can think of for a guy to talk about someone as much as he talks about you."

"If I could just—"

"At first, I thought it was because he was into you. And I mean, I'd *get* it if he was into you." He gives me another long, lecherous look up and down. "But then I started to realize it's because you're a serious pain in the ass." Dion rearranges himself against the door-frame. "Aren't you the one who threatened to go to the dean about us?"

"That's between me and Ross," I say.

Dion's head bobs as if he's considering this, but then he seems to decide and centers on me again. "I don't know. I'd say it involves me, too, even just from that same pain-in-the-ass perspective. It's the little things, y'know? Like ... Ross never checks the room phone, so he never has to deal with the messages people leave on it, pretending they're not who they actually are." He raises his eyebrows at me. "But guess who *does* check the room phone?" Dion sticks a thumb into his own chest. "It'd really make my day if 'those people' would stick to calling his other numbers. *God.* If I have to hear one more bitchfest about him leaving various girlfriends alone — not that *you'd* know anything about that, *Aubrey...*"

"Where is he?" I demand. "Where's Ross?"

"Not sure why I'd tell you that. You want to meet with Ross, call him like everyone else does."

I hold up my phone, which got quite the workout before I came over here. Dion's flattering himself if he thinks I didn't try every possible way to reach Ross before resorting to this one.

"I've *been* calling him. And texting. He hasn't replied. Usually he gets back right away."

Dion shrugs as if to say, *Well, then, there's your answer.*

We lock eyes for a few moments. I try to study Dion's, feeling like there are things he's not saying. Does he know something? About me? About anything? He's Ross's roommate; Ross must tell him things. Apparently, I'm a pain in the ass, but right now Dion looks like he might also think I'm something else. Which, of course, I secretly am.

"We done here?" Dion asks.

Are we? I'm not sure. I'm not even sure why I came in the first place. I'm no dummy; it's pretty clear that things with Ross are cut and dry — not exactly a trail of mysterious breadcrumbs to follow. Everyone but Miranda saw the writing on the wall weeks ago. Ross was clearly going to break up with her, but then like so many cowards, he got weak. He took the easy way out, obeying what felt best at the time. Collateral damage came with it. Everyone ended up more traumatized than if Ross had just been a human being and ended things with Miranda instead of playing his little, weak-willed games.

Really? says a voice in my head. *That's a laugh, Aubrey: YOU talking about anyone else's weak will?*

My mind goes to the photo Miranda sent — the one that

seemed to show four letters and a plus sign carved into the wooden floor. Is *that* why I came? It can't be; I'm not even sure the "letters" were really letters, let alone those *specific* letters.

Exactly, I think. *So tell me, genius: How could Miranda's photo-stalker have anything to do with Ross? Sure, Ross has a Skor phone (not that Miranda has any idea), but you and everyone else have been texting him on his iPhone all week. You tell yourself you have strong instincts, but is instinct REALLY the reason you came? Isn't it more likely that you're grasping at straws: trying to make Ross the bad guy because denial won't let you look in a mirror?*

As if reading my mind, Dion says, "You're not really here for *Ross*, are you Aubrey?"

"I just want to know where he is. I just want to talk to him."

He smirks like he doesn't believe me. "Oh, yeah? About what?"

I want more than anything to give Dion a good answer just to wipe that knowing smile off his face. But what exactly should I say? That I came here because instinct told me to? That I want to yell at Ross for ghosting Miranda — something that's not only not my business, but also something I've been actively campaigning for: to break them up? It's definitely not because of the photos Miranda forwarded me. That would be the worst thing of all to right now — the one thing that would prove I'm making things up just so I don't have to admit the truth.

Oh, hey, Dion, I wanted to ask. Do you know anyone who's been sending my friend creepy pictures? No, I don't *think it's something she should handle herself. Yes, it* does *necessitate my involvement — me, who knows nothing about it. Yes, my asking you is perfectly logical.*

"Just tell me what you really came for ... *Aubrey.*" He sneers. "Because who knows? Maybe Ross isn't as tight-lipped about his business as he should be. And maybe because of it, I can think of a *third* reason he keeps talking about you."

"Never mind. Sorry I came."

"You sure? If you're honest about what brought you here today, maybe we can even help each other out."

I turn away, furious. But there's nothing I can say in response, is there? I shouldn't have come. I have no leg to stand on, and Dion damn well knows it.

"Better get back to it!" Dion calls to me as I walk away. "Get out there! Be an eager beaver! Just because it's Christmas Break doesn't mean there's no need to study!"

I walk on but he keeps shouting.

"Gotta keep those grades up, am I right? Just about anything could yank that scholarship right out from under you!"

My feet stop. I look back. The hallway stretches between us, all taupe walls and decorated doors.

"Anything," Dion repeats, wearing a too-wide smile.

Looking eye to eye, I know now that Ross has talked to Dion about me in far, *far* too much detail. Things I want nobody to know. *Ever.* Things Ross found out, because a guy in his position is always looking for leverage, just in case.

I'm almost to the end of the hallway now, emotions coming in a tsunami. I feel the need to get out of here, to run to somewhere normal and innocuous like my desk at the student information office. I want to work all break long. I don't want to go home; home's where the bullshit is. I feel transparent, like everyone can see right through me. Emotions war: frustration, betrayal, guilt, a sense of unworthiness, and most of all a certainty that I shouldn't be here, in the exalted halls of this college, and that everyone around me is inches from coming to their senses and throwing me out.

I thought I'd gotten away? Thought I'd fought and clawed and made a new and better life? I guess I was kidding myself. Will things ever change? Or is this all people will ever see when they look at me — just one more piece of trash?

"AUBREY!" Dion calls.

I spin, half angry and half broken. Tears of fury spill from my eyes, but from this distance at least Dion can't see them.

When I look back, Dion's holding up his phone.

"Keep something in mind, will you?"

I wait.

"If you call the dean's office about us again," he says, "whoever comes to check on Ross will also find a whole lot on *you.*"

Chapter Thirteen

I don't remember going to sleep.

I was preoccupied headed back to the dorm, unable to think of much other than my carefully balanced world falling to pieces. It left me in a weird trance state, sending me through my usual chores on autopilot. I know I took Abby into the central courtyard to pee. I know I fed her. I know I set my duffel out again to pack ... though looking back, I doubt I was packing to go home. I don't want to go home, but thanks to my talk with Dion, I also don't want to stay here anymore. And so I packed mindlessly, not thinking, obeying some primitive and unthinking urge to get the hell out of Dodge. To just leave and go ... *anywhere else.*

I suppose my brain thought that running away would solve everything. It should know better. I ran away from home a lot as a kid, but I always ended up back where I started. Then I ran away to college, hoping to erase who I'd been and become someone new. And look well that's turning out?

Dion's voice in my head: *Just about anything could yank that scholarship right out from under you.*

I'm kidding myself if I pretend Dion knows nothing. All I can hope for is he isn't annoyed enough to cause trouble. Ross must have all sorts of problematic stuff on me hidden away in his room. I can only pray they'll keep their mouths shut. I think I'm okay with Ross; he and I have mutually assured destruction. But Dion? I've got nothing on him. Dion could explode everything if he wanted, just to be an asshole.

I must have fallen asleep at some point, though, because my ringing phone wakes me up. I check the time on the wall clock before answering, fighting the confusion that always comes when I nap. I haven't slept long. It's just shy of 1 p.m. On Friday? Yes, my confused mind says it's Friday.

"Hello?"

"Oh, good. You're alive."

I want to swear. Damn naps. Damn confusion. Normally I'd at least look at my phone before answering it. Normally when my mother calls, I just let her go to voicemail.

"Oh. Hey, Mom."

"I noticed you're not home yet."

"I texted you that I had to work and might have to wait until tomorrow. I didn't say for-sure I'd come back today. I didn't even say it'd be *for sure* at all."

"Now, what kind of a selfish thing would that be, to not come home at all?" Mom says, a latent gasp in her voice. "You're not that selfish, Aubrey. We have all sorts of things that need doing around here. You know I can't get around much anymore. My diabetes."

I sigh. "Mom. If you'd at least listen to your doctor, you can still—"

"Easy for you to say. You don't have a chronic disease. I do. I raised you. Spent everything we had on you. Nobody knew you were coming when I got pregnant with you. In truth, we couldn't afford a kid, but we managed just the same."

I resist the urge to argue. I'm used to this by now. My mother constantly reminds me that I was an unexpected pregnancy, even though she really means flat-out *unwanted*.

"I took care of you, Aubrey. Now it's your turn to take care of me. Grandma's welfare benefits won't last forever. I sacrificed every-thing. Don't you dare turn your back on your poor mother now."

Why not? She turned her back on *her* mother. Grandma, whose welfare benefits won't last forever, has been dead for six months, having been mostly forgotten in our finished attic for the last years of her life because it was cheaper than a nursing home.

I don't know the details of the fraud that's kept Grandma's checks coming to our mailbox, but I'm not surprised Mom found a way to scam the system. She's brilliant in some ways, stupid in others. She roped her only child in on the many cons she pulled throughout my teen years, and now I guess *I'm* supposed to pull the cons and give her a percentage. And it's not like I can tell her I'm sick of committing fraud. Sick of lying all the time. I've just had to back away from her instead of confronting her directly. For four months now, I've been trying to cut my family off ... but they keep clawing their way back in.

At least I don't have to worry about my parents revoking my tuition when I finally excise them like a bruise from an apple. *They* don't pay tuition. *I* do. Every cent was earned through endless childhood ventures — anything I could do to earn a buck just to get the hell out of that house. The lion's share keeping me here is paid by my tennis scholarship, and Mom can't ruin that for me. No, it seems I'm working overtime to ruin that one for myself, with Dion on the assist.

"So," my mother says. "You'll be home this evening."

"No, not today. I'd get there too late."

"Selfish," Mom scoffs.

"No," I say, finding my control wavering as it always does. Thinking fast, I spin a lie: "I promised a friend I'd help her move a dresser into her dorm room before I left. That's tomorrow morning."

"Uh-huh. What friend?"

"Miranda."

I can almost hear Mom's *gotcha* grin. "You said Miranda was going somewhere with her parents."

Shit. I forgot Mom managed to get me on the phone last week, and in that conversation, I mentioned Miranda's trip. I don't think I gave her the timing, though. If I did, Mom knows Miranda actually left school on Sunday, planning to spend a few days at home before heading up the cabin in the woods. Hard to use her as an excuse if she's been gone for most of a week.

I'm committed now, though. I'll just have to hope I wasn't specific.

"She hasn't left yet," I say, crossing mental fingers. "She's leaving tomorrow, after we move the dresser."

"Well ... who's going to make my dinner?"

"Can't Ted do it?" I'll skip the obvious answer: *How about YOU?* My mother is far from incapable. Far from immobile. Oh, sure, she'll eventually lose both feet if she doesn't start taking her diabetes seriously, but for right now she's just incredibly lazy. She's one of those self-imposed helpless people, flat on the couch so much she's growing into it.

"*Please.* Ted can't make toast. Besides, he has his poker game."

Ah, yes. The poker game. Mom says it like it's a friendly weekly get-together with friends, but actually this is how my stepfather makes money. He's a card mechanic, hired to deal for illegal poker games and stack the deck in his employer's favor. I've been waiting most of my life for him to be killed or arrested.

"I can't get out of here tonight, Mom. I'm sorry."

"Such an ingrate. We always gave. All you did was take."

"It's *one day,* Mom," I say, but I'm fighting very hard for it to *not* be just one day now that she's giving me the thumbscrews. The flimsiest excuse for staying, I intend to grab with both hands. That's my big job overnight: to find an excuse my mother might believe at least a tiny little bit for why I can't come back over break.

"Can't trust you to do what you say even after all this time, can I?" my mother says. "I thought I taught you better. I guess I was right, never letting you get a dog."

I look at Abby, who I waited until college to get even though I'm not allowed to have pets. I'm best when I'm painted into a corner. I didn't even ask about dogs; I just got Abby and knew I could make it work. I'm good at manipulating people. Good at pulling a scam. I'm ashamed of it, but I was taught by the best.

Abby makes a small grumbly noise, as if she heard and agrees Mom is full of shit. It makes me want to tell Mom that I *did* get a dog and if I have to go there for winter break, she'll see my dog firsthand. I stop myself, though, knowing I shouldn't poke the bear. It's easier to walk away from my mother than to fight with her.

"I'll call you in the morning," I say. "Give you an update on if I can still come to the house." The words I choose are telling. Ever since I left for college, I've said *come to the house* instead of *come home*. I didn't even notice I was doing it.

"*If?*" Mom says. "You mean '*when*.'"

"I mean 'if.' I'm juggling a lot of things here. It's possible—"

"*No*," Mom says, her voice gaining an edge. "You listen to me, Aubrey Jane. I told you: You left us high and dry, going off to New York. But okay, you had to have it your way. I suppose there's not anything I can do about it. But you *will* come back summers, and you'll come back for breaks, and once you're done out there 'finding your fucking self' or whatever it is, you *will* come back here after you graduate, to your family who sacrificed everything for you, and you *will*—"

"Bye, Mom." Then I hang up.

The phone rings again right away. I can almost feel the anger wafting from it like heat. Maybe I should have let her finish before hanging up, just to avoid a hissy fit. Or maybe this is the beginning of the end of all of that. Maybe this is me standing my ground, pruning my mother back one manipulative word at a time.

The vibrations end as the call goes to voicemail. I get a notification moments later that Mom's left me a message. I won't be listening to that one.

Abby comes over, sliding her head beneath my dangling hand. I look down. She raises her gaze and says, *"Hula Hut,"* which is a new one on me.

My eyes go to the window, which has a view of the quad if you turn your head just right. Looking out on it now — still mostly green, though a freeze is coming — feels like seeing an oasis in the middle of a life-spanning desert. I feel like a woman dying of thirst, desperate to reach salvation — and, once there, to hold onto it with both hands. I'm barely out of that house. Barely away from those toxic people. The bonds holding me to my old home are stretched thin after four months of slow distancing, just about to snap. I like where I'm headed. Miranda says I'm a whole new person here: all the best of High School Aubrey but with fewer and fewer of her neuroses. We've both blossomed away from home, but the difference is that Miranda's home can maybe be fixed. Mine is broken forever.

I can't leave college. I won't. I refuse. I'm not going back to my old home, and no stoner roommate of Miranda's piece-of-shit boyfriend has the right to say otherwise.

Screw you, Dion, I think. And screw you, Ross.

Dion's right: there's stuff in that room that could cost me my scholarship.

I guess that means I'll just have to go in there and get it.

Chapter Fourteen

It's hard for me to focus. Always has been. I'm a high-strung person juggling a million thoughts at once, and the only thing that narrows my mind enough to let me work is Adderall. Mom wouldn't take me in for an ADHD diagnosis, so as with most things, I undertook it myself. I'm not a doctor. Not even pre-med. I took a risk when I started buying ADHD meds from the black market (from Ross, who's been selling lighter drugs since high school), but what the hell? My whole life has been about risk-taking anyway.

At first, taking Adderall worked great. But then I started to have trouble sleeping — especially when I took it in the afternoons and evenings, needing to study but without enough energy to do so. Because I get no support from my parents (really the *opposite* of support; they're like trying to swim in lead boots), I've spent the first semester working thirty hours a week just to keep up with bills. Add tennis practice to that, and gym conditioning, and matches, for which we often have to travel. Schoolwork has to fit somewhere atop all of it.

Stimulants did the trick for my frenzied life ... until I had to sleep. To solve that particular issue, I started taking Xanax at bedtime. *Also* bought from Ross on the black market. Mixing

Adderall and Xanax probably isn't the best idea, but my life right now feels like triage: I just need to keep the balance, and screw everything else. I'll do whatever it takes to stay in school, keep my grades up, and cling to that tennis scholarship. Worrying about my health can come later.

Now, still seething after the call with my mother and willing to do anything to stay away from her for pretty much forever, I text Ross for the fourth or fifth time today. It's my Hail Mary attempt to address Dion's threat to expose me as an illicit drug-buyer. Of course it fails. Of course the text, like the ones I sent earlier today, goes unanswered.

That's not terribly unusual. If Ross is in one of the college buildings — especially one of the basements — bars don't exist. Even *with* bars, he's clearly avoiding me. Obviously. He is (was?) dating my best friend, and she won't listen when I tell her he's bad news. Yes, I know how much of a hypocrite that makes me. I don't care. Miranda doesn't have my same dependencies, nor does she need to know I have them. Or all the other things I feel incredibly guilty for not telling her, especially after last weekend.

I try calling Ross after my text fails. I'm sent directly to voice-mail. I leave him a message even though there's no point.

"Hey, Ross. It's Aubrey. Call me back. We need to talk."

I hang up wondering why I bothered. Ross knows I don't like him with Miranda. Never have. The three of us went to high school together, but even back then I kept mostly out of his way. I never liked the guy. *Never.* He dealt a little in high school and ramped it up in college, but that's not even my problem with him. I've done some shady stuff to stay afloat, and in my mind it's all just entrepreneurism. Ross is a "dealer lite," not some big shot. He sells party drugs and college drugs, none of the hard stuff. He doesn't carry a gun. My problems with Ross, for Miranda, are only *somewhat* related to his dealing. I'm more bothered by the fact that he's a Titanic asshole.

Sighing, I try texting Ross on his Skor. It's the number that clients like me have: the phone Miranda doesn't know Ross owns, but also the reason I know about Skors in the first place. This time the text spins for a long time but doesn't bounce. I wait. The text is in Skor's cloud and out of my hands. All I can tell from my screen that Ross hasn't seen it yet. Wherever he is, even Skor can't reach.

Normally, I'd be patient. Ross doesn't always answer right away — especially these past few days, while he's been responding to everyone but Miranda. That's from his iPhone, though ... and that's weird, now that I think about it. Not weird that he's been answering iPhone texts (except to Miranda, and to me this morning), but weird that he *hasn't* been answering Skor texts. I texted him Monday about a refill, then forgot after I found a few extra blister packs I didn't know I had. Only now is it dawning on me how unusual it is for Ross not to answer something like that. I'm a client rather than a pest when I buy from him, and Ross is serious about clients.

So I actually *call* him on the Skor just to see what happens. Of course I get voicemail: my chance to play a role, because I don't want him to know the real reason I'm calling.

"Ross. It's me, A. I need a refill. Two, actually. ASAP. Let me know." I try to sound desperate, even though I have plenty of both meds left.

I frown at my phone after hanging up, unsure what do next. In truth, there's nothing I *can* do. Ross might see dollar signs and call me back, but there's every chance in the world he'll ignore me given recent events. He and I have unfinished business. Between the last time he sold to me and now, a very large elephant entered the room, and that elephant is all about Miranda.

I wish my damn phone would ring. I wish he'd reply to my texts. My heart starts pounding. If I can't talk to Ross about what Dion said, I'm back in the middle of no-man's land.

Dion's words return to me, threatening to snitch. It makes me wonder if the two of them have something brewing. Has Ross's operation expanded? Does it include his roommate now? If so, is there a reason Dion got mad and started making threats when all I did was ask questions? Dion strikes me as paranoid — the kind of guy who doesn't like *what-ifs* — who really hates waiting for loose ends to become a problem.

That could be bad for me, if Dion sees me as a loose end.

It's okay. They can't pin anything on me. Dion's blowing smoke. You can hurt them a lot more than they can hurt you.

But is that true? Maybe I'm being paranoid, but the fact that nothing came of my tip to the dean suggests maybe Ross is big-time enough to have bought himself protection. If that's true, anything I report to the college won't come back to hurt them. *They* can hurt *me*, though. Plenty.

I head back to Ross and Dion's dorm, hide behind an out-jutting corner in the hallway, and dial the number to their room phone. It rings all the way through to the point where I could leave a message if I wanted to, but I don't. I just need to know if anyone's in the room. If one of them is, they usually answer the phone. The fact that nobody picked up probably means the coast is clear.

I call again just to be sure. Ringing counts the seconds as my mind spins into paranoia. Do the terms of my scholarship allow them to drug-test me? I think they might. I don't feel like I have a problem, but that's what every addict thinks. A drug test would be fatal for me. Who knows if Adderall would register or if the scholarship committee would care, but Xanax, at least, is commonly abused. If the athletic department had reason to check me, it'd all be over. Goodbye college. Goodbye good job in an exciting city away from home ... and hello Mom and Dad's house for the rest of my life.

My call goes to voicemail again. Nobody's home. I pause to consider if I'm really desperate and daring enough to do what I'm about to do, but who am I kidding? This is *me* we're talking about.

I glance up and down the hallway, then listen hard to hear if any creatures are stirring. The entire wing sounds empty; the trilling of the phone when I called was like a record scratching in a silent bar. It's Friday before break, and there were no classes today. Most people left last night. Only people unable to go home (plus Dion, it seems, because even shut-ins need drugs) remain.

What I have in mind is kind of stupid. All it'll take to be seen is for someone to poke their head out of a room. Once someone sees me, it'll be clear what I'm up to. Even so, I guess I'll just have to chance it. Just have to try.

My dorm is a carbon copy of Ross and Dion's. The layout, decor, and construction are all the same. And so before I came over here, I spent time figuring out how to break into my own room, knowing the things I learned would allow me to break into this one. I'm glad I practiced, because it's not straightforward. You can't just stick a credit card in the jamb, and despite my snoop's reputation, I have no idea how to pick a lock.

So I have this contraption I built, which worked on my door but couldn't possibly be more obvious in use. It's an L-shaped thing made out of straightened coat hangers. I rush down to Ross's room, say a silent prayer that I was right and that they're not actually inside, then slide the long end of my device under the door.

Once the long end is under, I rotate the short arm of the L so the long end stands up on the other side of the door. It's exactly tall enough to reach the door handle, which is the kind you push down instead of turn like a knob. There's a deadbolt you can lock from the inside, but it won't be engaged if the boys aren't in there. The other lock is engaged by a knob from the inside or a key from the outside. To *unlock* it from the outside, you again need a key. But here's the good part: If you're inside and the door's locked, you only need to push down on the handle.

It means that if I can push down on the *inside* handle from *outside* the door, I'll be golden. That's what my weird gizmo is for.

Working blind, remembering how clumsy this was back at my room, I try to feel around until the loop at the top of my L-device slips over the handle. It rattles as I try to find my spot, sounding like a big hamster in its cage. I'm sure someone will bust me, but finally I feel the loop slip home.

I pull a string that runs along the L to cinch the handle and tug it downward. At first, I think I don't have enough leverage, working through the gap under the door, but then something pops and the door moves a little bit toward me. *I'm in!*

Down the hall, a handle rattles. Someone's coming. I shove my lock-picker the rest of the way under the door and dive inside.

It's a moment before I exhale. I was somehow sure Dion would be in here waiting for me, getting his fists ready while watching my contraption open things up. He's not, though. Everything's quiet.

Don't get too comfortable. You have no idea when they'll be back.

A quick check tells me I don't need to worry about Ross. His dresser drawers are slightly open, and I know from having been here on Sunday night that some of his clothes are gone now that were here then. His sheets have been thrown upward as if he took something from under the bed. That'd be his suitcase. As a whole, the scene tells me Ross packed his bags and went home for break — not to class like Dion told me.

I move fast, sticking to Ross's side of the room. I glance at his shelved coursebooks, leafing through the pages to see if he's hidden business paperwork inside. After, I search the drawers and find a few spiral-bound notebooks. They're math and history and one comically shitty sketchbook. I search the rest, looking through the scant belongings that fit in a dorm room. It doesn't take me long, and there really aren't many places where things could be hidden — except the vents, which I shine my phone's flashlight into and come up empty.

There's nothing here. No register of who Ross sells to and what they buy. No evidence they could use to hurt me. But then again, what did I expect? It's not 1980. Did I really think Ross kept his records in a Rolodex? Did I really think I'd waltz in and find *The Big Book That Proves to the Scholarship Committee that Aubrey is an Addict* sitting on his desk, ready for me to steal to make the world right again?

My shoulders sag. I'm an idiot. Ross probably has all his records on his phone like a normal person. Or even better: Ross has nothing that incriminates me at all. Dion was probably bluffing. He doesn't like me and what he sees as sniffing around his business. I thought I read his body language right; I thought he kept glancing into the room while taunting me as if something incriminating was sitting right there. But I guess I was wrong.

Now I have no idea what'll happen. I'll just have to wait and hope Dion says nothing. And—

A frown touches my lips. I've just spotted something strange on the built-in bulletin board. Ross and Dion have made abundant use of the thing, with multicolored pushpins holding up all sorts of party fliers, photos, and numbers on napkins I assume came from girls they met while drinking. Over all of it, though, as if added recently, is a printed-out email.

An email I've seen before.

It takes me a second, but then I recognize the Airbnb logo and the single photo showing the listing in question. Below the photo, Ross has written himself a note: *6 hours. Leave 10 am = avoid rush hour.*

I rip the paper from the board, careless that I'm leaving evidence I was here. I stare at the corner, looking for the time and day this was printed. He printed Miranda's dutifully forwarded reservation email this past Monday at 8:14 a.m.

Monday. 8:14 a.m. That's when Ross printed out Miranda's email, then tacked it up so Dion would know where he'd gone.

I do the math. What time did I... ?

My jaw drops.

"Oh," I say. "Oh *shit.*"

He's not at school. Hasn't been since Monday. I just assumed he was still around, but no: He left *days ago*, meaning the thing I think he might be doing might already have been done. Or *should* have been ... but something there doesn't quite fit, either.

Instead of going home for break, he drove up to Miranda's parents' rental ... and based on the timing, I'm horribly positive I know why.

Chapter Fifteen

ROSS

AN UNCERTAIN NUMBER OF DAYS AGO

At first, I have absolutely no idea what's going on. I wake up, but I'm not in bed. My face is pressed into bare wood. Which is strange. Usually, I don't sleep on wood.

I blink. I try to turn my head, but something hurts. My neck? Yes, my neck hurts like a bastard. My brain is really, really foggy. I'm dizzy and very little makes sense. I puzzle and puzzle, but nothing slots into place.

What's this thing around me? Around my face and *almost* limiting its movement ... but not really?

I blink again. My brain doesn't want to engage, so I clench up and focus, trying to force it to do its job. It's like I'm underwater. Which would make sense, because it's dawning on me as I come back to life that every sound is muted. Am I wearing earplugs? Do I usually wear earplugs when I go to sleep on the freezing wood floor of some sort of rustic outbuilding? I can't remember. What day is it? The last I recall, it was Sunday. No. *Monday*. I know I left somewhere on Monday because I was worried about rush hour coming out of a city, and that wouldn't happen on the weekend. Not sure where I was going, though, or why I went. I remember a distant sense of white-hot urgency — a feeling that I needed to get wherever-it-was as soon as possible. But why?

I wait, but my mind provides no answers.

Is today still Monday? I don't have a clue. It could be Tuesday. Or Saturday. Or Christmas. Is it Christmas? When *is* Christmas? Is it in the winter? I'm pretty sure it's in the winter. Thinking is hard, with this fog and pain and big holes in my memory. Why don't I remember anything? Do I have amnesia? If so, how did I get it? Can you catch amnesia like a cold? I don't think you can, but right now anything could be true.

I just know that on Monday morning, I was at college. I go to college. In ... New York? And right now I'm in...?

(ask again later / cannot predict now / reply hazy, try again)

Noncommittal responses rise in the darkness of my mind like the answer-giver floating in indigo liquid inside a Magic 8 ball. I don't *know* where I am right now. Not yet. It's such a cliché.

So get up, Ross. Get up and walk around. You like travel. Wherever this is, it's a whole new place.

But no. Unfortunately it seems I've been tied to a chair. That's really unfortunate. And unusual. I don't think I sleep on wooden floors, tipped over on my side and left that way so long I'd swear I can feel a bedsore developing. And I *really* don't think I do it tied to a chair.

"Hello?" I try to say.

But it comes out muffled. The source of the thing I felt around my head has made itself known. It appears to be a gag. Not a ball in my mouth, but instead the kind that's tight through the center of the mouth, leaving my lips free. I kind of wish I'd thought to cover my lips entirely when I put this gag in my mouth and tied myself to this chair before going to sleep on the floor of what I now think is a toolshed. Or at least that I'd applied some ChapStick. I could have gotten chapped lips with all this carelessness. It's cold as brass balls in here.

In *where*, though? What is this place?

I remember driving. It feels like that was earlier today, but I don't think it was. I think I've been here for a while now — days, maybe. On Monday, I wanted to leave by 10 a.m. That time sticks in my head: *10 a.m.* Why? I'm a late riser. Typically when I wake up with my face bruising against a freezing wooden floor and with what I'm now realizing is a pretty serious headache, I sleep in. Even a 10 a.m. departure is early for good old Ross. I don't normally bind myself in rope just to wake early, allowing myself enough time to drive all the way up to...

(reply hazy, try again)

Okay, still not ready to answer that one yet. It's okay. I really know nothing, so I've got plenty of other things to think about while I'm waiting for that domino to fall. I don't know why I'm so hazy. I feel like I'm trying to think my way through a big, sticky wad of gum.

It's not normally this way, right? Usually I can think. I'm pretty sure that in my normal life, I know a bit more about what's going on than I do right now.

Inventory. Do some inventory. See what you still remember.

So, okay. My name is Ross Ehrlicher. I own a Chevy Camaro. It's ... blue? Yes, I think it's blue. I remember a blue car. I drove that blue car to ... to wherever I went. I parked it, and I walked across a small gravel parking lot. Or maybe smaller than that — just a parking pad, large enough for three or four vehicles. Where is my car now?

I seem to remember someone taking my keys. I remember them wanting to move my car. I assume it was a valet. And that means I'm at the kind of place, right now, where you'd get a valet. I'm a freshman at ... somewhere. Some college. I drove far. My girlfriend is Miranda Wimberly. She's brunette. With an overbite. No, no, the overbite is someone else. That's ... Andrea? Alyssa? Someone whose name starts with an A.

Oh. And I did something bad. I don't know what it was, but I definitely did something. The A-name girl? Thinking about her stirs vague feelings of ill-at-ease, but right now I can't connect them to anything. Because my memory is so completely fucked. Why is my memory fucked?

Roofies. Someone gave you roofies.

Yes. That's right. Now I remember. I'm starting to suspect I didn't put myself in this situation. I'm starting to suspect that sleeping on a wooden floor, tied to a chair and gagged, seemingly tipped onto my side instead of sitting upright, in a place so cold I can see my breath when I exhale — I'm starting to suspect it's not how I usually roll.

Maybe another person was involved. I remember drinking something, and after I finished drinking it, I realized too late that I'd been roofied.

Rohypnol. Illegal in the US, but really good for sleep. *So* good for sleep, in fact, that people who take it tend to sleep whether they want to or not. Then they wake up with big holes in their memory, right? I'm not sure why I know that. I feel like maybe it was mono-logued to me. Or maybe I just figured it out. It's correct, though. It strikes me as more than right.

Someone made me sleep.

After tying me up.

Why? I'm such a nice guy.

"Hello!" But thanks to my gag, it comes out more like *HFFFLLW! Think. Come on, Ross — think!*

But I don't think.

I pass out again instead.

Minutes later. Maybe hours later. Hell — maybe a day or more later. I can't tell by the sun, because I don't remember where the sun was before, the last time I was conscious. It's hard to guess the sun's position from where I am, anyway. I'm still on the floor. How the hell did I end up on the floor?

(ask again later)

But no. Nobody accepts "Ask Again Later." Everyone knows that.

I got the best toy in the world when I was a kid. A Magic 8 Ball. It was psychic. Seven years old and I unwrapped it at Christmas, from my Aunt Marie, I think. Mom and Dad both rolled their eyes because they're both doctors, both science types, and to science types, the idea of psychic toys isn't fun; it's misleading. They didn't let me believe in Santa, so they definitely weren't going to let me believe in this.

But I knew the truth. All throughout that first Christmas, when I was seven, I silently asked my Magic 8 Ball questions.

Will I get that video game I wanted?

And the ball said: *As I see it, yes.*

I wasn't sure why the Magic 8 Ball felt the need to qualify its affirmative. There was no opinion — no "as I see it" — involved. I opened a flat rectangular present and there the game was, plain as day.

Will my parents burn the turkey?

Yes, definitely.

And although it didn't technically burn, it did cook too long and dried out so much it was like chewing on shoe leather. I decided that was close enough.

Can I get out of helping with the dinner dishes?

Outlook not so good.

Will I be famous and marry a supermodel?

Don't count on it.

I'm still hoping the 8-Ball was wrong about that one, and maybe it'll turn out to be. I'm only nineteen. I've still got plenty of time to meet and marry supermodels.

Nobody accepts *Ask Again Later* from a Magic 8 Ball, though. Everyone who gets that bullshit answer just asks again right away. So I think very hard about my situation. About why I'm here. About where the sun was, if I saw it last time, and maybe even how much time has passed. Who leaves someone tied up in a shed in the cold? Maniacs, that's who.

Something rattles nearby. My mind works harder than it should to categorize the noise. My brain still isn't working. It's working better than it did before, but my memory is still nothing-doing. I understand how doors work, but it's seconds before I realize the rattle is the undoing of a lock.

My view of the door is sideways and low. I can't really turn my head to look up because of the gag and because something in my neck still hurts. I feel like I've been beaten. Badly. The cold has camouflaged the swelling in my jaw and the bruising on my side, making everything numb. Pretty sure I got my ass kicked, though. I can't feel one of my arms; *that's* how numb I am. I can't *feel* it, but there's still a dull throb there, as if the throb is subsumed by the cold but hasn't entirely made it go away. It hurts. Now that I'm thinking about it, what I *can* feel from the arm I'm lying on — the one I mostly can't feel at all — hurts. The ropes tying me to the chair prevent me from looking myself over properly, to assess my damage.

The door cracks open. It's light outside but overcast. Chilly breeze enters my space, informing me that as cold as I've been, the outside is still colder.

Boots step toward me, but I can't look up to see whose they are. They stop a foot from my face. My cheek is so cold it's like my mouth is full of ice cubes. I think maybe my lip is bleeding ... or was, until the blood froze solid.

I'm yanked upward. My world rotates ninety degrees. The next moment, I find myself sitting upright on the chair, but even though it's unusual to be tied to a chair, at least more things make sense now. I can see more of my surroundings, and I don't have to work, mentally, to rotate what I see into an upright configuration, so it makes sense.

Now I see a workbench. Tool chests. The space is medium-sized, and I'm in the middle. The area around me has been cleared, presumably so I don't hurt myself by falling on tools. Or maybe so I don't procure any tools and use them to escape.

Escape? Is that what I'm supposed to do?

(signs point to yes)

A man squats in front of me, lowering himself enough to look me in the eye. He's not really engaging with me, though. His look is more assessing than that. Like I'm an object — some inanimate thing he's come to inspect.

But then he does talk. Directly. To me.

"How are you feeling? How's your head?"

He lowers my gag so I can answer.

"Someone hit me." I'm not sure if that's true, but it feels true.

"I didn't give you much. I don't want you to forget. I don't know how much it takes to make you forget. You just need to rest. Nobody wants this. I just need you calm."

"Calm?"

"Yes, calm. Do you know who I am?"

(don't count on it)

But I don't say no. I think instead. I don't want to give up. I'd rather go down trying.

"Do you know why you came here?" he asks.

"You brought me here." ... *whoever you are.*

"No. You came here." The man cups my face in his hands and straightens it. I'm having trouble holding my head up. I'm very tired. He slaps me lightly, the way you do when you want someone alert. "You started this. That's only fair. You have to understand that we didn't have a choice."

"Oh," I say.

"So. Do you remember why you came?"

"Miranda."

"That's right; you wanted to see Miranda. So you remember who she is?"

"I'm not stupid."

"No. But you *are* coming off of Rohypnol."

"Rohypnol? Why Rohypnol?"

He scowls. "You know goddamn well *'why Rohypnol.'*"

I don't. Not with this fog-brain of mine. I wish I did.

"I didn't give you much. I just wanted you calm. Do you remember how you were, Ross? Remember how you weren't calm earlier, and refused to listen?"

"I'm calm," I insist. I've seriously never been more chill about anything.

"You're calm *now*. But." He lifts his shirt. On his right side, his ribs are red and beaten. A bruise has started to form. "Remember this? Remember how it happened?"

"I hit you."

The man nods. I'd guess he's in his upper forties or early fifties, with salt-and-pepper stubble. I know him from somewhere. Vaguely. As if he's someone linked to someone else. A second-degree acquaintance. I get the feeling when we met, which was maybe earlier today or maybe yesterday, it was the first official time. Before that, I knew *of* him, but didn't really *know* him. I remember hitting him now. With ... *with a baseball bat?* That doesn't sound like me. It's so rude. I probably didn't make a good first impression.

"That's right, you hit me," the increasingly familiar man says. "Do you remember why?"

I shake my head. It's a mistake. My neck still hurts.

"It was a misunderstanding," he explains.

"Me hitting you with a bat was a *misunderstanding?*" I ask.

"It came from one, yes. You hit me because you misunderstood something I said. You misunderstood what I was trying to do. Do you remember, Ross? It's very important that you remember. My wife gave you some Rohypnol dissolved in water after I got you under control, but it should have just been enough to calm you down. We don't get much internet up here so I can't be sure, but from what I was able to find, I think that with this amount, once you wake up the rest of the way, most of your memory will come back. It's very important that your memory comes back, Ross. It's very important that we talk about what you did."

"What *I* did?" I look down at my bindings. I've been tied to a chair. To keep me from scooting the chair toward all the tools around me, one of the legs has been drilled through and secured to a chipped-at bit of rebar in the middle of the floor, where boards give way to a concrete foundation. I imagine the tying-up was done after I was unconscious. I remember a rush to this man's actions — his actions, and his wife's. I think I caught them by surprise. I think they did the best they could with what they had.

"Yes. What *you* did. This?" He gestures at my bound-up predicament. "I didn't want to do this, Ross. You didn't give me a choice."

"What did I do, then?"

"You don't remember?"

I think about it, trying hard. The fog is starting to open up — enough that I remember emotions and snippets, if not a lot of specific events. The first emotion I remember was, of all things, *guilt*. But why would I feel guilty? I think I felt it on my way here rather than after I arrived. I remember repentance. Then ... betrayal?

I'm beginning to feel that something happened that really turned things around on me, and I didn't like it at all. I do remember anger. I do remember swinging a bat. But I also remember this man's hands on me, rough and furious, and I think I might remember being punched. A lot. But still, it's all so strange. There's a picture in my head of this same man, looking me square-on like he is now, his eyes wide and eminently reasonable. This is a man you believe when he talks to you. A man who can tie you up, then explain how it's entirely your fault.

"You don't remember," he repeats, and this time it's not a question.

The man

(Mark? Is his name Mark?)

looks at his watch. Then he looks to the door, which he's left open, and now I see a woman there, too. His wife. They're a couple. I don't know how I know them. I don't know why I chose to visit. She's not dressed for the weather. She's wearing some sort of house dress or nightgown, a coat pulled over top of it. Her eyes are red and timid, maybe worried. She's not wearing a hat. Steam rises semi-transparently from her head: heat escaping because she hasn't prepared enough for the cold.

"Mark..." she says to the man. Then she stops there, as if every bit of whatever-this-is has become too much for her. Behind her, strung between two leafless trees, is a clothesline strung with clothes. Some of those clothes are mine. Or just one item, one thing among the others. Just a light jacket. I got blood on it; that I remember. I threw it off and tossed it on the floor. They must have washed it, so it didn't look so murdery. Strange, to tie someone up and then hang their laundered clothing out to dry. It's almost like they're new to this. Whatever *this* is.

"You don't remember anything," Mark says, and this third time it's *like* a question without really being a question. I'm supposed to confirm or deny.

"We have to move him," says the woman.

"No. No, we don't have to do anything with him." Mark looks me in the eyes. "Do we, Ross? We just have to talk. I want to straighten out this misunderstanding. I really do. Sincerely. Things got out of hand, was all. This is fixable. It's fixable." The way he says it twice, I feel like he's talking more to himself than me or her, willing "it's fixable" to be true.

"Mark ... if his arm..."

The haunted way she says "his arm" makes me turn despite the discomfort in my neck. Intuition and memory are suddenly very insistent. It's suddenly vital that I get a look at the limb that I was too numb to feel earlier. Now that I'm upright and that arm isn't against the freezing floor, I'm starting to feel it again. It hurts. It hurts very bad, but only up high. I don't feel anything below the shoulder. I try to see it, but it's wrapped back and out of sight. The more I focus on it, the more I feel it throbbing like a bastard.

But then I twist much farther. Far enough, finally, to see.

The arm in question — my left — isn't wrapped behind me after all. It's also not numb. Turns out, the reason I can't feel it is because it's *not there*. It's been cut off. Amputated. A tourniquet's tied above the severance point, maybe six inches above where my elbow used to be.

I start to scream.

"Ross..." Mark says.

But I just keep screaming.

"*ROSS.*" He sounds frustrated — inconvenienced by my pain and disfigurement. I half expect him to look at his watch, waiting with ill temper for my hissy fit to be over.

Horrid memories begin to return, but only in fragments. Their disconnected, unexplained nature makes them even more terrifying, although what I know is terrifying enough. I don't yet remember why or how or when or what circumstances surrounded it ... but I am absolutely certain that wound, when my arm went missing, was cauterized to keep me from bleeding to death. I am absolutely certain it was done by sticking a cast iron pan into a broiler, then pressing it against my flesh.

I scream and scream and scream.

"Stop," Mark says.

He looks more flustered than angry. He keeps darting glances all over, wondering what to do about this ruckus I'm raising. But my damn arm's been cut off. Of course I don't stop.

"Stop! Be quiet!"

"You cut off my arm! You cut off my fucking *arm!*"

"I had to! You were going to kill me!"

"I'd never kill you! I'd never kill anyone!"

"Q-quiet," he stammers. I can't read his emotion. This could be intimidation, or it could be the beginnings of fury.

"Get away from me! *Let me go, you fucking psycho!*"

"I SAID QUIET!"

"Mark..." says the woman behind him.

"Let me go! Let me go! YOU TOOK MY ARM!"

"SHUT YOUR GODDAMN MOUTH AND LISTEN TO ME!"

He hits me with his fists.

Once.

Twice.

Three times.

I stop screaming. I'm whimpering now, trying to keep my mouth shut. But my arm. My damn arm. What happened? How am I here, and why is any of this going on?

Then Mark steps back, and I can see that my face has lacerated his knuckles. It looks like he reached into a bag of glass. He takes a breath and looks away, then smooths his hair back using his bloodied hand. A smudge of red smears across his forehead.

"Mark!" the woman shouts.

He looks back at her. "Remember how it started," he says. "Remember what he is."

He's huffing and puffing as he wipes the blood from his knuckles. He's the very picture of a sociopath trying to convince himself he's the right one here.

"We just need to talk this out, Ross and I," he says. "That's all.

We just need to settle down, keep from overreacting and screaming and causing a fuss, and talk like two rational human beings."

The woman — Willa, her name is — seems to doubt that's possible. She says nothing, afraid of both of us.

"My arm," I mutter — softly, so he won't hit me again. *"You cut off my arm."*

"And do you remember why?"

"What's to remember? What explains *cutting off someone's arm,* you freak?"

Mark pulls the gag back up over my mouth. *Into* my mouth. Now all I can do is moan.

"He needs time," Mark says to his wife. He pulls his jacket bottom down with both hands, composing himself. He runs a second hand over his hair, making it neat again.

"But Miranda..." Willa begins.

"She won't be here until Friday." He looks at me and says to Willa, "Ross can stay out here a while longer. He needs time, to think about what he's done."

Chapter Sixteen

I sleep on and off. When I wake for what seems the definitive time, I'm relieved to find my mind is my own again. The cloud that was muddying my thoughts earlier is, as far as I can tell, gone.

I remember everything now. I remember showing up at the cabin. I remember things spinning out of control. I even remember the arm. God help me, I remember being seared, to stop the bleeding, with that branding-hot pan.

It hurts, but it's like I've gotten used to the pain. The woman, Miranda's mother, came back during my delirium and offered me Advil of all things. She said she had nothing stronger — nothing to dull the pain of a missing limb, a smashed-in face, and who knows how many other injuries I've sustained. Just Advil. I told her I wanted a dozen of them.

A dozen? Isn't that too much?

I told her who cares; obviously they were going to kill me anyway.

I mainly said it to see how she reacted. She seemed shocked. That's good. It suggests, as I sort of figured, that they don't know what to do with me yet. Killing is just one choice of several, and one they'd rather not think about too much. If she'd just nodded when I said the kill-me thing? *That* would be reason to worry.

I caught them off guard; that was half the problem. I understand that now. This was never going to be a picnic in the park, but things might have been different if they'd at least known I was coming. Nobody expected me to show up for their little vacation — not the parents, not Miranda, not anyone. *I* didn't even expect me to show up. If Sunday night hadn't happened, I wouldn't have. I came because of conscience ... not that I ever had a chance to play nice and make amends.

Problem was, Miranda wasn't at the cabin like I expected. She left school Sunday, and her Airbnb email showed her parents' check-in as days earlier, but I guess she went somewhere else before driving up. Mark said they weren't expecting her until Friday — which, I've deduced with my excellent tied-up detective skills, is still two days from now. Would've been nice if she'd bothered to tell *me* that, dammit.

A scowl forms on my face. I'll bet *Aubrey* knows where she went. Miranda didn't tell me her full plans, but I'm sure she told Aubrey, who's got her nose in everything. But did Aubrey mention Miranda's side trip to *me* when I saw her last? Of course not. I'm good enough to sell her white-collar study drugs, but not good enough to date her best friend.

Bitch.

I should have turned around after showing up Monday and learning Miranda wouldn't arrive for four more days. Or, I should have been apathetic and stayed at school like Dion told me to. I knew Miranda's parents disliked me, but I didn't know how much. It's possible they didn't even know Miranda and I were dating. Could that really happen? Is Miranda really so ashamed of me that she never let them know? I'm not sure. All I know is that the timing seems to suggest it. Mark and Willa were cold when I first showed up, but the more I said the sorts of things boyfriends say about their girlfriends ... well, that's right around the time Mark *really* flipped out. I *had* to grab the baseball bat by the door — the same bat that made him grab the machete. He was coming at me with fists up, just for saying I loved his daughter. I had to stop him some-how, right?

That was my mistake: not reading the signs, not seeing how Mark's blood boiled at the sight of me. Instead my dumb ass tried to make nice, figuring I'd soothe bad blood while I had them alone.

Yeah. That worked well.

I didn't know that loving his daughter was a crime, but clearly it was. We started arguing right from Hello, then ramped up the more I said about wanting to see Miranda. Mark came at me, yelling, and I forgot all about being civil. It became physical within minutes: Mark with the first blow, not me. It was a mistake to even try. Miranda said he had a temper. I guess I should have known better.

We could have stopped at any point, but instead things just got worse and worse. Mark kept accusing me of crimes — things I'm not even sure I did. Pride got in the way. I refused to back down. At some point we crossed a line. *Me*, yes. But *them?* Absolutely.

You cut off a guy's arm and he's going to go to the police. That's why Mark tackled me and Willa tied me up. Now, they don't know what to do with me. The entire situation has called their bluff. *How far would you go when push comes to shove?*

Ma and Pa are thinking hard right now, trying to figure that out. I don't plan to make things easy for them.

When they first came to check on me, I was loopy. Now, I'm sharp as a tack. I remember every bit of what Mark wants to "dis-cuss rationally." I know enough to understand why this happened from their perspective — maybe even to see his side of things. But that doesn't make him right. It doesn't make me wrong. Not even close.

Mark Wimberly has a police record. Miranda told me about it. More than once, he was arrested for assault. Me, I've got skeletons in my closet, but that right there is the difference: They're *in my closet*. Not out in the open like Mark's are, ready to work against me once someone calls 911. I've got more leverage on this family than they have on me — at least where the cops are concerned.

Mark seems smart; I'm sure he's figured that out by now. That's probably what he's been doing while I've been in this shed: thinking, maybe discussing options with his wife. Mark's a hothead, but I doubt he's a killer. Few people are. That gives me a tenuous advantage. I don't have to be a victim here. I can still control this situation if (and this is a very big *if*) I can get myself out of it.

Today is Wednesday, I think. They've had me tied up for two days, doping me with roofies between meals, water, and using a gross bucket latrine. I've been high all that time, giving them space to consider their options. But now, the roofies must have run out. Now I'm clear and will stay that way. That's good news. If they were sure about killing me, they'd have done it already. What's more, my newly clear mind gives me options. They've been able to feed me like a docile pet before now, but from here on out, I'll have words and logic and threats to use against them.

So how should I play this? Should I act cocky, telling Mark he'll never get away with killing me? Or should I play innocent instead, promising I won't tell anyone what happened if they let me go? Will he believe that? Can he possibly believe that *I* believe it? A cut-off arm is pretty hard to explain. I can imagine a world in which I blame it on an accident, but would anyone buy it? And if so, would I *want* them to? *These bastards took my arm.*

I need to think carefully. Either way I've got a negotiation ahead of me, and nobody wins an angry negotiation. But will I be able play it cool, pretending to agree to disagree on the whole hacked-off-limb thing? By Friday morning, we'll need a decision. They'll want whatever-happens to be finished well before Miranda arrives, so they have time to clean up the mess ... whatever *that* ends up meaning.

Wednesday afternoon to Friday morning. I have 36 hours to figure out what to do.

I peek out the window, but it's facing away from the cabin with very little to see. The sliver around the shutter is too narrow to spy much more than trees. I can see the supports holding up the raised bridge I crossed on my way here, but that's about it. No other homes in sight.

Think, Ross. Think!

I've been testing my restraints on and off, trying to loosen them since my first awakening. I try them again now just to be sure, but nothing's changed. They feel tied by a sailor. Any wiggling I do only tightens things up, probably by design. I'll only waste energy trying to work my way out.

Think.

I force my breath toward calm. There's no rush. I need to take my time and do the *right* thing, not just *some*thing. 36 hours; that's what I've got. For most of that time, I'll be completely alone. They don't enjoy checking on me, so they'll do it as little as they can. What can I do out here while nobody's looking?

I take in my surroundings, looking for weaknesses.

The shed door is locked from the outside. The walls seem well-built and unrotted, so even if I got free, I'd have to cut my way out, raising a ruckus. My bindings are solid, the knots like nothing I've seen before. Willa clearly knows her way around a rope.

Can I cut my restraints? It's just rope, and I'm in a toolshed.

True, but my chair is sturdy, not flimsy like a cafeteria-style folding chair. The way it's fastened to the floor means I can't scoot it, and the fact that it's tied to rebar instead of wood means I can't yank a board free. It's maddening: I'm in a toolshed, surrounded by saws and screwdrivers, but they're way too far to reach.

So, what? You're just going to give up?

I fidget even though there's no point, because doing something futile is better than doing nothing. I test my bindings where they're tied to the chair, wondering if I can break through a weak weld. I hop up and down in the chair, seeing if my tie to the rebar will loosen. It makes a lot of noise — like pipe banging on pipe — but neither Mark nor Willa come running. They must figure we're in the middle of nowhere, hearable by nobody. And they're exactly right.

After a bunch of hopping, something happens. I see the concrete chipping. I'm making headway! It lasts for a handful of seconds, but then the chair leg snags on the rope holding it to the rebar and tips me over. After that I'm on my side again, face pressed to the wood beyond the concrete piling. I can tell the crawlspace beneath the floor isn't insulated. Frigid air blows up at me through the cracks while a weathervane creaks outside.

"Fantastic," I mutter. The room does not respond.

But what's this? I feel something in my pocket, pressed between my leg and the decking. I look down, unsure what it might be. It's too hard to be my wallet. I can still feel my wallet in my back pocket anyway, softer and more yielding than this. They didn't search me. Things happened too quickly for that. Emotions rose. Everything was *react, react, react* — no time for thinking. They could have searched me after I was tied, but I can see in their eyes how repugnant all of this is to them. When they're not in here, they're trying very hard not to think about me at all. To pretend none of this happened. It's almost like they're willfully blind, hoping I — and the problem I represent — will go away if they just keep their heads in the sand.

I imagine Willa: an ordinarily passive person Mark knows better than to leave alone with me for fear I'll appeal to her sense of sympathy. And I imagine her saying, *Mark, did you remember to take his wallet?* This while he's wiping my blood off his knuckles. This, as he does whatever-he-did with my severed arm. Where is it now? What does a person do with an arm, anyway? Throw it in the garbage? Toss it into the brush for vultures to find?

They took my iPhone. Of course they did, even though there's no service. Miranda's dad sounded so proud of himself, using my face to unlock it so he could respond to text messages so nobody knows I'm gone. Has he been texting Miranda as me, when there are bars enough to do so? Will he be that bold?

But it's not the iPhone I feel in my pocket. It's my Skor phone: slim enough to not create a bulge. Nobody expects a person to carry two cell phones.

I shimmy my upper body, trying to rub the bottom part of my pocket against the floor while leaving the upper part open. At first nothing happens, but then the phone moves, squeezed out like pinching the base of a pimple. It doesn't take long before it's laying there beside me.

Not that I can reach it. Or free my hands (ahem: *hand*) to use it even if I could.

There's a small amount of give in the rope. So I smear my arm, shoulder, and side against the ground while using my core to take weight off my hips and legs, torquing sideways to half-lift the chair. This done, I contract like doing a crunch. With most of my weight on my upper body, it's the lower half that moves. The chair stays tight on my ass, but my little curl-up maneuver brings it with me when I pull my knees toward my chest.

The sideways chair legs rake the boards as they move. The sound is like a big wooden rasp. But it works; my knees slap the phone and send it two inches higher, toward my abdomen.

Good work, soldier, I think. *Now repeat.*

I scooch up, using the little bit of slack in the rope holding the chair to the deck. Once my knee is again just below the phone, I try again. My whole body contracts, this time knocking the little burner phone a good six inches.

Once more. I get another six inches this time.

Now that I'm out of slack on the rope, I wiggle my way back down. The phone stays where I've nudged it. Once I'm back in my original position, it's right by my face, in the hollow between my chin and neck.

Okay. Now what?

I hear footsteps, then a hand slapping the shed's side. Someone's right outside the door.

"Settle down in there," Mark's voice says through the wood. "You'll just tire yourself out. Nobody can hear you."

He says it like a parent at the door of a child who's up too late, so I half expect him to go away without coming in. But that would be dumb. What if I got free? He has to check, so I'm sure he will. He'll open up, and then he'll...

!!! The phone !!!

Alarm surges through me. I hear Mark punching numbers into the lock on the door, suddenly panicked. My captor will be inside soon, looking down at me and what I've done. Once he spots the Skor, he'll take it. I screwed up, making enough noise for them to hear. All I've done is expose my one last chance, for whatever it's worth.

The door unlatches. Hinges squeak. All I can do is lunge forward with my chin, use it to tuck the phone tight against my neck, and hope he doesn't see it.

I look up with my eyes only, not trusting myself to turn my neck and expose what it's hiding. I see Mark standing behind me with a machete — the *same* machete, I think, that cost me my arm. It was probably meant for trail-clearing, left by the owners. I guess this time Mark wanted to be ready in case I'd slipped my bindings. Or to do a bit more home surgery, so I'll be symmetrical.

"And now you're on the floor again."

I don't dignify that with a response. I'm too busy trying to hide the phone, hoping against hope he doesn't see it.

"Fine," he says. "But I'm not doing this again."

He squats. Alarm bells scream inside my mind. He's going to pull me upright like he did before. Fat load of good my neck will be as a shield when it's no longer on the ground. He'll practically slip on my burner phone as he walks toward the door. And then what? Death?

Do something! my mind screams.

"So how hard is it, Mark?" I ask.

He stops with his hand inches from the frame of the chair.

"How hard is it, to not keep drinking when you have a bitch for a daughter?"

"Watch yourself," he says. I can tell he's forcing himself to be a bigger man than he actually is. He's angry, but not allowing himself to be. He's probably telling himself right now that *of course* I'm lashing out. He's holding me prisoner. He needs to let it go. To let me have my tiny little victory before he disposes of me.

His hand wraps the chair frame, preparing to lift me even after what I said. His muscles tense. The chair rises a fractional inch. My face lifts just slightly, parting company with my little black phone.

"She hates you!" I blurt.

The chair stops moving. I can't see Mark's face.

"Laughs at you, too," I go on. "She knows you'll never stay sober.

She told me you have an anniversary coming up. One year." I force a laugh. "Never made it past a year, have you? I guess not. Because you're a coward."

No movement. I can feel his cloud of anger.

"Of course you made her life hell," I say. "I would, too. You know, it's funny. I'd *never* be with someone like your daughter if it weren't for the sex. She's too much like you. She's weak. And cruel. We laughed and laughed about your so-called 'sobriety' last week, when we were in bed together. In fact, you know what *I* think, *Mark?* I agree with Miranda. She said you were *made* for failure. *Designed* for it." I laugh again. "Go on. Celebrate your anniversary with a cocktail, you *fucking drunk."*

That does it. He lets go suddenly, and I drop the inch I was lifted, my face crashing back to the floor. I feel the phone move under me, but it stays hidden. It's halfway under my cheek, smashing teeth against my inner lip.

I wait for him to kick me — or, worse, to use the machete again. He's to my rear; there's no way I'd see it coming. I brace, and I wait, and above me I can sense Miranda's father more than hear him.

But he doesn't kick me. He simply says, "Enjoy your night." Then something cold douses my head, plastering my hair to my face. "And enjoy your water."

His footsteps retreat without hurry. The door squeaks open, then closes. The lock engages.

My heart hammers as if it's just woken up. It's cold enough out here that the water he poured might give me hypothermia, and it'll be all for nothing if he just soaked the phone I'm hiding.

Carefully, I move my head around until my hair stops dripping. Only then do I pull up and use my chin to nudge the Skor out from under my face.

The floor around it is dry, shielded by my head. The phone's screen is smashed from its last concussion, but it's still powered on, still working fine.

We're in business.

Chapter Seventeen

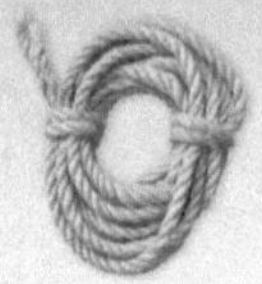

But of course it's not that easy.

The Skor got pretty busted up during my beating and now it doesn't work properly. I knew the screen was smashed, but it turns out the keypad was, too. None of the buttons work — something I discover only after using my teeth to pull a splinter from the floorboards to use as a dialing wand. I can't press 9, I can't press 1, and I certainly can't combine them into 911. Not one of the buttons will go down. Or rather, they're all *permanently* down, the entire front of the thing looking smashed with a hammer. And of course I can't talk to it like my iPhone, working it by voice.

A text comes in. I can barely read the screen, which is far smaller than a smartphone's and with one tenth the resolution. It's an order. My customers all use code numbers, and this one is from Lionel Graves. He wants some Oxy. Dumbass. I don't even sell Oxy. You want weed? You want uppers to study or downers to sleep? For that stuff, I'm your man. I've got mushrooms. LSD. MDMA. The fun stuff, nothing harmful. Nothing I sell even has a lethal dose, except for the benzos. I'm the good guy. A romantic. I made a mistake and came all the way up here to make things right — not just with Miranda, but with her folks, too. And look what being Mr. Nice Guy got me?

The last reception bar vanishes as the screen dims. Who knows how long ago Lionel sent that text? If I were able to reply — if the keypad of my phone wasn't smashed to shit — who knows how long it'd take for my text to upload to the Skor cloud and send?

Up here in the armpit of New Hampshire, we put the "asynchronous" in "asynchronous communication," bro. You wanna text me? Cool. I'll get it sometime this year.

All my squirming around on the floor has me exhausted. I'm parched. Worse, the water I should have drunk — that instead, Mark poured over my head — has frozen my hair into an ice helmet. I wonder if I'm getting delirious.

Delirious, or just hilarious? Ha ha, thanks; I'm here all week.

Until I'm dead.

Focus. Focus or you'll lose your mind. Or, you know, give up. Just go ahead and die right now.

I wonder if my coat is still in the car, or if my car is still where I parked it. Did they already move it, hiding it like they hid me? Maybe they rolled it down the cliff and into the river. That would be badass to see. If it happened, I'm sorry to have missed it.

Ross. You're losing it. You have to focus.

I blink, trying to snap-to. My voice of reason is correct; I *am* starting to lose it. I've been here for a long time without medical attention. My wounds throb on and off despite the numbing cold. I'm intermittently lightheaded, as if I lost too much blood. Could I have an infection? It's impossible to say; I'm so cramped that even my uninjured parts hurt. Makes sense that I would, though. Cauterizing my arm would seal and sterilize it, but that's not the only place he drew blood.

I should have let Mark lift my chair upright. The phone's too busted to use. If I'd let him find it by lifting me off the floor, I'd be sitting properly right now. I'd have water in me instead of ice on me. Maybe they'd even have brought me food.

Too late for that now. Everything outside is dark. Has been for what feels like a very long time. The adults went to bed, leaving the naughty kid in the outhouse.

What time is it, anyway?

I poke the phone with my mouth-stick. It's 11:43 p.m.

I consider spitting the stick across the room. What's the point? I can't press any of the numbers. The selection buttons are all that work, but what good are they? It took me a useless forever, but I've already looked through the menus. Using my stick and this broken piece of crap, I can redial numbers I've called before, but that's beyond useless because even Skor's persistent-send feature doesn't work for calls ... if I could even *make* calls, which thanks to the lack of bars, I absolutely can't. I can take photos with its zero point zero micropixel camera. Or, lastly, I can change the brightness of the backlight. Yay.

I poke something and the camera's shutter clicks. The screen shows me my photographic masterpiece. Congratulations to me; I've managed to take a photo of a big black-and-gray field of nothing.

But then: *Hang on.*

I can't sit upright, but I can twist my torso a little — a move I keep doing just to keep cramps at bay. I do it now, though, so I can look more down on the camera instead of sideways at it.

I've got the thing wedged against a chip of wood; that's how the camera had room to take an incredibly terrible photo instead of just shooting directly into the floor. I poke it flat onto its back now, rising above it to look at the spiderwebbed screen.

Now that a photo is in play, the phone is giving me a new set of menu options. I didn't know it did that. Though, why would I? Most burners don't have a camera. I've certainly never thought of using mine.

There are three options in rectangles on the bottom of the little screen. I can use the select pad to move between them using my little stick. They are: *Save. Discard.* And *Share.*

Curious, I poke it over to Share and hit the Go button. The photo minimizes and the screen fills with a digital number pad.

Holy shit. When you share a photo, you don't use the number buttons to tell the phone where to send it. Instead, you use this onscreen thing. I poke around using my stick, practically giddy. I can't call 911, but I can text them a photo!

I try. Nothing happens. It seems 911 doesn't accept photos from strangers. Or (and this strikes me as more likely), Skor probably doesn't allow users to send them in the first place. It's a criminal's phone, sold as if anyone who isn't doing something illegal might care about NSA-level anonymity, GPS obfuscation, standard text-message remailing so addresses can't be traced, and all sorts of other law-dodging crap. Wouldn't want to involve 911 in that, now, would we?

The police station, then.

If I had their number and service, I'd call the cops instead of sending pictures. But again, the pad is broken. All I could do (if I had their number) would be to send a blurry picture of nothing, seeing as this particular Ansel Adams can't use his hands to work the camera. Besides, you can't trace a Skor without the SIM ID and a warrant — and again, the GPS on the thing is deliberately shielded. Some cop would get my picture, maybe try to see where it came from, then would ultimately consider it as just another crank who's sending the cops things they don't want or need.

I don't have contacts programmed into this phone. I can't; it'd be a violation of my dealer's code of ethics. Because yes, I have a code of ethics. My clients don't snitch on me, and I don't snitch on them. Hence everyone having an untraceable customer number that I've memorized but never written down. Hence my never, *ever* being so dumb as to store their names and numbers in a phone that was built to be disposable.

Okay. Then send pictures to a random number. They're texts, so Skor's tech will send them through eventually. Someone will think it's weird. Someone will at least poke around.

But will they? We live in an apathetic society. I've never even seen someone react when a car alarm goes off. We all assume calls for help are someone else's problem. So is there a point?

I can't send real messages; I'd need the broken keypad if I wanted to type letters. All I can send is photos. And I can't *arrange* the photos; I'm lucky I can take them at all. If I had my hands, maybe I could write something and then take a picture of it. But what options do I have without that? This felt like something I could use, but as with everything else it's useless.

Unless...

What if I send a photo to someone who actually knows me? Maybe that's at least one step farther from apathy.

But after a long time thinking, I can only come up with four numbers I know by heart. The first two are mine — the Skor's plus the one that rings the iPhone Mark and Willa took from me. The third is my mom's old number, because she made me memorize it when I was a kid. That number's long gone, but the last number could actually help me. I know Miranda's number because I was with her when she finally got her own cell plan. I showed her a mnemonic to help remember the new number — and so, like getting a contact high, I remembered it, too.

I bring up the photo. Hit Share. Enter the number. The picture goes into the queue and begins its persistent-send thing. After that I exhale long and slow, preparing to shut my eyes and find out later what happens.

But before the screen even dims, the queue empties. A bar comes and goes. The photo's been sent.

I shake off fatigue and lift my head. What will Miranda think when she gets it? She doesn't know this number, or even that I have a second phone. I felt some hope before sending the photo, but that hope is already half-gone. A dark and grainy photo of nothing, sent by what she'll think is a random number? What kind of cry for help is that?

I can do better. I *have* to do better, if I want a shot at survival.

And so as exhausted as I am, I pick up my little wooden stick again, working it into position between my teeth. I wiggle forward, then do my best to scratch a message into the floor. It's wood on wood, so by the time I'm done (three hours later, by the way; *you* try using your mouth to write on floorboards with a toothpick), I've only managed to shallowly scratch four letters with a symbol between them: our initials, like a lovebird carves into a tree.

When I scoot back to try and take the picture without using my hands, the shitty little camera can barely see what I've written.

"Barely" is being generous. But it doesn't matter; I'm too tired to do more now. I've lost blood; I'm probably only conscious thanks to adrenaline and shock. I'm well past my bedtime. Or my on-the-floor-in-the-cold time.

I send the photo anyway, its message all but invisible. Unlike the last one, this picture enters the queue and stays there. It might send overnight, if a bar appears. It might send tomorrow. Or never.

I'm too tired to care.

But even so, there's still one thing to do. Mark left me tipped over because I made him angry, but he won't leave me this way forever. That means I still need to hide the phone. It takes work, but I use my chin to nudge it away from me and under a rag beside a dust-covered paint can. It's at the limit of the range allowed by the rope, but I'll be able to stretch enough to get it again when I need to. Skors have incredible battery life. I'm not too worried about it running dry. They basically put a smartphone battery inside a junker that uses a hundredth of the energy.

Once the phone is tucked away, I scooch myself back to where I was, centered over the foundation pylon and far enough from my hiding place.

The last wave of fatigue hits me. I collapse more than sleep.

Chapter Eighteen

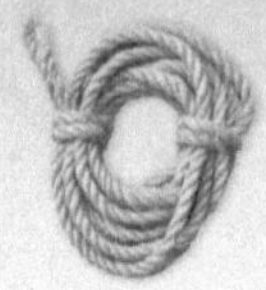

My eyes open slowly. I assumed I wouldn't be able to sleep trussed like a turkey, but it's already morning. *Late* morning. The sun shines through a crack beneath the shutter, slicing a dust-filled beam across the far wall, hot and yellow like a racing stripe.

Between me and the window, Miranda's father waits on a chair.

"Good morning." His voice is flat, like a recording.

He rises. Blessedly, he lifts my chair upright. There's a small pause as I start to tilt, as if Mark is waiting to see if I'll wise-off again. I won't. My side is entirely numb. Stay where I was any longer and I'd lose more limbs.

My chair settles, square to his.

"If I untie your hand, can I trust you not to do anything stupid?"

I nod. I swallow. My throat is sandpaper. The air's warmed a little, though. It must be above freezing. My hair is wet instead of frozen.

Mark reaches into his pocket, pulls out a knitted beanie, and puts it on my head. Then, with watchful and wary eyes, he slips my gag down and unties my remaining hand. It's the right and I'm right-handed. Thank God.

Still eyeing me, Mark steps back. Slowly, to show him I mean no immediate harm, I remove my arm from behind my back and shake it out in an attempt to dislodge the pins and needles. It doesn't work well. I open and close my fist, feeling like I've been attacked by a porcupine.

Mark moves back, then sets a piece of peanut-butter-covered toast on the floor atop a napkin. He's not even giving me a plate. Plates can be broken, used as tools or weapons. I get a cup, too, but it's soft plastic, almost rubbery — the kind of thing you'd give a toddler. He nudges both toward me using the toe of his scuffed snow boot, keeping the flopped-up edge of the napkin between shoe and food for cleanliness reasons.

I bend down to take what he's given me. I drink greedily, shove the toast into my mouth, then drink again.

"Not too fast. You'll get sick."

"And you care if I get sick?"

"We got off on the wrong foot, Ross. Nobody wanted this. It just happened."

"So that's what this is? An unfortunate misunderstanding?"

"Oh, *I* understand plenty," he replies. "*I'm* extremely clear on who you are. It's you who's out of the loop."

My brow wrinkles. "What the hell does that mean, 'You're clear *who I am*'? Who am I, Mark? Don't be shy. Am I a drug dealer? A petty criminal? Don't hold back. *Please.* Tell me *who I am* that I deserved to *have my fucking arm cut off.*"

Then I wait, genuinely curious. Mark just stares, looking like he wants to say something. He wants to say it *badly*, but for some reason he's holding back. Why? Given how much hatred is in his eyes right now, he must have a powerful reason for keeping his mouth shut. Does he think he saw me cheating on Miranda while he was drunk in a bar, but can't say so because he can't admit drinking? Because shit, man ... that never happened. I can't imagine *what* he thinks happened.

Our stand-off goes on for a while. It's the strangest thing, watching him. Part of Mark clearly wants to cut more parts off of me, but a saner, more logical, more forward-thinking part of him holds the evil part at bay. He thinks he's got dirt on me; that much is clear. I just can't imagine what it is, or why he won't say. I wish he'd give me whatever dumb theory he has, because then I could debunk it. I'm not perfect, but I've never made mistakes where fucking Mark Wimberly could see.

"What?" I prompt. "Why do you hate me so much? What do you think I did?"

"You started dating my daughter."

"So fucking what?"

Again I see him hold back. His teeth flash subconsciously, but he takes a breath and puts his inner beast back in its cage.

"Things got out of hand," he says.

"I see. And now you're sorry."

"I wouldn't go that far."

I shake my head, so furious and indignant that I feel like screaming. "You're a monster. And now you want me to absolve you. Do you really expect me to say you're *not* a monster?"

He sighs as if tired of all of this. "Ross..."

"Miranda told me about you, you know. About how you are. She said you've got two faces. 'The sweetest man.' 'The most horrible man.' How does it feel, to know your daughter had to balance her feelings about you between love and fear?"

"I'm not that man anymore. I've changed."

"Have you?" Again I look at my stump of an arm, then my many other bruises. I can feel the way my cheek is larger than normal. All evening, the movements of my jaw had me accidentally biting my inflated lip.

"You started shouting," he says. "I didn't know what you were going to do."

"*Please.*" I sneer. "I started shouting because *you* started swinging. Just like you used to do when Miranda was little. *Twice.* How are those assault charges treating you, you brown-bag drunk?"

I think Mark might react to that, but he just exhales as if it's all so regrettable. "You can believe me, or you can not believe me, but it's true. I don't like you, but all things considered, I wish I hadn't hurt you. Not like this."

"'Like this' meaning 'in a way that's about to get your ass busted.'"

"We'll see," he says. And the eyes flash again.

I scoff.

"But none of that really matters, does it?" Mark says. "The question, Ross, is what we're going to do now."

"Finally got to thinking, did you? Did it finally dawn on you that you're completely and totally fucked?"

"Let's not get ahead of ourselves."

"No," I say. "Let's. Let's get *really far* ahead of ourselves. *Weeks* ahead. *Years* ahead. What are you going to do now, *Mark?* Are you going to kill me? Are you really stupid enough to think you can sweep murder under the rug, then go back to your life and family like nothing's changed?"

He says nothing.

"Or is your plan to keep me in your shed forever? Although I guess it's not really *your* shed, is it? This place? I know it's a rental."

"It's not a rental. This is my father's property."

I laugh again. "Bullshit. How do you think I knew where to come? Miranda's a real good girl, Mark. Very responsible. She brushes her teeth every night before bed ... and when she goes away for a while, she lets all her friends know where she's going to be. Hell, I tacked the reservation email she sent me up in my room at school. Plain sight, for everyone to see. You're here for ... what? Two more weeks? *Then* what? Are you planning to smuggle me back home? Keep me in your basement, like a pet?" I scowl and shake my head. "You did this on someone else's turf, at a place everyone knows you rented. So I guess *that's* what you're going to do next: You're going to get fucked ... *Mark.*"

Emotions war on his face. He doesn't like the way I'm talking to him, but he knows I'm right and that he's in trouble. It doesn't matter that nobody planned this; the deed is done. It just happened, like he said. We argued, we fought, tempers were lost, violence was had, and then suddenly our little spat became something much, much worse.

Baseball bats were grabbed. Machetes were grabbed in response. Nobody meant to use them until we both started swinging. The difference was that after I broke Mark's ribs, I flinched. Mark did not. He wanted to kill me even before I hit him; that much is clear to me now. I still don't know why. All I know is that when he came at me, he came possessed. Possessed and strong and stupid like ... well, *like a drunk*. Cutting me the first time didn't back *him* off like hitting him backed *me* off. Instead, it made him swing the blade again. And harder. As if he was in a frenzy, as if bloodlust had taken him over. The machete went into my arm bone hard enough that I heard it crack all the way through. Maybe in some primal, inebriated part of his brain it made more sense to finish the job and patch the wound than try to repair it. Why wouldn't he, after how bad he cut me? Post-chop, my left arm became a ham hock dangling from a stubborn piece of sinew.

It probably wasn't after things were triaged — the bleeding stopped with the sear of that cast-iron pan, all blood mopped from in front of the cabin — that reality probably came crashing down for Mark. He handled the problem that arrived unexpectedly at his door ... but then the solution became a much worse problem.

"It was self-defense. You came at me with a bat."

"*Your* bat. Which I took from you."

"But who swung first?"

"*You!*" I blurt. How could he believe otherwise?

"Self-defense," he repeats lamely.

"Okay," I say. "Self-defense. Sure."

"It's true."

"Fuck you it's true. You were drunk. We both know it."

"I wasn't drunk. I haven't had a drink in almost a year."

I laugh. "Whatever you say. So how about the part where instead of taking me to a hospital or calling the police, you locked me up in here?"

He exhales. "That was a mistake. Things happened too fast. I wasn't thinking. Now it's too late to take back."

"You're finished. You know that, right? You've already got two strikes with the police. This time they'll put you away until you've got great-grandkids." I use my lone hand to count off crimes that weren't self-defense at all — the ones he made choices to commit. "Kidnapping. Torture."

"I didn't torture you."

"Missing arm."

"That happened in the fight."

"Not the part where you cut off the rest of it. Not the part where you burned me with a red-hot skillet."

"To stop the bleeding!"

"Not the part where you stuck me in a shed, didn't feed me, and didn't give me water for the first day. Not the part where you hit me again. And again. Not the part where you knocked me over and left me that way overnight, in the cold, with my head covered in ice."

"What's done is done."

"Yeah. That's *exactly* what I'll tell the jury."

His jaw works. I don't know what it means, nor how to play him. I'm working on instinct here, unsure whether threatening Mark until he lets me go is better than being meek. I didn't know this man before Monday. I only knew he never liked me near his daughter and had a nasty temper. Miranda said her father always regretted his actions in the morning, though, no matter how upset he'd been the night before.

In the mornings, he's always sorry. Always wants to make it right.

I hear her words in my mind, wishing she was here right now.

Mark still hasn't said anything. He's still thinking, trying in his chess-player's way to decide the best way out of this. Watching him, I wonder if I've read the situation wrong. I expected repentance and regret, but what I see on his face right now is something different. He's cooler than I figured. Calculating. It's an icy kind of calculation, too: the kind that separates emotion from fact, willing to make the choice that serves him and his people best no matter what it might take, what it might cost.

Maybe I shouldn't be issuing threats. Maybe I've just given him a great reason to kill me.

"Look," I say. "I guess you're right. Where we are is where we are. Doesn't matter how we got here."

Mark says nothing.

"No matter what happened before now, there are only two options: You let me leave, or..." I hide a swallow, wanting to be as logical and unemotional as he seems. "...or you don't."

He nods.

"I'm sorry. I shouldn't have said what I said. I won't tell anyone. I promise. Just let me go. I'll make something up. We can work together. You and me. We've both got something to lose. We'll come up with a story. Both of us. Together."

He looks at my arm, then my eyes. That's when I realize how badly I've screwed up. Mark came in wanting to do what I just proposed, sensible or not, but my words before now have made him unsure. I should have kept my temper. I should have pretended that peaceful agreement was all I wanted, too. I could break my promise and go to the cops *after* I was free. He can fink on me all he wants because *I* got into a fight ... but *he's* the one who cut off a limb and held me prisoner.

"You're lying," he says.

"What? No! I want out of here! Why would I do anything other than what it takes to leave?"

He stands and comes at me. I resist, but he has no trouble re-tying my freed hand.

"Hey," I say. "Come on. Put yourself in my shoes. What would you do if you were me? Would you hold a grudge if it meant staying here? Wouldn't you do *whatever it takes* to end this, even if you hate it?"

He crosses to the shed door. Puts his hand on the knob. Turns it. The latch disengages, the door swinging open to Thursday morning's winter sun.

"Mark!"

He looks back.

"I swear I won't say anything! You can ... I'll sign something, okay? Some sort of testimony. Get it notarized; I don't care! I'll put it on paper. I'll swear on my mother that you never touched me!"

He looks at me for a long time. It's a chilly, assessing kind of stare. He's sizing me up like meat. That's when I realize: I'm not a person to him right now — just a difficult puzzle he somehow needs to solve.

He exits. The door closes.

I decide he's going to kill me. The calm I've so delicately held evaporates, and I start to yell. I'm in panic fire now, shouting everything at him I can think of. It doesn't even make sense. Am I offering surrender? Compliance? Revolt? Justice from beyond the grave? I have no idea. My life is flashing in front of my eyes.

"I'M ALL OVER THIS PLACE AND YOU KNOW IT!" I scream after him. "My blood's on the stoop! My DNA is all over the living room! All over *in here!* What if they track my phone? What about people who come looking for me? Do you think they'll have to look far? *People know where I am! THEY'LL COME LOOKING FOR YOU! YOU CAN'T GET RID OF EVERYTHING!"*

The door clicks again. A moment later, it opens.

"Good," I say, relieved to see Mark's face in the gap. "Let's both just take a breath. There's still a way to make this work."

He crosses to me. Without a word, he tugs my gag back into place.

I scream as he leaves again, but this time my shouts comes out as a low drone, inaudible through thick walls over the gurgling water pump, over the sound of river rapids in the valley below.

For two or three hours, I worry and cry. You'd think I'd have more of a spine, but my bravado left when I saw that final look in Mark's eye. It's true that he's not a murderer. It's true, probably, that he can be kind, with a big heart and a bigger soft spot, assuming he's not drinking. But it's *also* true that his hand has been forced. He's between the proverbial rock and hard place. He's not a killer ... but this one time, I suspect he's realized he might have to become one.

What choice does he have? We'd be kidding ourselves to pretend this can go away. It's gone too far to take back. Mark knows it, I know it, and now I'm quite sure *he* knows *I* know it. And so, like any logic-minded protector, he's in there steeling himself for what must be done.

I tip myself onto my side, then wiggle until I'm able to fish out my hidden phone and poking stick. The photo did send overnight, but I doubt it matters. The message I tried to carve into the floor is barely visible even in bright morning light, so there's almost zero chance Miranda saw it — if she even looked at the picture from an unknown number to begin with. Most of what I "carved," seen plainly now, turned out to just be moving dust around.

So now what? Do I even have options at this point?

The best I can manage, in terms of broadcasting my location, turns out to be a clumsy picture aimed toward the window crack. But what can anyone see through that crack? From down this low, just the top of the bridge and some trees are visible. Even if my location *could* be identified from the photo (it'd have to be visual; Skor's "privacy" means no GPS tags on its images), there's nothing in-frame that screams help is needed.

I check the phone's time: just after noon on Thursday. Miranda is supposed to come up here tomorrow, on Friday. That's the deadline. It means I'm probably going to die today. Maybe tomorrow, if I'm lucky.

The truth of it makes me cry again. I want to shout; I want to be bold and brash; I want to find strength enough to flex and tear through my restraints, burst through the wall of the shed, and run away. Or better: burst into the cabin and give Mark (maybe Willa, too) a taste of what they're planning to give me. But I can't do those things. All I can do is sit here and wait to die. They've tied me too well and taken away all my possibilities. This isn't the movies. Nothing will miraculously save me.

After a few minutes of sobbing, even catharsis loses its catharsis. I've soon enough got no bad feelings left to purge, and when that happens, I'm actually bored — sort of wishing Mark would come in and threaten me again so at least I'd have something to do. A person can't feel sorry for themselves forever. So here and there, I find impotent resolve again. But what exactly can I do?

Something. Anything.

Even if it's useless, I've got to try *something*, or I'll go out of my mind. But what? I only have the phone and a splinter of wood. All other tools are inaccessible, and there's no point in whining about it.

So what can I do with my dumb burner phone?

I can send photos. But only to Miranda or strangers.

They say a picture speaks a thousand words, but I've tried my hand at putting *actual* words in a photo and come up empty. I'll have to be creative. Without hands. Or being able to reach anything. While on my side tied to a chair, because I'm pretty sure the next time Mark comes in, he won't pick me up. He'll kill me instead.

I need as shocking picture as I can manage, given what I've got. That's the only way to get Miranda's attention, and I desperately need her attention if she's going to get curious enough to ask some questions.

My eyes don't travel far before they find something shocking enough: my stump of an arm. It looks dog-chewed and incinerated. Red-hot cast iron pans aren't standard medical tools for cauterization, and Willa left chunks of red flesh at the end while playing horror movie nurse. I can see a big artery in there too, burned closed but still like something from a Halloween display.

There's still something missing. It hurts like hell, but I slap my arm hard on the ground a few times until it starts bleeding a little. I bleed theatrically where the camera will see it, to paint as gruesome a picture as I can.

I wish I could hold the phone to really frame the picture right, but all I have is my face and my stick and an atrocious camera to work with. I do my best but end up with what looks like a picture of a steak that went halfway through a paper shredder, plus the blood and one of my feet that ended up in the frame. But will anyone know what this is? You can't tell from the photo that my stump is even an arm. Or, for that matter, human.

But: *Unsettling? Gross?* Oh yes; it's both of those things.

I send it to Miranda. The sky is clearer than usual, so it goes right away.

Too bad that by the time she gets here, I'll already be dead.

. . .

I HEAR A CAR ABOUT A HALF HOUR LATER. ITS ENGINE IS FAR away, but clearly approaching. Who could be coming? There aren't any houses for miles.

While I'm thinking, the shed door bursts open and both Wimberlys storm in, their eyes wide with panic. I can still hear the engine very low behind them. That confirms what I thought: It's not *them* in the car. Someone else is here.

Mark pulls something from his pocket. It's a stun gun. Where'd he get a stun gun? He must have gone into town. Always a planner, he must have thought he'd need it.

I don't have long to wonder, because Mark jabs the stunner hard into my chest. There's a sharp buzzing sound, like a single coordinated bleat from every bee in a hive. My mind goes blank. My muscles tense. The pain and alarm of being stunned is immediate and total. Seconds later, I can't move no matter how hard I try. Then Willa's behind me, untying my ropes. Her hands move fast, deft and knowledgeable.

They pull me from the chair, dragging me across the wood floor like luggage. Inside my shirt, the Skor rattles against my bare chest. Good thing I chin-bumped it there instead of toward the rag by the paint can this time, because now I and the rag are far apart. There's rush and panic in their motions. Have they heard the car? It sounds like it's far off, maybe as far as the road. What do they have in mind?

"Not there," Mark says of the place Willa's preparing to re-tie me, closer to the tool bench.

"Where, then?"

"Just not there," he repeats. "He'll be able to reach the tools."

"Then I'll hog-tie him. Hands to feet." She blushes a little and corrects herself: "*Hand* to feet."

The car's engine pauses like it's confused by the driveways, then revs as the driver finds the right direction. There's another commotion outside, too: animals, I think, running through the brush. The car must have startled them. I think it's a group of deer, now creeping past the outside of the shed. The Wimberlys' panic just adds to their confusion. Whatever's going on, it's taken everyone by surprise.

"Hurry!" Mark shouts.

"Well?" Willa says, angry because something beyond both of them — out there in the world — has made them afraid. "Have you made up your damn mind?"

"About what?"

"About *here!*" she says, indicating the sturdy, quadruple-bolted pole squeezed beneath the bench. "If you don't want him visible through the window, this is the only spot!"

I try to move. To roll. All I can do is drool, but it must be too much motion for Mark. He stuns me again and I pee my pants. Oh well.

"I just worry about the tools." He shoots a glance outside, toward the sound of distant wheels on gravel. Through the open door, I see the clothesline beyond. Now some of Mark's clothes are hanging, but it looks like attempts to get my copious blood out has failed. Even the socks, hung with the rest, still have big pink stains on them.

That's evidence, sucker, I think in my dizzy, drooling state. *Better burn it or it'll turn around and burn you.*

Deer stutter past the doorway. They seem in a hurry to get somewhere — or, more likely, *away* from somewhere — but that doesn't stop them from turning to look at the three of us with curiosity.

"Fine," Mark says, eyes bugging. "Tie him under the bench, but do it so he can't get at any of the tools."

"You're sure?"

Willa's eyes go toward the sound outside. I follow her gaze to see that one of the deer — a buck — has gotten more curious than the others and is now nosing around the clothesline. Poking at Mark's jeans, his jacket, his shirt.

Mark nods. "As long as he can't reach anything, yeah. It's safer under there. Can't see under the counter from outside. He can't flop around in the chair and make so much noise."

Joke's on you, I think. *I've got a phone in my shirt. It's shit in terms of calling for help, but if I can fish it out, I can bang it against the pipe. That's noise. Bitch.*

"But what about...?" Willa trails off.

"We'll have to figure it out later," Mark answers, presumably talking about my forthcoming execution or extrication, whichever they decide. "Somehow we'll have to get her to leave for a while so we can move him."

Willa's already retying me. It takes seconds. She's good; I'll give her that. But her face is worried. She doesn't like this one bit.

"Move him where?" Willa asks.

"I don't know, okay?" Mark's eyes are seriously freaked out. The pressure of the approaching car has him rattled and at loose ends, his careful plan suddenly in tatters. "I don't know what we'll do, and I sure as *hell* don't know why she's here already. Does it matter? Let's just get her settled in. Get through dinner somehow. And then—"

Mark's interrupted when Willa gives an inarticulate shout. I look where she's looking, now almost entirely hog-tied with my back rounded into an arch. It seems the buck that's been nosing around the clothesline has managed to spear a bloodstained shirt with one of its antlers. A second later, it spooks and runs off.

I try to smile, but the palsy hasn't left my face. That deer's about to blow this case wide open. Running away with my blood on a shirt? *Run, Bambi, run — all the way to the forensics team!*

Mark moans. He rises to his feet and starts giving orders while inching toward the door.

"Finish tying him, then go around and enter the cabin through the rear. I'm going to try and get that shirt back. Make sure his knots are tight. I'll stall her. Hurry!"

Mark runs, grabbing a big plumber's wrench from the workbench on his way — presumably to bash the deer or give himself a heart attack trying. Willa opens her mouth to ask where he's going, but he's already gone.

Good luck, asshole. Your old, slow ass ain't gonna catch a deer.

My paralysis wears off as Willa double-checks her work. She's as good this time as last; there's no chance I'll reach anything not attached to me. Maybe I can shake the phone loose. Forget about anything else.

She looks me in the eyes when she's finished, and in that moment, I decide I might be able to sweet-talk her. Mark's the bully; his wife is being pulled along for the ride. I've seen the uncertainty and fear in her from the start. I moan a little, bouncing my chin in the sign language of the bound.

She lowers my gag. "What?"

"There's still time to take this back. Don't let him do this, Willa! He's—"

She slaps me hard across the face. When I come around, her eyes are no longer soft, but now hard like diamonds.

"Don't you *dare* try to take back what you did, you bastard," she snaps. "Don't think we don't know!"

My mouth hangs open. Willa stands and goes.

Outside, I hear running feet and rolled-on gravel. Sticks crunch. The engine is closer now. Wheels roll slowly, pause suddenly, and then I hear Mark's voice but not his words. After, I hear Mark running at the cabin and yelling loudly for his wife to make ready. Meanwhile the car continues toward the cabin, parking close by.

A door slams. Feet walk: smaller, less lumbering this time. And that's when I realize a miracle has happened, and I might be saved after all.

It's Miranda. She's a fly in their ointment, having arrived a full day early.

Chapter Nineteen
AUBREY

Friday Afternoon

My mom hates it when I let Abby ride in my car. She's got long black hair that I suspect is just sort of piled on rather than anchored at one end, considering how easily it falls out. I'm always finding clumps everywhere, including and especially in the shotgun seat of my car. Still, I take her pretty much everywhere because she can't stand being away from me. At home, if I go to the end of the driveway to get the mail, she scratches the door and barks until I return. And if the door's unlatched, watch out: she'll run right at me, ending in a tackle.

I look over as we cruise north. *"Waffle,"* she dog-grumbles.

It's a good point. "Of course," I tell her. "But I have to try."

Mom hates that I let Abby ride because of all the hair, but I don't even give tiny, fractional shits what Mom thinks about what I do with my car. As with everything of value in my life, I got it all by myself. I won my own tennis scholarship. I applied for the loans that cover my remaining tuition. I bought my car, gas, and insurance. No wonder I need Adderall. There's not enough time in the day for all the financial scrambling I've had to do, thanks to sub-par parenting.

I reach over and pet my dog's head. You have to pet her in the right direction, or she'll get Flock of Seagulls hair. Abby loves being with people, but the way she feels about other dogs is how I usually feel about other people. We were made for each other.

My phone rings. It's Mom. She and Dad have been tag-teaming me the entire time I've been driving north, and that's three hours so far — already halfway to Miranda's parents' rental. The official story is that I'm now in an area with no cell service rather than ignoring them, which is actually what's going on. I left them a message hours ago explaining that I have to do what I'm doing (I've got no choice but to help Miranda through a crisis, so I regrettably can't come home for Christmas after all), and that where I'm going is way up in the middle of a foothills forest. I told them I'd probably lose cell service right away. Turns out I was right, as far as they know. Not a single call from my parents has made it through, seeing as I haven't been picking up. I'm completely, totally, on-purpose incommunicado.

The ringing ends. Mom's call goes to voicemail. Not long after (4:36 p.m., according to the clock), two notifications light up my screen: a missed call and a message. According to my official story, I might not be able to listen to that message until the new year because Verizon's giving me fewer bars than I give shits. Such a shame.

"They just won't give it a rest," I tell Abby. "They call and call and call. I mean, come on. Take a hint, why don't you?"

"Rollover," Abby agrees.

Static interrupts the radio. Time to change it again.

My Bluetooth is on the fritz, so for the entire drive I've been listening to a series of local radio stations. I get about an hour on each one, but then I leave the broadcast radius and the signal fades. Now that I'm three hours in, the stations are getting to be less and less my style. Last round I could only find country, gospel, and a banjo station that doesn't know it's making a cliché of itself. This time, who knows what I'll hear.

I hit Scan. It goes all the way through the FM dial without stopping on a solid station once.

"AM it is," I say. Great. Now all I'll get is NPR.

When I hit Scan on the AM dial, I get a station right away. The signal is strong and clear, broadcasting a report by an obnoxious-voiced weatherman.

"—a hard freeze overnight and into Saturday morning, so bring in or cover your summer plants, y'hear? We'll spend today's daylight hours in the high thirties, but I'll tell ya, *cuz*, it wouldn't be a bad idea to stay inside around the fire anyway, because sun or no sun, the white stuff is on its way. The winter storm we've been predicting now looks like it might come ahead of schedule. That's more of a sure thing for folks up in New England, where they got a half inch of ice last night into this morning and are getting a preview of the snow as we speak. If you're traveling up that way, you'll want to be careful — maybe put the chains on the tires early, if you know what I mean. Expect mountain passes to become dicey, or maybe even close."

A female voice cuts in — another stock radio personality. "So you're saying I should cancel my waterski lesson?"

The forecaster laughs. "Cancel the waterskis, pick up the snow skis."

"All right, will do. And speaking of skiing, the Winter Olympics committee today announced its decision to—"

I turn the radio off, feeling uneasy. I grew up in the north and know how capricious its weather can be. I may not have to worry about snow yet, but it sounds like I will in an hour or two. *Something* cut off yesterday's call to Miranda's landline. The weather forecast just said her area got an ice storm overnight, so I'll bet a falling branch was the culprit. Ice this morning, snow accumulating now ... It's not exactly Miami weather I'm driving toward, and even the patch ice I've run into so far has me nervous.

When I stopped for gas a half hour ago, I was shocked and a little alarmed to see how cold it'd gotten. It's like fingers snapped, turning things from late autumn to full-on winter. I brought warm clothes, of course, but cold is only half the problem. With the front that's coming through, the winds have kicked up. I already don't like driving these foothill roads, even *without* wind trying to blow me into the abyss.

So why are you going? I ask myself. *You could still decide to tolerate your parents over break instead of all these Ross-and-Miranda shenanigans. At least you'd be tolerating them without this much driving — ideally in front of a nice, warm fire.*

But I know damn well why I'm going, and it's not just to avoid Mom and Dad.

I hear Ross's voice from the dungeon of my memory: *This was a mistake.*

Monday morning, that was — so early the sun wasn't up yet. It turns out Ross got in his car and started driving north just hours after he said those words to me. I feel like that should offend me, the way he scrambled off like fleeing a crime scene, but instead I feel robbed of my own regret, my own guilt.

Sleeping with Ross *was* a mistake. It was also a complete and total surprise. I woke up rubbing my face, staring at the sheets, fighting to remember what happened after we started drinking. I've only been blackout drunk once before. Hell of a time to do it again.

I'm sorry, Ross told me. *You have to go.*

When he said those words, I thought they were connected: He was apologizing for asking me to leave. Now, though, I think they were two separate statements:

I'm sorry. And because I feel sorry, you have to go.

The reason I "had to go" turned out to be because *Ross* had to go — not that I knew he'd left until today. I've been assuming he was still on campus, not gone from it for four days now. He *is* gone, though; I verified with his RA that Ross left Monday morning. He slept with me, kicked me out, then immediately hopped into his shitty little car like Sir Galahad hopping onto his trusty steed. That's Ross for you. He thinks apologizing — if done sincerely enough, which in this case means "in person, probably on his knees" — makes up for everything.

Will Miranda forgive him if he shows up, confesses, and begs? I don't know the answer to that, but I do know how bad it'll make *me* look. Ross makes a mistake and says he's sorry. Meanwhile, I've been trying to understand how it happened and find a tactful way to tell Miranda that hopefully won't make her shun me. Unfortunately, Ross saw fit to ruin that plan for me. After he apologizes, the fact that I delayed at all will look like I've been trying to get away with it. He's throwing me under the bus to save himself. That's *really* what his trip is about.

To say I've been sweating my eventual confession to Miranda is a vast, *vast* understatement. For that reason I've taken all this time so that I can find the right words, not because I'm trying to hide what we did. I just don't see how it could have happened — why the deep-down part of me would *let* it happen.

Is self-sabotage to blame? God knows I've struggled with self-worth thanks to Mom and Dad. Was that it? Was that why I got drunk, went crazy, then carpet-bombed the only meaningful relationship I have? I just know I'd never intentionally hurt Miranda. I'm not even attracted to Ross. I went over to buy more Xanax, had a bunch of drinks, then woke up in his bed. Shouldn't I get a pass if I didn't mean to, didn't want to, and still don't get what drunken urge made me do it?

That's why I didn't mind Ross ghosting Miranda, even if our little indiscretion was almost surely the reason. That's why I wanted Miranda to talk to *me* before she talked to *Ross* — so that when the hammer started to fall, I could at least try and cushion it. A cowardly part of me hoped Ross wouldn't say anything at all — that he'd just ghost Miranda forever, letting me get away with my crime. Of course I'd eventually come clean, but giving cowardice its moment at least bought me some time.

That's all over now, though, because Ross isn't trying to hide what we did. Nope; instead he's planning to use it as a shield. He'll sacrifice me, probably saying I seduced him.

This is all *so Ross*. I should have known he'd wake up with buyer's remorse, immediately sick with regret, because feeling regret is better than risking blame. I should have known he'd immediately look up Miranda's Airbnb address, then run to spill his guts. And now look: That's exactly what happened.

No.

It's like something's speaking up inside my head.

No, that's not what happened, Aubrey. You're jumping to conclusions because you're edgy. Ross didn't go to see Miranda — not yet, anyway. If he had, she'd've mentioned it when you talked to her this morning. The working theory says he left Monday morning, meaning he'd've been there Monday afternoon. Miranda didn't arrive until yesterday. He beat her by three days.

I frown, squeezing the wheel. It's true. Maybe Ross didn't go to Miranda's cabin after all. Just because he printed out an email doesn't mean he took a trip. He wrote on it that he needed to leave at 10 a.m. to avoid traffic, but he might just have been using Miranda's email as scrap paper for unrelated reasons. He could have gone somewhere else, still hiding his secret the same way I have. The fact that he wrote his note on the Airbnb email might just have been a coincidence.

But again something in me says, *No.*

No, Ross didn't go somewhere else. Your gut is right about his destination. Your gut is right about the reason he went. What you're wrong about is something else.

But what else is there? What else is wrong?

I'm not sure. I've been so preoccupied with Ross's dick move (hogging all the regret, thereby making me look like an uncaring whore) that all the nonsensical loose ends flew right by me. I haven't given them any thought. Everything points to Ross heading out hours after we parted, but for some reason he never actually connected with Miranda. *That's* what's wrong. *That's* the piece of this that's missing.

I frown, thinking.

Ross didn't know Miranda was planning to spend a few days at home before she went to the cabin. When he got there and found her absent, he must've been surprised. Maybe he turned around and decided to try again after she arrived, but he'd've had to talk to Mark and Willa to find out when that would be. I doubt Mark and Willa would talk to Ross. I *definitely* don't think they'd tell him exactly when to come back to find their daughter, considering how much they hate him.

Then maybe Ross never reached the cabin. Maybe he had an accident along the way.

But that's not it, because he's texted me since he left. Ongoing texts from Ross are why I assumed he was still on campus.

I pull over, then pick up my phone to peruse our text thread. Maybe I missed something — some sign that he'd hit the road, that he was planning to tell Miranda about us. But nope, there's nothing. My texts from Ross have actually gotten blander, vaguer, and less Ross-like since I last saw him. I didn't want to commit "we slept together" to a text message, so mostly I just tried to see if he'd answer me using vague pokes of my own. His responses, to those pokes, are too cheery. Too tone-deaf, considering the elephant in the room between us. He's been using a lot of bright and sunny language, which isn't usually his style. He's commented on the weather. He's even using old-school emoticons: a colon and a parenthesis to indicate a sideways smiley face instead of proper emojis.

I put the phone down, stare straight ahead, and feel my face go blank. My head starts to shake slowly side to side without my intending it. Something fishy is going on here, but I can't figure out what it is.

"Mudflap," Abby says, looking concerned.

"Yeah," I tell her as I put the car in Drive and pull back onto the road. "I know."

I know, but I don't know at all. Truth is I'm driving in blind — no way anymore to call ahead — because I need to try and talk to Miranda before Ross does, to do whatever it takes not to lose her. But truth is also that something about this is still wrong ... still prickling every bit of what Miranda calls my "annoying meddling detective bullshit."

I went looking for Ross on a hunch. Those were his and Miranda's initials carved into the wood, so with Miranda gone, Ross felt like as good a place as any to start. It's because I went, and because Dion more or less threatened me, that I learned any of this.

Coincidence?

Maybe. But weird, not-quite-right things about Ross keep

crossing streams with weird, not-quite-right things about Miranda, which in turn keep crossing streams with weird, not-quite-right things about the photos someone keeps sending.

Photos with Ross and Miranda's initials in them. Coincidentally.

But that's the funny thing about coincidences: Once you put enough of them together in one place, they start to feel a lot less coincidental. So: What *is* going on at Miranda's cabin? What's going on with Ross? I have no idea ... except that I know damn well I don't like it at all.

Snow is coming. There's no landline up there anymore. No cell service, effectively no texting, no communication in or out of my best friend's isolated little bubble. I'm more than halfway there already: closer to completing this fool's errand than letting it go. My alternative is spending winter break with my parents ... and, more likely than not, giving Ross a chance to exonerate himself for our misdeed by pointing fingers at me.

That right there is the reason I'm on this errand: If I'm not around to defend myself when Ross bares his soul, I might just lose Miranda forever.

I make a lot of mistakes. I'm miles from perfect. I might even be a terrible friend, since it's cheap to blame the Ross thing on alcohol. When I arrive, Miranda might come at me with both fists because I'm wrong, I'm bad, I've betrayed her, I'm the devil and she never wants to see me again. We all know how poorly Miranda handles jealousy.

But my gut tells me none of that's happened yet. Ross hasn't confessed. Instead, he's still up north somewhere, maybe waiting in a motel for Miranda's arrival so he can drop the bomb he came to drop. He won't know exactly when she's coming, though, because her parents would never tell him, and that gives me a very slight advantage because I knew her plans in advance. Ross won't break his ghosting just to ask her whereabouts ... so maybe if the timing's *just right* I can slip in before he tries again, beating him to the punch. Maybe there's still a chance — a *whisper* of a chance — that I can make this right.

I glance over to see Abby's big brown eyes staring at me in a way that suggests she can read my thoughts.

"I already said *I know*. We talked about this, and I told you: *I have to try*."

Abby still looks skeptical. *"Rochambeau,"* she replies.

Chapter Twenty

ROSS

THURSDAY AFTERNOON

'm saved! Miranda's arrival means I'm saved!

Of course I try to scream, but of course the gag prevents me. I tip my head side to side, shaking it, stretching my jaw around the fabric in my mouth — any movement at all that might shift it so I can yell.

Rapidly opening and closing my jaw makes it inchworm down the back of my head, lower and lower. I keep doing it, hoping that at some point it'll fall around my neck. Once that happens, my mouth will be free to shout all I want. But it's too tight to simply fall from between my lips. If anything, it's a little tighter where it ends up: front end in my mouth, back end at the bottom of my hair-line. Try as I might, I can't scream at all.

I listen as Miranda walks around the cabin, waiting to hear her enter the house or for her out-of-breath parents to meet her in the driveway.

No matter what happens, this is good, I tell myself. *They were supposed to have a whole other day to decide what to do with me, but now that Miranda's here, they're out of time.*

Miranda's smart. She'll be able to tell that something's wrong.

She's a curious person. Sometimes even a suspicious person. I can hear her now, still pacing, still not opening the cabin door. I think she's alone. I don't hear other sets of footsteps and I don't hear voices.

I need to make noise. Draw her over here, *especially* if she's alone. When Miranda opens the shed door and sees what her parents have done to me, it'll all be over. I'll win. They'll lose. I'll live and they'll go to jail. Because she loves me.

I don't have to tell Miranda about me and Aubrey until this is over. Even when I do tell her, it'll be okay. It's all explainable. Aubrey is ... well, we both know how Aubrey is. She's really messed up. Has those terrible parents — way worse than Miranda's parents, kidnapping and torture aside. No wonder she acts out. She's been flirting with me for ages. All it took to loosen her inhibitions was a little intoxication. I was already smashed. Super drunk at the time. As soon as she no longer had the excuse of sobriety, Aubrey was all over me. I should have resisted, I suppose. I should have done better. I know I'm weak. I can only hope — can only beg, like I came here to do — for Miranda to forgive me.

Hog tied, I can barely move. My remaining hand and feet are tied together, and all of that is fastened to a sturdy pole holding up the workbench above me. I try to wiggle and make noise, but all I get are the light squeaking sounds of my sneakers against metal. So I hop instead, trying to rack my skull against the bench's underside. It's too high; I only manage to hit it once and am rewarded with double vision. The tools on top of the bench don't even rattle, which I hoped they would — for noise, or maybe I'd get lucky and a saw would fall into my lap.

I scream past my gag, trying to thrash. My nose racks the bar. My legs kick something small and metallic on the floor nearby, sending it rolling. My bleary eyes follow, seeing it's not a screw or washer. It's my ring. The special one I wear around my neck on a leather shoelace. I'd been wondering where that went. The lanyard must have broken when that pair of assholes dragged me in here, rolling into the shadows.

Now my head hurts and I've accomplished nothing. I need to *do something*. But what? Tied as I am, my Skor phone is useless.

Don't worry about the phone. Miranda's right outside, by the parking spots.

I try again to scream. It's muffled, but maybe I can muffle loud enough to get her attention.

The door opens. Covertly. Mark's face peeks in, and I say around the gag, *"Fuffa fuffa biff!"*

He ignores my profanity. Contrasted with the deadly stare he gave me earlier, this is an extremely businesslike Mark. He's composed and calm, with eyes of ice.

"I dow Mawawa ith—!" I blurt.

"Quiet," he says. "Yes. She's here. I'm very agitated right now. I suggest you shut your fucking mouth. If you don't — if you keep doing things that might bring my daughter into this — I will cut you in half. It was better for you when we had the luxury of time."

That's all he says. It's all he has to. I wasn't sure if I believed he could kill me before, but I believe it now. Miranda's arrival hasn't ruined his plan. It's made him desperate, less likely to think before acting.

He goes to the water pump, situated in the corner of the shed closest to the drop-off above the river. One insulation-wrapped pipe runs up through the floor to its intake. Another leaves its discharge end, also through the floor. That end, I assume, meets a buried water line to the cabin.

Mark grabs a wrench. I'm sure he'll beat me to death with it. But he doesn't. Instead, he loosens something on the pump. When it kicked on before now, the pump made a polite, silent humming sound. Now when it kicks on, it rattles like a machine going to pieces. It's audio camouflage — a background metal-on-metal rattle loud enough to obscure any sounds I make.

Mark points at me with the wrench.

"Maybe you can find a way to be louder than that pump," he says. "If I were you, I wouldn't try. Maybe she'll hear you and come running. But then again, I might hear you first ... and I'm the one who knows the code to the door."

He leaves. I hear him take the long way around, traversing a short, wooded path that circuits the cabin the way Willa must have gone to enter from the rear. Shortly after, I hear them call Miranda inside.

The cabin door closes, and I forget all Mark told me.

I scream and scream and scream.

It grows dark. Eventually Willa brings me a sandwich on a paper plate and a water bottle with a built-in straw. She puts both on the ground beside me.

"I need my hand. You have to untie me so I can eat."

"You'll manage." And then she's gone.

I do manage. Sort of. "Manage" implies minimal adequacy, not a superior (or even acceptable) way of doing things. People *manage* to scrape by despite poverty. My idiot brother *managed* to get into the lowest-rung college before I stepped up and did a whole lot better. By that definition, I *manage* to eat and drink. I have to suck the sandwich toward me, inching at it with prehensile lips. I manage the water bottle the same way.

Uncomfortable but at least sated, I try to roll back to my starting position but fail entirely. Gravity helped me get down here, but I lack the leverage to get back up.

Everything hurts soon enough. I don't fall asleep so much as pass out from the pain.

Unconsciousness lasts until morning, although in the meantime I did enjoy a night full of terrible dreams in which I was, you know, tied to a post in terrible pain.

The sun inside the shed is like yesterday: all dust-filled sunbeams. The air is different, though. It smells colder, if that's a thing. My sense of touch is less reliable, on the temperature front, than smell. That and hearing. Everything outside creaks in the wind now. I hear a few branches break and crash. I think we might have had an ice storm last night. It must be beautiful outside.

I can't really feel anything, having laid this way all night long. If I have hypothermia, it's systemic instead of giving me the cute little *brrr* and shivers people normally get from being cold. My thoughts hurt. My eyes are confused. I feel like throwing up, but also like passing out. It's all pretty great.

Atop this, I can't move. At all. Overnight, in one of my dreams, the pump fell into a weird running resonance and made a racket that I was too messed up to hear in a conscious way. In my dream, I seem to remember hearing Miranda come outside, into the dooryard near the shed. Then I heard her parents, who'd come out to check on me (and maybe the loud-ass pump) but stopped short because of Miranda. That's when I realized she's not saving me. She's making it worse. Because after the middle-of-the-night meet-up disbanded, Mark and Willa must have decided it was too risky to check on me after all. I'd been inches from being put in a more humane position ... until Miranda showed up.

Damn you, Miranda.

I think I might be delirious. Or maybe Miranda is. I can't think straight at all right now, but neither can she and she doesn't have my excuse. Because honestly: Who thinks the family vacay I've overheard and imagined must be going on inside the cabin could be *even remotely normal?* She should have demanded to know what's going on by now. She should have snooped around, trying to figure out what they're hiding.

My Skor phone vibrates inside my shirt: a new text message I can't look at. Then it actually vibrates as it full-out rings. RINGS. The sky looks pretty clear through my sliver of window despite the cold, so I guess it got bars enough for a phone call.

I smash myself against the bar, then the floor, trying for anything that will depress the right buttons and answer the call. Of course I'm not that precise. I've been trying the rub-and-hope maneuver on and off, and all I've managed to do is take pictures of the inside of my shirt. Maybe they even shared; who knows? If they did, they'd be going to my most recent contact. To Miranda.

Hey baby, here's that inside-the-shirt nude pic you always wanted.

I want to laugh, but it's not funny. Then it suddenly is. Yes, I'm definitely in delirium here. My cheek has been flat on the floor so long, I've probably got frostbite. I definitely can't feel the skin there. I've gotten used to seeing the world sideways, though; that's good news at least. The floor is to the right. The roof is left. Straight ahead and slightly left is my crack of a window.

I'm going to die here. It no longer feels like such a bad thing, given what's happening right now.

In the shadows is my ring: silver and gold bands intertwined, topped with three blue stones. I really liked that ring. I never really showed it to anyone because it was too small to wear on my finger and honestly a little girly for my tastes, but I still loved it; at least I knew it was there. I remember the day I got it. I remember the feel of it in my hand. I even remember the way I felt: a semi-guilty decision, my brain saying, *Okay, I'll take it.* I shouldn't have. I really shouldn't have. But hey, sometimes a guy has to spoil himself. And really, why do I care about poor decisions, whether they're spending my tuition money on club-hopping or getting some silly little ring? You're supposed to experiment in college. Try new things.

That's all I did — that and love Miranda.

I'm deadly sorry I betrayed her trust. I was weak. Aubrey made herself irresistible to me. I was going to make up for it. I didn't try to hide the truth, not for a second. Shouldn't I get some sort of karmic credit for that? The second I woke up with Aubrey beside me, I felt sick. I'd made a terrible, terrible mistake. I made her leave right away. I asked myself how honest I was willing to be, to make this right, and after realizing I couldn't call Miranda to confess and beg forgiveness, I got right in the car. That's how much it meant to me.

I'm a good man. Really. When I screw up, I fix it. Miranda knows that. Lord knows she's seen me screw up in other ways. But she always forgives me. That's what we do.

It's only a matter of time now. But I've lost track of days and weeks and years to all this suffering presence, so I don't actually know when *now* is. I should know, though, and so I think. I picture a calendar and try to decide what day it might be.

I decide it's Friday: the day I die.

. . .

SOMEONE COMES TO FEED ME AGAIN. FINALLY, I'M SITTING upright again, this time on the floor instead of a chair. I don't know who it was that did any of it, but either Willa or Mark stun-gunned me before releasing my bindings and re-tying them to give me a little more room. I think all the stunning — plus the cold, blood loss, and probably infection — is messing with my head. It's getting hard to tell if I'm awake or asleep.

What do I care? I can't feel large sections of my body and my pants long ago became my toilet. In retrospect, I'll bet they wish they'd found a way to make that not the case, but what's done was done. Kind of no point now.

By midday, snow begins to fall. I can see flurries through my tiny window, in front of the frame of the canyon bridge.

Miranda's voice enters the dooryard, or maybe the parking spot. Her parents are out there, too. I've lost the ability to understand spoken language unless someone *E-NUN-CI-ATES VE-RY LOUD-LY AND CLEAR-LY,* so I have no idea what they're saying. When it's over, Miranda drives away.

Almost immediately, Mark and Willa storm into my shed. It's *my* shed now. *Bitch.*

"I'll jolt him," Mark says, pulling the stun gun from his coat pocket. "Just cut the ropes. Faster that way."

I look at Mark and grin stupidly. Then I say, *"Oh, please."*

Willa looks me in the eyes and says to Mark, "What's wrong with him?"

Mark shrugs. "I'm no doctor. Shock?"

"Shock doesn't last this long."

"Some sort of a breakdown? Who cares?"

"Well, now, hang on," Willa says. "If he's having a breakdown, maybe we can..." She raises her eyebrows.

Mark shakes his head. "Absolutely not."

"I'm the motherfucking president," I say. It just sounds funny. Everything is funny right now because nothing matters anymore.

"See?" says Willa, indicating me and my proclamation.

"He's faking."

"What if he's not? Mark, I don't want to do this."

"Listen to your wife, *Mark,*" I say like a slur.

"What if he *is?*" Mark retorts.

"We should call Asham."

"Asham?"

"Yes! He'd know."

"Oh, for..."

"Mark. I'm serious."

"I see. Okay, let's pretend we *could* reach him. What do you want to tell him, exactly? Asking him to get on board with this might be stretching our friendship a little too far."

"Make something up." Willa hesitates, then adds as if with inspiration, "Tell him we found a hunter who's been wandering around, lost in the woods! Say we just need to know how to treat him. And to do that, we have to know if we can trust what he's telling us, because he sounds kind of confused."

"Willa..."

"Asham's a doctor!"

"A doctor now, a witness later!" Mark looks at me, exasperated. "Who cares what's going on with this asshole?"

"I just want to know what people do when they get all dehydrated and confused in the woods like that," Willa insists. "Do they get crazy and tell crazy stories? Can you believe anything said by someone wandering around in the woods? Look at him, Mark! He's lost his mind! If nobody can trust anything he's saying, maybe he's not a threat."

Mark looks like she's just said the dumbest thing ever. "You want to let him go. And what? Just hope nobody believes him when he comes back at us with lawyers blazing?"

"If he's had a legitimate mental break, maybe it won't be an issue." She comes upright so she can put one hand on her hip and give him The Look. "I know it's a longshot, but we can ask. I just want to *ask,* just in case it's an option. That's all."

I wish I could say I'm doing the possum thing, fully sane right now and playing games so they won't kill me. That's not the case. Or maybe it is. Probably not. I don't know; what do you think, elephant?

"It's too risky no matter *what* Asham says." But now Mark is looking at me as if he sees Willa's point — the one about *just trying.* Just asking. Just doing *anything* to delay what they must otherwise see as inevitable, even if it's not a real chance, even if it's only procrastinating something unpleasant.

"Just call him."

"On what? The phone's out."

"Take the Jeep," Willa says. "Drive out until you get a signal on your cell."

"Absolutely not. We needed to find a time to move him out of the shed, and now we've *got* time while Miranda's in town. That big storm's coming, Willa. *Tonight.* I don't think we'll get another chance."

Willa shakes her head.

"She's already suspicious!" Mark goes on, frustrated that Willa doesn't share his urgency. "She keeps asking me about the shed. 'Why are all the utilities in the shed, Dad? Can I watch you fix the furnace?' Why would she give a shit about the shed? And why did I say the junction box was out here? I wasn't thinking straight. I'll have to make something up, but we can't just keep telling her 'it's nothing' for two weeks."

Willa looks resolute. I'm guessing she's hit her limit, so she's dug in firmly. I suppose they might be planning only to move me instead of kill me, but maybe not. Where would they put me, if it's just a move?

Personally, I like this whole crazy hunter idea. Let me go. I swear I won't tell a soul.

"Hear hear," I say, voicing my general support. They just look at me briefly, then again at each other.

Mark extends a knife to Willa, presumably to cut my ropes. He's still got the stun gun at the ready with his other hand, but then Willa pushes his stunning hand back.

"Miranda will be gone for hours. The snow's barely coming down so far. You can drive out, make a call, and be back in a half hour. I just want Asham's opinion, okay? I'm *just a tad* uncomfortable, Mark. I can't sleep. I don't see it getting any easier if we keep playing house with our daughter for two weeks, smiling over dinner and acting like everything's normal. So if you don't mind, I'd like to exhaust every alternative option before we do..." She looks at me, then back at Mark. "Whatever we end up having to do."

Mark's eyes are angry, caught in the middle.

"Whatever we end up having to do..." Willa says more firmly, "... because *you lost your temper.*"

Mark looks at me. I see how trapped he is. She's got an ace to play with him, and she's just played it.

Mark stands, reluctant but apparently willing. Soon enough, I'm alone again, still bound and gagged with the door re-locked, watching and waiting to the accompaniment of wheels on gravel.

Chapter Twenty-One

The door opens again in no time. One moment I'm lightheaded, seeing shadows come alive, forgetting whether it's night or day despite all the sun (sun means daytime, right? It's knowledge from another life), and then the next moment, Willa and Mark are here again. It's a rip-off. My messed-up mind skipped right over the part where I could have rested without them around. Stupid brain, only showing me the bad parts.

After that, life comes in a series of short video clips. If I've got the delirium that Mark, Willa, and the seven goblins sitting in the corner seem to think I have, that would explain it. After four days of pain, trauma, dehydration, and terror, my consciousness has stopped being a movie and has become a best-of reel instead. Usually I experience a day from A to Z with all the long, boring parts in between, but this time I'm only coherent(ish) for the high-lights. It's a real time-saver.

Mark and Willa enter. They're as frenzied as before, presumably because time has passed and they feel short on what little time remains before ... before what? I don't remember. I only remember that someone left a while ago. It's important to my captors that they finish dealing with me before that someone returns. Who? Why? It's all a mystery to me anymore.

(Miranda. You're thinking of Miranda, you fool.)

There's a jump cut in my thought-stream. Suddenly my legs are free and they're being careful to stay behind me because they think I might mule-kick them if they're in front. It's a laugh. I forget what strength is, other than I used to have it but now I don't.

Jump to some words being spoken. An argument had. I've still got my legs free, but nothing's happened with my hand, which is tied around behind me and then to the post, keeping me plenty incapacitated. They've forgotten about me so they can bicker about what to do with me. I try to pay careful attention because the question of what happens next does, apparently, have some relevance to my life. I can't pay attention, though. Attention, like strength, is something I no longer have.

Jump cut. I'm on my side now. The world is tilted. I'm certain that today never happened, and that I was never picked up after sliding to the floor back when there used to be a chair involved. I feel a line of drool making its way down from my lip. I can see my ring again. Three blue stones. Twined gold-and-silver band. It reminds me of a girl. That's why I have it.

Jump cut. Willa and Mark are still talking heatedly and I'm still halfway bound. I have no idea how much time has passed since they returned. Mark's temporary absence, in the car I think, had something to do with an ashram. I think ashrams are where monks live but I can't quite remember. He was going to call one of them. Why?

After that, I hear a car's engine. I'm pretty sure I'm imagining it, because neither Mark nor Willa look up — not even when I hear gravel under tires instead of just the engine itself. A car door closes. Feet walk. None of it must be happening, because Mark and Willa still aren't reacting. All they can hear are each other's voices. They're still arguing, still wondering if they have to kill me or if there are other options on the table.

At least, I *think* that's what they're talking about. But what do I know? I thought I heard a car — that whoever-it-was is coming back to the cabin. But obviously that's wrong. If Mark and Willa heard those footsteps nearing the door, they'd stop arguing and start covering. That's what they've been doing for however long I've been in this place, but they're not doing it now.

I'm convinced all of that is true, but it turns out not to be. Miranda's parents have been so careful to keep me hidden, but all it apparently took to trip them up was one good argument. They were so preoccupied yelling at each other that they didn't hear someone return in their car. They didn't hear them exit, or walk across the driveway, or arrive at the open door to the shed, where they are right now.

It's Miranda. At the door. Looking at our tableau with shocked eyes.

"Mom? Dad?"

The jump-cuts stop now that Miranda's in the doorway. My brain seems to know how important this is, so it's returned my cognition and focus.

My captors spin toward her, limbs freezing in the positions they happened to be in at the time. Miranda's frozen, too: mouth open, unable to believe what she sees. All of us pose like department store mannequins, immobile far longer than logic should allow. I can only conclude they've forgotten how to move. Willa and Mark's eyes, trapped in immobile faces, dart like mice as they peek at one another uncertainly, afraid to flinch.

"M-Miranda!" Mark stammers. "This isn't what it looks like!"

Miranda rushes forward. She elbows her parents aside, either failing to notice one has a stun gun and the other a knife or just not caring. A second later she's kneeling beside me with my face in her hands. Against my freezing skin, they feel like fire. Her expression is like nothing I've seen before: bewildered, hurt, crushed, horrified, maybe even ill.

With her familiar hands on my skin, she's close enough to smell. The world seems to change, then. My head feels instantly clearer. Hallelujah — I can think again.

Miranda doesn't seem to understand what she's seeing. At first, she reacts just to my presence, here in this inexplicable place. Then her eyes to go my bound arm and the remains of cut ropes on my recently unbound legs. Only after does her brain show her the worst of it: the horrible, otherworldly thing her parents did to my severed arm. I watch her struggle to accept what she's seeing. It doesn't come easily. Injuries like mine are things you hear about on the news. Maybe you see them in movies. But nobody ever, *ever* expects to see them in the flesh ... no pun intended.

"What the hell is going on?" she asks of them. *Demands* of them. Her voice is strong. Furious. "Why is he here? What ... *What the hell happened to his arm?*" I can't tell if she's angry, disgusted, or just overwhelmingly crushed. I only know that fury and tears are warring within her, trying to decide which gets preference. It's all too much, seeing my stump and seared flesh and all this dried blood. *"What have you been doing to him?"*

"Look," Mark says. "I know what you must be thinking."

She snaps, close to screaming. *"WHAT,* Dad? *What* am I thinking? Am I thinking this looks like a murder scene? Is that it?" She half-stands from her crouch, laying my face down gently despite the fury of her other movements. Her eyes are wide — almost bugged-out wide. Spittle flies from her lips with the force of her words.

She looks to her mother. "I knew you hated Ross. But..." She stops, unable to find words. "This is..." Again, she stops. "Untie him. *Now.*"

"But—"

"UNTIE HIM!"

"Miranda, you don't know the whole story!" It's Mark this time, but I think of Willa too, slapping me and telling me she thinks she knows about something I supposedly did.

"What justifies this, Dad? Was it just a misunderstanding? Tell me, huh? Tell me what I don't know!"

He hesitates. He looks at Willa. It's not that he's got nothing; it looks more like even now, what he's got to say isn't for his daughter's ears.

"We were just looking out for you," he says lamely.

Miranda laughs. The laugh becomes a mighty scoff. "Right. Like always. Like when I was eight and you beat the crap out of Mr. McCafferty for no good reason."

"There's another side to that story," Mark says.

Miranda looks incredulous. *"Another side.'"*

"You aren't a parent, Miranda! You can't know how it is! You'll do anything for your children! Anything it takes!"

"That was for *me? That's* why you beat up Mr. McCafferty: *for me?* Oh, and this"—she waves an arm around the shed—"this is for me too, huh? *I don't want this, Dad!* How can you possibly think I want any of this?"

"Miranda—," Willa tries to say.

"Or was it because you were drunk," Miranda continues, saying it like a statement instead of a question. "Maybe that was why. Drunk my whole damn childhood. Drunk when you beat the crap out of the neighbor and made my best friend move away. Is that how you 'look out' for me? Every time I see Cassie even now, there's this *thing* between us. We *just* started talking again, you know. Just now, after ten damn years. You know, it's funny," she says, *faux-*thoughtful. "I never had to wonder if my dad could beat up my friends' dads like most kids wonder on the playground. I actually *knew*, thanks to Jim Beam and Budweiser!"

"Miranda," Mark says, "Cassie is—"

"She was my best friend," Miranda finishes for him, but then something changes on her face. She hesitates and looks at me — something about Cassie, something about me, something she's setting aside to process later.

"You can't understand!" Willa blurts.

But Miranda is nodding as if she has them on the ropes. "Oh, I understand. I understood as soon as I went into the utility closet to turn off the water when the pipe broke. I guess you managed to find where the owners kept their liquor, huh?"

Mark's eyes darken. "I didn't touch it."

"Sure. Sure you didn't. Almost made it this time, huh, Dad? *Sunday*. You only had to make it two more days to have a full year, but I guess self-sabotage is too strong. Now look what you've done. Who do you look out for more? Me? Or your precious booze?"

"He's not drinking," says Willa, her voice small.

"I said untie him. *Now.*"

Mark stares Miranda down. Right now, he's calculating every-thing he's tried to calculate over the past few days, only now with a whole new variable. Does he really have any choices left? Now he *can't* kill me and think it'll solve the problem. Not unless he wants his daughter to hate him forever, or unless he plans to kill her, too.

Rock, hard place, I think. Even exhausted and beaten and on-the-floor as I am, I smile a little at this unfortunate shift in Mark and Willa's fates. *Checkmate, sucker. You lose, and I win.*

Very slowly, Mark takes the knife from Willa and moves it toward the ropes still holding me to the workbench post. *It's happen-ing.* Miranda's saved me, same as I thought when she got here!

The relief is so intense, my body won't let me feel it. I watch Miranda's face even though she's still glaring at her parents. My love for her has never been so pure or so grateful. It's all right there, in her angelic profile.

Then something catches her attention. Her head turns. I'm looking at the back of it as she kneels near me, as she half-crawls forward and reaches for something. I still can't see her face, but I can see what she's picked up. It's my ring. She seems fascinated by it, pulling it out of the shadows and turning it to see all its sides. I'm not actually sure why, other than curiosity. She recognizes the leather lace because I'm always wearing it, but I don't think she's ever seen the ring that hangs from it — not this closely, at least. I always wear it under my shirt. It's private: special to me, and not for public eyes.

Miranda studies the ring for a long time. When she's done, she turns to me again. She looks different now, and I don't understand her expression.

She stands from her crouch. When she glances back at her father, Mark relents. He turns one last time, moving the knife's tip until it's touching my bindings.

"Wait," Miranda says.

Mark pauses. In the silence, his eyes go to the ring he's just noticed Miranda is holding. His face changes too. Willa freezes, confused. All three of us look at Miranda. At the new, strange, unreadable expression on her face.

Then she looks me in the eyes but speaks to her parents. Her look is hard and unyielding.

"Keep him tied," she says.

PART III

Chapter Twenty-Two
CASSIE

FOUR MONTHS AGO

I'm putting my record collection in its place of honor when someone knocks on the door. It's not completely closed (because my new roommate didn't bother when she left, but really because the sparse dorm room feels less lonely if I can hear others moving in), so the knock comes off as docile. Our new RA, Millie, who smiles enough to fart rainbows, introduced herself by walking right in. Compared to Millie, this visitor is as timid as a mouse.

"Come in?" I say it like a question because everything so far has been administrivia. I imagine this is yet another student volunteer or freshman advisor, here to tell me about meal plans, forms that still need filling out, or that most dreaded of first-night events: an icebreaker. If that's what this is, I'm making an excuse. Moving day is hard enough without having to tell strangers which animal I relate to and why.

The door opens slowly. As it does, the chaos outside increases in volume. Everyone's been going up and down out there all day: rolling carts from end to end and banging suitcases into walls.

When I see who's there, my first reaction is shock. Seconds

later, though, shock is tackled by something closer to relief. Everyone says you make friends fast in college, but I've spent the hour since my aunt left wondering if I'll be the exception. My roommate is a cheerleader type and I'm the type with Bauhaus on vinyl. I've been fighting a belief that there's nobody here for me, and I'll spend the next four years in this sad little room alone. No wonder the newcomer feels like water in the desert.

"Miranda?" But yes, it's really her. "Miranda Frickin' Wimberly! Don't tell me you go here too?"

She's still at the door, not knowing what to make of my reaction. I guess I don't blame her. It's been ten years, and the last time we talked was when she gave me a Get Well card for my dad. She left crying. I never summoned the guts to contact her again.

"Yeah…" she says.

She's still awkward. Still shy, given our history. But it's okay; I can do this for both of us. I'm not usually the forward type, but I'm just so happy to see a familiar face among all these strangers. So I rush her, and before she can resist, I'm strangling her with a hug.

"Oh my god. I'm so happy to see you. *So happy,* Miranda!"

"You are?"

I roll my eyes. "Fuck you, bitch. Sit down!"

I'm smiling when I say it, but Miranda still looks confused. I have to keep in mind how long it's been. *Fuck you, bitch* might be an endearing expression with my high school friends, but Miranda missed my formative years. I don't think I used that expression back when I was eight.

I clear a chair of clothes so Miranda can sit, then plop into my roomie's desk chair across from her.

"I didn't know you were at Fordham!" I say.

"I guess we sort of lost touch," she replies.

"You should have told me." It's striking me how much I needed this today. It feels like I'm on a euphoric drug, already making me laugh just because. "Or maybe I should have told *you*, if I'd known you were here. Oh my God, Miranda. It's been way too long. How are you?"

"Good?"

"Are you sure?"

She finally cracks a smile. *"Good,"* she repeats. "Made it through high school. At least that's a thing."

"Jesus. How long has it been?"

"Years."

"A *lot* of years."

Miranda looks conflicted again. "Look, Cassie..."

I see where she's going and shake my head, businesslike. "No. Forget it. Today's not about that."

"I should have called you."

"You were eight."

"I didn't *stay* eight. I thought about you all the time. I just..."

"I said forget it. The past is the past."

She smiles, but it's uncomfortable. She's been carrying an albatross all these years. I see that now. I want to assure her it's nothing, it's no big deal, but it seems that's only true for me. Miranda felt guilty from Go, as if she — not her father — was the one who caused all our problems.

"So..." she says, looking up at my collection. "You're really into music, huh?"

I nod. "Deeply. Best thing about going to college is the record stores. When I was sixteen, I pretty much only took my headphones off to sleep. Sometimes not even then."

"It's your happy place, huh?"

I almost laugh. My collection is almost entirely goth rock from the 80s: Joy Division, The Cure, The Smiths, Siouxsie and the Banshees. "The opposite, actually, but that's a good thing. It got me through some shit. It's funny, but the more depressing the song, the better it made me feel."

Another awkward moment. *Way to go, Cassandra. She was loosening up, but now she's thinking that what her dad did was the start of your depression.*

"We *all* go through some shit," I say. "My mom was a big help. She's..." I sigh. "She *was* one of the good ones."

"I heard," Miranda says. "I'm so sorry."

Seeing Miranda's sympathy almost makes me cry. It's only been six months since Mom passed. I put up a front and pretend I'm over it, but obviously I'm not and probably never will be.

"How's your dad?" she asks.

"Also dead."

"Oh. I'm..."

"Cancer," I say. "Two years ago. It's okay. Really." What I don't add is that unlike with Mom, I wasn't sad to see him go. He used to beat the shit out of me, starting when I was in diapers. I hated him for it, but at least he made me strong. There've been a lot of things in my life I wish hadn't happened but that made me strong.

I uncross my legs and sit forward, elbows on knees. This is no fun. I have to break the chain, or this little reunion will sour before it has a chance to begin.

"Hey," I say.

Miranda looks me in the eyes.

"Let's talk about it."

"About what?"

I smirk. "I'm serious about letting it go. You, on the other hand..."

Her face breaks. She looks away as a tear spills. I was wrong about her arrival at my door today. I thought it was a casual visit: an old friend popping by just because. But it wasn't casual at all. Somehow Miranda found out I was going to her same college, and I'll bet anything she's spent the time since preparing for this moment: building it up, making it more emotional than it has to be.

I'm over it. Really, I am. I've thought about that night over the years, and I'm convinced Miranda's father did our whole family a favor. Something about being beaten nearly to death rattled my dad's cage — enough that he didn't hit me for months afterward. It resumed after we moved, but there were a lot of toxic things about our old life that moving helped reset. I got a whole new start in a whole new school twenty miles away. Until I was sixteen and life turned upside-down again, things were better for me other than the beatings. My only real regret was losing Miranda.

She's still fighting emotion, so I take both of her hands.

"Or we can *not* talk," I say softly. "Just know it doesn't need to be a thing. I really mean that, okay? Frank was..."

I stop and sigh, wondering if we need to get this personal this quickly. Nobody but my doctor — who tried to tell CPS, who ultimately did nothing — knew about the abuse before now.

"...he wasn't a very nice guy," I finish.

I can see her wanting to ask me what that means. There's probably a lot that Miranda wants to ask right now: what "shit" it was that music got me through three years ago, for instance. She won't ask right now, though. We're freshly reacquainted. Plenty of time later to plumb the depths.

"How *is* your dad?" I ask her.

"Better," Miranda says. "He's sober now."

"Really? That's great! For how long?"

"Beginning of the year, I think?"

"Good for him," I say. I'll keep my doubts about this eight-month sobriety to myself. Once I was old enough to hear it, my mom told me something Miranda doesn't know I know: Mark Wimberly has tried and failed before. He blew his first attempt that fateful night ten years ago. Frank McCafferty was unlucky enough to be there his first night off the wagon. "And your mom?"

"She's gotten into sketching."

"Like, art?"

"Yeah."

"Art's good. It's cathartic."

A silent beat follows. She might be reading too much into what I just said, assuming art has been catharsis in the troubled life she thinks her family gave me, or that I'm suggesting her mom needed art to get through life with her dad. I hope we can get past this part quickly. I'm not carrying baggage anymore, but Miranda's weighed down with it. Personally I'm just happy to have a friend — my *best* friend once upon a time, back with me again.

This time Miranda breaks the quiet. Her eyes tick down, toward my neck. Then she leans forward and slips a finger under a leather string tied around my neck. She uses it to slip the necklace from under my shirt, then gives a small, surprised laugh as she looks at what's hanging there.

"C for Cassie," I explain, looking at my charm as well.

"It's not that." Her lips are kissed with a nostalgic smile. "I half-thought you were still wearing your ring."

"Rings go on fingers."

"That's not how you wore it back then. Do you know which ring I'm talking about?"

I don't answer right away. I know *exactly* the ring she's talking about, but it has two meanings to me now, not the single meaning it used to. It was a pretty thing — the perfect embodiment of what young girls think of when they think *extravagance*. I still remember its every detail: three blue stones on a band made of braided gold and silver. It had an inscription inside: *I will love you forever. Dad.*

Back in the Miranda days, I wore that ring around my neck because it was too big for my fingers. Years later, I put it back around my neck after my fingers grew and the ring became too small. The emotions involved are complex. I loved my ring, but that same love sometimes made it hard for me look at it. My father bought it for me. My *real* father. He guessed the size of my adult fingers back when I was still a baby — that's the story Mom used to tell. I wish she'd told me more because later on, "fatherhood," with Frank, meant nothing but pain.

"Yeah," I tell Miranda.

She spies my jewelry box. She should know it; it's the same one we painted together as kids. She reaches for it, finally giddy, but I speak before she gets there.

"I don't have it anymore," I say.

Miranda turns. "You're kidding. You don't have *your special ring?* We used to play wedding with it, it was such a big deal. What happened?"

"It's complicated."

She looks at me then, and I hope she'll read my face and know not to keep asking. Truth is, a guy has my special ring. Truth is, I'd really rather not to talk about that guy right now — *especially* with Miranda.

She stands up suddenly. I just watch her, until she extends a hand for me to take.

"Acai," she says.

"What?"

"We need to get acai bowls from the cart outside the student union immediately," Miranda says with a grin. She pulls me upright. "Come on. My mom's credit card is buying."

I WISH I'D REALIZED EARLIER HOW MUCH I MISSED MIRANDA. I should have reached out. It would have been easy. I feel like a different person around her, as if I've slipped back into younger and more innocent skin.

We settle in the quad's bright sun to eat our bowls, and I feel like I should be wearing a child's flowery dress instead of a black skirt, concert tee, and black polish and lipstick. Sitting with Miranda, it's like I can see myself from the outside, and what I see is a girl angry at the world. I suppose she has every right to be, but "the way I am," until now, has never felt more like a statement. Or a performance.

"Did you know my friend Aubrey?" Miranda asks.

I shake my head.

"Oh, that's right. I guess I met Aubrey in middle school. You were gone by then." She shoves berries, oats, and Nutella into her mouth. I can't believe I've never had one of these bowls before. "I'll introduce you later. She's a pain in the ass, but you'll love her."

"'She's a pain in the ass but I'll love her,'" I repeat.

Miranda nods. "If you have anything on your police record, you'd better tell me now. If you don't, Aubrey will sniff it out."

Something occurs to me, so I elbow Miranda conspiratorially. "Hey," I say. "Remember Julia?"

Miranda rolls her eyes. I guess that's a yes.

"Did you know I moved right by her?"

"Oh my God."

"Exactly," I say. "She lived like two blocks away. Went to my high school."

"*Double* oh my God."

"You should have seen her humble-brag game. It got real when she hit puberty."

"Hang on," Miranda says. "Are you telling me she actually got *more* insufferable?"

"Oh yeah. Insufferable *like a ninja*. She never stopped telling me all the ways she was better than me, but she got so much better at it. Her brags somehow always made *me* look bad. But the things she bragged about? They were bullshit. That part never changed."

Miranda snort-laughs. Oh, the times we had, hating Julia. One of her moves was to tell Miranda how crappy her inline skates were compared to her own, but the difference was that Miranda could actually skate. It never dawned on Julia that "being better" wasn't compatible with "having no ability whatsoever."

"She sucked so bad," I say.

Miranda nods. "Facts."

I scoot closer and lower my voice. "Hey. Did your school cafeteria serve those rectangular pizzas? You know the kind."

"Yeah," Miranda says, wondering why I've changed topics so randomly.

"So get this. One day at lunch they were serving those pizzas. For some reason Julia really likes them, so she bought two. A girl I know at her table told me they were joking about it, like why would anyone want *two* of those things? Julia said she could eat a hundred, she loves them so much. One thing led to another, and she got up to go buy more pizzas as part of the joke. But the line was closed, so she couldn't."

"This is thrilling," Miranda says.

"But then someone was like, 'You can have this one' and gave her theirs."

"Okay."

"But the pizza *wasn't* theirs. Apparently, it was from two lunch periods ago, left on a seat. Everyone thought everyone knew that, but Julia ate the pizza before anyone realized she didn't know how old it was."

Miranda leans in, on the edge of her seat.

"It wasn't a big deal, though. Not until sixth period."

"What happened in sixth period?"

"That's when the food poisoning kicked in. I was there. I'd noticed her squirming like she couldn't sit still, but then suddenly there was this huge farting sound. Like, I swear it went on for hours. Like a butt-based foghorn."

Miranda guffaws.

"Everyone looked right at her, but Julia tried to cover like it hadn't happened. Then it happened again ... only this time, it wasn't a fart."

"Oh God."

"But she *didn't leave class!* That's the crazy part. You know how she is. She had to be right. 'Right' in this case meant not admitting to pooping yourself so much it squirts down your pantleg while everyone's watching."

"Hey!" Miranda shouts, but she's laughing same as I'm laughing. "I'm eating here!"

"It just kept coming. And coming. *And coming.* It sounded like her ass was trying to call a flock of geese."

"GROSS!"

Miranda throws napkins at me. I throw them back. We both devolve into explosive laughter after that — the kind where you can't catch your breath.

It dwindles by degrees. When we finally come back to our senses, we're heaving like we've just run a marathon. A quiet afterglow follows, and it's like we never broke up. On my side now, I roll toward her with my head propped on hand and elbow.

"I missed you," I say.

She's touched enough that she doesn't answer right away. Instead, she gives the emotion a beat. In that beat, I almost want to add, ... *and I needed you.* I don't say it because she already feels guilty and the flip side of needing my friend during my hardest years is the fact that the friend wasn't there. It's true, though. I needed her. I needed every decent soul I could get.

"I missed you, too."

"Remember Ross?" I ask.

"Remember him? I'm *dating* him!"

I feel a blip at that, too, but I cover it right away. I guess I shouldn't go down the path I was going to go with that one, now that I know they're together. I was hoping for some good old fashioned hetero girl bonding on the whole Ross issue, but maybe not. I had a thing for Ross once. A *big* thing. Feels wrong to mention it now.

"What?" Miranda asks.

"Since when?"

"It's brand new. Three weeks?" Then she says again, "What is it?"

"I'm just surprised," I say, but my facial expression tells the rest of the tale. I should be smiling about this odd surprise, but instead I'm straight-faced as if it's something we'd better be careful discussing.

"Bad surprise?" Miranda asks, reading me easily.

"Surprise surprise," I answer. "Did he tell you we used to debate music together?"

Pause. Then: "What, when we were kids?"

"In high school. We had this music trivia club at my school, and your school was one of the only others in the area that had the same thing — like Quiz Bowl but cooler. We had crosstown matches all the time. Ross never mentioned it?"

Miranda shakes her head slowly. Some of the rapport we've built over the past hour has just been restricted, like when a bank holds funds until a check clears. "No."

"Oh," I say. "Well ... after I moved, I didn't see him again until our freshman year and the club started up. Maybe he didn't say anything because he didn't remember you and I used to be friends."

"Maybe," Miranda says.

Another long, awkward beat passes between us. This shouldn't be an issue (I haven't even talked to Ross since our season ended, before he and Miranda got together), but Miranda's weak spot has always been her relationships. I saw it in person back when a peck on the cheek at recess meant she and Roy Trundle were married, and Ross told tales of Miranda's jealousy a few times when we talked, though always about other guys, not Ross himself.

Truth is, though, we didn't *just* compete in music trivia. I don't really want to say that now. We were friendly — flirty, even. I lied earlier, and now I'm glad I did. I know for a fact that Ross remembers me and Miranda being friends, because we talked about her even though it now seems Ross never talked to Miranda about me.

Why? The unknown of it has me off balance. Even though the weirdness between me and my ex-best friend kept us from reacquainting, I always took comfort from assuming Ross was the bridge between us. I never specifically asked (the reason I couched my first question as *Remember Ross?* instead of *How about that Ross?*), but given all he told me about Miranda over the past four years, I just assumed he was doing the same about me. Now I know otherwise, though: Ross and I got close, and he kept me a secret. Maybe it's because *they* weren't close until they started dating; I have no idea. What matters is that now they're intimate, and I'm something Ross kept from his girlfriend. Not exactly the vibe I was hoping to create here.

Looking at Miranda now, I know why Ross never said anything to her. *This* is why. She might get the wrong idea. Or, in the case of two separate times we made out at parties, she might get exactly the right idea.

"You and Ross?" she says.

"Friends."

She's trying to act casual, but I can see the jealousy. You don't want to make Miranda jealous. She'll bite your head off. "Weird that he never told me. Weird that he wouldn't remember we were friends."

Shit. That's a trap. All I've said is that we played on competing teams, but I'll move from evasion to lying if I hide the extent of our relationship now. We were just friends. Friends who made out twice. Friends who never dated and never slept together — not because Ross didn't want to very badly, but because I slammed on the brakes. That should count for something, right?

Relax, I tell myself. *She wasn't even dating him then. And it was at the start of high school, not the end. It's not like you've even spoken much over the last few years. Back when Ross liked you, you weren't even this goth girl with hard edges. He probably wouldn't even want you now.*

"*Moderate* friends for a while," I say. "Mostly freshman year of high school. We got along. But then things changed the way they do, and it was more like acquaintances. It's not like we hung out."

"So you *didn't* hang out."

"Well, not after freshman year. Some of sophomore."

"He's here, you know," Miranda says.

"Where?"

"At Fordham."

"You're kidding."

"So you didn't know?"

I shake my head.

She's staring at me now. Assessing me. Probably noticing how despite the fuck-off way I dress and do my hair, I've been told I'm cute in a pixie sort of way. She's probably wondering if I was Ross's type. If I might *still* be his type. If, basically, she should consider me a threat.

Finally Miranda shrugs, then takes a big scoop from her acai bowl. Something snaps, and once again we're just two old friends eating treats.

"My parents don't like him," she says, casual again. "Ross."

"That sucks," I say. I'm still watching for eggshells, but I think she's let it go. For now.

"He's sold some drugs. Light stuff. You remember his background."

Yeah, I do. When we were little, Ross *literally* came from the wrong side of the tracks. There were train tracks through our little town, and it was pretty obvious which side was the bad one. I shouldn't complain about my parents because Ross barely *had* parents. He could have turned out a full-on criminal, but instead what he became was a gray-area entrepreneur. The stuff he sells falls under the umbrella of "it's technically illegal but really shouldn't be." He scrapped because that was the only way he could survive. I don't hold it against him.

"That's why your parents don't like him? Because he sells drugs?"

"It's not really like that," Miranda counters. "You say 'sells drugs' and you get a picture of what that means, but that's not what Ross does." She takes another bite, and I can tell now that all our tension from earlier is over. "But yeah. I think that's why."

"You *think?*"

Another spoonful. She responds with her mouth full. "Who knows? *Parents.*" She rolls her eyes again. "Like Dad wasn't way worse when he was drinking." She gives me a glance, probably not intending to say what she just said to me of all people. "They know about a thing Ross did in high school. A weed thing. But they had a problem with him even before that. Especially my dad. Dad *hates* him."

"He's just protecting his little girl."

"No," she says. "I forgot to mention: They don't know we're going out."

"They don't know you're going out?"

"Mmm-mmm. I plan on keeping things that way for as long as I can. They'll find out eventually, but right now I'd rather not have the hassle."

"Then maybe your dad is protecting his little girl *in advance.* Like, he can tell Ross likes you, so he's being Papa Bear ahead of time."

"So now you're defending my father?"

I hold my hands up in surrender. "Okay, then he's an asshole. What do you want from me? I was just thinking there's two sides to every story."

"Were there two sides when he beat your dad almost to death?" Miranda asks.

I grunt. Miranda grunts. Apparently, we've reached an impasse wherein we can only communicate like apes.

We're finishing up when a round blue thing lands between us. Pattern recognition kicks in and I see it for what it is (a rubber ball made to look like the earth, with blue oceans and raised green continents) only after it's too late to brace for impact. I try to move back, but the next thing happens too quickly to shield myself.

A large black something bowls into our space, annihilating everything: the remainder of Miranda's bowl, my napkins and detritus, the few items we'd taken out of our backpacks as we caught up. It comes with a grumbling, snorting sound. The attack is a frenzy: all limbs and long hair. I definitely take a dog butt to the face.

Then it's over and a black dog plops contentedly between us. It puts the ball between its front paws, chewing on the thing as if we're not even there.

Feet approach. A shadow falls over me. Miranda, with eyes on the dog, speaks without looking up.

"Cassie, meet Aubrey. Aubrey, meet Cassie."

"Heya," says the newcomer, sitting to make a triangle.

But now we're all ignoring this huge black-haired monster loudly chewing on rubber between us as if everything is normal.

"And this is Abby," Aubrey tells me, "annihilator of picnics and destroyer of balls."

Abby takes one of her ball's green continents between her teeth and wrenches until it rips off. I look at Miranda, but all she can do is shrug.

"Welcome to Fordham," she says.

Chapter Twenty-Three
MIRANDA

I stand at the picture window, turning the ring over and over with my fingers. Outside, snow falls in large, beautiful flakes. I keep trying to pretend Ross isn't tied up in the bedroom (no need to hide him in the shed anymore) with one arm cut off by my father. Pretending isn't as hard as you'd think. The truth is too crazy to be true.

The lights flicker. That's been happening for a while now. It seems likely we'll lose power in all this snow and ice.

My mother approaches. "Miranda..." she says.

I don't look back. "Are you going to try and explain it?"

She doesn't answer. After a few silent seconds, I turn to find her frozen by the tone of my interruption. I can only imagine how I must sound, how it must surprise her. They expected me to be shocked by what they'd done to Ross, or at least afraid of it. The last thing they expected, I'm sure, was approval.

Don't let him go. Keep him tied. Mom stares at me like she'd stare at a stranger. The way she looks, it's like she's afraid of me.

"I'm serious," I say. "Is that why you're here? To explain?"

She opens her mouth twice, closes it twice. Finally she sighs. "I don't know what to say."

We watch the snow.

"Ross was wearing this, wasn't he?" I show her the ring. I've threaded it back through its broken leather lanyard, which is stained with blood.

She nods.

I turn the ring over again, my eyes refusing to leave it. "He's a bastard."

"He thought he was protecting you. Everything he does, whether the rest of us understand it or not—"

"I'm not talking about Dad. I meant *Ross* is a bastard."

Mom seems reluctant to agree. She must see the murder in me. What Ross got was nothing. The way I feel right now, I want to do worse.

"I'm sorry you ended up involved in this, Miranda," she says.

"I'm not," I say. "Did you know we were dating?"

"Not until he came to the door."

"I was hiding him from you. I thought you'd disapprove."

"Honey..."

"I thought you'd say he was bad for me. You always hated him. I thought you'd bitch until I couldn't take it anymore. I imagined all sorts of ways you'd give me a hard time. How you'd give *Ross* a hard time if I ever had the guts to bring him home. But have to admit: I didn't think you'd do *this*."

"Things got out of hand. Your father..."

I hold the ring out for her, dangling from its bloody string. "Do you know what this is?"

She takes it, then looks at it properly. It's a blast from my forgotten past. I haven't seen it for over a decade, but my hands remember it like yesterday. I've worn that ring many times, though back then my fingers were too small for it. I thought the intertwined gold and silver band looked like snakes hugging. Its three blue stones reminded me of sapphires, of pirate's treasure.

"It's Cassie's," I tell her.

"What?"

"It's Cassie Grey's ring."

"Are you sure?"

"Look at the inscription," I say. "I'm sure."

I watch Mom while she considers the inscription, curious at her reaction. Before I said the ring was Cassie's, she looked at it like she'd look at a pebble. Now, though, she seems dire somehow — troubled, distracted; it's hard to say. I can't read her face. I don't think she knows the ring specifically, but there's something in her eyes just the same.

"Does it mean something to you?" I ask.

She hands it back. She's guarded when she says, "I don't think so."

"Does it mean something to dad?"

"What's it mean to *you*, Miranda? Is it like how we used to give varsity jackets to our sweethearts back in my day? Is *that* why you're so mad? Because you think Ross and Cassie are ... *together?*"

Yes. I *did* think that. I thought it months ago. I thought it yesterday, when Aubrey told me they'd been emailing. Now, however, what I think is so much worse.

"He always liked her, Mom. He had all the years Cassie and I we were apart to drool over her. Maybe I should have known."

"Miranda..."

"I'm not mad at you. I should be, but I'm not."

"You have to understand," Mom goes on. "Your father and I..."

"I said I'm not mad." I look her in the eyes. "Hey, look at the bright side. We're the same now, aren't we? I guess you'll finally have to admit I'm an adult now, just like you. What's more adult than joining your folks in torture?"

"I don't like it any more than you do."

I turn to face her. "That's what you're not getting, Mom," I say. "I *do* like it. He's getting what he deserves. So that's another grown-up thing, isn't it? What's more adult than a broken heart?"

"Is that what this is to you?"

"It's a lot of things."

"You aren't making sense. I think you're in shock."

I look at the ring one more time, then pocket it. I know *exactly* what it means that Ross had this ring. *Exactly*. And yes. I'm shocked enough for all of us.

Time passes. I forget Mom is there again. For a while it's just me and the snow. I'm trying to decide what to do next. I've already revisited the owner's closet with its wet bar, where I poured myself a drink to take off the edge.

"Miranda?" Mom says.

But I just look into the cold, swirling darkness outside, where a full moon paints everything ghostly yellows and blues. The window I'm standing in front of is poorly insulated. From my perspective, it seems that the window is radiating cold the way an air conditioner does, but that's not how it works. Cold is actually the absence of a thing, not a thing itself. It means the window isn't radiating cold so much as stealing my heat away.

Cold. Hot. There are at least two ways to look at everything. Two sides to every story.

"Miranda," Mom repeats.

"I heard you the first time."

"We never meant for this to happen."

"You mean you never meant for me to find out."

It all makes sense now. All I had to do was pull off my blinders and get out of my own way. Finding Cassie's ring in Ross's possession didn't tell me anything new, not really. All it did was remind me to see things from a new perspective. I shouldn't be surprised. This was inevitable. More than inevitable: *DONE.* This isn't a new deed. It's the husk of something done a long time ago.

This is how I live, Aubrey tells me. Always just a little bit in the past, always responding to threats only after the threat is gone.

"I texted Aubrey," I say.

"What?"

"I said I texted Aubrey. I wasn't specific. I just told her we needed help."

"Miranda ... for God's sake, *why?* What if she calls the police?"

"I told her not to. I told her to call me if she's able. I said it was life and death."

Truth is, I didn't really text Aubrey *nothing* so much as I texted her something that, in Aubrey's hands, will function as a clue. I don't know why I did it, other than it felt right. I can't decide what comes next and I don't trust my parents to decide, so I guess I made Aubrey the tiebreaker. Texting Aubrey was my way of casting a lifeline, so we're not the only ones inside this bubble.

My mind goes to Cortes, who burned his ships after reaching the New World so there'd be no turning back.

That's when I realize why I did what I did. Texting Aubrey casts our die. It ties our hands. It burns our ships so there can be no turning back — no putting our heads in the sand and pretending nothing happened. My text to Aubrey ensures that the one thing that *can't* happen next is nothing at all.

I don't want this to go away now that I understand what it is. I've committed us to facing what should have been faced long ago.

"H-*how*, though?" Mom stutters. "There's no cell reception in the storm."

"I used Ross's phone."

"*We* have Ross's phone."

"He had a second phone. A burner. You should have searched him. It works different from an iPhone. I checked a few minutes ago. I don't know if Aubrey has reception enough to get the message, but I know it sent. It's only a matter of time."

Now Mom's at the window beside me, looking toward the long, snow-covered driveway. Between the moon and the snow, it's beautiful.

She shivers, but not from the cold. There must be eight inches out there now. It's dawning on her how trapped we are. There are no signs the snow stopping. No signs it's slowing down.

I watch a tear fall. Mom wipes it away.

"I don't know what to do," she says. "Your father won't listen. He thinks we can solve this, but I just don't see how. When you were away, he drove out and called Dr. Khan. You remember Dr. Asham Khan?"

I nod. I don't call him "Dr. Khan," though. To me, he's always been "Uncle Asham." He and Dad went to college together. When my cousin David went into the hospital with an unspecified illness, it was Asham who helped us save his life. David's mother, my Aunt Lucy, lived two states away and refused to come to visit. Aunt Lucy was ashamed that her son had attempted suicide, but until David regained consciousness, she was making all his decisions from afar — including the decision not to tell us what was wrong. Asham broke all sorts of hospital rules to tell Dad the truth, and because of it, we — not Lucy — were able to get him the help he needed.

I get why Mom's mentioning Uncle Asham. When we needed his help, he cared more about "what's right" than some dumb rule ... but this isn't HIPAA privacy rules; it's a kidnapping and a cut-off arm. I don't think Asham will help us with this one.

"Dad didn't tell him anything!" Mom says, reading my reaction. "He told Dr. Khan that we saw a hunter stumbling around disoriented in the woods. Ross was acting disoriented in the same sort of way before you showed up, like he didn't know which end was up. I wanted a medical opinion on whether we could maybe just let Ross go. Maybe he wouldn't remember what happened, or nobody would believe him if he did."

"Mom..."

"I know. I know. He's not confused anymore. I'm not saying I want to let him go now. I'm just saying I'm open to any option that's not..." She doesn't want to say it — doesn't want to sully her tongue with talk of murder. "...not *excessive*. Can you think of anything, Miranda? If you were able to get a text through, and if Dr. Khan *already* knows something's going on, then *maybe*..."

I wait. Mom hangs on that last drawn-out *maybe*. Then she sighs, crumples, and practically collapses into a chair.

She wants my company, but my insides boil with turmoil. So I walk away, leaving her, and tread to the front door. I open it, step onto the covered porch, then take more steps until I'm beneath the falling snow. It's the kind that begins to cover you right away. Within seconds, my head sports a beanie made of fluff.

I look down the long, blue-shadowed driveway. The snow is deep enough to bury half my calves. When it blows, I can see nothing at all.

The truth is, I'm not sure why I texted Aubrey. I'll never have enough bars for her call to get through, so all I've done is worry her. I gave her no details — nothing that could get us in trouble. So what was the point?

You did it because Aubrey's comfortable. Aubrey's familiar. Unlike some people, Aubrey has never and would never betray you.

Why did I contact her? Because she's from my normal life. Same as Dr. Asham Khan is a confidant from my parents' normal life. Fear makes us reach in vain for what's normal.

Behind me, the lights flicker again.

I wonder, standing in the snow with blood on my hands, if I'll ever feel normal again.

Chapter Twenty-Four

AUBREY

When morning comes, I stop wondering if the piece of shit motel the weather forced me into last night will allow a late checkout. It's clear that nobody cares. It's a visually offensive strip of flat-roofed craptastic, and I'm sure the other rooms are empty or occupied by people who live here. Also drug dealers. The *hard* kind of dealers. Not weed and Adderall like Ross handles, but heroin, crack, and meth. I fell asleep to the sound of a woman having a seizure in the next room. I assumed she died, but then I heard her this morning, asking someone where her needles went.

I part the blinds and peek outside. The snow that began falling overnight hasn't slowed. So much for my game plan. I stopped last night because of road ice, figuring I could kill time here until the plows caught up and cleared the streets. They haven't caught up, though, because the snow's done such a good job of maintaining its lead. How annoying. I slept here in hopes that my situation would improve overnight, but instead it's gotten worse.

Should have kept driving despite the ice, apparently.

I can't get a good cell signal anymore, and of course there's no wifi. Even the TV doesn't work. I'm flying blind, operating on the last weather forecast I heard. Without bundling up and starting my car to hear the radio, I won't get a fresher one. All I know is that the snow Miranda's place started getting yesterday is here now too. Who knows how much worse it'll be up north.

The solution, of course, is to stop going north. I'm outmatched and should bug out, driving south instead. I should do it *now*, before the snow gets deeper. If I head south, the roads will start improving in a half hour or so.

That's what I *should* do. But I won't.

Because that itch still has me. That damnable, unverified, unsubstantiated feeling that lives in my gut and nowhere else: a sense that something is horribly, horribly wrong with this entire situation.

My mind floats back to the photos Miranda sent me. To the texts she received. I think about her parents and the weird behavior Miranda described. By themselves, none of those details mean much — but combined, they make a puzzle that doesn't quite fit. There's a piece missing; I'm sure of it.

"Tell me I'm crazy," I say to Abby. She's curled up on the floor like a big, hairy cheese doodle. "Tell me I'm being dumb right now for even considering this, and we can both go home."

"*Robocop,*" Abby mutters.

She's right.

Damn the snow. Damn the hatred awaiting me, when I show up and have to tell my best friend I slept with her boyfriend. Those things matter less than this creeping, lassitudinous dread creeping up my spine. Logical or not, I'm certain something in Miranda's world has gone terribly awry.

Call the police if that's what you think, says the last bit of sanity inside me. *Don't go there yourself, alone!*

Okay. And tell them what, exactly? That my intuition is acting up?

What I'm thinking is idiotic. I grab my keys and do it anyway.

TWO HOURS LATER, I'VE MANAGED TO DRIVE ALL OF FIFTEEN miles. The idiot level has blown sky-high. Back at the motel, I could still kind of justify what I'm doing. Now, I'm mentally ill to try.

There's nobody on the roads. When I was still on the expressway, there were at least semis and pickup trucks screaming by and shivering the air around me as I tried to stay in the tire ruts. The semis were heavy enough — and had so much road contact with those eighteen wheels — that a little snow was no big deal. The pickups were dicier, but my beat-up Camry made even the lightest trucks look sure-footed. I was definitely foolish for driving the expressway, but at least I had company. At least I wasn't the only crazy one.

Now, though, I *am* the only crazy one.

By the time I finally see the conjoined KFC and Starbucks as promised and pull gratefully into the parking lot, I'm exhausted. White-knuckle driving is nonstop exercise that works both body and mind. There are no wandering thoughts when you're white-knuckling. There's no checking out — just constant checking in. My shoulders, neck, biceps, and forearm muscles feel like someone's tightened them two or three sizes. My hands have formed video game claws so cramped, I doubt I could hold a Coke without dropping it.

It's been a rough couple of hours. I was just a few miles from the motel when I first got stuck.

It happened so casually — not traumatic at first. I was creeping down a four-lane road and needed to change lanes to make a turn. The act of moving from one set of worn-down tire ruts into the next required rolling over the compacted, ice-clump-strewn row of snow in between. Then my tires slipped. The slip became a skid, and soon enough my front wheels were halfway into the median. My front-wheel-drive car lodged in slippery ice-mud, and after that, pressing the accelerator did little more than dig ruts.

I looked at my phone. In situations like this, all the plows in any given area are usually occupied with pulling dumb assholes like me out of ditches, but there was little else I could do but call roadside assistance. But of course I was already in the boonies — not a bar of cell reception in sight.

I tried to rock the car back and forth in the ruts, careful not to floor the accelerator and make them deeper. Without a second person to push while I pedaled, though, I got nowhere. I could move about an inch, no more.

Lovely.

I fought to stay calm. I knew how to do this. Because my dad sucks, I know how to do a lot of things. A tree fell across our driveway once, and I was the one to chop it up with the chainsaw. Mom's van was running rough a year or so ago, so I watched YouTube videos until I learned how to check and change the spark plugs. That's me. That's Aubrey. I don't take a back seat. My friends think of me as a bulldog: traits they often call intrusive and nosy. The upside, though, is that my confidence is always up to the task. That's what happens when you can only count on yourself in life.

And so at that point, I got out of my car, hugged my not-entirely-substantial-enough winter gear around me, then opened my trunk and scoured it for anything I could use to gain traction. I wasn't fully off the road; only my drive wheels were in the muck. I just needed to close the inches between the bottom of my wheels and the bottom of the ruts I'd carved, plus put something under the tread to give the drive wheels traction.

Tire iron? Maybe.

Wheel jack? Nope.

Jumper cables? I'd just rip them apart ... and besides: In all this cold, I might end up needing them.

I tapped the trunk's edge, peering in and thinking. My fingers were already freezing. I didn't bring my big thick gloves, nor a decent hat. My coat was a ski jacket with a sweater and shirt underneath — not really warm so much as weatherproof.

Stay cool, I told myself. The pun wasn't intended.

I was just about to try and wedge the tire iron under one of the wheels when I struck paydirt. A few scraps of leftover 2x4 lumber were still in the trunk from the time I (not my father) built a set of sawhorses to do the porch soffit repair that nobody else was going to handle. Two of the pieces in my trunk were around eighteen inches long. Perfect.

And traction? I'd already solved that one: The bag of dog food I stopped to buy yesterday would do. *Sorry, Abby. I'm a bad dog mom.*

I looked up to see that she was watching me with encouragement from inside the car. It gave me the will to go on.

Wedging the 2x4s under the wheels — with a bit of dog food for grit — did the trick. I jumped out after I'd gotten the car back on the road so I could grab the two-bys from the mud. You never know; I might need them again.

Once I was mobile, I started looking for a place to turn around. I'd been stupid, but now I saw the error of my ways. I'd been ridiculous to keep driving north. It was time to bail whether Miranda's situation worried me or not. And so I drove on, intending to give up, but there were no turnarounds. The road had grown desolate, beginning to wind and turn as I entered the mountain foothills instead of heading straight. That scared me. Foothill roads aren't always salted. They aren't always plowed. If I kept going, I might be in some serious trouble.

A place to turn around. Find one.

But there were no crossroads. No restaurants, truck stops, or gas stations. There were technically a few places where travelers could cross the median and drive in the opposite direction, but the plows that'd come through hadn't cleared them. Instead, they'd blown all the accumulated snow and ice onto those crossovers. If I dared enter one, I'd never get out.

So I kept driving.

The second time I went off the road, it wasn't my fault. I'd only seen three cars in the past hour, but this time, one of them came at me with a wheel on each side of what had once been the center line, following directly behind a plow. On seldom-driven roads like the one I was on, plows mostly just knock a strip through the center: a single pass, not a pass back and forth. It makes sense to drive in the middle of the road when things are that way, but it's a problem when two cars meet, one headed each direction.

The plow moved without a problem, but the driver behind it wasn't as agile. He stayed where he was, his face visible to me as an alarmed moon through the windshield. I tried to inch away, but there wasn't room. I ended up with my right-side wheels in deeper snow, starting to swerve even before we reached each other. My front end swung toward the other car, then away. For long seconds I was sure we were going to crash.

My bumper missed his by inches. Time slowed. I saw the other driver gesticulating, mouth open and yelling. After we passed each other, I saw his middle finger pressed against the glass. His horn saluted, long and insulting. Then the snow swallowed him ... and meanwhile, my car continued to slide.

I struck the berm hard. Piled-up snow rained onto my windshield. It wasn't precisely a collision — more a muted *FOOMF* as my front end rammed nose-first into a drift. My body slammed forward hard enough to check me against the seatbelt, but not quite hard enough to set off the airbag.

The car fell still. I lifted my head to see that one hand had hit the blinker, its metronomic clicking the only sound inside the car. Yellow light, distributed by the snow over half of my Camry, flashed on and off. The covered windshield was dark. By now, the sky was starting to darken as well.

Abby, unhurt, had been sleeping in the passenger foot well. She licked her lips and gave me a look that asked why I'd done such a thing.

I turned off the blinker. The world went silent. That's when my mind activated and began explaining just how screwed I was.

No cell service.

Nobody around.

Thin coat, thin gloves, thin hat ... and nothing warmer in the trunk.

Quarter tank of gas ... *maybe*. After that, I wouldn't even be able to run the heater.

I wasn't a hundred percent sure where I was, either. My GPS had stopped working long ago, but I'd had enough foresight to buy a map from the motel office. Having the map brought me to eighty percent sure where I was. Okay, seventy percent. Fifty at the lowest.

Someone tapped on my window. I looked in my side mirror to see that that the plow I'd passed had come back, now parked behind me with its big lights flashing.

I rolled down the window.

"Looks like you got yourself in a little bind here," the driver said conversationally.

Relief quenched most of my panic, the alchemy of emotions almost causing me to burst into tears. The driver tugged his hat down over his ears, which were sizable. He was a thin, wiry type, like beef jerky in human form.

"Say. You want me to pull you back onto the road?" he asked.

"Oh my God. Yes. Please. Thank you."

With a businesslike nod, the driver disappeared. He retrieved a heavy chain from the plow's side compartment. I listened as he clanked it into place at my rear. This done, he returned to the plow, hooked up the other end, then backed up to pull the chain taut. There was one quick shudder, and suddenly we were back in business.

The plow driver returned to my window. Before I could thank him again, he said, "I'm sure you know there's a travel advisory."

"Yes. Yes, I know. I kind of got stuck in this." It was true; I just left out the part where I *was* safe and then decided to drive right into a snowstorm.

The driver pointed at the road ahead. Flakes swirled hypnotically in my headlight beams, like a snow globe that never settles.

"Restaurant up ahead. 'Bout two-three miles. I just went past it and yep, it's open. You'll wanna pull off there. Wait this out a little."

"Is there a place to stay?"

"No, but my cousin works at the station. Probably the only gal there today, actually, on accounta they live one block down. She won't give you no hassle. Not much of a conversationalist, her, but she'll give you a chair, let you watch the little TV they got behind the counter if you want. Shoot, I'm sure she'd offer you her couch to sleep on if this goes in the shitter and we can't get ahead of it."

"Thank you," I said.

"Now. Pull in behind me, willya? Be there in two shakes."

"You're going to escort me there?"

"Ayuh."

"Weren't you going the opposite direction?"

"Well, yeah, I was. But I got this rule about not leavin' people to die on the side of the road."

"If it's just two miles..."

"Don't fuss with me, now," he said. "That big cat there"—he pointed, apparently meaning his plow—"she's got feet like a mountain goat. Ain't gonna cost me more than ten minutes off my run to head back, and ain't gonna take you more'n five if you're right behind my wake. Just don't get too close less'n you want a shitload of salt in your face. You got me?"

"I got you," I said gratefully.

Without another word, the driver climbed into his plow, turned around, and cut a sure-footed path for me all the way to the KFC/Starbucks combo, both of which were open as promised.

When the plow then swung back to continue his job on the roads, I considered asking if I could follow him the rest of the way. He'd been going south, after all, and that's where my dumb brain finally admitted it had to go — unsettled feeling about Miranda's situation or not.

But before I could ask anything, the driver honked and waved, and seconds later even the swirling yellow lights of his flashers were devoured by the storm.

As expected, the two restaurants — joined and inter-accessible like a miniature travel plaza — are deserted except for the clerk. I understand now why the plow driver thought only his cousin would be here: One person can run both counters if they have to, especially with nobody around.

I wish he'd given me her name. Or *his own* name. I feel like I need a hookup here, to introduce my presence and my desire to stick around for a while. The girl looks friendly enough, though, and not a whole lot older than me. Given the driver's apparent age, I assumed his cousin would be a 40-something lumberjack type. I know you shouldn't judge people by their looks, but in this case I already have. I've judged the clerk friendly. She even smiled my way when I entered — warmly, not like obligatory customer service.

My phone vibrates in my back pocket as I'm walking between rows of chips and candy bars. I don't even remember slipping it in there when I got out of the car, which is still running outside with headlights and heater on, Abby watching me from the front seat until I summon the guts to ask if I can bring her inside. I also don't recognize my phone's vibration as being a text message at first. My brain's too fried — too filled with thoughts of death by crash or frostbite — for that. I'm on the dark side of the moon right now, not navigating anything like the real world. Look at me: preparing to hole up with a stranger because I have no other choice.

But then I think: *There's no cell service. How the hell did I just get a text?*

I pull the phone out, sure it's not a text but instead something like a low-battery alert. But nope, it's a message. And it's from...

...Ross?

I frown at my phone long enough that from the corner of my eye, I spy the plow-driver's cousin looking at me, wondering what's up with her only customer. It's thoughts of weirdness that make me force my legs to start walking again.

But *yes*, I see as I pass the chip section and move toward the miniature cereal boxes: The text *is* from Ross. And that's weird, but not as weird as *which* Ross number just used to text me: not his iPhone, but the burner he uses for dealing.

I open the message. Even though it's from Ross's phone, he's not the one who sent it. It's actually from Miranda, which is strange. She doesn't, as far as I know, even know that Ross has a burner phone.

I stand in the aisle and read Miranda's message twice. It's not a good message. In fact, it makes me feel unstable on my feet — enough that I try to grab a shelf to ground me. I miss and knock a little box of Wheaties to the floor.

The message reads: *It's Miranda. Call me as soon as you can get through. I can't say why on a cell phone. Don't tell anyone else. Please. It's life and death.*

I stare at the screen. When did she send this? Given the way Skor phones work, she could have sent it hours ago. *Days* ago.

A chair's squeak and movement in the background tell me the clerk is wondering about me again, coming forward this time to see if I'm drunk, high, or about to throw up all over her nice clean floor. I can't think about that right now, though. My mind is busy running through permutations. Considering my options, which just became a lot simpler ... but also a whole lot worse.

"Are you okay?" the girl asks me.

I look up. She has kind eyes.

"Do you have a landline phone?" I ask.

"Yeah, but it's out. The entire valley's out. Heard it on the radio." She ticks her head toward the counter, where I see a small dedicated news-and-weather radio. Live in these parts and I guess you take your weather pretty seriously. That's something I can now appreciate better than anyone.

"Do you have cell service?" I ask. "Or service at home?"

I feel faint. It's getting harder to hold myself upright. It's delayed shock, I think: my brush with death catching up with me. That plus this new wrinkle really packs a wallop. It must show on my face, because the girl's kind eyes crease with concern.

"Sorry, no," she says. "You hurt or something? There's a doctor in walking distance. As long as his lights are on, he's open."

I shake my head. "How about police?"

That makes her eyes widen. She wants to ask why I'd want police, but she just says, "Fifteen miles down Vallejo Street. Wish I knew someone with a CB."

The text is still on my screen, throbbing like a toothache. I can't reply. I can't call — not Miranda, not anyone. There are no police nearby to ask for help. There might be others around who'd do the job — big strong mountain men with shotguns, maybe — but Miranda's made it clear: *Tell no one.* There's no way to clarify why with her, or ask if it's okay to make an exception. For all I know, I'd only turn her bad situation into something worse by doing so.

Whatever's going on, I'm the only one who knows anything about it — the only one who *could* know, unless she happens to have the local police number memorized. If I remember right, you can't dial 911 on a Skor — if Miranda even has service, which I doubt because she's resorted to using the Skor in the first place.

I — little old stranded Aubrey, here in her Camry with its shitty snow footing — seem to be all Miranda has. And that leaves me with only one impossible, worse-than-terrible option: *Somehow, some way, I have to continue north in this storm. Somehow, I have to get up there.*

It's not fair. I've always had to make my own way in the world, and now it's come down to this. I've never felt more alone.

A hand lands on my shoulder: feather-light, but almost too much burden for me to carry. I think I might collapse. It would be a blessing, to drift into nothing at all.

Instead, I hold my footing and look at the clerk.

"You're in trouble, aren't you?"

All I can do is nod.

"I don't guess you can tell me what it is."

I shake my head, but this time it's the girl who nods. Something secret enters her eyes — something I know by instinct she's never let anyone see before.

"I've been in trouble," she says darkly. "I know how it is when nobody has your back. If you can't tell me, I understand. I won't ask. But I won't tell you your business either. Whatever you need, you need. Whatever anyone else thinks, they don't know what they're talking about. Everyone's got secrets. People can't judge — not when they don't know it all."

I watch her for a moment. She nods so slightly, it's almost imperceptible. It's her sign that I have permission: a clean slate to confess anything I want.

My lips are chapped and hard to move. "I need to get to my friend's place off of Old Route 4," I say. "Today. As soon as possible."

She looks at my car, still with Abby inside. At my inadequate snow tires, and the fact that I had to follow a plow into the parking lot. My best guess says Miranda's place is another twenty miles on, through one of the worst snowfalls I've ever seen.

Another beat of silence passes between us.

"Come with me," she says.

Chapter Twenty-Five
ROSS

Everything hurts. It's not lack of sleep that keeps making me tired so much as whole-being exhaustion.

Holding my awkward posture takes energy. Resisting pain takes energy. Understanding the upside-down nature of night and day takes energy, but of course I've been in and out more than just night and day. At first, they drugged me, and then they held me in the freezing cold — which, again, took a lot of energy just to keep from dying. I even have to expend energy to keep myself sane. I've found that I can pull myself from the kind of delirium I felt earlier if I exert all the will I have ... but, again, doing so exhausts me.

I'm weak. When they moved me from the shed to the bedroom, they had to support me like a wounded warrior. I'm sandbagging a little (if I ever see a chance to get free, I'd rather surprise them with a bit of saved-up energy), but it's *just* a little. Mostly I want to sleep. And so mostly, that's what I do.

When I come to, I think at first that I'm alone. A small, low-wattage incandescent bulb throws yellow light from a bedside lamp too far away for me to reach. There are no other lights in the room, and the blinds are drawn, so I dismiss the shape by the window as a pile of coats. But then it speaks, and I realize it's Miranda. I can't see her. Her face is in the shadows.

"'I will love you forever,'" she says.

I strain to sit up. With my good arm fastened, I fall right back down.

"I'll love *you* forever, too," I say.

But she's not professing her love; she's reading the inscription on my ring. When she leans forward into the lamplight, she's holding it up. Her face is the opposite of loving.

"Where did you get this ring, Ross?"

"I don't remember."

"Don't lie to me."

"I'm not lying."

"How could you not know where you got it?"

I shrug. "I know a lot of people. I lose track of who gives me what."

She looks away, shakes her head like she's disgusted.

"I'm not lying, Miranda! I don't know!"

"You're always lying!" Her voice thickens, as if with frustrated rage. *"You've never told me the truth!"*

"What? Where is this coming from?"

She gives another harsh, furious shake of her head, turning away to look toward the window.

I make my voice soft. "Miranda, I love you."

"Bullshit."

"Whatever I did to make you this mad, I'm sorry."

She laughs at me: one short, cruel bark. I can hear angry tears trying to take her over.

"I'm here in the first place because…" I start to say. But then I stop. Telling her I slept with Aubrey is maybe not the best idea right now, even though clearing my conscience was the reason I came. "…because I wanted to make sure you knew that I loved you," I finish.

"Came all this way," she says with disbelief, "just to deliver a Hallmark moment."

"Look, I don't understand what's going on here. I don't know why your dad attacked me. I only know he tied me up after he real-ized he'd gone too far. All I did was come to the door. I wanted to see you. I had to be near you."

"For no reason at all," Miranda says, thick with sarcasm. "Not because you felt guilty for what you did with one of my best friends."

I feel a shiver. "Who?"

"You tell me."

"Dammit, Miranda. If you have something to say, just say it! Can't you see I've been through enough?"

She stands up, then begins to pace. It's too quiet in here; every tick of her shoes on the floorboard is rendered with the detail of an auditory sculpture. The snow is an acoustic blanket, dampening every echo. You'd think you wouldn't be able to hear the absence of sound, but you'd be wrong. I've been hearing it for days: all that snow outside, piled on us like judgement.

"Please," I say. "Please help me get out of here."

She comes closer. She runs her fingers along the stump of my severed arm, and I flinch. It wasn't done cleanly: all those seared-shut veins and dangling ligaments. I'd expect her to recoil, but instead her touch is almost tender.

"Please, Miranda. You see how much he hurt me."

But it's like she doesn't hear me. "This ring," she says, looking at it once more before pocketing it. "It meant something to someone."

"Yes. *Me.* It means something to *me.*"

"Because of where you got it?"

"I told you. I don't remember where I got it."

Miranda nods. Then she gives a bitter laugh.

"It's all so clear to me now," she says. "You lie, and you lie, and you lie. Half the time you probably don't even think of what you say as lies. You're always the victim. You've always got some sort of justification for the things you do. Worst of all, you *believe* those justifications. You don't even know when you've done something wrong."

"I don't lie," I say.

"Then *who gave you the ring?*"

"Why does it matter?"

"BECAUSE IT MATTERS! Because I know the truth and here you are, LYING TO MY FACE!"

Very carefully, I say, "What do you think you know, Miranda?"

She walks closer. Stands by the side of the bed. I wait, watching her and seeing the myriad emotions fighting there for dominance.

"Bastard," she says, and slaps me hard across the face.

MIDDAY ON SATURDAY. EVERYONE'S QUIET. I DON'T KNOW WHAT time it is, but with my windows blacked out, it feels like the middle of the night even though I know it's not. Normally at this point I'd get out of bed, use the restroom, then tuck back in. Seeing as they didn't provide me with facilities, though, I just pee where I am. Screw 'em. Worst-case scenario, I've just left a bit more DNA evidence for those who come to investigate my murder. Best case, I've still ruined the mattress. Cost them their security deposit, those assholes.

Ghosts whisper in the eves. Ice-covered branches scrape the cabin's side like long brittle fingers. The lights in here flicker from time to time. I think it means power is failing; soon we'll be shut down and freezing. From my position tied wide on the bed, I see the silhouettes of snowflakes, coming like thrown confetti. Wind at the eaves makes the shriek of a banshee.

I'm going to die here.

It hits me as a statement of bald practicality, not a threat. I'm no more afraid than I was moments ago, thinking it. I'm just suddenly resolved. Suddenly convinced. It's a relief, in a way, to no longer wonder if anyone — like Miranda — might yet come to save me. I know now that I'm alone.

Somehow, some way, I have to get free. I have to get out of here while I still can.

I scan the room. I tug lightly at my bindings, considering my options. They tied me with the same rope they used before, and just as tightly. I do have the one arm free, but seeing as it's only half an arm, it won't really help. There's not much slack in the ropes. Not nearly enough to curl up so my bound hand can untie my feet or vice versa.

I test to see how far I can move, careful not to tug too hard and tighten the knots. I have about six inches of play — just enough to scratch my nose when it itches. If I scooch down so my hand's rope is tight, I can move it six inches toward my feet. But what good is six inches? There's nothing within six inches to reach.

I run through my options.

Can I break the ropes?

No, I'm not Thor.

Can I untie the knots?

No, because I can't reach my foot knots with my hand, and my cauterized stump has no fingers. I don't have enough slack to reach the knot at the bedpost with my teeth.

Speaking of teeth, can I bite through the rope?

Not a chance. That was the first thing I tried, but it's wound nylon or similar — more like climber's rope than something fibrous like twine. I can't clip through any of the individual strands with my incisors, let alone all of them.

Can I slip the rope off of my wrist or ankles?

No, though at first, I thought otherwise. Willa tied all the knots on the far ends and put them down near the lower part of the frame, not up on top of the mattress. I can't reach the knots to work them, but despite appearances, the simple loops of rope on my skin can't be slipped. At all.

Can I ... move the mattress from beneath me so I can reach the knots down by the frame?

Um, right. I'm grasping at straws now.

Maybe I can rattle around. Break the bed frame so the rope comes free.

But that's not possible, either. The bed is solidly built, not loose at all. The one time I tried yanking hard enough to rattle it, Mark came in and held a knife to my throat until I stopped.

Then I have to find something sharp. Something I can use to cut the rope quietly.

But what? It's not like they left letter openers in the bed. I've already felt around all I can, looking for sharp metal edges or screws

I can loosen and use like tiny daggers. There's nothing. I also can't break the wood and use the splinters. The bed's wooden parts are made of oak or something just as strong.

I try for a little while longer to get my wrist free, but Willa's work is far too good. And so, furious and frustrated, I do the most mature and productive thing I can do. I throw a tantrum.

It lasts maybe ten seconds. For ten seconds, I thrash and scream and whip my head around and pull the ropes as hard as I can. Then I settle, and Willa pokes her head in, and we just stare at each other for a little while until she sees I've gotten it out of my system and leaves. It's not until after the door is closed again that I feel the sting of rope burn on my wrist. It's raw there, skin worn down, and...

But it's not just rope burn. There's a tiny scratch on the heel of my palm, looking and feeling like a papercut.

What cut me?

I think for a while, then get an idea.

I turn my head to the side, then pull my wrist close enough to brush against my ear. It's not the kind of flesh-to-flesh pairing a person makes under normal circumstances, but it's exactly the kind of contact you get from thrashing around.

I was right, I realize. It was the back of my ear stud that scratched me.

And as it turns out, six inches of slack is plenty to reach down and pull the sharp little stud free.

As encouraged as I was at first by the ear stud discovery, I'm demoralized a half hour later. It's like I'm in one of those movies where a guy tunnels out of prison using nothing more than a cafeteria spork. It's going to take forever. I won't let myself believe what feels truer than that, though: that it's going to take *more* than forever. A dark part of me is sure that no matter how long I do this, I'll never cut myself free.

Don't think about how far you still have to go, I tell myself. *Just keep going.*

Pessimism aside, I actually have managed to scratch a small gash in the rope, cutting some of the individual fibers. It's not exactly prison break material, but at least it's something. I might only be a hundredth of the way through the rope, but at least I can do math with 1/100th that I couldn't do with zero. If I keep cutting nonstop and don't sleep, I'll be through the rope in two days. You know, after they've already killed me.

I said don't think about it.

An hour later, after another tiny amount of progress, I realize I can wedge the back of my hand against one of the dowels on the bed frame and rub the rope across the earring instead of the other way around. It's still slow work, but faster than before. I feel more and more of the fibers breaking away, the cut deepening. The problem now is the stud on the back of the earring, which keeps bending. It might snap away. How far am I through the rope? It's hard to crane my head and see, but my fingers guess it's maybe twenty percent cut.

I settle into a rhythm. Moving my hand back and forth makes the bed shake, but there's a sweet spot: fast enough to make maximal progress without the whole thing squeaking. It's dull work, and my tired mind wanders.

I think of Miranda.

What's wrong with her? I thought I was saved when she found me earlier today, but sometime in between, she's changed her mind and gone sadistic. Clearly, she thinks she knows something, but she won't say what it is. The ring seems to mean something to her, but if she was sure of what it was, she'd say so.

That means she's bluffing. It's a girl's ring, and here I am wearing it around my neck. I guess that drove her to conclusions, especially since she's always been the jealous type. But again, she's full of shit. I got that ring *years* before we started dating. Truth is, I've worn it on and off forever, though I keep it under my shirt. She's the jerk for not spotting it before now.

I should have said it was my mother's. Too late to say that now, I suppose.

I saw at the rope and think. I think and I saw the rope. The feeling is that I'm dulling the earring while sharpening my mind. But that's okay. It's a good thing, really. I'm going to need all of my wits to get out of here even if I *do* manage to cut through the rope.

Mark is crazy. He's the biggest threat.

Willa supports him, but she's not aggressive, so I figure I can bowl right through her. It's easier now that their actions have given me no reason to hold back. There's rough stone on the fireplace; I figure I can slam Willa's head into it and that'll be all she wrote.

That leaves Miranda: the wildcard. Can I plow past her the way I can with her mother, or will she be more like daddy? I'm honestly not sure. The scene she happened upon in the shed would chill anyone's blood, and at first, she reacted like any sane person would. Then she saw the ring, and maybe she even knows it's Cassie's, though I can't imagine how. Cassie wore it around her neck, too, but there's no way Miranda ever actually saw her with it. Miranda and Cassie fell out of contact when they were both little, and clearly the ring is sized for adult fingers. There's no way Cassie owned it all those years ago.

But even if Miranda knows, so what? Has she decided I'm screwing around, and cheating justifies joining the crazy crew despite her having every chance in the world to be part of the sensible side? It doesn't make sense. That's why she's a wildcard: because I think she might be crazy.

If she flips this easily, then who knows? *She* might come at me with a machete if I make a move, same as Mark did.

Hours later. I can see around the blinds that the sun's out, though it's a muted sort of sun, made soft and diffuse by the still-swirling snowstorm. I can't see outside, but there must be a foot or more of snow out there by now. Nobody's coming at this point, if only because no one can. I'm on my own. Best I make peace with that before I plan any further. Dion might work out where I went if he sees the email I tacked on the board, but Dion's also a stoner idiot. If he figures it out, he won't assume I'm in danger. And even if he *does* assume I'm in danger, he won't involve authorities because half the shit on his side of the room is illegal or contraband. I'll be saved by a flock of eagles before Dion.

It's fine. The rope is halfway cut now. It's going faster, now that I've found my rhythm. If I can get through the rest of it, I should be able to reach down and untie my legs. If I manage that soon, I think I'll just pop open the window and run. Mark leaves his car keys inside his car when he's at home or a home-substitute; I heard Willa yell at him about it. He drives a Jeep. I saw it when I came in. A Jeep might be able to get through this snow. At least I have to try.

Thinking of escape (even though a fully cut rope is still hours away) makes me almost giddy. I've forgotten what it feels like to be a normal person without all this agony, all these hideous pains. The last time I felt that way was when I rang the cabin doorbell with a big dumb smile on my face. That feels like a very, *very* long time ago. I remember being optimistic as I stood on the stoop, waiting for someone to answer. I assumed it would be Miranda. That's why I stopped along the way and bought her flowers.

But it wasn't Miranda who answered the door. It was Willa, and apparently Miranda wasn't even around. At first, I don't think Willa recognized me because the context was so wrong. Mark did, though; he rose from his chair and came right at me. But I knew ahead of time there was a chance the parents would answer. I knew they didn't like me. That's why I had a little speech prepared. I'd just tell them how I believe in old-fashioned things, and I really wanted to get parental approval now that I'm dating their daughter.

That, I see in retrospect, was my mistake: announcing that I was dating Miranda. I assumed it was old news, but no: turns out I was telling them something they didn't already know.

Goddammit, Miranda. Hiding our relationship from Mommy and Daddy like a guilty little secret, were we?

After I said Miranda and I were a couple, something changed on Mark's face. He stopped marching toward me with purpose and started *running* toward me with purpose. He pushed past his wife and punched me without preamble. I staggered; that's when I tripped over the baseball bat that'd been leaning by the door. I picked it up without thinking, but seeing me wield it only made Mark angrier.

Melee. Chasing. The machete.

Looking back, I never had a chance. Mark saw me, then immediately wanted me dead. That's how crazy this family is. And so, considering my forthcoming revenge, my attitude becomes *good fucking riddance.* Miranda wants to make me jump through hoops before she'll *refrain from torturing me* over some jealous theory she has? Screw that. Once I've cut my bonds, I'm headed for the window and then the Jeep. After that, I'm hauling ass toward the road. If I get stuck, I won't be any worse off than I am now. But if that Jeep actually makes it to the end of the driveway? If the road beyond saw even one pass by a plow?

If that happens, I'll haul ass into town. All anyone will have to do is look at me to know the Wimberlys are the bad guys. Some helpful citizen will rush me to a hospital, then send the cops here.

As soon as I get out of here, the Wimberly clan is going to fry.

I want to escape quietly ... but if they make me fight, I'll fight. I might even enjoy it. Might even be *hoping* they try to stop me. I'll turn the tables. Do to them some of what they've done to me.

Who would blame me?

Who would arrest me, if I kill my captors while fighting back?

Chapter Twenty-Six
AUBREY

The vehicle I'm driving is called a Polaris. The plow driver's cousin — Charlie, her name was — told me that as long as I returned the thing intact, she'd only charge me for gas. I left my driver's license, a credit card, and the keys to my Camry, and no matter how charitable she's feeling, I'm going to pay her heaps when this is over. She's still taking a big leap, trusting me in this weather.

I couldn't stop thanking her. It doesn't matter that her father's bait-and-hunt shop rents vehicles like this all the time or that I offered to pay her price. It doesn't matter that in all this blizzard, nobody else was going to rent the ride I've taken anyway. What matters is that when I needed help most, someone believed me.

It's simple, Charlie told me. *Key to turn it on. Gas and brake. If you can drive a car, you can drive this. Just make sure you turn it off when you get to where you're going. Wouldn't do for the battery to die and leave you stranded.*

The Polaris is as easy to drive as Charlie promised. It's lighter than my car, but a lot more sure-footed. The model I took, unlike some of the others her father had for rent, has been fitted with big snow treads like a snowmobile's and has two extra gas cans strapped in the back. Unlike a snowmobile, though, it's got an enclosed cab and a heater, although the heater doesn't work that well. Charlie said it'll do forty or so on hardpack with the treads, probably closer to twenty in fluffy snow like we've got. It's going to take me a bit to reach the cabin, but at least now I've got some confidence I'll get there.

Abby looks at me from the bumpy passenger seat. The personality hair over her eyes forms an emo curtain — perfect for the concern in her big brown eyes.

"*Gallagher,*" she tells me.

"I know."

"*Monkwort.*"

"I said I know!"

I don't really need a backseat (or, in Abby's case, passenger seat) driver right now. The Polaris is a much better snow vehicle than my Camry, but that doesn't mean I'm relaxed. Every muscle from my scalp down to the tips of my fingers is working overtime, bracing me for what feels like an inevitable slide or collision, treads or no treads. I hope that doesn't happen. Charlie told me that unlike the main roads I've driven so far, the smaller roads between the gas station and Miranda's cabin aren't maintained when the snow starts falling. The plows don't even try. After the snow ends and the highways are clear and salted, *then* the plows might start working up here — but until then I'm on my own: one lonely idiot and her dog going up the country in a suicide run.

Charlie gave me an extra coat, hat, and heavy gloves, and she even had a pile of blankets in which Abby's cocooned herself in the passenger-side footwell. If we get stuck, though, the extra warmth will only delay the inevitable. If I go off the road up here, no friendly plow driver will come along to help me out. We'll just have to hole up and pray. Vainly, I suspect.

Abby seems to be thinking about saying more, but she keeps her silence and lowers her head. I should have brought a ball for her to chew on. She loves balls, but they're also her pacifier. Chewing on balls is a way for her (but unfortunately not me) to find calm.

The digital speedometer says 22 mph, about as predicted.

My mind goes to Miranda's last text, to which I've been unable to respond. Texts don't go through. Calls bounce. Obviously.

Please. It's life and death.

Twenty-two miles per hour. Whatever's going on up there, I can only hope I make it in time.

THE WINDSHIELD IS A SHOWER OF ALL-WHITE CONFETTI — A snow rave thrown by a colorblind party planner. To see the road, I have to ignore the huge flakes close to my face and somehow see *through* them, wholesale, to the vista ahead. It's not easy. I can't focus for long, and it's giving me a headache.

Keep going, Aubrey. Miranda's counting on you.

It's all that keeps me driving. Even though the few houses along the road seem to have lost power, they pull me like beacons. Inside, those powerless places are still warmer than where I am. Soon, there won't be any houses at all. I scouted the place ahead of time on Google Earth, and up in Miranda's neck of the woods, all I could see were trees.

It's a lonely thought. I push it out of my head. My focus wanders from the road, and soon enough I'm thinking about Miranda's plea again.

Please. It's life and death.

What could possibly be life and death, but also something she didn't want to say over text? If someone was hurt, she'd say so. She'd tell me to call 911.

I can't say why on a phone. Don't tell anyone else.

When do people clam up? I ask myself. When do people refuse to talk where they might be overheard or overseen? The answer's easy: *When they've done something wrong. When they want to keep a secret, because the secret might hurt them or someone they care about.* Is it possible that's it, that once again, Miranda is covering for her asshole boyfriend? Did something go bad, and Miranda's worried that if the cops come, Ross will be in trouble? If that's it, I'll be pissed. Ross *is* the trouble. If I'm risking life and limb and it turns out it's *him* I'm saving, I'm seriously going to blow a gasket.

I just don't know. I don't know and I can't find out ... and yet here I am about to burst into some clusterfuck without a clue what it is. They don't know I'm coming. Probably only Miranda knows I'm even supposed to call.

Please. It's life and death.

All I can do is keep the road ahead of me, watch the maddeningly slow progress of the odometer, and wait to find out.

MY EYES TICK TO THE DASHBOARD. I HAVEN'T BEEN PAYING attention to what's there other than noting my speed once in a while (25 mph seems to be the max I'm going to get) for two reasons. The first is that my borrowed coat has a huge, fur-lined anorak hood that I've kept up because the Polaris's heater is either on the fritz or not that great to begin with, and seeing past the hood gives me tunnel vision. The second reason is that over the past half-hour, I've become terrified to take my eyes off the road. I'm on the final leg now, and I might as well be a polar explorer breaking new ground. The so-called "road" feels more like a suggestion than anything official. I'm aiming for the spots ahead where there are no trees, hoping that's close enough.

While the road's been busy vanishing beneath all this untrodden, unplowed, undifferentiated white, the shoulder on my left side has been busy becoming a deep valley. I've got the vehicle as far to the right as I dare, but even so, the drop-off feels uncomfortably close. For short stretches — probably places where the folks who made the road two hundred years ago ran into too much rock to pick-axe through — the path is only one car wide. If I encounter an oncoming driver in those places, I'll have to finagle backward or forward until I find one of the designated spots they've cleared to pull off the road. There aren't many pull-offs, but I think it's because there aren't many people on these roads even in summertime.

I'm not really at risk of needing to pull over and let someone pass. I've seen nobody and expect to see nobody. That makes driving more straightforward, but it's far from good news. If I slip into the ravine, it'll be weeks before anyone finds me.

Abby dog-mumbles from the footwell. I wish she'd stop staring at me like I'm holding her hostage.

I'm wearing Charlie's huge gloves, so the reason my hands feel numb must be the tension in them, not the temperature. I'm gripping the wheel so hard, I half expect to break it. My neck hurts from holding it perfectly, unnaturally still. I must be doing something with my face the whole time — grimacing with concentration, perhaps — because even my headache has a headache. Atop all of that, my eyes hurt from the glare. The snow's falling steadily enough to block most of the sun, but it's still there, probably as high in the sky as it's going to get.

What time is it getting to be, anyway? I'd look at my phone's clock if I wasn't terrified of driving into the ravine. It feels like I've been at this forever. I spent my Saturday morning in a fleabag motel, nearly died by the side of the road, then started doing the insane thing I'm doing right now ... so, I figure several months have passed since this morning, right?

Five minutes further on, the road tilts uphill. Alarmingly, my treads don't dig in right away, raking the ice beneath the snow before finally catching. The treads are far superior to my tires (daresay I'd be dying by now, if I'd taken the Camry), but suddenly it's hitting me that they're not infallible. Not when the vehicle is heavy enough to sink all the way down to a hard and slippery surface instead of churning its way through pliable snow and dirt, anyway.

The treads' hesitation lasts only a second, but it makes my heart slam in my chest. It slams harder when a second patch of ice causes the left tread to spin while the right one keeps its traction. During that harrowing moment, uneven propulsion turns the nose of the vehicle toward the drop-off. I slam the breaks, slide another few inches, then overcorrect by terrifying instinct. Soon I'm fishtailing. Who knew you could fishtail in a tank?

Easy, I tell myself after I finally bring the Polaris to rest. *Just go slow. Your vehicle was made for this.*

I take another deep breath to steady myself. Before putting the Polaris in reverse and pressing the accelerator (I figure it's best to point the nose *away* from the cliff before proceeding), I peek at the dashboard I've been ignoring. The speedometer says zero, of course, but it's another dial that catches my eye.

The gas gauge has gone all the way down to E. Beside it, a little orange light has illuminated — the light that says, *Hey dummy — you're about to run dry.*

My heart threatens to speed up again, but there's no need for that. I'm carrying extra gas. Based on my map, Charlie said she thought I could get to the cabin okay without refueling, but it looks like I wasn't that lucky. Pouring gas into the tank *after* reaching the cabin would have been better than filling up roadside, but oh well. Just one more hardiness test for Good Ol' Aubrey.

I sigh. I wish I was new to this kind of thing, but thanks to Dad, I'm not. He made me capable of anything, just by never being there to help me out.

The gas cans match the Polaris as if they came with it. They're the 5-gallon flat kind that look more like giant plastic cereal boxes than rusty cylinders. Both are held fast by thick rubber straps with fat tabs on the end, and you secure them by slotting the tabs into recessed notches on one side of the trunk. Even though I watched Charlie load the cans, I'm somehow sure they'll turn out to be empty. They aren't, though. That's just paranoia, threatening again to undo me.

The gas cans share a pair of rubber straps, both held in place by the same set of restraints. I pop out one rubber strap, then the other. The first can slides free, tips over, and slaps the cargo bed of the Polaris with a hearty thump. That's when I finally notice how much my hands are shaking. I try to control them, but I can't.

It's because I'm cold. That's all it is.

Oh, bullshit, I think. *It's because you're* scared, *girl; that's what's going on. You've been scared for more than a day now — 24 bona fide hours of fright. Or maybe longer than that, because let's admit it: Your decision to run up here alone wasn't based on logic. It wasn't even based on a desire not to spend winter break with Mom and Dad. Now that we're up here alone together,* the sensible person inside me says, *maybe it's time we face some facts you've thus far been avoiding. You're here because of pattern recognition and stupidity: pattern recognition because that detective mind of yours has known something's wrong for a while now, even though you still can't say what exactly it is. And stupidity, because...*

Well, I don't really need my skeptic to complete that one, do I?

Personally — and with no offense intended to the voices in my head — I'd use the word "dedicated" instead of "stupid." Other words I prefer include "insistent," "single-minded," or even "stubborn." I knew without asking that the creeping feeling I've had ever since Miranda sent me the pictures someone's been sending her meant something, but because I couldn't articulate *what* it meant, I knew I couldn't ask anyone else to help me. I've spent my life being the way I am, so I've learned what's worth sharing with others and what's not. Rallying support and assistance based on "a strange feeling that nobody else thinks is strange"? That's *never* been worth sharing. I've learned not to bother asking. Now, I just pattern-match beneath the level of conscious awareness ... and if something seems amiss, I don't plan and I don't ask. I just *do.*

But yes. I'm scared. I'm *very* scared. Thinking it now makes the emotion double back on itself like its own support team, making my fear even worse. This is why I haven't let myself see it before now. Back when I could still give up and go home, fear might have stopped me. That would be unacceptable, because I'm certain help is needed.

I focus on my shaking hands. They shake less, but don't come close to stopping.

"No point in chickening out now," I tell the whistling wind while Abby, on the seat now, watches me. "The way back isn't any shorter than the way there."

I'm not sure if that's true, but it seems true. I'm reasonably certain the station where I met Charlie is the same one from which Miranda called me on her way up. She said she had a half-hour left from there, but that was a dry-road estimate. Over winding roads, I'm guessing a half-hour by Miranda time meant twenty miles or so. According to the trip odometer, I've already gone twelve. My 22-

mph clip has been woefully inconsistent, and I've had to steer around some big drifts, so those twelve miles took about an hour. With the weather and roads both worsening by the minute, eight miles might take an additional hour. I can already see the way drifts ahead have turned the nice, mostly flat slope of the road into topography that looks like wedges laid on their sides. Charlie tossed a snow shovel into the back "just in case." I'm glad now that she did, seeing as I might have to dig through some of those drifts before I can drive.

It won't be another hour if that's true, says that annoying voice inside me. *If you have to dig as much as it looks like you will, it could be two hours. Or three.*

I look behind me, wondering if twelve miles back to the station is any smarter. It's not, because now that the wind's picked up, those same drifts are behind me, too. I'm screwed no matter what I do. Stranded in the middle of nowhere in a winter storm, hours from rest and assistance.

I stand tall, trying to summon courage. Still forcing my hands not to shake, I reach for the toppled can.

A Polaris gets good mileage, Charlie told me. *In dry weather, one gallon of gas would probably get you where you're going. In this, maybe two gallons. Between the two cans, you've got ten gallons. I'd fill the tank for you, but our pump's frozen up. Normally my dad'd take a torch to it to unfreeze it, but that's not such a great idea with gasoline. The tank's low, but I'd guess there's at least a gallon in there, probably more. In your shoes, I'd go now instead of filling it up here. If you can get to your friend's place without opening one of the cans, maybe they've got gas to fuel you coming back.*

Why go to all the trouble? I asked. *Why not just pour one of the cans into the tank now?*

Because gas is gold in this weather, Charlie said. *The more you can keep in reserve, the better.*

I pull the can toward me. She was saying that the weather out here is so dangerous, I'd be wise to use any other source of gas and consider the cans only in case of emergency. If I can make it to the cabin without refueling, it would be better to ask Miranda for a fill-up than deplete what I've got.

I remove the cap and lift the can, then realize I haven't opened the Polaris's gas tank yet. I set the can in the snow and do so. That's when I realize the place I've parked has much worse traction than I thought it did, because treads or not, the Polaris starts to skid on the ice bed beneath the snow. First, it's just a creaking inch. Then it's six more.

"No no no no ..."

Something breaks free. I rush to follow, tripping over the gas can and kicking it onto its side as I scramble after my vehicle. The slope beneath me is slight, but it's plenty slippery for treads to slide on ice — especially because I now see that up ahead, wind has scoured away the snow and left solid ice as the driving surface. Soon the Polaris is picking up speed, making its way forward. I can see Abby inside, wondering why she's leaving without me. She's standing up, walking around, wanting nothing more than to come out here and join me. Doesn't matter whether it's better inside or out; Abby always, *always* needs to be by me. It's pathological.

"NONONONONO!"

I grab the flopped-down tail gate, deluded somehow into thinking I can hold on, dig in my heels, and stop the slide with force. I'm immediately disabused of the notion, the pebbly surface of the bedliner-coated gate ripping at the fabric of my gloves as the machine slips right through them. I've still got the ravine to my left, running in short, precise steps so I don't slide into it. But I've got another problem now, much bigger than my slipping: If *I* fall, I might be able to catch myself because the ravine is deep but not too steep. The same can't be said for the Polaris, though. And if *it* goes into the ravine? Well, that wouldn't be good.

"GODDAMMIT STOP YOU PIECE OF SHIT!"

Abby's on her feet, watching me through the back window. She's wagging nervously, trying to understand.

Throwing caution to the whooping polar wind, I rush around the left side of the vehicle as best I can, sure I'll fall down the hill any minute. I don't, though; I reach the door and pull it open. I have to shove Abby away as she tries to come at me.

My left-side tread begins to skirt the drop off. I'm still hanging halfway out, knowing I'm out of time. I tense my body, stabbing at the brake with one foot while I turn the wheel with the other. It's a complicated maneuver, seeing as my butt is outside the cab rather than in its seat where it belongs.

It's a near thing. I'm hanging out like a stuntwoman, my world full of the sounds of chaos and rattling. I think to look back, hearing the smooth sliding of plastic on bedliner, and watch helplessly as my second gasoline can slips past the lift gate and off the rear. I wonder if I should hop back out and go after it, but then the decision is taken out of my hands.

The can hits the ground once, then rebounds sideways. I watch it bounce all the way down into the valley until it's out of sight, somehow irrationally sure it'll blow up when it reaches the bottom. But I can't mourn that can. I can't even take the time to see where it might have gone, and I already know the driving wind will erase its path almost immediately. I still have a vehicle to wrangle ... and so I do, throwing myself into the cab so that my momentum — not really my strength — forces the wheel to turn.

The front treads catch. The slide arrests and then changes direction. As before, in my Camry, I'm swung hard to one side. The Polaris heads back onto the road instead of into the ditch, and seconds later we come to a sudden but soft stop in a windshield-high snowdrift.

"*Sandile*," Abby says, deeply bothered by what's just happened.

"No shit," I tell her.

It takes fifteen or twenty seconds for the shakes to hit me, but when they come, they come hard. Suddenly everything I've been holding back hits me all at once. I almost sent my dog tumbling down a hillside. I almost fell down one myself. I nearly lost my ride, the only thing keeping me from freezing — literally, maybe, because there's not a house in sight. It's not even the first time those things have nearly happened today. I almost died (or was stranded, leading to death) twice before now. That doesn't even account for the bad tidings I'm rushing to Miranda to help with in the first place. She herself said it was life and death.

I hug Abby hard. I think I cry a while, though it's hard to say.

The heater is still running. We could just stay here, in our little cabin with an engine, until this whole bad dream blows away.

Except no. Because gas.

That snaps me out of it. The engine is still idling, wasting fuel. In my mind's eye, I watch the black plastic can as it tumbled its way down the slope, sure already that it's not worth trying to find it — and definitely not to rappel down and recover it if I could.

Not wanting to risk the ice we've just come through, I carefully retrace my steps. Abby, still in the vehicle, protests — unwilling as always to be more than ten feet away from me.

I march toward where I left the first gasoline can — the one I was preparing to pour into the tank when this whole thing started. I try to remind myself what Charlie said, about how a single gallon of gas would probably get me where I wanted to be. I've still got five gallons left, and I can siphon gas at Miranda's even if they don't have a can.

"I'll be okay," I say aloud. "I'll be fine."

The wind steals my words before I can hear them. It's like talking with earplugs in. It's mockery, I'm sure: nature saying that I can keep telling myself whatever I'd like — any pretty lies, in all this snow, to make myself feel better.

"I will," I say, as if the wind cares.

I stop when I step on something that feels too artificial to be a rock. Curious, I duck down and brush away the snow.

It's the gas cap. Not the one to the Polaris, because that one's on a short strap so it can't get lost. No, this is the cap from the gas can. I remember now: I removed it before realizing I still had to open the Polaris's tank, then set it on the deck for safekeeping.

Oh no. Oh God. There's no lid on the gas can.

My head whips forward, eyes scanning for the black, rectangular specter of the can. I don't see it at first, but then I do. It's a travel can, made with a low profile. Low profile means it's tall but narrow. And what do I remember feeling when I started to chase the Polaris? Oh, right. I remember the feel of my foot, kicking the thing over.

I rush forward. I find the can fifteen feet ahead, lying on its side.

The snow beside it reeks of fumes, its color amber and mostly melted. A crazy part of me wonders if I can still use the spilled gas by scooping up the snow. It's just got a little extra water in it now, right?

I pick up the can. It lifts sickeningly easily — not the heavy burden it was when I pulled it off the deck.

My stomach plummets. I shake the can, then look inside. The lip around the spout saved a cup or three from spilling, but that's about it.

I return to the Polaris feeling like the walking dead. I pour what's left in the can into the tank and re-cap it. When I restart the engine, I find that the amount I've added at least turned off the low-gas warning light, but not by much. On and off already, the light flickers as if just waiting to come back on.

I want to give up. I want to cry. All the gas I have is now in the tank, and already it's almost out again.

I drive on. Maybe I'll make those last eight miles or so, or maybe I won't. All I know for sure is that I'm on my last strike ... and if my gas runs out, I'll die.

Chapter Twenty-Seven
CASSIE

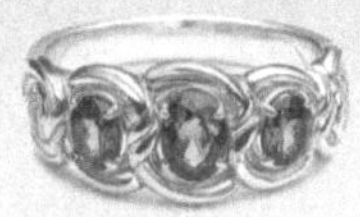

TWO MONTHS AGO

"So what you're saying," Miranda tells Aubrey with a dramatically raised eyebrow, "is that you were wrong."

"I wasn't wrong."

Miranda puts a hand on her chin and bobs her head, acting like she's trying to understand something complicated. "Okay. So you were *right?* Your suspicions that your mom has a gambling problem and blew the rent money were *spot on?*"

"Shut up."

"I'm just saying. It's *gotta* be the second one, right? Because this is *you* we're talking about. This is *Aubrey.* Aubrey's *never* wrong when she starts climbing up everyone's butt and following a series of clues ... *right?*"

Aubrey crosses her arms. "I said shut up."

Miranda smirks. She won't shut up and she'll never let it go — not now that we have a chance to rub Aubrey's irritating habit right back in her face. Neither of us cared about her recent quest to bust her mother, but that doesn't mean we won't make fun of her until she can't stand it anymore now that the quest has hit a dead end.

Doing so is symbolic. But it sets precedent for the future. It was

Aubrey's mom in the crosshairs this time, but it's been Miranda before ("The Case of Who Stole Aubrey's Last Chicken Strip at Dinner on Tuesday") and *of course* it's been me. When we first reacquainted last month, there was a moment where Miranda seemed sure I had my hooks in her boyfriend — that while we were estranged, Ross and I got closer than Miranda would like. Turns out, Aubrey took Miranda's case without anyone asking her to, poking around in my business until she decided that either 1) I *wasn't* actually after Ross or 2) I was hiding it well enough that even Aubrey's inner Holmes got stumped. Apparently, both were acceptable, though I'm pretty sure Sherlock would never settle for a draw. Personally, I think Aubrey just got to like me during her investigation and gave me a pass. It's no fun busting a friend.

"Aubrey was right," Miranda says to me, rubbing it in. "She's always right, isn't she, Cass? We're so lucky to have her. Without Aubrey's crack skills, everyone around here would get away with everything. Thank God we have someone with such perspicacity in our midst."

"What's perspicacity?" Aubrey asks.

"I don't know," Miranda counters. "Why don't you start an investigation and find out?"

Aubrey throws her pillow. Miranda, who saw it coming, deflects with one of her roommate Suni's pillows. The thrown pillow deflects and lands on Aubrey's dog Abby, who thinks it's a game and begins to wag her entire back half. I've never seen a dog so exuberant or flexible. When she gets excited, she wags hard enough that she sometimes hits herself in the face with her own butt. Girl could be a contortionist.

Laughter begins. It takes long minutes to peter out, and when it does, we're all staring at the ceiling: Aubrey on her bed, Miranda on Suni's bed, and me on the floor atop the pillows they've already fired as spent ammunition.

There's a quiet moment, and then Aubrey says, "I guess my mom's not a degenerate gambler after all. I got confused because she sucks in so many other ways."

"At least she doesn't care what you do with your life," Miranda says.

"Yeah, that's a great trait in a parent," Aubrey replies. "Apathy."

"Hey, it's better than micromanagement. Trust me."

Aubrey rolls onto one side, engaging fully. "Okay. You want to play this game? Is that seriously what you want?"

"What game?" I ask.

Aubrey doesn't seem to hear me. She tells Miranda, "Before I left for school, my mom said, 'Don't bother coming back if the Devil turns you into a whore.'"

"Woah," Miranda says. "Warm up with some gunplay first, will you? Don't start by dropping a nuke."

"You think *that's* a nuke?" Aubrey laughs. "Oh, how little you know, my friend."

"You want *me* to start pulling nukes?"

Aubrey laughs harder. "Oh, like *you* have nukes."

I sit up. With the beds they occupy on opposite sides of the room, my spot on the floor puts me right in the middle. "What are you guys talking about?" I ask.

"Oh, I *have* nukes," Miranda tells Aubrey, still ignoring me.

"Please. What nukes do you have?"

"My mom retracted my Fordham application after I submitted it," Miranda says. "She rewrote my essay."

"Oh, boo hoo."

"She rewrote so that it was all about 'conservative family values.' It contains the line, 'It's time we give America back to Americans.'"

"No way," Aubrey says.

"Way. And I mean, I guess there's no *overt* racism or queerphobia in 'my' revised essay, but I *was* courted by the skinheads after getting settled."

"There are no skinheads."

"Oh, there are skinheads," Miranda says.

I'm still confused. Finally Aubrey takes pity. "It's something we do sometimes," she explains. "It's called Butthole Roulette."

"Nothing to do with roulette, though," says Miranda.

"Also, it's only about *one* kind of butthole. Not just any butthole. Parental buttholes."

"It's a working title," Miranda says.

"So it's just basically bitching about your parents," I clarify.

"Everyone 'bitches about their parents,'" says Aubrey. *"Amateurs* 'bitch about their parents.'"

"This is next level," Miranda explains.

"Total warfare."

"Because my parents are so much worse than Miranda's, it's a joke."

"Or so *Aubrey* says," Miranda tells me, eyeing her friend, "because *she's* never lived with such masters of passive aggressiveness."

Aubrey rolls her eyes. "Oh, right. It must be so terrible to have parents who actually care what happens to you. I'm sorry you've had to live under so much proper guidance."

"You wouldn't call it 'guidance' if you had to deal with it."

Aubrey scoffs.

"You'd call it what it is," Miranda goes on. *"'Control.'* I don't think you had it so bad, Aubrey. Sure, your parents didn't pay attention to you, but at least that means you can vanish and never hear from them again."

"Oh, I'll *hear* from them no matter what I do," Aubrey counters. "All my life, I'll hear and hear and hear."

"Yeah, but you could change your phone number and move away. They won't expend the effort to find you. You're already self-sufficient, so who cares? It's not like your mom and dad are going to get off their Barcaloungers and chase you. One quick cutting of ties and then you'll be free forever. My parents, on the other hand..."

"What about them?" I ask. I was eight when I last interacted with Mr. and Mrs. Wimberly. Other than Mark beating Frank nearly to death, they seemed okay. Miranda even said her dad's not drinking anymore.

"Oh. Cassie. You have no idea."

"I know I have no idea. That's why I asked."

"They're *interested* in her," Aubrey explains, indicating Miranda. "Terrible, isn't it?"

"They're not *interested in me*," Miranda says, staring Aubrey down. "They're trying to *sculpt* me into the perfect embodiment of what they think a 'proper daughter' should be."

"Whereas all mine did was to completely ignore me, forcing me to fend for myself."

"And now you're eighteen. Now you're free."

Aubrey laughs. "Oh, their abandoning *me* doesn't mean I'm allowed to abandon *them*. To thank them for all their years of neglect, I'm supposed to spend my adult life taking care of them. They're glad I'm in college. You know — the college I paid for by myself? They don't *seem* glad because they spend so much time telling me I'm only here to have sex and drink and generally pave my path to Hell, but they know it'll pay off when I have a higher salary for them to mooch off of."

"True," Miranda says. "At least I'm not going to Hell. At least I'm not a Jezebel."

I sit up straighter, setting my pillows aside. "I want to play."

"Oh, such a nice girl, Cassie," says Miranda. "You don't want to sully yourself with our dirty parental skirmish."

"Sully?" I say. "You're assuming I won't just annihilate you."

Aubrey and Miranda exchange a look. "Look who's talking a big game," Miranda says to Aubrey.

"Thinks she can hang with the big dogs," Aubrey replies. "How cute."

"Look, I don't want to have to do this," I say, "but my dad used to get violent." It's heavy, but I say it lightly. This is just a game with a dark sense of humor, after all.

"Used to?"

"He's dead," Miranda tells Aubrey. "I told you that."

"Didn't your dad beat Cassie's dad up when he was drunk?" Aubrey asks.

"No, he was sober at the time," I say.

"I meant *Miranda's* dad was drunk."

"Oh, right," Aubrey says. "I confused one drunken assault with another drunken assault. I keep forgetting how many champions the three of us had as parents."

"My dad never assaulted anyone while he was drunk," I say. "That's how you can tell them apart."

"Well," Miranda says. "Except assaulting *you*."

She probably shouldn't have said that. It's incredibly personal and incredibly offensive. But that's the name of this game, right? *Maximal parental offensiveness?* Aubrey already told us her mom said not to come home if she became a whore. It's like one of those gross-out games, except replacing "gross" with "terrible, scarring, and child-endangering."

I shouldn't laugh at what Miranda said, but I do. It's about time all the terrible things in my past were used for something positive. Dark humor for the win.

"I've got scars to prove it, bitches," I say.

There's a long beat of silence. Then, unable to believe I just turned a lifetime of abuse into a joke, they both explode with ashamed laughter.

"Seriously, though," Miranda tells Aubrey when it's over.

"Seriously?" Aubrey says. She's rolling with the punches, but before now she's only heard my backstory secondhand.

"Seriously," I say. "Although technically, Frank was my stepfather. I called him 'Dad,' though."

Miranda shifts on the bed, coming up on one elbow. "I didn't know that back then. Growing up, I thought he *was* your dad."

"Nope. I never knew my dad." The fun evaporates as if it was never there, and suddenly I'm looking at the floor, drawing patterns in the all-purpose carpet. A cloud of melancholy forms above me, as out-of-the-blue as a sudden summer storm. It doesn't rain sadness on me, not yet. I feel its presence just the same. "Never got in touch. Mom wouldn't talk about it. I think she knows stuff, though. I ... I get the feeling that under different circumstances, things might have been different for me."

From the corner of my eyes, I see Miranda and Aubrey exchange a glance. I feel bad; I know I just ruined their game. We all had bad parents. For a while, it's fun to laugh about it, to pretend it doesn't hurt. Aubrey's are angry layabouts with hardline religion. Miranda's are serious helicopter parents, and that's the best-case scenario, when Mark's not busy drinking. Even Ross had it bad, never knowing his dad in the way I never knew mine. I don't want to make myself special, seeing as everybody hurts.

I try to fight the cloud that's forming, but it seems this was all it took to provoke the catharsis I've worked so hard to prevent. I can feel it coming. If I don't dodge quickly, it's all going to come out here and now. I don't want that. Poor Aubrey is new to me. I don't want her saddled with this.

"It's fine," I say, refusing to wipe my eyes because I know what it'll look like.

A hand rests on my back. I'd expect it to be Miranda's, but it's actually Aubrey. "If your dad left and never looked back, you're probably better off without him."

"That's just it," I say. "He didn't get in touch, but I think it was only because my mom wouldn't let him, not because he didn't want to. Because ... see ... he gave me this ring..."

All at once, the dam breaks. There's no warning. One moment, I feel fully in control — fully able to explain to Aubrey that no, I know my father wasn't a total deadbeat and I have evidence to prove it — but then the next moment there's no control at all. All I had to do was voice that one word. All I had to say was *ring*.

Suddenly I'm sobbing. Sobbing and sobbing and sobbing: one of those runaway crying jags that feels like it'll never end. It's not just my parents. It's not just the memory. There's something else here, buried as if it might magically stay that way. Something I never talked about. Something, truth be told, that I never even admitted — not even to myself.

"Shh." Now it's Miranda who's at my side with her arm around me, offering comfort and suppressing alarm. "It's okay."

"It's not okay. *I'm* not okay."

I can't see her face, but I'm sure she just looked at Aubrey very seriously. I know how this must seem. They're concerned, but they're probably also afraid.

All thoughts of hiding what's now trying to emerge from within me vanish. It's like a birth whose time has come: You can't just clench really tight, trying to stop the inevitable. This should have come out years ago. Now, it's coming whether I want it to or not.

The thought makes me cry harder. My stomach hurts; I feel hollow all the way to my core. It dawns on me how hard I've worked to repress this. Three years ago, my attitude soured, and I started wearing black, started looking down when I walked and pushed away those who wanted to be close to me. It was the only way I could hold my armor. The only way I could go on pretending nothing had changed. If I admitted the truth, I'd have to admit that what happened to me was real, not just a mistake or misunderstanding. Denial was my shield ... but I can't hold it now.

And so by degrees, I tell them both. I tell them how, three years ago, I went to a sophomore party, laughed and danced and stayed up too late, then woke in the morning with a bastard of a hangover with no idea how the previous night ended. There was just one problem: I don't drink. Never have. I greeted the day in a spare bedroom of the host's house, sore and bleeding below the waist. I told myself I was just forgetful. I told myself I got a contact high from all the weed in the air — weed I didn't actually smoke. *That's* why I woke up with my panties missing and no clue who did it to me.

I had a bunch of pretty serious-looking bruises on my side, so my overprotective mother made me go to an Urgent Care. I never told her what the doctor suspected after she examined me. Instead, I told her some drunk guy got to roughhousing. That's how I got all those bruises.

"Jesus, Cass," Miranda says when I'm finished telling the story — once my agitation's dropped a few notches. "Didn't the doctor have to report it, if you were raped?"

I shrug, then blow my nose. "I told her not to. I said I had sex with someone that night, and we were playing rough. I told the doctor my mom would kill me if she found out, so please don't tell her. Maybe they're supposed to say something to the parents in a case like that — I was only sixteen, after all — but I guess I made a pretty good case. A *really* good case. I don't know if this makes any sense, but I *couldn't let* it be true. Like, for my own protection, you know? I wasn't just telling the doctor a story. I was telling the same story to *myself*, and that meant I had to do all I could to make it sound like a real story. So for instance, they drew blood when I went in. I knew someone drugged me because I didn't remember what happened, so I got ahead of it and invented an excuse. Before the doctor could ask me about the drugs in my system, I told her that we were *taking* drugs. On purpose. I told her I must have overdone it. Took a little too much Ecstasy, even though I've never done a drug in my life. I don't like the idea of altered states. I like — I *need*, after Frank and his beatings — to feel like I'm always in control."

New tears come. I wipe them away, angry that they keep returning.

"I couldn't let it be true," I repeat. "I couldn't be the girl who went to a party, drank something that someone must've given me, and woke up the next day not remembering. The reality of it was so disturbing, I had to fight it. Had to deny it. So I lied."

"But you think the doctor knew?"

My head bobs. "She knew. But since I didn't know who did it and wouldn't press charges anyway (because if I pressed charges, I'd have to admit it happened), she let it go. Or *sort of* let it go. A really nice policeman came in to see me while I was there, careful not to let my mother see him. That happened because the one thing I *do* remember, and mentioned to the doctor, was a really vivid dream where I stabbed someone with a pen. I don't think it was actually a dream. I think that when the guy started pushing me down, I pushed back. I think that's why I have the bruises: because he didn't like that very much. I think I stabbed him with a pen, because it's all I could reach." I touch the outside of my thigh. "Here."

Miranda and Aubrey wait for me to go on. Their eyes tick to the closed door, hoping Aubrey's roommate won't return before this is over.

"The policeman was really diplomatic. I think he understood how it was for me, not wanting to remember but still maybe wanting something to be done about it. He said that a few of the doctors were out in the other room talking about me: my doctor telling a few of the others. Saying, 'Hey, there's this girl in my exam room, and she was drugged and raped, but she won't admit it.' There's nothing they can do in a case like that, but they wanted to — they *really, really* wanted to. The cop didn't work at the Urgent Care and they didn't call him in. He said he was visiting Mercy General, which is attached to the clinic. He was there to see a friend who'd been shot a few days earlier, and one of the doctors asked if he wouldn't mind talking to me. So he did. But he was really cool about it. Asked if I could weigh in on a 'case.' That's the word he used: 'a case.' He said there might be someone around who got stabbed in the leg with a pen at the same party I attended. Would I by chance know anything about it? Because it'd really help him out."

I laugh, but it's bitter.

"As if the pen-stabbing was a big crime and my intel might help crack it," I say. "Oh, but I went right along with it. I let myself believe that's really what he was asking, because by then my denial was in full gear. I told him I didn't know anything. Because I didn't. As far as I was concerned, I went to a party and then I fell asleep. I had a dream about some guy and a pen in the leg. Maybe I tripped over a piece of furniture and got bruised up; by then I was telling myself that, too. I just wanted to go home because it was no big deal, but unfortunately my crazy mom made me go to the clinic."

Aubrey scoots closer. "You know, there might be a record of that. Someone stabbed with a pen..."

Miranda joins in. "My parents know a doctor at Mercy General. He's like an uncle to me. If I asked, he might be able to check the records. See who came in that night to be treated for—"

"No," I say.

"But if this guy raped you."

"It was three years ago. I just want to move on."

"But what if he does it to someone else?"

I keep shaking my head. "I said no. I can't go through that again. There's nothing to be done anyway. You know how hard it is to prove a rape even right after it happens? *Three years,* guys. I didn't even let them do a pelvic exam, so there's no proof. No documented injuries other than some bruises on my side. No DNA."

"Then at least *you'd* know who it was. At least you'd have closure."

"Why?" I ask. "So I can spend the rest of my life furious at some rando from my high school, knowing I can never do anything about it?" I shake my head definitively, not bothering to add the other thing: that in a window of lucidity, I *did* later call the hospital and invent a story about a friend who'd been stabbed in the thigh with a pen, just to find out. I learned it was a quick in and out at Mercy's ER, for the guy with the stabbing. He didn't use insurance. No records were kept.

"But—!"

"*No,* Aubrey," I say, staring hard at her. *"Don't.* I know you're going to want to run off and start looking for clues, but don't. I'm serious."

Aubrey looks away.

"Aubrey? I mean it. Promise me. Promise you won't go snooping around. This is *dead and buried.* You hear me?"

Aubrey mumbles a promise. I stare at her again until she sighs, then nods more sincerely.

In the quiet that follows, I exhale loudly a few times. Then I lean myself against Aubrey's bed, trying not to think too hard about this skeleton I've let loose from my closet.

"I'm sorry," I say. "That was a heavy thing to lay on you all at once."

They trip all over themselves to tell me I shouldn't be sorry, that I should trust them and lean on them, that I shouldn't feel the need to keep secrets — especially secrets that eat me alive.

"I'm sorry anyway," I tell them. "I didn't even mean to go there. It caught me by surprise. It's just that we got to talking about my real dad, and that's emotional for me *anyway*, and..." I sigh again, surrendering.

Silence returns. Then Aubrey — who should know to let the topic rest, but who also can't help herself when there are loose ends to connect and puzzle pieces to put together — sits upright. Very subtly, Miranda's eyes tell her not to say what she's thinking ... but this is Aubrey, so she says it anyway.

"Hang on," she says. "How's *your dad* connect to *your rape?* Do you think it was somehow him who..."

I laugh a little — not at the subject, but at the absurdity of her question. "No, I don't think my birth father was at Rob DeVaney's high school kegger."

"Then why... ?"

"Oh," I say, understanding. "Because of the ring. My dad gave me a ring before I was born. Gave it to my mom to give to me later. Miranda knows all about it. I used to wear it around my neck because it never really fit my fingers. It had an inscription inside, from my real dad, saying he'd love me forever. I always used to wonder about that. If he'd *love me forever,* why wasn't he part of my life?"

"But I still don't see how that has anything to do with... ?"

My hand goes subconsciously to my chest, where for so many years I wore that ring. "Oh. I didn't say, did I? I was wearing it that night. I always wore it." I pat my shirt, where the ring used to be. "But that morning when I woke up, it was gone."

Their faces sour. It's a violation atop a violation.

"The bastard who raped me," I say, feeling a snarl form on my lips. "He took my ring too, like some sick trophy."

Chapter Twenty-Eight

MIRANDA

"Open your eyes," I say.

I don't know if Ross is actually sleeping or just pretending. He could also be passed out. If what Dad did to him with the machete — or what Dad and maybe even Mom did to him otherwise — got him infected, he'll be warm to the touch. Considering how long he's been here, he might be *hot* to the touch. Nobody will need to kill him if that's the case. If Ross has blood poisoning this far from a hospital, he's already dead.

I could easily find out if Ross has a fever. I won't, though, because it disgusts me to touch him.

I lean in. "Open your eyes, you son of a bitch, or I'll close them forever."

Ross's eyelids flicker. They open. It takes him a second to register the ring, returned to its familiar leather lanyard, because I'm holding it so close to his face. When he sees it, it's like something flying right at him. He flinches hard, rattling the headboard.

"Careful," I purr. "You might just make my decision for me."

At first, he doesn't understand. Then he does. I'm holding one of the kitchen knives to his throat. He might not be able to feel the subtle edge where it presses into the flesh just below his Adam's apple. There's not much to do up here, now that we all know the task ahead of us. I've spent most of the day making myself certain. All the while, sitting in Mom's sunroom, I've been sharpening this blade. It became a game. Could I hone the edge so finely that I could barely see it? The answer was no, of course, but by now I could slice a roast just by setting my knife on top of it.

"Miranda." His eyes are huge. His throat moves as he swallows against my knife, testing its razor-sharp edge. He looks afraid. Afraid, tired, and confused.

"Don't lie to me," I say.

"You haven't asked a question."

"Then tell me the truth. Without a question."

"What are you talking about? The truth about *what?*"

My head shakes slightly. My lips press together. The way he pretends ignorance infuriates me. I want to cut him just so he knows I'm not a fool.

"Yes. That's it," I tell him. "Make my decision easy."

Ross scoots back another inch, glares at me, and half yells: "Miranda God dammit *I don't know what you want me to say!*"

I consider his face, still pressing with my knife. Mom and Dad don't know I'm in here. I don't know how they might change whatever I'd do on my own, so I don't want them around to find out. Instead, I want this moment to be solo and therefore pure. I want to see what happens if I test Ross all on my own, without parental influence — whatever that ends up meaning.

I don't know why Dad snapped so completely on Ross, unless I know *exactly* why: He's an alcoholic; he knew the combination to the closet where the owners keep their booze and went a little bit crazy. Maybe I'm a fool for thinking there might be another explanation. Dad is kind and gentle when he's sober, but I know better than anyone that he becomes a beast when he drinks. And so maybe Dad, steeled by more secret booze, would see what I'm doing now and join me. Mom's another story. I don't know why Mom allowed Dad to do this, unless it all devolved too quickly for her to stop things until they were too far gone.

For now, it's just me and Ross. Just the two of us, having a heart to heart.

I shake the ring. I let it swing to hit him on the bridge of the nose.

"I want you to tell me where you got this."

"I told you I don't know!"

"I want you to tell me where you got it," I repeat, "and I want you to tell me of your own free will. You can keep insisting you don't know if you want, but don't think I'll believe you. Denying just insults me. It just makes me madder."

"Miranda," Ross says in his most reasonable tone of voice — the one he uses when he's being slippery, when he's trying to turn bull-shit into roses. "Look at me."

"Oh, I'm looking."

"I'm telling you the truth. I have a bunch of rings at home. I collect them. Someone found that one on the quad and gave it to me. I don't remember who, but if you can get internet service, I can find it out because I know it was someone from one of my classes and I know they asked me over email if I wanted it."

"You're lying."

"I'm not lying. You've seen my collection. It's in the box I keep by my bed. I *swear* you've opened it before. Don't you remember?"

My teeth are pressing so hard together, I think I might break them. "Stop it. *Stop trying to gaslight me.*"

"Miranda, we can still make this right. I know how it must look to you, but I swear on my life that's not how it is."

"Good," I say. "Because *your life* is exactly what's on the line."

"I told you: I can prove it."

"You *claim* you could prove it. *If* we had internet. Which you know we don't have." The lights flicker again. "Convenient, that your proof can't be accessed."

"But it's true," he says. "I promise you, with all the love in my heart, that what you're holding is just a ring to me." His eyes widen, innocent. "Why won't you tell me what it is to *you?*"

For the briefest of moments, I wonder if there's any chance that what Ross says is true. I didn't grow up around liars, so I never understand them. I'm naive in that way: willing to believe someone if they promise me hard enough, because only psychopaths will lie to your face. What if Ross didn't take the ring from Cassie and someone else did? What if whoever took the ring lost it somehow? What if, after they lost it, Ross ended up with it? It's an incredible series of coincidences, but Ross's slippery eyes swear to me that coincidence is exactly what happened.

I shake it away. I press the knife harder into his neck.

"I don't know what to do with you," I say. "My parents don't know, either."

"Then let me go. We can work it out."

"If we let you go, we put ourselves in danger. If we don't, we become murderers. I've been thinking about it all day, Ross. All day, all night, and then all day again. No matter how long I thought, there was no good answer. So I made myself a deal. I decided that if you'd at least admit what you did, we could talk. Because that way, we'd be on even footing. It'd all be out in the open. I decided, in other words, that the only *for-sure* here is that *if* you keep on lying, there's only one choice to make. And so I'd like to promise you something, while you're making all these promises to me. I promise that if you tell me the truth, maybe you'll live. I also promise you that if you don't ... you won't."

"I know you, Miranda. You're not that cold."

"And now I know *you*, Ross. I know *exactly* what you're capable of. What I need to know is whether or not you'll admit it ... or whether you'll keep hiding like a coward."

He goes still. I can tell he's taking me seriously now. He's dug in pretty deep on his lie, and because of it he's probably reluctant to change his story. But unless he's as big an idiot as he seems to think I am, he *must* know by now that I don't believe a thing he's saying. Truth is, I don't know if I can cut a man's throat in cold blood like I've threatened to do. All I can hope is that Ross doesn't force me to find out.

"Okay, okay," he says. "That's not how I got the ring. I just didn't want you to get the wrong idea."

I meet Ross's eyes. I've been turning this part of things over and over as well. As of two months ago, Cassie had told nobody about her rape — not her friends, not her parents, not her doctor ... not even herself. She's spent three years living in denial, trying to pretend it never happened. I don't think, in the past two months, that's changed.

Cassie doesn't know who raped her and hasn't tried to find out. I'm the only person who knows the story *and* that Ross has the ring. I'm the only person who knows what the ring meant before to Cassie and what it means to her now. Ross has none of that information. He took the ring while Cassie and I were estranged and can't possibly know how long she's had it ... or that I'd know it, immediately, on sight.

He can't know I know. He thinks *nobody* knows. He thinks he's safe. That's why his next words are crucial. If he actually admits what he's done, it will be voluntary: uncoerced by my knowing. Only then might I be willing to bargain with him. Only if he tells me what he doesn't know I *already* know will I consider letting him go.

"It's Cassie's."

"And?"

"She gave it to me. As a friend."

"Bullshit."

"It's not bullshit. Wait until the snow melts, then drive out and ask her."

"You're just stalling for time. You're saying that because you know I can't call her now."

"That's not how it is."

"What would you say if I told you I *already know* whether she gave it to you or not?"

Uncertainty enters Ross's expression. "What do you mean?"

I pinch the ring's band between my thumb and forefinger, letting the leather necklace hang. I hold it in front of Ross's eyes.

"Cassie's had this ring since she was born. You made a big mistake, taking something so significant as your trophy."

"*Trophy?* What do you mean, trophy?"

"After you raped her."

His whole demeanor changes. He goes from afraid to somehow aghast. If he's lying to me now, he deserves an Academy Award.

"What the hell are you talking about? I'd never rape anyone!"

"She told me the story."

"Then she's full of shit! I never touched her!"

"Never?"

"Fine! Fine! We made out! It was long before we started going out! Years after she moved away! How the fuck was I supposed to know you'd have a problem with it?"

"With rape?"

"I DIDN'T RAPE HER!"

"Just stole her ring, huh? Then lied to me about it?"

"I lied because I knew you'd react like you're reacting right now! You want to call people psychos, Miranda? How about you look in a mirror?"

My insides boil. Emotions roil like ingredients intermingling in a stew. He's so irate. So convincing. Yet I know. I know what's true.

Too little, though, says the nagging voice in my head. *Too little and too late. Here we are again, reacting to danger long after it's over — right, Miranda? Everyone knows how jealous you get. Is it really so impossible to believe he lied because he's afraid of you?*

"Don't," says a male voice.

I look back. It's my father. He's at the door. It's still swinging behind him, so I know he hasn't been there long.

"Don't believe him, Miranda."

My head whips back and forth, looking from one man I don't believe to another. Ross is lying about the ring and about Cassie. Dad, though, has spent his life lying to me about drink and what it does to him.

"Why did you do this, Dad?" I say, more confused than ever.

"Because he deserved it. Because he's a danger to my little girl."

"I'm not your little girl," I say, trying not to see the way our conflict gives Ross an encouraged expression. "I can take care of myself."

"You don't know what's going on here, Miranda."

"Dammit, Dad. Stop babying me. I know. *I know!*"

He's calm, nowhere near aggressive. "You don't. Not really."

"Have you been drinking?"

"No."

"You're lying."

"Of course he's lying!" says Ross.

I swing around so fast with my knife, I almost eviscerate him by accident. *"YOU SHUT UP! SHUT YOUR FUCKING MOUTH!"*

"I'm not lying, Miranda," Dad says from my other side. "My name's Mark and I'm an alcoholic. It's been 364 days since my last drink, and I made a promise to my family that I'd make it to one year tomorrow."

"Liar. *Liar!*" Ross shouts.

"Listen to me," Dad says, his tone more reasonable than reasonable. "I'm not drinking. I started this and I'll finish it. I did what I did sober. I did it with a goddamn good reason, and I'd do it again."

"He's full of shit, Miranda," Ross says. "Look what he did to me. Because I *came to his door!*"

"That's not the full story, Miranda." He extends a hand slowly and I quickly see why: I didn't mean to, but I'm pointing my knife at his stomach as often as I'm pointing it at Ross. "Hand that to me. There are things here you don't understand."

"Dad ... He..." My resolve is crumbling. I came into this room so sure of everything, right down to a willingness to end Ross's life if things turned out wrong. Now I know I was bluffing. What Ross said is true: I'm not so heartless as to kill someone in cold blood, no matter what he did. Or what I *think* — but am no longer one hundred percent sure — he did.

"He raped Cassie," I finish.

"I know."

"You *know?*"

"He's lying! He's lying because he's drunk!"

Compared to Ross's shouting, Dad feels eminently reasonable. He watches me with steady eyes — not a drunk's eyes at all.

"You have to trust me, Miranda." He tips his head toward the door, meaning I should leave so I don't have to witness what he came here to do. "I need you to go out into the living room and sit with your mother for a while. Face the window. Don't look back. Don't look back until I tell you."

My gaze moves from Dad's face to his side, where his hands dangle. He's holding a small knife, smaller than mine, plus a bag of plastic zip ties that I recognize from the toolbox in the owner's closet. He probably means to cut Ross's ropes, re-tie him for transit, then take him out into the woods. It must strike him as the only viable option left. No choice is a good one. My father's last desperate fatherly kindness, it seems, is to spare me the sight of it.

Gently, he takes the knife from me.

"Go," he says.

There's a flurry of motion. Before I know it, Ross is sitting up, then scrambling as best he can to the edge of the bed. His hand is free, his rope cut somehow. In seconds he manages to untie one foot, and because they were a single bound unit, the other comes free as well. I see how exhausted and weak he is. This is all adrenaline: some instinctual reservoir of resolve he's found, his body finally sure the alternative is death.

Dad reacts, but not quickly enough. Ross half-falls toward a basket atop the dresser, snatching a sharp knitting needle. It's made for yarn work instead of impaling, but it looks sturdy enough for both.

He points the needle at us with his remaining arm, leaning against the dresser for support. His arm stump presses into the dresser's top as best he can, needing its bulk to keep from falling.

"Give me your keys," he says.

Dad's watching him, less than totally concerned. If Ross lunges, he'll fall on his face. We could out-maneuver him at half speed. The only thing I'm a little worried about is the direction of that knitting needle. He's aimed and braced it very deliberately, knowing his limitations. If he falls, chances are he'll stab me on the way down. I can't step back, because the open door has me wedged into a corner.

"I said give me your keys."

"I don't have them."

"Then get them."

I start to move.

"Not you," Ross says. "I'm talking to Daddy."

"They're in the Jeep," Mark says. "You want them, get them yourself."

Ross's eyes go to me. There's a tiny bit of pleading left in them — one small spark of the man I thought I was in love with.

"I'm telling you the truth, Miranda," he says. "Can't you see that? Why would I lie now? I'm free. I've got all the leverage." He's overstating that last one, but I'd still rather not be stabbed. "I could admit everything now, if there was anything to admit. You have to believe me. It's *me*, Miranda. It's Ross."

"Don't believe him," my father says.

"He's the one you shouldn't believe," Ross says, still braced against the dresser with his needle out like a jousting lance. "Who's lied to you before? Who's tried twice to get sober, then proven he doesn't have the stones? That wasn't me. It was him."

"There were reasons I fell off the wagon before," Dad says, speaking to me but with his eyes unblinking on Ross. "Reasons I stayed *on* the wagon this time."

"Oh, for Christ's sake. He's drunk right now!"

"I'm not drunk, Miranda."

"Come with me," Ross says. Ross *pleads*. "You aren't like them. You don't *want* to be like them."

"You have to trust me," Dad says. "Don't believe a thing he says."

Ross scoff-laughs. *"Me?* Look who's talking. I'm not the one with self-restraint issues! I'm not the one with a history of sudden and unexplained violence!"

"Not unexplained," Dad says. Then he looks right at me. "Not unexplained," he repeats.

"We have to go now," Ross tells me, his rushed panic competing with my father's calm voice for attention. "Getting the Jeep out of the driveway will be rough with all this snow, but I think maybe we can make it. If we're lucky, the roads might be decent enough for a four-wheel drive. It's a risk, but we have to try. I'll die if I stay here much longer, Miranda. You have to help me. You can save my life. It's the only way out of this for you. I'll tell the cops you helped me.

They'll see the truth. I'll tell them that when your father finally came in to kill me, that's where you drew the line."

"I knocked him out with Rohypnol," Dad says.

I turn my head and look at him.

"Roofies," he elaborates. "I can show you the blister packs. They're still in the kitchen." He makes a *faux*-quizzical face. "Why would I have *roofies* lying around ... unless someone brought them here with him?"

I turn back to Ross. His face starts to melt.

"There have always been reasons for the things I've done, even if you've never known what they were," Dad says. "I always had a reason to protect my girls."

Girls. Plural. It makes me look through the gap in the door, searching for my mother. Where is she in all of this? It feels a stretch for Dad to claim he protected her too, not just me. If anything, he put her in danger. He nearly ruined Mom's life before he nearly ruined mine.

"Please," Ross says, though his face knows now that he's been caught out, that he's lost this game.

I'm still holding the ring, though my hand long ago forgot it. Dad reaches out now, and quietly takes it from me. He holds it in the palm of his hand and looks at it with an expression I've never seen on him before.

"*I will love you forever*," he says.

"That's sweet," Ross says, "but—"

He stops when my knife hand seems to rise on its own. Its tip presses an indent into his bloody shirt.

Because I understand now. This must be how Aubrey feels, when all the clues finally slot into place.

Dad didn't know Ross had the ring with him. I found it first, then watched him react with surprise. I've held onto it since. It's never left my possession. Dad never looked at it closely ... and yet, from where the ring is now in his palm, there's no way he could be *reading* the inscription.

He could only know what's written inside Cassie's ring if he put it there to begin with.

"You'll do anything to protect your girls," I say, looking at my father. Repeating his words, with new meaning.

I understand now.

Girls.

When Dad used the plural, he didn't mean Mom.

Chapter Twenty-Nine
MARK

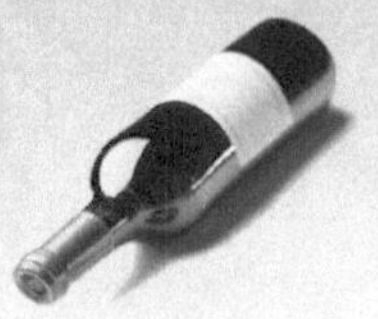

TEN YEARS AGO

A hand settles on my shoulder. I'm handcuffed to the hospital seat's armrest, so it's awkward to look up. I see my friend Dr. Asham Khan standing above me in scrubs, looking down kindly.

"I told them you'd be good if they take those off," he says, meaning the handcuffs. "Do you promise to be good?"

It's been hours since they brought Frank McCafferty into the ER. Hours since I got in my own car to follow the ambulance, then was spared a drunk driving charge to go with the assault charge they slapped on me when I arrived by Willa, who's since left me for the cafeteria. She understands why I did what I did, but she still hates it. I made her a promise eight years ago, but proximity keeps making a liar out of me. I thought I could stick to my own business, and most of the time I can. But today was a bridge too far. Bad news got me drinking, and once I started drinking, the devil took over. It wasn't wise, what I did to Frank, but I'd do it all over again.

It's been hours since I came here. Plenty of time to sober up.

"I'll be good," I tell Asham.

He looks at the policeman standing by the doorway, then ticks his head toward me. The cop comes over and removes my handcuffs.

"Mr. McCafferty really isn't pressing charges?" the cop asks.

"He's really not," Asham says.

"After *this?*" He shakes his head. The cop is young — too young to know that even Mark Wimberly, with all the evidence against him, is supposed to remain innocent until proven guilty. He sneers at me. "I heard you beat that guy in front of your own daughter."

"That's exactly what he did," Asham says. "Now. If you'll give us a second?"

The cop throws me a final hateful glance, then exits the waiting room. It's almost 2 a.m.; nobody else is here. If Frank's not pressing charges, the police will probably leave. Get a good night's sleep at home with their families. I wish I could do the same, but I know I won't be sleeping tonight.

"What did you say to get Frank to drop the charges?" I ask once we're alone.

Asham sits next to me. We're not doctor and drunk now — just two friends like we've always been. "I told him I know Cassandra's pediatrician and heard about some suspicious injuries."

"Cassie doesn't have a pediatrician. Molly won't allow it because of Frank." These are some of the many unfortunate things I learned today. "She just does first aid whenever he hits her and hopes nothing too bad happens."

Asham nods. "That's why saying I knew her pediatrician made him drop the charges."

"So you threatened him."

Asham shrugs. "Wrath of Khan. Of *Dr.* Khan."

"Really? 'Wrath of Khan'?"

"Oh, come on. White people love *Star Trek*. They get such a kick whenever I say that." He leans back and stretches. "You know, Mark ... a more productive way to deal with child abuse is to alert someone, not deal with it yourself."

"I was drunk."

He slaps me on the back once, hard. It's a gesture that says, *You fucked up, and you're a mess, but you're my friend and I love you anyway.* "I know you were drunk."

I rub my face. This is all too much: the cops, the shame, and the inability I've had to look in the mirror ever since blowing my sobriety just two weeks before my one-year anniversary.

"I didn't know for sure that he was beating her until today. But then this morning I was talking to the neighbor on the other side, and she said something I couldn't explain away ... and something inside me just snapped. I knew I shouldn't drink, but the stress of knowing and trying not to react got to me. I fought it for a long time. It was 11 a.m. when I found out that bastard was laying hands on her, and I made it until ... what? Three o'clock or so? By then I'd decided to call CPS, but I needed to calm down first. And so God help me, I went to a bar."

"You needed to calm down, huh? And a bar was the answer?" His head bobs sarcastically. "How'd that work out?"

"If I hadn't seen Frank ... If I'd just made the call and handled it from arm's length..."

Asham leans forward, then looks at me earnestly. "Yes, Mark. But you *did* see him, didn't you? That was always a risk. You know you can't hold your temper when you drink. As someone who pissed you off whenever I insisted you clean up your side of the room in college, I know that better than anyone. You know what I think? I think you *wanted* Frank to come out of the house. You ran into the door of your garage, which is right next to his garage. Then you made a spectacle of yourself at the mailbox in front of his house, under a streetlight, making a lot of weird noise so he'd see you out there. By the time he came over, you had all the excuse you needed."

"He's been beating Cassie for years, Asham. *Years.*"

"I know. I mean, I didn't know before, but that is how these things work."

"If you'd known, would you have told me?"

"Of course I'd've told you. That's what I promised eight years ago, and I keep my promises. I'll always tell you if I learn something about Cassandra that you need to know. I'll always keep your secret.

Always help you both however I can. But Mark…" He sighs again, finally sitting back. "I can't help if you break the law."

"It was justified."

"That's not how justification works. If Frank was hitting you and you hit back, *that's* justified. This was vigilantism."

"Cassie can't protect herself. Nobody stands up for her."

"That's why *I* just stood up for both of you. I put my neck on the line, Mark. Everyone thinks you beat up an innocent man who was just minding his own business."

"But she's my *daughter.*"

"Yes. She is. I know that and you know that. Molly knows that. I guess Willa knows it too. But unless you want to tell everyone else, this is going to keep looking the way it looks."

We go quiet. I tied this noose myself. I didn't want to, but I did. Molly was on marriage number one when we had our affair. Obviously, I was with Willa. It happened while she was pregnant with Miranda, when she was yelling at me more than usual about my drinking and wasn't interested in sex. I was weak and stupid, and life's made me pay the price since. I came clean to my wife and for some reason she found a way to move on, but Molly refused to tell her husband. Molly wanted me out of her life, but ours was an affair of convenience: nothing more cliché than screwing the neighbor, mostly because she was there and lonely. When it ended, neither of us had enough money to move away. We agreed to stay neighbors and just behave ourselves. I kind of liked it, actually, because staying next door let me keep an eye on my second daughter even if I could never acknowledge her.

In the end, though, being close to Cassie was what undid me. I was never able to keep emotional distance, even before today. I'd sit at the window for hours and watch her play in the yard, hoping nobody saw and thought I was a creep. It's been so hard, telling nobody — Cassie most of all — that I'm her father. I never felt differently about Cassie than Miranda. I'd do anything for either of them. Tonight, I did just that.

I wonder what she'd think of me, if she knew. The ring I gave her was intended to show Cassie that she wasn't abandoned. I asked

Molly to make sure she understood that her father was absent *not* because of neglect, but because of circumstances surrounding her conception. That was the plan, but life moves on and plans fall by the wayside. Molly married Frank, and Frank was a monster, and to deal with it I did what any father would do: I protected my little girl.

My face goes into my cupped hands. Soon enough, I'm sobbing quietly. The weight of what's happened and the futility of the future are on my shoulders like bricks made of lead. I doubt Frank will touch her again — at least not for a while — but now Cassie will be afraid of me. Miranda, who I remember seeing through the window after my fugue, will be afraid of me, too. I can never tell either of them why it happened. I made promises too, and it's my burden alone to keep them.

Again Asham's hand is on my rounded shoulders, offering comfort.

"I don't know if you believe me," he says, "but I really do understand. Being a dad means doing what's best for your kids, not necessarily what feels good or even what other people call 'right.' There's loneliness to it. But I want you to remember that even if it turns out that everyone, including yourself, hates you for this, you did your best. I want you to remember, when all's said and done, that *this was the best you could do.*"

"Except call CPS."

He slaps me affectionately again. "Except that. But even so, they'd understand if they knew. Willa will forgive you. I think Molly will forgive you, too."

"And the girls?"

"If they knew your side of the story."

"But they won't."

"Probably not," Asham tells me. "But I'd argue that makes what you did *more* brave, not less brave. It's easy to do the right thing when everyone agrees it's the right thing."

I lift my face from my hands. I must look a mess. I've never been so ashamed.

"So it *was* the right thing?" I ask. I need to hear a yes. Maybe there were better things in an ideal world, but right now I need more than anything to hear that in *this* world — the world in which flawed Mark Wimberly lives with his disease — this was as good as I reasonably could have done.

"Can you keep a secret?" Asham asks.

I nod.

"I'm a doctor. I've dedicated my life to healing people. I swore an oath to do no harm, and *officially* I think violence solves nothing. But that's the academic answer. If I was actually in your shoes, and it was Jamila he'd been beating? In that case, I think I might be the one handcuffed. Not in the hospital, but in the morgue."

I wipe my eyes and shake my head. "I almost made it to a year before falling off the wagon. *Almost.*"

"And you can start over tomorrow."

"I don't think I can do that." I really don't. It might be years before I'm fully sober again, if ever. I've tried before, many times, but I only ever last a week or two — a month, if I'm lucky.

He puts his arm around me. "Then I'll be there. For you, but also for Cassie. You don't have to be her father alone, Mark. I'll be your second, if you want me to be."

"You'll protect her? You'll watch over her?"

Another nod. "I told Molly that if she doesn't start seeing a pediatrician, I might have to make some calls. They'll do it. They'll get her a proper doctor. When they do, I'll have the inside scoop. Because you know me. I'm a networker. I know every doctor in town."

What he's saying is actually comforting. The medical community has Cassie's back from here on out. We're in this together, Asham and me.

"If anything happens to Cassie and you can't be there..." Asham says. "If that happens, my friend, *I'll* be there to tell you the score."

Chapter Thirty

MIRANDA

We must look like the third act of a Shakespearean play. I'm wedged in the lee of the room door holding my butcher knife, its tip in Ross's chest. Ross still holds his knitting needle, still leaning on the dresser for support and pretending he's the one in control here. Dad's behind, watching us. We're at mutually assured destruction right now. Someone sneezes, and Ross and I might just stab each other.

But I don't feel threatened. None of my usual emotions fit anymore. The moment I've just had is one in which everything changes. You go through your life believing one thing, but the truth lies elsewhere.

I didn't live next door to my best friend all those years ago. I lived next to my half-sister.

"Cassie's your daughter," I say. "*You* gave her that ring."

Dad doesn't precisely nod. Nothing moves, but something about the way he's looking at me answers in the affirmative.

"Wait. What?" Ross says.

"So ... that Fourth of July..." I say, realizing the way a traumatic event in my life lines up with one in Cassie's, "the last time you tried to get sober..."

I let it hang. My father's drinking has always been like swimming in a pool that's too cold. If he gets drunk and stays drunk, it's almost the kind of thing you can get used to. Problems come when he gets *out* of drinking, gets sober for a while, and then jumps back in. *That's* when it shocks the system. Twice now he's sworn off booze, climbed out of alcoholic waters, and spent nearly a year lounging sober on the deck. Twice then, he's fallen off the wagon and rolled right back in. That's when the worst things happen.

The first time was when he beat Frank McCafferty. The second was July 4th three years ago. Both failures of my father's sobriety, I realize now, had something to do with Cassie.

That year, Mom and I drove to a fairground to watch fireworks. Dad was going to come with us, but he got a phone call that stopped him. I didn't know who'd called, but Mom said Dad had an emergency; he had to run into town to meet with a friend. By the time he arrived at the fireworks hours later after that meeting, he was completely soused. He was furious and out of sorts, but I never knew why. I only knew that his plan wasn't to stay, but instead to grab something from the car and rush off again. That's not what happened, though — not that Dad was pleased by the change in plans. Mom pulled him aside and they argued, and in the end, Dad didn't leave after all. He was unsettled and angry the rest of the night, unable to sit still. We watched starbursts in the sky while he wandered and drank, wandered and drank. He ended up in a fight with a beer vendor and got arrested again.

"It was Uncle Asham who called me before the fireworks," Dad says now. "He knew my secret. He told me Cassie had come into the Urgent Care attached to the hospital because she'd had an accident at a party, but the examining physician was sure something different had happened." His gaze flicks to Ross, and the reasonable tone in his eyes turns to hatred. "Cassie wouldn't admit it, but the exam was definitive. She'd been raped."

Again he stares at Ross, impotent with his knitting needle. I stare at Ross too, and it's then that his face turns to shock.

"And you think it was *me?*" Ross says. "*This* is your proof?"

"I already had *my* proof," I tell him, taking the ring back from my father and displaying it for Ross. "Now we're talking about *his.*"

"But! But!" His eyes dart from one of us to the other. "This is ridiculous! Even if someone did rape her, are you saying she claims for sure that it was me?"

"She doesn't know who did it," I tell him icily, "because she was *roofied*. Someone slipped one into her soda."

"I keep Rohypnol so I can sleep!" Ross blurts, remembering what Dad revealed earlier: that it was Ross's own roofies, appropriately enough, that my parents used to sedate him in the first place. He looks from me to Dad, Dad to me, getting no reaction. "If she passed out, it was because she was drunk!"

"I talked to Asham," Dad says, speaking to me as he answers. I think that's deliberate: answering me instead of Ross because it's the only way to control his temper. "He said Rohypnol can hide inside the effects of alcohol. If you drink a lot, you might not even know you were roofied because you just think you're drunk. But in this case, there was one problem with that excuse."

"Cassie doesn't drink," I say.

"What? Yes she does!"

I look at Ross evenly. *"No she doesn't.* She's had too much trauma. Trauma from sons of bitches like you. She doesn't drink because she always wants to stay in control."

Ross's facial acrobatics begin to move into the absurd. "This is ridiculous! Look at you!" He turns to Dad. "Is *that* why you did this to me, you piece of shit? Did you *hack off my goddamn arm* because you think I hurt your precious little princess?"

"Not exactly. My wife stopped me from going after you on the day you hurt my youngest daughter," Dad says, finally looking at Ross. "I did what I did when I found out you'd come for my eldest, too."

Something drops in the pit of my stomach. I hadn't put the rest of it together, but that fits. I didn't tell Mom and Dad about Ross. I hid our relationship from them because I knew they hated him, though I never knew why. When Ross came to the door and announced that he and I were together, I can only imagine my father's rage. He'd gotten one of Dad's girls. No way he'd be getting the other.

The knitting needle has become pointless and pathetic in Ross's hand. He must see how trapped he is, even though I'm still technically at his mercy, stuck in the door's swing as I am. The needle droops, hanging sad toward the floor. Black char marks from his cauterized arm stump make a mess of the dresser's top. It looks like a charcoal drawing.

"Miranda," he pleads, "think about what he's saying! Something happened to Cassie, and he just assumes *I'm* to blame? You said yourself Cassie doesn't know who did it!"

"I asked around," Dad says. "*You* invited her to that party. *You* gave her a ride."

"That doesn't mean I—!"

"And while you were there, you were on top of her all night. Kept cozying up, trying to kiss her. Getting *really* close. Nobody thought she was into it, though. But then suddenly, both of you disappeared at exactly the same time."

"That doesn't mean shit!"

"Maybe not," Dad says. "But then my doctor friend told me someone came into the ER around the same time as Cassie. He had an unusual wound — the kind that doesn't happen very often, and so is easy to identify. That wound told the doctors all they needed to know, but that there was nothing they could do as long as Cassie wouldn't admit what happened. They couldn't even tell *her* because the consequences for violating patient privacy are so severe. But I will say this: The guy with the weird injury?" Dad points. "His description sounded a lot like you."

"Stabbed with a pen," I say. Then I look to my father. "Right?"

Dad nods. We both stare at Ross.

"It wasn't me," he says.

"Then show us the outside of your thigh," Dad tells Ross. "Prove there's no scar."

For the first five or ten seconds, there might be something Ross could say to explain his way out of this: some further doubt we're unable to explain away. But after fifteen seconds — *thirty* seconds — of confused sputtering, he's given himself away.

Ross's eyes dart to the window. My eyes follow, spying Dad's Jeep through the gap. That's when Ross must decide he won't be explaining his way out of this and needs to change his plan from bargaining to escape, so he leans hard into the dresser, using his weight to tip it. It balances on its corner, then crashes into my side, pinning me in the corner behind the door.

Dad reacts, but not quickly enough. When I'm hit, I drop the knife I've been holding. Ross manages to scoop it up despite his weakness and pain, and seconds later he's ten feet from us, brandishing the blade as he circles around and waves Dad away from the exit.

"Keys," he says.

Dad has his hands halfway up, but he's still holding that little paring knife. His eyes are hard, his mouth a thin line of hatred. He doesn't respond. Doesn't react at all.

Ross whips the blade around so it's pointing at me instead.

"*KEYS!*"

This time he answers. "I said they're in the Jeep."

"You keep your keys in the car?"

Dad's stare is as cold as outer space. "My wife hates it. Step into the other room, Ross. See if she has anything to say about it."

That makes Ross consider. He's forgotten about my mother. The wind outside is loud, but maybe she's heard some of this. She might be waiting in the living room, a weapon at the ready.

"Yell to her," Ross says. "Tell her not to interfere."

"I don't know that I can tell her anything," my father replies. "She was almost as furious about Cassie as I was, and Cassie's not even her daughter. Now that you're a threat to Miranda, though?" He makes a sarcastic *Phew!* sort of sound. "Ever run across a mama bear protecting her cub?"

Ross shakes the knife at me. "Do it. Yell out."

We stand at impasse. I listen to the wind and whistle of the snowstorm, half thinking I can hear something mechanical beneath it. It reminds me of before, when Ross was in the shed and I thought I heard clanging, or a pump sound, or maybe the low rumble of an engine. I strain to hear, but whatever it was — if it ever existed — is already gone. The wind is just too loud, like the rush of a river and the scream of a thousand tortured souls.

I hear a heavy thunking sound outside, muted by white noise. Then again nothing.

"I said *do it*," Ross repeats.

Dad doesn't move. I think he's trying to outlast Ross. Ross has been tied to a bed or a chair for most of a week now, and during that time he's been beaten and lost a limb. It's taking a lot of effort just to hold himself upright. Make this standoff long enough, Dad seems to figure, and he'll simply fall over.

Ross understands, though, so he inches closer to me, using the righted dresser, again, for support. Now he's close enough to draw blood.

"I mean it," he growls.

A beat. Then without moving his eyes from Ross, Dad says, *"WILLA."*

"Louder."

"She was going upstairs to sleep," Dad says. "She's not out there, idiot. She's taking a nap. So go ahead. Run to the goddamn Jeep."

"She couldn't sleep through this," Ross says.

"Of course she could. The room's all the way in the loft, and just listen to the wind. She probably hasn't heard anything."

For someone so ready to go, Ross now looks reluctant. "You're trying to trick me."

Dad sighs angrily. "Think about what you're saying, you stupid asshole. I don't *want* you tricked. I want you *out of my house.* So like I said: Go ahead. *Take* the damn Jeep. You'll never make it anyway. You'll drive off the road, get stuck, then die out there because you're too weak to do anything about it. You think I want to stop you? You think I want my *wife* to stop you? Please. I want you to *go.* You leaving solves so many problems."

I think I hear something from the main room. Is it Mom? Over the whoop of the wind, I swore I just heard a floorboard creak.

Ross's jaw firms. With his eyes as wide open as they'll go, it makes him look crazy. Manic. He's thinking about what Dad said, realizing his only options are poor ones.

"Good point, Mark," he says, moving behind me and shoving me out of the corner at knifepoint. "I guess I should take someone along to help me with my escape."

"Fuck yourself," I say.

Now he smirks. "There's that dirty talk I like so much."

He pokes me with the blade. He looks to my father, who raises his hands a little bit higher. Ross gestures at Dad to stand back, so he does. After that, I'm walking ahead of Ross, the knifepoint in the small of my back. I can't see him behind me, but I can hear the shuffling stutter-step of his gait. If he had a second hand, he'd be holding my shoulder for support.

I pass the threshold, then spot something out of the corner of my eye.

Or some*one*.

I flick my eyes sideways and see that it's Aubrey. The sounds I thought I heard must have been her arriving while we were fighting. Mom didn't hear our situation, but Aubrey did ... and now she's in the main room, hiding behind a drape.

Ross doesn't see her as she steps out behind him, raising the same baseball bat Ross used on my father days ago.

"Surprise," she says as she swings.

Chapter Thirty-One
AUBREY

But I don't hit Ross in the head like I planned. I don't know what's going on, other than it's no good and Ross is the bad guy, and so I decided after I saw the bat against the wall to clock him now and sort it out later. That's not what happens, though. Ross is barely ambulatory, and as I swing my weapon, a stutter-step saves him. One leg buckles, his torso drops, and instead of striking his skull I connect with—

(oh jesus oh shit)

—with a blackened stump where his arm should be. What grotesque shenanigans have I missed? What the hell's happened here?

It's still a hit with a bat, though, and I've hit him somewhere tender. He was leading Miranda from the bedroom at knifepoint, but that's over now. His other hand can't hold the blade. My blow knocks him into a stumble. He manages to keep from falling, jittering sideways instead in something that looks like an old-timey stage routine. A china cabinet stops him. He collides with it, and its glass front explodes.

Miranda *does* fall, upended by Ross's sideways exit. She falls in his direction, hits the couch, then hits the floor. I see her head pop up, but then she runs away — seemingly toward the kitchen. I'm left with Mark and Ross, both gaping at my sudden arrival.

"Aubrey?" Mark says.

Something shoots past my face, nearly cutting my cheek open. It turns out to be a plate, thrown like a frisbee. Ross, beat to hell and clearly running on adrenaline, has managed to regain his feet and is now raiding the cabinet for weapons.

Mark turns toward Ross. Ross manages to fire off another ceramic frisbee, its dead aim striking Mark's temple.

Mark slumps, unconscious or maybe even dead. Ross turns on me with another round cocked and ready. He flexes to throw, but then a door opens upstairs, and Miranda's mother appears fully dressed, her hair a mess. She startles when she sees, all at once, what's happening below.

She lets out an involuntary bleat. Instead of throwing the plate at me, Ross throws it at Willa. Willa is too sleep-addled to dodge in time, but from so far away Ross's aim is terrible. The plate detonates nowhere near her.

Thinking fast, I lunge for the couch Miranda fell into, wondering at the same time where Miranda's gone. I think maybe I can hear her near the kitchen, throwing heavy things onto the floor. No time to wonder at that now, though. I grab one of the big square couch cushions and run at Ross before I can think too much about it. It works; he throws a new plate and it hits my shield, falling to the floor useless.

With Mark down, Miranda gone, and Willa still gaping like she's half-asleep at the top of the stairs, it's up to me to handle Ross. He's faster than you'd think, though; understanding that plate-throwing is now useless, he's gone for something else. A new weapon.

God help me, it looks like a machete. My only choice is to commit to my charge. My only chance is to close the distance between us before he can wind up and swing.

Ross manages a slash, but only halfway. Momentum throws me and the cushion into him, again slamming him into the cabinet. For a moment I think I've got him, but then my legs tangle in his and we both go down.

Ross takes advantage. Somehow, he rolls us; somehow, I end up on the bottom. I raise my knee like my self-defense teacher taught me and connect with Ross's testicles, but some trick of fury makes him immune. He's nothing but stress hormones now, with nothing left for manly pain.

He works the machete around from beneath himself, then raises it where I can see it.

"Of course it's you," he says. "Meddling bitch."

My eye spies the blackened arm stump. I twist hard, throwing a right hook into the flesh there.

Ross howls. He rolls halfway off, and I scramble free, scampering on hands and knees. Seconds later Ross has my feet, though, and I have to kick one free before kicking him in the face.

I'm up, then down as I see Mark on his feet again with a bloody hairline. He's got the bat I used earlier, and I've leapt right into his swing path. I manage to dodge, but my interference makes him whiff: nowhere near Ross. The force of the swing twirls him around, binding him up, and Ross takes advantage.

He runs for the door. I tackle him, we roll again, and then we're on our feet trading tussles.

Mark runs at us. Ross shouts like a karate master as he raises the machete, meaning to cut Mark in half.

But then the whole world shudders. A deafening *BANG!* stops us all in our tracks, frozen like a game of Red Light.

Porcelain tinkles to the floor. I can't hear as well as I used to; now it's like I've got wads of cotton in my ears. It takes long seconds to understand why: Miranda's standing at the front of our fighting group, holding a revolver over her head. The light fixture above her sparks and hisses: aftermath of her warning shot.

"Let's all just take it easy," she says, "and see what happens."

Chapter Thirty-Two

ROSS

Miranda lowers the gun from overhead, then points it at me.

"Miranda," I say.

"Ross," she answers.

"You don't want to do this. You don't want to hurt me."

She pulls the trigger. Whether by luck or design, she barely misses. She aimed down, maybe for the floor or maybe for my foot. All I know is there's a chunk missing from my floor: a divot less than one inch from my toe.

I swallow.

Mark looks alarmed. He's inching toward Miranda like he might be afraid of her. He says, "Where did you get that gun?"

"Owner's closet. Next to the vodka. You didn't know?"

"I did my best not to look at the vodka when I went in there for tools."

Something obnoxious passes between them. Miranda half-smiles at her father, as if she's proud of him for averting his temptations.

"Well, that's just precious," I sneer.

Miranda raises the gun. The muzzle is pointed at my chest, and I decide she didn't miss me earlier on purpose.

"Why don't you give that to me, Miranda?" Mark asks.

"I got it, Dad."

"At least point it away from him. It's cocked, so it's on a hair trigger. You're worked up. You might shoot him by accident."

"Or on purpose."

Aubrey steps toward Miranda. "Maybe you should listen to your dad."

Miranda wordlessly reaches into her pocket. She pulls out the ring I wore for three years and puts it in Aubrey's hand.

At first Aubrey doesn't understand. Then her eyes go wide and her mouth becomes a big wide O.

"Ross had it," Miranda says.

Aubrey's apparently part of the pick-on-Ross club too. She stares daggers at me and says, "You son of a bitch."

"Give me the gun, Miranda," says Mark, reaching now.

"I said *I got it.*"

"You weren't kidding about life and death," Aubrey says, looking around.

"It's complicated."

I eye the front door. It's right there. If the group will just shift a little, I can put myself in front of it. With the right distraction, I can maybe even go through it. I don't think Mark was lying about the keys being in the Jeep; it's too weird a thing to say randomly. I'm weak on my feet, but my adrenaline high is still strong enough to push me when I need it, I think.

I start to move, causing the standoff circle to move with me. I keep looking at the door, noticing a bonus there: When Aubrey came in, she didn't close it. Probably wanted to spare the noise, once she saw what was amiss. That means I don't even need to mess with the handle — or, God forbid, the lock. One good turn of Miranda's head will give me the time I need to slip out. After that, how much *more* time will I need? I can probably manage a decent sprint to the Jeep. Will she shoot me in the back? I'm still not sure. I give my odds as 50-50.

50-50 is better than dead, which is what you are right now, I think.

It's true. I maneuver myself as close to the front door as I'm going to get, then wait for a chance. One will come, I'm sure of it.

The room has settled a little, or at least as settled as a standoff can be.

"I *knew* something was wrong here," Aubrey says.

"Something was wrong," Miranda echoes, still with the gun on me.

"I couldn't get a signal. There was nothing I could do from where I was. All I could think to do was come and see if I could help. Somehow."

Miranda nods. She did need help, and she got it. If not for Aubrey, I'd already be out the door with her by now.

"I can't believe you were able to get here," she says.

"I got hold of an ATV called a Polaris. Barely made it, though. I've got *no* gas left. *Literally* on fumes. Thought I'd die by the side of the road." She sighs. "It's a long story."

"Listen to the two of you," I say. "One with a gun. One running through the storm to save everyone. Meanwhile I've been held hostage and tortured ... but it's all just a big game, isn't it? What do you think is going to happen when I get out of here? Back in the real world, do you think the police will say you're heroes?"

"What makes you think you'll get out of here?" Miranda asks.

I'm so sick of this. I spread my arms wide and say, "You want to shoot me? Okay, fine. *Shoot me.*"

Her face darkens as I call her bluff. The pistol doesn't waver, but she doesn't pull the trigger. It makes me wonder if I could just walk out of here, no distraction needed. If she didn't shoot me just now, why do I think she'd shoot me as I leave? Hell, Aubrey even brought me an ATV.

"Screw this," I say. "I'm out."

I take a step toward the door. Miranda shoots the doorframe.

I turn. I glare. That was a warning shot, nowhere near me. So I try it again — another step toward the exit — but this time she shoots so close I nearly lose a finger.

"*What the hell do you want from me, Miranda?*" I demand, turning and furious. "Okay, so I did something wrong. *Says you.*" My lip curls up like a snarl. "Even if you *could* prove it, which you can't, look what *you* did. And I do mean *all* of you." I take my time, pointing directly at all of them. "Hell, I'm willing to take my chances. Let's go to the cops and see what they say."

"Let's," Willa says, but she says it weakly, so I spin on her.

"Yes, *let's!* Do you think you're going to get off scot-free? Is that the way the law works? Eye for a supposed eye? Think you can just go to a judge and tell them I had it coming? Enjoy prison, Miranda. You'll get to go to the big-girl one, seeing as you're an adult."

"And you. You'll go to big-boy prison," Aubrey says.

I feel like walking over and punching her. Aubrey shouldn't even be here. I've never liked her. *Never.* Always with her nose in everyone's business, always poking around where she doesn't belong. She's hot enough to bang, but terrible to be around.

It's petty, but I can't help myself from saying the first thing that comes to my mouth to shut her up.

"Why *are* you here, Aubrey?" I ask. "Did you come to confess like I did?"

Miranda's face shows confusion. She looks at Aubrey. "Confess what?"

"Nothing. I'll tell you later."

But that only eggs me on. This might be the only victory I get today, so I plan to milk it. If I'm going down, at least one other motherfucker's going with me.

"Because you're definitely *going to confess*, right, Aubrey? I mean, *I* couldn't confess because Mark took me aside to show me what visitors get in this family, but *you* talked to Miranda a bunch of times since Sunday, I'll bet. So *surely* you told her, right? Seeing as you're best friends and all, you wouldn't dare keep such a terrible secret."

"What's he talking about, Aubrey?"

I watch Miranda's gun. This is working, though that wasn't my intention. Miranda already suspects something, and Aubrey's reaction isn't making her suspicion go away. It's absurd, to think of these things right now ... but from where I'm standing, I don't need anything more than fifteen seconds of distraction. A girly argument will do nicely.

"It's nothing."

"If it's nothing, tell me."

"Miranda," says Mark, "whatever it is, let's keep our eyes on—"

"I said *I got it, Dad.*" She looks at Aubrey. "What's he talking about?"

Aubrey doesn't answer. I think: *Gotcha.*

"I guess she didn't tell you, then," I say. "Me and Aubrey? We kind of had a *thing.*"

"A *thing?*"

"Figure it out, Miranda. You're a big girl."

Her eyes don't want to believe what I've said. She turns to her friend. *"Aubrey...?"*

"This isn't important right now," Willa says.

"Aubrey?" Miranda repeats, speaking more firmly.

Aubrey looks like she's swallowed something sour. Her eyes are two white mice, trapped in cages.

"Miranda, for Christ's sake," says Mark.

"You slept with him?"

"No!"

"Yes," I say.

"It's not what it sounds like."

"It's *exactly* what it sounds like," I tell Miranda. Then I make my voice lecherous. "And it was *goooood.*"

Chapter Thirty-Three

MIRANDA

The gun doesn't know where to point. I think it has a mind of its own. I know I'd never shoot Aubrey over this, especially with everything else that's going on ... and yet, the muzzle keeps drifting her way.

I point it at Ross. I point it at Aubrey. It's as if I'm deciding which life to end.

Ross. If you're planning to shoot anyone, Ross is who you shoot.

But that's logic talking. My logic isn't doing too well these days. Logic took a vacation when I nearly ran my father over while he was chasing a deer. I moved out of the logical world entirely when I came to the shed door and found my one-armed boyfriend held captive by my otherwise mild-mannered parents. I understand a lot of the *whys* now, reaching all the way back to when I saw Dad almost kill the neighbor ... but that information is new and hasn't fully settled. I'm tired and stressed and freaked out and scared and even spooked by the snowstorm. I'm not wearing my logical pants right now. Right now, I'm wearing raw emotion. I'm wearing amygdala — the part of my brain dominated far more by primal things than sense.

She slept with your boyfriend.

It shouldn't matter — especially now — but it does. I find my finger tightening on the trigger, then remember my father's note about pulling it accidentally. I focus on aiming at Ross. Ross has earned punishment three or four times by now, whereas Aubrey's guilt is new. Although ... I still can't shake the thing Ross said, about how it happened Sunday. I've talked to Aubrey since Sunday. Has she really been betraying me the whole time?

Calm down. It doesn't matter.

It doesn't. Not now. I know it couldn't possibly matter less with so much on the line. But I'm just so worn-down. So scared. So stripped down to my very last nerve after two days in Hell.

Ross's eyes flick while my gun is drifting. I see it, and I see what he means to do, but my head's too distracted to react in time.

He springs, moving like lightning for someone so beaten. He leaps toward Aubrey and the next thing I know he's behind her, using her as a human shield. He never let go of the machete; it just got less dangerous after I bested him with a gun. Now he's holding it to Aubrey's throat, backing toward the door.

"Okay," Ross says, peeking out from behind her. "Now's your chance. How mad are you? Mad enough to shoot her?"

"Miranda..." Aubrey says, but Ross tightens up and the blade on her neck stops her.

"Shut up," I say. I don't want to hear from Aubrey right now. I don't know how I feel. I'm just happy my hands seem to have figured it out, sighting the gun on Ross's peek-a-boo head instead of the big target of Aubrey's torso.

Ross stays behind her, keeping low.

"Drop the gun, Miranda. I don't think you'll shoot me, but I'd rather not find out."

"Screw you," I say.

Ross drags the machete across Aubrey's throat. It's light and away from the arteries, but she bleeds a little just the same. She's trying to be strong, but a whimper escapes her. I hate myself for it, but I want her pain to stop. God help me, I'm siding with my betrayer.

I hold onto my weapon for a few more seconds, then drop it.

"Kick it here."

I kick the gun toward Ross, and he picks it up. He elbows the door open and tosses the machete out into the snow, then steps away from Aubrey just in time. I noticed the way her arm tensed, bent at the elbow, ready to strike. She lets it hang as Ross backs away and out of range. Lucky bastard. If he'd kept holding her, he'd've gotten an elbow in the gut by now.

As he moves into the doorway, he trips over his own feet and almost falls down. The doorframe catches him, but the stumble reminds me just how gassed Ross is right now. He blinks in an attempt to focus, his eyes threatening to roll back without control. It strikes me how hard he's breathing as he fights to stay conscious and standing.

Dad half-steps forward, but Ross has more than enough control left to turn the gun in his direction. There's a beat as Dad freezes. Then Ross smiles.

"Well, look at this," he says as if he's a newcomer to his own standoff. "Look how things ended up for me and you ... *Mark.*"

Dad still seems to be considering tackling him. He probably figures Ross only has one good trigger-pull in him, with zero fight beyond it. The problem is that one good pull. Bullets still beat a fistfight.

Seeing her husband under the gun makes Mom yelp. She scampers down the stairs to join us on the first floor. Ross flicks the muzzle toward her, but Dad yells to stop him.

"ROSS!"

Ross swings the gun back toward Dad.

"That's right," Dad says, waving at Mom to keep her distance. "Keep it aimed at me. The door's right behind you. Go ahead. Nobody will stop you from leaving."

But Ross doesn't leave. He's in charge now and must feel like gloating. It's three on one and he can barely stand, but the blue steel weapon he's holding still trumps everything we've got. It's clear he's enjoying this — this sudden reversal of fortunes. For days, my dad has made the rules. Now Ross is the big man, and he's going to milk it for all it's worth.

"Were you going to kill me?" Ross asks. "In cold blood?"

Dad doesn't answer.

Ross sneers. "Well, guess what, *Mark*? Maybe I *did* do what you think I did to your daughter. His eyes flick to me. "Maybe I'd even do it again. I'm going to go free, you know. So maybe somehow, some way, we'll meet again."

I'm the one thinking about tackling Ross now, though I'm afraid he'll shoot one of us if I try. I want to claw his face. I want to rake his out eyes with my fingernails. *He did it. He really raped Cassie.* How didn't I see through this psychopath? How did I let him into my life, my family, my bed?

"You won't go free," Dad says. "I'll make sure of it."

Ross thinks, then nods. "You *will* make sure of it, won't you?"

The lights flicker like a horror show. Dad's face is strong. Unafraid. Willing to do whatever it takes.

So Ross shoots him in the side. Then he rotates and shoots my mother, too.

I cry out. I rush toward my parents as they hit the ground, but Ross yells to stop me. I look up, feeling lost and confused and like I'm tumbling into a bottomless pit. I can't take any more of this. A pool of blood is spreading on the cabin floor, and I can't do anything about it. I'm paralyzed with every emotion at once ... but very quickly, anger grows stronger than the others.

I turn to Ross, planning murder, and see that he's pointing the gun at me now. His face is strange. He doesn't look like a bad guy all of a sudden — just a nineteen-year-old kid again. The weight of what's happening might be settling into him, becoming real. It all happens while he watches me, his expression weak and nostalgic.

"Ross," I say. "Don't do this."

We stare eye to eye. Unspoken words pass between us. His mouth opens two separate times, but twice it doesn't know what to say. But then his expression hardens. Determination eclipses his doubt and his focus returns, calculating and shrewd. It's dawning on him that he just shot two people. He must be planning to claim self-defense ... but that won't work if he leaves witnesses.

"Ross," I say again.

He shakes his head, negating something unknown. All he can say to me, as we face our blighted ending, is "I'm sorry."

He pulls the trigger. The hammer falls and I flinch ... but instead of a boom, I hear a click.

Six shots. The gun is empty.

The power finally dies. The lights go out, and our whole world turns to darkness.

Chapter Thirty-Four

It takes a moment before my heart remembers to beat. It seemed at first that the gun didn't fire, but I guess it actually did, because here I am, in the nothingness of death.

Then sense returns. The power just gave out; that's why I can't see. I know there's a moon outside, but its light is too dim to register. Maybe the snowstorm is obscuring it. Maybe it's hidden behind a cloud. Or maybe it's just me, with my unadjusted eyes.

There's yelling. I can't tell who it is, though maybe some is coming from Aubrey, or maybe some from Ross. Maybe even some from me. My loss of vision has compromised everything. I'm scrambling now, already stressed beyond belief, just to find my bearings.

You were standing by the couch. Ross was by the door. Aubrey was ... I don't know where Aubrey was. And oh God...

The next thing comes as if from a bulletin, as if I didn't just live it for real:

Oh God — Ross just tried to kill me.

Someone's stumbling around me not far away. I lose track of sounds, of voices, of coherent thoughts of finding my way. The shock of nearly dying and going instantly blind drain away, and that's when my scattered brain remembers the other thing. That's when I remember my parents.

On my knees. Feeling someone moving nearby, hearing someone run into things and mutter and grunt. Crawling. I can't think of anything else other than finding them, wherever they are. I've already turned a few times, unsteady on my feet with no sight to ground me. Where's the living room? Where's the kitchen? Where's the door?

I hear scuffling and shouting behind me. Something metal clangs. I hear Aubrey and Ross's voices, fighting somehow, but that's another world — a world for people with unshot parents. I flinch as something heavy thuds against my arm and slides to the floor, realizing as I crawl over it that it's the revolver Ross tried to kill me with, useless now that all shots have been fired.

Most revolvers only hold six shots, I think as I crawl, reminding myself it's true, and that I'm only alive because I fired four times before Ross picked it up. If it wasn't a revolver the owners stored in their closet, I'd be dead right now.

I feel something wet and warm. Inches farther, I feel a soft form like a sandbag. When I touch it, it retreats from my touch and makes a sound like a whimper.

"Mom?" I whisper.

She doesn't answer so much as groans. But at least she's still alive.

"Is Dad—?"

A light blazes before I can finish my question. When it does, I see that I'm at my mother's waist and it's her shoulder that's bleeding. Dad is beside her, right where he should be. I think he's alive too, though his wound is in a much worse place: on one side of his torso. I doubt Ross got his lung, and he definitely didn't get his heart, but kidneys and intestines are still up for grabs. I'm thankful that Ross is in the condition he's in. Even good shooters have trouble hitting targets using one hand, and Ross's single remaining hand was far from steady.

Activity from the rear finally makes me turn. I nearly slip in blood, realizing my crawl here has covered my hands and lower legs with it. I look up to see Aubrey holding a camping lantern from the end table by the door. Ross has her in a headlock, squeezing her neck hard enough to break it.

In the high contrast of the light, Ross looks like a maniac. The recessed parts of his face are pitch black, while other parts are bleached white by the lantern. His eyes are huge and wild. His teeth are gritted, lips pulled back.

"Good girl," he growls to Aubrey. *"Hold it steady."*

Aubrey looks more terrified than when he had her with the machete. She must have taken the lantern and turned it on at his command, and there's zero doubt or resistance in her eyes. I feel it too: Ross's last-chance desperation, turning him more dangerous than ever. He might be ravaged, but he's using all the adrenaline he has left, and it isn't screwing around. Those stories you hear, about little old ladies lifting cars to save infants? That's the influence I see in Ross, and Aubrey sees it too. Right now, I think he could pop her head right off. It would be like squeezing a tube of toothpaste until it bursts.

"Stay right where I can see you," Ross says to me, as if I'm a threat.

He drags Aubrey out into the snow like she weighs nothing at all, his eyes scanning the ground. At the edge of the porch, he slams Aubrey into a post and kneels quickly while she's still disoriented. When he comes back up, he's got his machete again. At her throat again. This time, he's not bluffing. Or in control, I suspect. The thing Dad said to me, about firing the gun by accident just because I was so keyed up? That's the way Ross looks right now, in terms of slitting Aubrey's throat open from ear to ear.

He drags her to the vehicle she must have driven here, the one parked beside Dad's Jeep —she'd called it a Polaris. It looks like an ATV crossed with an earthmover: a little tank with windows, all of them fogged from the inside.

"You'll need the keys," Aubrey says, understanding that he means to take it. It's far better than the Jeep.

He gives a sinister laugh that doesn't sound like Ross at all.

"Oh, I'm not going alone," he tells her. "You're coming with me."

Chapter Thirty-Five

I'm on the porch, as close to Ross and Aubrey as I dare with my bloody hands up, palms out.

"Let her go. Leave and tell people whatever you want, but let Aubrey go."

"Really? You want to save her? This whore?"

Aubrey whimpers. Her eyes tick to the cabin, to the Polaris, to me, to the Polaris again as we cross the dooryard.

"I *can't* let her go," Ross explains, slamming her into the vehicle's side, causing a dark shape to move in its cabin. "Look what those bastards did to me, Miranda. Thanks to your parents, *I* definitely can't drive."

I want to shout him down, with those same parents very much on my mind. I don't, though. I need to stay focused. We're in a snowstorm, in the dark and without power, and a rapist and three-time would-be murderer is about to escape with someone I feel I should help despite what she did to me.

Ross tells Aubrey to open the passenger-side door. When she does, she does it strangely: stepping back as the door swings, keeping herself between it and Ross. Seconds later I understand why: For reasons unknown, she's brought her dog with her. She bounds into the snow in a whirlwind of black fur, then turns back, excited to finally be set free.

"Abby," I say.

The dog looks at me, then Aubrey.

Panic tears threaten. There are too many crises, and I can barely keep myself together. I try to focus on the one and only thing I might be able to do for the Good Guys in the moment, seeing as there's nothing I can do to stop Ross. I can at least get the dog safe. I can at least do my best to keep Abby from going to Aubrey — or, worse, to try and protect her. She's not an attack dog. She's fiercely loyal and can't stand to be away from her owner, but she's still a big softie. If she challenges Ross right now, he'll hurt her.

"ABBY."

Miranda sees what I'm doing. With her voice full of terror, she whispers to her dog, telling her how fun it will be if she goes to Aunt Miranda.

Abby comes halfway. I close the distance and take her by the collar, then back up and shut her inside the cabin. I have to press the door twice before it sits right; the damn latch always wants to stay open. While I'm there, Ross yells gruffly for me to grab them some coats, hats, gloves — and for Ross, socks and boots. I split the difference between rushing (because he's got Aubrey) and taking my time (to stall, hoping for something, *anything* to pop up and save us). It's strangely comforting to be distracted gathering gear for a full minute or two. For that time, I can lose myself in searching with a flashlight and forget all that's gone wrong.

I'm reminded of reality only when, two separate times, I almost trip on the mostly unmoving forms of my parents in the middle of the floor.

"Don't do this," I say, pushing the gear at Ross. He shoves it into the rear, apparently planning to dress warm as they go.

"I have to. Don't you see that I have to?"

"We can figure it out." I tick my head toward the cabin. "They're not dead. You didn't actually kill them. Just let Aubrey go and let's talk."

Ross seems to consider, but obviously things are already too far gone. His momentarily softened expression hardens again, and he shoves Aubrey into the cab. I keep watching for opportunities, knowing it won't be hard to best him if I can just keep everyone away from the machete he's holding, but Ross knows it too and is being careful. Instead of putting Aubrey in the driver's seat and circling around to let himself in the other side, they're both getting in from the passenger seat: Aubrey first, sliding down so Ross can enter. That way he's never too exposed.

"Please," I say, pleading as I come around to the vehicle's side.

"This is how it has to happen," Ross says. "This is what you've forced me into." He grins, and I don't like that grin at all. It's the look of a crazy person. "But it's okay. It'll all be fine, won't it? We'll just trust the process. Trust America and its great legal system, y'know?"

His grin grows wider as he works things out. "The way I figure it, I was helpless. *Tied to a goddamn chair in the cold* for days. Nobody let me go. Nobody was *going* to let me go. And why? Because you think you can prove that I raped someone *three years ago?*" He laughs. "Good luck."

I don't want to think about what he's saying, but I do. It's true. Rapes are hard to prove even in the moment, let alone years back. Cassie didn't file any charges. She didn't even admit to herself that it happened for a long time, let alone to anyone else. It's an impossible situation. Everyone knows Ross did this: Dr. Khan, the police at the hospital, my parents, Aubrey, me. Hell, Ross even admitted it. And yet nobody will ever be able to prove a thing. Maybe that's why Dad did what he did: Vigilante justice was the only justice he had.

If Ross didn't commit a crime in the eyes of the law, even the few things we might have been able to justify — if there were any — can't be justified. This week will look exactly the way Ross paints it: My alcoholic father with a criminal record for assault kidnapped my boyfriend, then did terrible things to him. That means if Dad lives, he'll go to prison. Maybe Mom as well. Hell, I showed up and told them to keep him tied instead of letting him go. Does that mean I'll be arrested, too?

Everyone will end up paying for this. Everyone but the guy who deserves it.

I lock eyes with Aubrey. I have no idea how to feel about her. My emotions are a stew, totally irreconcilable. I want to hate her, but I can't shake a feeling that I'll never see her again.

"Miranda," she starts to say from the driver's seat. She stops when Ross jabs her in the ribs with the machete.

"Let her talk," I say.

"Goodbye, Miranda," Ross says, using his leg to jerk the door closed.

I step forward and grab the door before it slams. Then I move to within a few feet of Ross, close enough that I could grab him by the Adam's apple. He's in charge; I know I can't stop this or he'll kill Aubrey. But I also know he only has one hand, and it's already in use.

"I said *let her talk.*"

Ross stares me down, knowing I've called his bluff. I can't attack him, but there's nothing at all he can do to keep me from standing this close, or from holding the door he wants closed. From defying him, just to defy him.

I look at Aubrey, prompting her to go on.

"I'd never betray you," she says.

"What?"

"I'd never betray you," she repeats, and I realize she's near tears of regret even as her life hangs in the balance. "I don't know how it happened. I don't understand how it *could* have happened!" She swallows. "You know better than anyone that I'm fucked up, but I'm not *this* fucked up. I've never lost control that badly before. I wouldn't! You mean everything to me, Miranda. You're the family I never had. And so I—" She half-stutters, knowing Ross's patience will only last so long and she's got a blade at her belly. "I just need you to know how beyond-sorry I am. I'd *never* intentionally betray you," she says, still fighting tears, "no matter *how* drunk I was."

I don't know what to say. I feel tears, too. They could be for so many things. I want to reply, but I can't find the words.

Ross kicks me back with his foot, then uses it to yank the door again. He pulls the leg back into the cab and waits for the door to slam on its own momentum. It doesn't, though, because I catch it again.

"Ross," I say, leaning in.

He was looking at the door, which was supposed to close. Now he looks at me. We're inches apart.

I spit in his face.

Ross flinches as it hits him. Fury floods his expression, but he can't swipe at me without taking his weapon off of Aubrey. He can't even wipe my spit away. All he can do is stare at me while it trickles down his nose and cheek.

I slam the door before he can speak.

The engine starts. They pull away. I glance at the Jeep, knowing it's futile to try and chase them. The snow is deeper than the fattest part of the tires now. Even if Dad had chains on, which he doesn't, I wouldn't make it ten feet.

As Ross and Aubrey drive away through the falling snow, all I can do is to stand where I'm standing, feeling cold and alone, watching their silhouettes through the back window as they grow smaller and smaller.

Chapter Thirty-Six

The storm reasserts itself, stabbing at me with wind that feels like daggers made of ice. I'm not dressed for the weather. I hug my clothes tighter, take a final look at the taillights of Aubrey's weird vehicle, then turn with a heavy heart to go back into the cabin. In the cabin, there's no power but still some heat. For now, anyway.

The warrior inside me speaks up, protesting this surrender.

Come on, girl! Are you really going to give up so easily? Are you really just going to crawl back into your shell while they get away? You have to chase them! The Jeep is right there!

Yes, and there's a foot of snow with ice underneath. The wind is ferocious out here in the open. They didn't drive away fast, but the Jeep would be slower. Even if I *could* catch them, what would I do? How would confronting them out there end up different from what just happened here? There's no point, and I know it.

My mind doesn't want to hear the truth, though. I'm angry and sad and righteous and crushed and a hundred other feelings, but as luck would have it, every single one of them wants the exact same thing: *Find Ross. Destroy Ross. Save your friend.*

There's a tiny protest at that last one: Yet another part of me that doesn't quite agree, that tells me Aubrey's not my friend anymore. But no; that's not how it works. I keep thinking how she looked straight into my soul at the end, promising me she'd never do the exact thing she knows she's done.

I'd never betray you, no matter how drunk I was.

This right after she betrayed me. Yet strangely, I still want to believe her. It's a feat of denial, trying to accept both things — or perhaps more accurately, to disbelieve the truth in favor of Aubrey's promise.

I shake my head to snap myself out of reverie. What's done is done, on all fronts. It doesn't matter whether Aubrey screwed up or stabbed me in the back on purpose. I am where I am, and how I got here is irrelevant. It's time to stop wondering and pining and — yes, I feel it now — beginning to cry from the horrible dead end that my life has become.

For the first time, I let myself feel the weight of everything that's happened. Now that the adrenaline is gone and all that remains is triage, it's hitting me just how bad things are. I've been keeping it at bay so I can stay sane, but now there's no chance of salvation to distract me. There's no longer a chance of resolving this well. My parents have been shot, I'm basically alone, and the guy I thought I loved raped my sister and ran off with my friend. If I see him again, it might be from behind bars.

It's all so heavy. I'm carrying a backpack made of lead.

My eyes have mostly adjusted, so even after the Polaris's lights are out of sight, I can still see the cabin's entranceway in the moonlight. After I shut the door to keep the cold out, though, I'm back in black. The cabin feels like a tomb.

It takes me a moment to find the flashlight I used while gathering coats and hats. Before I do, I stumble mostly blind. I rack my calves into furniture. Something soft keeps brushing into me, scaring me to death. Only after the thing seems to grunt the word *Ibiza* do I remember that Aubrey's dog Abby is in here with me, both of us groping our way in the dark.

I train the light on Abby first, seeing how anxious she is. She's eyeing the door and then eyeing me: universal dog language for "I want to go outside." I won't let her, though. Maybe she has to pee, but I know this dog. Mostly, she wants her master. If I open the door, she'll run down the tire tracks, and I might never see her again.

I move to my parents. It's hard to inspect their wounds by flashlight, and Ross took the only lantern I knew where to find.

My dad tries to sit up. I push him down, but he keeps slapping at me, trying to find words as shock takes him over. At first, I just mollify him, trying to keep him still so he can conserve his energy. It's already getting cold in here — and *man*, it's going to get so much colder.

But Dad persists. Mom's coming around more now, too, and after a lifetime together, she understands him in ways even his daughter can't.

"He wants you to turn on the generator."

The generator! I'd forgotten all about it. Like everyone else, I've been watching the lights flicker for most of the day, wondering when line power would die. I knew the place had a generator, but part of me dismissed that knowledge when I saw how much they'd been lying about to cover up the fact that they were hiding Ross. I think I figured the generator was a ruse: one more excuse for noises outside; one more reason for Dad to check on something beyond our walls.

Hearing his request articulated by my mother wakes Dad up a little. His eyes clear, and this time when he speaks, I can hear him fine.

"Around the back. Sliding wood door."

He tells me how to open its enclosure and how to start it. I expect difficulty — just to make our situation more exciting — but there's none. It's easy as pie. Dad anticipated an outage, knew how important it would be to have power if that outage came, and prepped everything days ago. By the time I come back in, hot air is even coming from the vents. I remember Dad explaining something about that, too — about how something in the HVAC here makes it easy for the genny to run the furnace, when in other cases it wouldn't be so simple.

With the lights on, my medical assessment is much easier. Mom will be fine; she's in pain, but the bullet didn't even stay inside her. Dad's dicier, but I think even he'll be okay. Like with Mom, the bullet seems to have gone all the way through him. Ross got him in the side, just above the waist. I think the bullet might have a chipped his hip bone, but that's not a terrible thing. Bone is better than organs.

"Bad news, though," I say. I indicate the First Aid kit I've been using to clean them up. "No sutures in here, and you both need stitches. I think you can wait, Mom. I can clean it up and cover it with gauze. But Dad, unfortunately you'll need something else."

He half-answers. He's losing blood, weaker by the second. Apparently, Ross nicked an artery.

"Super glue?" he says.

"More ironic than that," I answer.

His wound has to be cauterized, just like Dad did with Ross's arm. Mom insists on handling it, probably thinking how much it would traumatize a daughter to cause her father so much pain. She does it with a heavy metal spoon heated on the stove. Not as bad as a cast iron pan, I guess.

Dad passes out when it's over. Mom collapses onto the couch, beaten from her own part in the effort.

I move away after ensuring they're as settled as they're going to be, trying to think. I glance back once before putting them out of sight, far from relieved at their conditions. Yes, they're both alive after being shot, and that's a big deal. But Dad's wound is sealed now, and that might mean all my treatment did was to seal bacteria inside. I'm a freshman, not a doctor. I don't know if the hydrogen peroxide and Neosporin I used beforehand was enough, or if the clock is now ticking on Dad's wound turning septic. Shut-in like we are, sepsis would be more dangerous than the bullet.

But I need to push all of that from my mind. I've done what I can, and now I need to process. It still feels like I'm slacking off by staying where I am, so I have to keep reminding myself there's nothing I can do. The Jeep is a hearty vehicle, but I'd need more than "hearty" to not get snowbound today. I have no idea where

Ross went, and his tracks were instantly half-buried by the wind. Besides, he's already been gone for...

I look at my phone.

...for six minutes.

I'm sure that must be wrong, but I know it's not. While I was crouched down and calling to Abby near the Polaris, my phone nearly slipped from my pocket. Its screen woke and I noticed that the time was exactly nine o'clock. It felt strange, for such chaotic events to be happening at such an orderly time.

I watch the time tick to 9:07, then pocket the phone. Time's slowing down; that's the problem. Everything has felt like running through tar, but at the same time, everything's urgent. I had to get the lights on quickly, but even my fastest felt like wasted time. I had to patch Mom and Dad quickly, so I ran through the whole thing, still feeling far too slow. Two minutes on the generator. Mom mostly handled the cauterization while I dealt with bandages and antiseptics. *Four minutes.* A lifetime of trauma, and yet four minutes of real time is all it took.

I move back into the living room, unsure what else to do. I find my father alone and hear a door close elsewhere in the cabin. Mom must be okay, if she's seen fit to crawl to the bathroom.

"Miranda."

I'm surprised to see my father conscious. Again I get that strange sense of time passing far too slowly. If he's awake, when did he have time to be passed out? I remember it happening. I feel like the three of us have been in this violent, blood-spattered room for days.

"Miranda, I'm sorry."

I move closer, sitting beside him, and take his hand in mine. *"Shh."*

"I never meant for any of this. It just ... got out of control." Then he corrects himself. *"I* got out of control."

"It's okay."

"I wasn't born with the 'control' gene, I guess," Dad goes on, wincing at the pain. "Never really had a chance once I met alcohol. And look what happened every time I tried to quit."

I actually *do* look back at what happened, now that I know more. I thought my father spent life flying randomly off the handle, but there was nothing random about it. My worst fatherly happenings — situations I always hated him for and saw no way to explain away, even though I tried — turned out to have explanations in the end. When he attacked Frank McCafferty, it was because Frank was beating his daughter. When he got drunk on the Fourth of July, it was because he'd just learned someone raped his daughter. This past Monday brought it all together: The man who raped his second daughter was now after his first.

Three incidents of lost control. Three reasons they happened.

"You're still sober this time, though," I tell him. "Right?"

He manages a wan smile. "I guess I am. This time, that bastard didn't drive me to drink."

We sit with that, both wondering if things would be worse or better if he'd fallen off the wagon this time.

"I'm sorry I blamed you," I say.

"You had reason to blame me."

"I'm sorry..." I feel myself choking up. "I'm sorry I hated you."

He puts his second hand over mine. "You had reason for that, too."

It's all true, and looking back it couldn't have been otherwise. What was he supposed to do after Frank? Tell me that my best friend was actually my half-sister? He'd kept that secret — painfully, as it turned out — for everyone's good. He always did his best, I suppose, even if it was terrible. I'm not a barbarian; I know full well violence isn't the answer. Still, these were the cards he was dealt ... and like any good parent, he did the best he could with what he had.

Face it, Miranda, I think. *You pretend you're enlightened and understanding, but actually you're as prejudiced as anyone. You'll give anyone the benefit of the doubt ... anyone except the people who raised you.*

For a few seconds, I resist that idea. Then I accept it. At some point I decided they governed me without reason, and after that I never gave them a chance. Dad's actions made it hard for me to believe he had purpose behind what he did, but he had purpose just the same.

I guess that when the people you love wrong you, you have to grant them just a bit more faith. A bit more benefit of the doubt.

Well. Except if they betray you.

Something tries to connect inside my mind. I feel like two wires in there are barely touching, sparking like mad as they try to complete a circuit. *Betrayal* has always been my biggest trigger. I react to thoughts of double-crossing like an allergy. My instinct is to snap first, think never. Talk about not giving the benefit of the doubt.

I think of Dad, whose intentions were unknown to me.

I think of Aubrey, who lied to my face.

I'd never betray you, no matter how drunk I got.

I want to believe her. Right now, more than ever, I want to see her side. If my father's behavior ended up redeemable, I'm dying to believe the same might be true of Aubrey. In one sense, it doesn't matter at all. In another sense, it's the only thing that matters in the world.

Things couldn't be more black-and-white. Ross is the bad guy, so by definition Aubrey is the good guy. I need to believe in goodness. I need to believe in my friend, if I might never see her again.

Those two stubborn wires continue sparking inside my head. An idea almost comes. I feel like Aubrey must feel so often: Like something's missing. Like there's an important detail I'm not quite seeing.

Dad keeps watching my face. I wonder what he's thinking as he watches me thinking. The last thing he said was that I had reason to hate him, and I haven't denied it. Does he think I hate him still? But no, I'm still holding his hand. The squeeze there tells him all he needs to know.

"What's going on?" he asks.

I don't know how to explain it. A wall is crumbling. All my firm-held resolve is breaking apart brick by brick. I feel like now — now that I have no parents to yell at, no boyfriend to save or hate, no standoff to survive — there's no need for all this strength. I've lost everything. *What's going on,* to answer Dad's question, is that I'm trying my best to salvage what I have.

I can't make myself believe that Aubrey didn't sleep with Ross. What I need right now, in the spirit of salvage, is to believe she didn't mean to.

But then it's Aubrey's voice that speaks up inside of me. She sounds snarky. Annoying. It's the way Aubrey always sounds when she's sticking her nose where it doesn't belong — when she's found some clue and appointed herself to a case.

You can't believe I didn't sleep with him, huh? my inner Aubrey says. *Come on, M. Try a little harder.*

It's such a strange thing, being doubted by myself. It's like it's really Aubrey in there, outside of my control. And she's not just working a mental mouth; I can practically *feel* her in there, trying to make sense of the wires that keep sparking. *What am I missing?* That's what Aubrey would be asking, if she was still here: *What am I forgetting? What am I failing to see?*

Nothing. There's nothing left to solve. Nothing left to see.

The wires spark. And spark. And spark.

"Miranda? What's—"

A lightbulb goes on. *"Roofies,"* I say.

"What?"

"You said you knocked Ross out with roofies."

Dad nods. "He wouldn't stop screaming. It was the only way to keep him quiet."

"And he brought them with him?"

"Yeah. Along with some condoms. Like that sick bastard was trying to paint a picture."

The wires inside me almost make a connection. I see a flash of an idea, but quickly it's gone. I focus. I think. I imagine I'm in there, trying to repair my disconnected synapses.

I'd never betray you.

Ross. Aubrey. Cassie. I see all three of them inside my head, trying to make sense together.

I don't know how it happened. I don't understand how it could have happened

Aubrey thinks I don't know she's on Adderall. She thinks I don't know she buys it from Ross. I let her believe those things because they embarrass her. Of course Ross sells here and there. Small stuff. Nothing that bothered me. I understand why Aubrey talks to Ross even though she hates him, even though I pretend to see none of it. It's for her meds. Meds she could get on her own now that she's eighteen, but habit is habit is habit, and Ross sells cheap.

You mean everything to me, Miranda. You're the family I never had.

Aubrey bought from Ross, and I never thought twice about it. Never questioned her loyalty before, even though I know she must see him regularly on the sly. Ross has always lusted after Aubrey despite hating her, but I knew there was no threat there. Aubrey's smart enough to hate Ross. She sees how he is. She saw through him, in fact, far better than I ever did.

I can imagine it now: how pathetic he must have been when they were alone together. Even when I was around, he was too overt with Aubrey, making jokes full of hints and innuendo. Whenever she went to buy from him, his advances-that-weren't-advances surely ramped up a notch. I can imagine comments he'd make and situations he'd engineer to be close to her. I may even have suspected as much subconsciously, but my usual hackles never went up with Aubrey because I believed what she so pointedly told me outside.

I'd never intentionally betray you ... no matter how drunk I was.

The wires connect. My head jerks up, and Dad blinks in surprise.

"Roofies. Ross had roofies."

"You said that," Dad says, not following.

"Were there a lot of them?"

"Enough. Half a blister sheet."

"*Half?* You mean he'd already used some of them?"

Dad waits, knowing my question was mostly rhetorical — that I'm already drawing my own conclusions. What Ross said about using them for sleep is bullshit. I know; I've slept in his bed. Other than self-administration, I can only think of one reason a guy might carry Rohypnol — and it's the same reason that Dad took as a smoking gun: proof, it seemed, that he's a date-rapist.

Cassie was three years ago.

It's *Aubrey* who lost her memory this time, waking up more

wasted and regretful than should have been possible with drinks alone.

"Jesus Christ."

"Miranda, *what?* What the hell are you thinking right now?"

"He roofied her. Dad — *he raped her!*"

"I ... I know. We knew that, didn't we?"

"Not Cassie. *Aubrey!*"

"You think that Ross roofied and raped *Aubrey?*"

I nod vigorously, already standing up. Dad didn't hear what Aubrey said to me outside, and I won't take time now to loop him in. I'm painfully aware of a new clock ticking. I don't know what I'll do yet, but I think I might know very soon. Now that the first sparking wires in my head have made their connection, a new connection is trying to be made. It's something else about Aubrey. Something that, like the roofies, I should have realized before now.

"What are you doing? Where are you going?" Dad calls after me.

"I don't know." But I'm agitated. Pacing. Restless. All the adrenaline that I thought was gone has returned, dying for an outlet. What am I supposed to do with this new information? It feels like I should be able to strike — to somehow make things right now that I know the truth. Aubrey didn't just get drunk. Ross slipped her drugs. *That's* why she did what she'd never otherwise do. *That's* why she woke up the next day, barely aware of what happened.

She was telling the truth. In the end, no matter how little she might want to, Aubrey always tells the truth.

"Oh shit," I say. Because I felt a spark. I understand now what my memory keeps trying to tell me.

I fumble for my phone, so nervous with my new realization that I almost drop it. The time is 9:11. Only four more minutes have passed, everything moving at the speed of paint drying.

I grab a coat and a few other things I absolutely need, then run for the door. Dad shouts after me, wanting to understand, but I don't have time to explain. It's been eleven minutes since Ross left with Aubrey. In Ross's perfect world, anything I try now would already be too late ... but this isn't Ross's perfect world.

With luck, they've already run out of gas.

With any luck at all, I might still be able to catch them.

Chapter Thirty-Seven
AUBREY

The Polaris is a beast. I'll give it that.

I wasn't inside Miranda's cabin for long. I've lost track of time and honestly couldn't say whether it was a half hour or a full hour, but in whatever-time-it-was, new snow and wind have almost completely buried the tracks I made coming in. They're visible mostly as shallow valleys in the snow ahead, nothing more.

Everything's much deeper, too: wind-blown, I think, rather than entirely sky-fallen. The sky isn't shirking, though. If not for the wipers, the windshield would be completely covered in less than a minute. Snow falls so thick, I can barely see ten feet ahead. The headlights don't help, because they illuminate the flakes more than the path I need to see. I'm tempted to turn them off and navigate by moonlight, but that's worse. Hard to believe anything could be worse than this.

The engine sputters. Ross, whose physical state is catching up with him now that we're away from the cabin, doesn't seem to notice. I can see an orange glow from the low-fuel light, but it's barely visible because I shoved a rag into the recess that houses the dashboard before starting the engine. I'd rather not remind Ross how low we are on gas. With luck, we'll run out. The worst-case scenario here would be us getting away. I'd rather take my chances in the snow than stay on this crazy train.

The engine sputters again. This time Ross looks up, but it's only to make sure I'm still sufficiently threatened by his machete.

"What road is this?" he asks.

"It's still the driveway."

"Bullshit."

"You drove here, didn't you?" I ask. "The driveway is over a mile long."

Ross looks around, as if for a clock. Ten minutes have probably passed, though there's no way to check. If his brain is still working, he's doing the math. Ten minutes to go one mile? People run faster than that.

"Drive faster."

"I can't."

He pokes me with the machete. I decide my best defense is offense, so I turn on him and unleash.

"Hey! Do *you* want to drive? Be my guest!" I take my foot off the gas, and we stop right away. "You think you can do better, then *fucking do better!*"

He looks at me, realizes he's barely in good enough condition to act as a crash test dummy, then grunts. I give him ten seconds more of temper, then start driving again.

He's right, though. I *could* drive faster. Truth is, I'm sandbagging. Truth is, I don't *want* to get out of here. My speed is plausible considering the depth of snow and our whiteout conditions, so unless Ross wants to try for himself, he doesn't have much choice than to keep believing me. I've been driving off the path on purpose, too, pretending I'm lost so I have to back up and turn around.

I'm freezing. The heater is on, but it's not doing much to warm the compartment. Ross pulled on his warm-weather gear right away. I'm still wearing what Charlie gave me a lifetime ago, but I still wish I had another layer.

The engine purrs. Hiccups. Purrs.

"I'll rat you out, you know," I say after a silent spell.

"Yeah, yeah."

"I know you raped Cassie."

"Good for you."

"You really think you can get away with shooting Miranda's parents?"

"Of course I can. Self-defense."

"And Miranda?"

"Miranda helped. What's the term? She 'aided and abetted them.' Besides. I didn't shoot *her*."

Not for lack of trying. The world froze for me when Ross pointed the gun at Miranda. He fired almost casually at Mark and Willa, but when it came time for Miranda, Ross raised the muzzle and aimed it at her head. I still feel the click of the hammer when it fell on an empty casing. He wanted to kill her. Not *wound* her, but *kill* her.

My best friend, dead with a bullet between the eyes.

I round a turn. Go off the path, get stuck, then turn around and get back on it.

We enter an open area away from the tree cover. The headlights flicker in time with a low cough from the engine. Ross finally understands, leaning over to peek at the gas gauge. He yanks away the rag, staring at the low-fuel light.

"Oh, right," I say.

The engine dies. The headlights turn off. Everything is silent. When the wind goes still, it's like there's literally no sound. The snow muffles everything. The world's become our private dark box: a cold and quiet tomb.

It's hard to see Ross in the darkness. I can't tell if he knows I sandbagged on purpose, encouraging him to abscond in the Polaris instead of taking his chances with the Jeep. In my defense, It was probably a case of six of one, half a dozen of the other. We'd still have plenty of fuel in the Jeep right now, but we'd've only gone a quarter as far.

I try to move, but I get a machete in the ribs for my trouble.

"Oh, *what?*" I say. "It's *over*, you psychopath. You think your big knife's going to mean shit when you freeze to death?"

He opens his door and then beckons — under threat of disembowelment — for me to follow.

"Let's go," he says, stepping into the darkness. "I have an idea."

Chapter Thirty-Eight
MIRANDA

This was a terrible idea. I shouldn't be trying to drive anywhere, but now that I'm in the Jeep, I refuse to surrender. I couldn't just sit around and do nothing. Not after learning what I learned.

Two roofies.

Two rapes.

Never mind a few counts of attempted murder.

Turns out Ross was the creep all along that Aubrey warned me he was. I refused to hear her, figuring that if anything ever went wrong with me and Ross, I'd learn it (and correct it) along the way. I didn't want to pre-judge him. Never mind that I've known Ross pretty much forever ... and, yeah, the signs were there.

I was too stubborn to listen. Too intent on trying to make my own choices. Too subconsciously insistent, I think now, on doing the thing my parents would hate most of all.

Am I really so predictable? Was I really so angry with the way they controlled me that I was willing to date someone terrible just to piss them off?

No, it's not like that.

And maybe it's not. Maybe I just sort of always had a crush on Ross, dismissing his flaws as "he's kind of a bad boy." Maybe the line between sensibility and dating Ross was a logical one, and I'm only deconstructing it otherwise because things went so bad. But still I have to wonder: that detective thing Aubrey does, where she can't help but assemble clues? I do that sometimes. I did it just now, in fact. It's the reason I'm doing what I'm doing in the snow, even though it doesn't make a bit of sense.

It's okay, I tell myself. *Just try to stay in the ruts.*

Remembering that the Polaris is almost out of gas changed everything. Chasing them far in the Jeep would be futile in this weather, but Aubrey made a big deal out of how close she was to not arriving at all: *I was literally on fumes*, she told us. Aubrey doesn't speak in hyperbole. One of her pet peeves is people who use the word "literally" wrong. If she said it back at the cabin, she meant it. She'd expect to shake her gas tank and hear nothing, because all the engine had left to burn was vapor.

I can't chase them to town ... but maybe I can chase them until they run dry.

How long will that be? I hope it's long — that Aubrey wasn't wrong about those fumes. It's nearly impossible for me to stay on the driveway, even with her ruts. For one thing, the Jeep is wider than the Polaris, meaning I can't use both ruts, just one or the other. My wheels spin in ways her treads won't. I keep nearly getting stuck in snowdrifts, gunning my engine and throwing up rooster tails behind me to get free. The windshield is mostly whited out. Thank God for the moon; when the snowfall slows a little, its glow is reflected by the ever-present whiteness.

It's slow going, but not as slow as I expected. I've got my phone propped in the cup holder, permanently lit up so I can watch the time. It's now 9:15, and the tracks ahead of me seem to be getting fresher. Driving in their ruts isn't entirely useless. I think — but don't dare hope — that I'm catching up.

My hope is dashed moments later when I exit a particularly dense copse of trees. Once out of it, the tracks almost entirely vanish. It means the "fresher" tracks I just saw only *seemed* fresh because the wind wasn't scouring them. Not so out here in the open ... where, I'm now realizing, I can barely see tread tracks at all.

I start to slide. There's ice under the snow.

"Shit."

The slide deepens. I move from deep snow into scoured-down earth, where the wind has blown most of the snow cover away. It'd be a blessing if not for the ice, which is thick here. Without snow to cradle my tires, I'm free to slide wherever I want, including sideways.

"SHITSHITSHITSHIT!"

I'm approaching the drainage culvert, helpless to stop myself. The brakes are beyond useless. I pump them anyway, even though I'm now sideways to the direction of travel. Obviously, nothing happens. The culvert looms. The corrugated-steel pipe at its lip is exposed: a dark gray spot in all this whiteness.

The Jeep's rear wheel slides off of the dome of the road, followed by the front wheel on the same side. God help me, I'm going to roll into the ditch sideways.

I brace myself: hands and feet. The car tips sideways, half-rolls, then stops with a heavy, shuddering crunch. I'm left breathless, wondering if I've survived. After a moment I realize I'm fine. I was driving slow. The airbags didn't even go off.

But now I'm on a tilt. I push the pedal, knowing there's no point, and of course the wheels just spin.

I kill the engine. Which kills the heat. I look back toward the cabin, which I can no longer see. That's not saying much, because I can't see very far, but I can see far enough to know that walking back in surrender is my only remaining choice.

I close my eyes and think an apology to Aubrey. *I tried, my friend. I'm sorry.*

But when I exit the Jeep through the passenger side, I realize I can see something after all. Behind me is the driveway to the cabin. But ahead, in the shadows, is a squat black form that can only be the Polaris.

Its doors are open.

From them, two sets of footprints lead into the woods.

Chapter Thirty-Nine

AUBREY

I keep looking for opportunities to get away, but Ross seems to have figured that out. I never thought he was smart, but there's no doubt he's cunning. Like a rodent, Ross isn't good at math or reading or talking about history. But damn is he good at solving whatever maze it takes to get the cheese.

I march ahead of Ross through the snow, holding the lantern we took from the cabin. It's the only way, because we'll never get anywhere if Ross has to hold my arm the entire time, keeping his weapon close enough to cut me if I try to run.

To solve the inherent problem with a me-in-front arrangement (namely, that the chances of me running are greatly increased), Ross has found a simple if undignified solution: He's got me on a leash. Abby's leash, to be specific. I took it off while we were driving and left it in the footwell, and now it's clipped to a collar Ross made for me from a pair of plastic zip ties he found in the back. I can't pull free without choking myself. Ross knows his strength is at a low point, so he's looped the leash around his hand almost in a knot. The same hand, since Ross only has one now, holds the machete. I've considered spinning on him, grabbing the leash with both hands, and pulling for all I've got, but if I do that, I suspect all I'll do will be to pull Ross toward me machete-first.

"I think it's that way," he says.

I don't think he's right. From the road, the driveway forks left to a neighboring house before forking right to the empty barn he wants us to reach. I'm pretty good with directions, even snow-blind as we are. My internal compass says it's the other way, so I say so.

Ross looks skeptical in the lantern light. "You're trying to trick me."

"I'm not trying to trick you. Do you think I want to freeze to death out here?"

Ross keeps assessing me, trying to decide the answer. It's *no*, by the way. I *did* want to run out of gas while we were still on the property, which is why I took my time and created so many false detours, but that was only so we'd have no choice but to turn back around. Ross may not be smart, but he's got that rodent's will to survive. We both want the same thing now, and "dying out here" hits the bullseye for neither of us.

"Fine," he says.

We resume walking, but doubt assails me almost right away. When the street-line power died, it killed the spotlight above the goat barn. That means I can suspect our direction all I want, but I can't see it. I'm trusting my gut, In truth, I know nothing.

I hug my coat closer, thankful that Charlie equipped me but still feeling frostbite.

Our survival clock is ticking. We could be headed into doom, and we won't know until we're dead.

Chapter Forty

MIRANDA

My flashlight is a big four-cell Maglite, heavy as hell. I keep extending it further in front of me to try and see more. It's not only futile; it's also an intense shoulder workout. I keep switching hands when one shoulder gets tired. The light isn't nearly as strong as it should be. I think the batteries are almost depleted. I keep having to slap the thing to wake it up, to brighten the beam enough to keep on going.

Going where, though? I've already lost my bearings.

I suspect I might be terrified, but as long as I focus on my job out here, terror retreats to the background. *I need to find Aubrey.* I keep telling myself that over and over and over. It shouldn't make a difference, now that I know what Ross did to her, but it does. I should want to save my friend the exact same amount as before, but learning her innocence has practically turned me into a martyr. Somewhere deep down, I think I might be okay dying if I can at least save Aubrey from Ross before I do. Because the way I feel right now, what's left for me if I *don't* find her? The future is bleak. This — this foolish quest I'm on right now — is the last thing I can grasp that feels anything like salvation.

Just follow the tracks. You can do this, Miranda — just follow their tracks.

For a while, I'm able to do just that. Ross and Aubrey abandoned their vehicle in an alcove, so the footprints leading away from it stayed fresh. There were two sets; I was strangely relieved to see that. My fears said maybe he'd killed her so he could get away solo, but no; I see a big and a smaller set of boots headed into the trees.

Why *into the trees?* I don't understand where he's taking her. I can only fear the worst: that the only reason Ross hasn't killed Aubrey already is because he plans to kill her later. The big chasm down to the river is in this direction, I think. What, do they plan to swan dive off the falls, going out in a blaze of glory?

I think I see light in the woods from time to time, but it's hard to tell if it's real or just a trick of my mind. The snow casts its own light, now that my eyes are adjusted to all this blue moon. I'd expect them to loop back to the driveway and return to the cabin, Ross assuming Mom and Dad are incapacitated or dead so he'd only have to face me. The cabin is the only warmth around for miles. Where exactly does he think he's going?

The terrain rises and falls. My calves are quickly exhausted from all the trudging and climbing. In snow this deep, nothing is really waterproof. Melted snow has soaked my jeans, my socks, the inside of my boots. It's so cold in there. I feel like I'm wearing bricks of ice.

On a hill, I look around. The wind blows. I hope to see some sign of them (Ross can't be moving that fast), but there's nothing ... except, maybe again that weird trick of might-be-light. I keep thinking I hear things when the wind rests, too, but sound under these conditions seems to come from everywhere.

I sigh and look at the snow from where I stand. Fear takes me.

Because although I can still see my own tracks behind me, there are none in front anymore. A small snowfall, probably kicked down by Ross and Aubrey, has obscured the tracks for twenty feet or so ahead ... and beyond that, the wind has done its job and erased them.

My own tracks, as I stand here and think, are dissolving too.

I shiver. And think.

I don't know what to do: Go on blind, or go back while I still can?

Chapter Forty-One
AUBREY

We stop short, our way forward blocked by a cliff's edge. It makes me laugh the desperate, futile laugh of the damned.

My famous self-sabotage is back with a vengeance. I haven't led us to the barn after all. Turns out I've led us to the top of an enormous bluff with a river at the bottom. From what I remember of the Google Earth shots of this place, the river is on the opposite side of the property from the pasture and barn. We went in exactly the wrong direction.

I may have marooned us, and if my guess of our position is correct, we're nowhere near anything that could help us. It's probably a mile to the barn from here, and at least that to the cabin if not more. I doubt we can walk that far anymore — probably not me, certainly not Ross. I'm finding my thoughts and movement sluggish, as if my core temperature is dropping.

Neither of our coats do much for the knife-edge of the wind. My guess is we're already dead. We just don't know it yet.

I laugh. It's a single exclamation, more like a bleat than anything human.

"What the fuck are you laughing at?" Ross demands.

"You. You and your plans."

"Where the hell is the barn?"

"Miles away. Miles."

He looks aghast. "You asshole. You've killed both of us, not just me."

I look to the side, leaning out against the tether of my leash. I want to see how far down the river is. If there was a stone nearby, I'd throw it in. The river — and the drop to it — are now far more interesting to me than Ross.

"What's wrong with you?" Ross asks.

But I just keep laughing. I'm delirious. I'm going to die, and I just don't care. The whole situation strikes me as ludicrous. Look at Ross: big man with the machete and the control end of the leash! He can barely walk. Barely stay upright. Right now, he's trying to look threatening — to stare me down so I know he's serious about hurting me, so I know who's boss. But given our situation, trying to be boss is so ridiculous, I want to guffaw. We'll be fucked a few different ways by nature before anyone's fucked by Ross and his power complex.

Am I really supposed to be afraid of him now? If that's what he wants, he'd better get in line. Hypothermia and a power drop to the river's bottom are both so much more real than the dictator Ross imagines himself to be.

A branch cracks. My eyes flick, and in the corner of those eyes I see Ross turn his head fully. Someone new has entered our midst. Someone I'm half-sad to see, because now she'll die with us, lost as I feel. Someone holding a big black flashlight, its beam off so she could approach by stealth.

Seeing Miranda, Ross yanks me toward him on the leash like a human yo-yo. I was wrong about his strength: He's still got it when it matters. Maybe "rodent" was the wrong metaphor for Ross's will to survive. I think now that "cockroach" is better.

Instantly I've got the machete to my throat again, but this time it means business. Its blade is against my trachea. My earlier mirth is gone; now I'm afraid all over again.

I try to elbow him in the gut, but Ross dodges. He punishes my insolence by cutting me. I feel blood flow into my collar. It's almost welcome in its warmth, but very quickly it freezes.

"Stay back," Ross tells Miranda.

"It's over, Ross."

He pulls me more in front of himself, hiding behind me like he did back at the cabin. Miranda barely reacts.

"It's over," she repeats. "Look at yourself. If you don't get inside soon, you'll—"

Ross interrupts, his voice harsh in my ear. I've never heard him this way. He sounds like an animal.

"I told you to *STAY BACK!* If I don't get inside soon, then what? I'll *die?*" He rakes the machete across my neck once more — enough to draw blood again. "So what? I'm dead already."

"We all need to get warm. Let her go, and I'll take you both back."

"You don't know which way to go."

She nods. "I do."

"We got lost. What makes you think that *you—*"

This time it's Miranda who cuts Ross off. Her tone is impatient, as if she's had enough of his shit and won't put up with it anymore.

"The trees are tapped. For sap collection," she says. "The tapped trees make a straight line. We just have to follow it back. We're not far. Ten minutes, we could be back inside."

"Which direction?" Ross asks.

"Don't tell him!" I blurt, but then Ross is strangling me again.

"Which direction," Ross repeats.

Miranda takes a step. Ross again tightens his hold on me, but Miranda keeps coming.

"No closer," Ross says. Miranda's not near enough to touch him, but in another few steps she will be.

"Let her go, Ross."

"I'll kill her first!"

Miranda seems to consider, then nods as if Ross has answered a trivia question correctly. He really will kill me; I see that now. He's got nothing left. For a while, maybe he could have pled his case to the cops or the courts, but that margin has grown slimmer as today's events rolled on. The cuts on my neck are new testimony against him ... along with some unknown ace I can see in Miranda. *She's learned something even worse about Ross since we left*, my clue-sense tells me. And the way she looks at me ... it's as if all's forgotten already. As if I never slept with her boyfriend at all.

Seeing recognition on Miranda's face — knowing that Miranda knows he's serious and is ready to kill me because he no longer has any way out — Ross smiles a cunning grin. I can't see it from where he's holding me, though. I have to feel the way his face moves, our skins deadly close.

"That's right," Ross taunts. "Back up unless you want her cut to pieces."

Miranda does. I see her mind working, trying to find a way out of this. I'm not sure there is one. Ross realizing how desperate his situation has become was maybe the *worst* thing that could have happened. He'll kill me without question if he has to now, just because he's angry. Because there's no consequence left.

"Okay," he says. His voice is very, very close to my ear. I can smell his breath. It's fetid, as if he's swallowed his own blood. "Here's what's going to happen. Miss Aubrey and I are going to get out of here. You're going to stay right where you are."

His head turns toward the woods behind Miranda. Because he's got me so close now, my head turns, too. I see the line of tree taps Miranda was referring to. They're like little spigots, embedded in the maples. That's where he's going to take me. That's where he's going to try and drag me with a blade to my neck the whole way.

"No," Miranda says.

"No?"

"You heard me. I know what you did to her. I can't let you do it to anyone ever again."

"Everyone's already heard your 'theories' about Cassie," Ross says. *"Boo-fucking-hoo."*

"I'm not talking about Cassie. I'm talking about Aubrey."

"I haven't done anything to Aubrey." He laughs, looking down at the cuts on my neck. "She cut herself shaving, is all."

"And I'm not talking about now. I'm talking about Sunday."

I dare to crane my neck. "What?"

"The half-pack of Rohypnol you had on you," Miranda says. "When did you use the rest?"

Ross clearly didn't anticipate the question. He doesn't answer right away. My mind, on the other hand, is ablaze. *Sunday?* I know what happened on Sunday. But what's it got to do with...?

No. My mind won't believe it.

"Or should I say," Miranda goes on, "*Who* did you give the rest to?"

I crane my neck further. Ross still hasn't answered. I have, though.

My inexplicable drunkenness after not enough drink. My total and complete loss of control. The way I can't remember what happened until it was all over. The way I betrayed someone I'd never betray, no matter how drunk I got. How haven't I put it together before now?

"You son of a b—!" I start to say, but Ross stops me with his deepest cut yet.

"Shut up," he says. Then to Miranda: "You can't prove a thing."

"Maybe not. But let's find out."

He laughs. "Then I guess my choice is easy. Nothing left for Ross out there in the normal world, is there? Even if nobody believes me, you'll do your thing, telling everyone what you think you know. And *you*..." He presses the blade into my larynx. "*You'll* do *your* thing. You meddling, conniving, in-everyone's-fucking-business-piece-of-shit. Tell me you won't." He lifts my face a little so I can see him, but he's no longer the man he was. He's pale, almost blue. His eyes are hard and half frozen over. I've always felt it would be a mistake to push Ross too far. Oh, he plays charming ... but beneath it is the kind of guy who snaps one day and shoots up a school.

"If you're going to do you," he growls to Miranda, "and *you're* going to do *you*," he growls to me, "then I guess all that's left is for *me to do me.*"

His elbow rises. What was once a limp arm flexes, tightened with the elbow up and out. He's going to slit my throat — for real this time.

Miranda sees what he's about to do and shouts: one hand up, coming forward to stop him. But it's too late; turns out Ross really was in charge after all. Miranda shouldn't have chased us. She's forced his hand, and now that Ross is backed into a corner, he's done with bluffing.

A branch cracks. We hear the thrumming of a strange machine — a *brum-brum-brum* sound rushing through the snow-covered underbrush. At first, I have no idea what it is, but I'm not imagining it; Miranda freezes and Ross freezes because they hear it too. It almost sounds like the galloping of a horse, coming right at us. But there's no horse here. The snow is swirling, and the woods are silent. Out in the woods, there's nothing at all.

Except a shadow: low, dark, and bullet quick. I catch sight of it far off, back the way we came, before it vanishes on the low side of a rise. It's moving fast. *So* fast. It comes like lightning, four feet kicking up snow along our footpath, following my scent to find its source.

I understand before Miranda or Ross because I've seen this before. In very different settings, but I've seen it before. Throw a ball for Abby, and she'll run like a big hairy missile. Because this is Abby we're talking about, and Abby loves balls.

Ross sees her too late. He should know to drop me and cover himself, but he doesn't. After all, we're alone out here … and only of us has balls to catch.

Abby doesn't run to me, the way I think she might. Instead she rushes lower, sinking her teeth into Ross's crotch and holding on for dear life. I fall away, safe, then watch the show. The machete is to one side now, completely forgotten. At first, I can hardly catch my breath. Can hardly believe it. My dog is the sweetest little girl — but everyone says that even the sweetest dogs know when to defend the pack.

She snarls as she rips at Ross's jeans. Pulls. Whips her head from side to side. Ross can only thrash, screaming. It's hard to watch, but I don't care enough to make her stop. I turn to look back the way she came. And to think I thought navigation in the snow was impossible? It wasn't impossible for a dog able to follow tracks to the Polaris, then scent to her best friend when she needed her most.

Miranda comes to stand beside me. "Oh. Right. The cabin door doesn't always latch. Silly me."

I move to call Abby off, but Ross gets free on his own. His crotch is covered with blood. Somehow, he manages his feet, and at first, I think he might try to run. I almost hope he does. The lip of the cliff is mere feet behind him, and the only other way out of here is through us: two women who'll never let him pass.

But he doesn't run. He can't reach us, so he turns his ire on the dog. He looks down as she snarls. Then he raises one leg, as if to kick her.

I shout, but for once Miranda doesn't wait until the threat is past to act. In the time it takes for me to open my mouth, she's cocked her arm back like someone throwing a fastball. Then, before Ross can kick, she hurls what she's holding for all she's worth. I see it as it spins through the air. It's her huge black Maglite, as heavy as a truncheon.

It hits Ross between the eyes. Startled, he falls backward.

Over the edge, down the cliff, tumbling past rocks until he reaches the bottom.

Chapter Forty-Two

It seems to me that Ross falls for a very long time. Too long, really. After the expected several seconds, it's as if I'm the one who starts to float and tumble. I don't need to imagine what it was like, to spin down end over end. Inside my head, I'm doing the same soon enough.

Without warning, my knees buckle and I collapse. I hit the snow in an untidy pile. My vision's gone fuzzy. I try to stand back up, but I don't understand why equilibrium won't hold.

"Aubrey? Are you okay?"

The voice comes from a million miles away. Down a long, dark tunnel studded with tiny points of light.

"I'm fine," I say. But my voice, too, is far away.

I honestly think I'm okay. I try again to stand, but now I can't tell which side is snow and which is sky. I'm cold. Colder than I should be.

A warm presence rushes forward and surrounds me. I can't remember why I'm down here on the ground. Even kneeling makes me unsteady. Even when I give up and let myself stay where I am, the whole world rotates.

Miranda's hands are all over me, at my neck and its many cuts most of all.

"Jesus. He got you, didn't he?"

"Who?" I ask.

My eyes drift closed.

I don't want to think about this anymore.

THE NEXT TIME I OPEN MY EYES, MY BRAIN IS A LITTLE CLEARER, but someone is strangling me again. I hear people talking. The voices are familiar. I think it's Miranda. Miranda talking to a woman. Her mother, I think.

My hand goes to my neck. Turns out nobody's strangling me. I've been wrapped with a bandage, and the bandage is extremely tight. It's hard to swallow.

The fog clears, but something's wrong; I'm too weak to move much. I roll my head to one side, wanting to see what Miranda's up to, but instead I see log-built walls and thick gray mortar. I've rolled in the wrong direction, more confused than I thought I was. I see a window. Outside is the front porch of what I now remember is Miranda's parents' vacation cabin.

Worst vacation ever.

On the porch is a child's sled. I seem to remember seeing it tucked inside a hunter's lean-to when I was out walking with Miranda's boyfriend Ross earlier, though I can't imagine why I'd be out walking with Ross at night. A spark of something in distant memory leaves me with a bad taste about that walk. It wasn't very fun, I don't think, or maybe it had ended badly.

I remember seeing the sled in the lean-to when Ross and I walked past it, though. I remember, later, being injured. Is the sled how Miranda brought me back here? Did I take a ride while I was asleep?

It's warm in the cabin. My skin prickles as it heats. The cold outside was terrible, but this actually feels worse. In the cold, I eventually went numb. Here, I feel like a frozen roast slowly coming to room temperature.

I roll my head the other way. Yes, it's Miranda who was speaking. Her mother is slouched in a chair, looking sallow, while Miranda paces the way she does when she's trying to think. Willa's wearing a bandage on one shoulder. That's nothing compared to Miranda's dad, though, who's listening to this conversation from the floor. All three of them are covered in blood. Mark isn't moving, other than the slow rise and fall of his chest as he breathes. A lumpy washcloth is on his forehead: ice, I'm guessing, to quench a fever.

I tune into Miranda's words mid-sentence, as she speaks more *at* her mother than *with* her.

"... than the carotid artery. I don't think I could have staunched it if it was her carotid he'd nicked. The bandage should slow things down but it's not stopping on its own. Mom? Are you still with me, Mom?"

"I'm sorry," Willa says.

"Don't be sorry. You're in shock, is all. I know it hurts, but I need you. If you can't walk, we're in trouble. I can't handle three of you all by myself."

"'Handle' how?" Willa asks, sounding more alert now.

"We need to get to a hospital."

I see more windows behind them, the snow still falling. The steady thrum of an engine drones from behind the far wall: probably the generator powering our heat and light. Injury isn't the only countdown here. Eventually fuel for the engine will run out, the heat will die, and we'll freeze. I'm coming around now, remembering what happened. I even remember the weather report. The next week calls for overcast skies and temperatures below freezing. Even if the snow stops, what's here already won't melt.

"How can we get to a hospital in this?"

"I'll siphon gas from one of the other cars and fill the Polaris that Aubrey drove here. We have to hurry. She keeps bleeding through her bandage. And Dad..." She looks down at him, but it's like she doesn't want to think about it enough to finish her sentence. "It's taking a risk to try the roads, but we can't just stay here. They'll..." But she doesn't want to finish that sentence, either.

"Arm," I say.

It comes out of me almost involuntarily. My body hurts and I feel dizzy, but my brain is coming back. It can't help trying to solve this puzzle along with Miranda, the exact same way it always does. I see pieces of a puzzle trying to fit, and right now one element is missing. We can run, but we can't hide. There are still crimes here — however justified — to answer for.

Miranda looks at me, then comes over.

"What did you say?"

I swallow past the too-tight bandage wrapping my neck. "You have to deal with Ross's arm," I say.

I FADE IN AND OUT. SOMEONE'S PUT A DIMMER SWITCH ON MY consciousness and blackout shades on my eyes. I can't control when I come and go. Sometimes I'm awake and aware for long, contiguous periods of lucidity, and other times I simply go away. Time passes the same in both places. When I'm not awake, I dream bizarre versions of what seems to actually be happening. It becomes tricky to tell what's real and what's not.

Watching Miranda leave for a tool locker in the shed and come back holding what looks like a ham hock with a wristwatch: *Real, or not?*

Being carried by Miranda and her mother into the Polaris, which I can only assume Miranda refueled and drove back here while I was sleeping: *Real, or not?* I'd absolutely think the former, but parts of it are surreal. Miranda can't carry me by herself, and her mother's right arm is useless thanks to the shoulder, so Willa carries my feet using a sling wrapped around her neck and back: an enormous Baby-Björn made from a bedsheet.

Rattling down the dark driveway in blinding snow, then detouring deep into the woods: Is *that* one real? Or not? If we're in such a hurry, it doesn't make sense to detour, does it? We end up at the cliff's edge where Ross fell to his death, parking so Miranda can get out.

Miranda standing at the edge, looking down, then tossing Ross's severed arm to land near his body. *Real, or not?*

It feels real, because Abby is between me and the window I'm watching through, nuzzling against me.

"Coyotes," says a voice to my left.

I roll my head to see Mark Wimberly, propped upright in the seat beside me. We're alone in the back of the Polaris. Willa is outside with Miranda, looking down to see if they hit their target.

"What?"

"Coyotes are hungriest this time of year," he says, sounding drugged. "Whatever they don't eat, vultures will."

I understand. I'm witnessing a first pass at explaining Ross's death: Poor bastard fell off a cliff and coyotes ate his corpse. But there are so many problems with that story. There's the state of the rest of us to consider: shot, shot, and cut. There's the state of the cabin and shed, filled with gruesome evidence. Most of all, there's the fact that Ross's arm was hacked from the bone by a big knife, not pulled off by animals.

"Nobody will believe he just fell, and that's all that happened," I tell Mark.

Mark is drifting. I'm drifting away again, too.

"It depends who investigates," Mark says, "and how closely they look."

That seems like thin reasoning to me: hanging our futures on a bullshit story and hopes that some dim-witted cop believes it without thinking twice. We need a better alibi. We need to hide the evidence. Ross was a multiple rapist who, in his last hour, shot two people, made sincere efforts to kill Miranda, cut my throat, and tried to kick my dog to death, but we can't prove any of it. *Oh, Ross raped girls? Prove it.* I didn't even wake up sore after he did it to me. It's going to look like I led him on, lied about being raped, then led him up to this honeytrap to die. Hell, *I* didn't even know what he did to me until Miranda figured it out. It makes me feel dirtier than dirty, learning I was essentially violated while sleeping.

Even if we somehow make it to a hospital — even if we do it before I bleed to death and Mark succumbs to infection — we'll be arrested soon after. We're murderers. Murderers and worse.

"Nobody will believe it," I say.

It's my last thought as I drift into another dose of nothingness.

. . .

THE POLARIS JOLTS TO A STOP. IT JARS ME AWAKE. IT DOESN'T DO the same for Mark, who's breathing deeply in a slow, hitching rhythm. Even the sounds of doors opening and slamming don't cause him to stir, though they happen right beside him.

Miranda and Willa — now starting to look as drawn and drained as her husband, though she's still on her feet — walk ahead into the snow. There's something in the road ahead. It's massive: half white and half brown. It's hard for me to understand at first, because it's too far away to be more than a horizontal series of shapes in the moonlit darkness. Then, as they walk along the thing, I realize what it is. It's a fallen tree limb, big enough to block the road.

They return to the cab, then re-close the doors.

"We'll have to go around," Miranda says. "That's all there is to it."

Willa looks at the dashboard clock. When she then turns around to look at Mark, she sees that I'm awake.

"How far do we have left?" I ask, too weak to lift my head properly.

"We've been driving for an hour," Willa says, frowning at Mark with concern, "and we've made it five miles."

I HAVE DREAMS OF CHOKING. DREAMS WHERE THE LIFE WITHIN me drains away like water from the bottom of a funnel. Dreams in which Ross still holds me death-grip tight, the kiss of cold steel against my throat. Dreams of Ross tumbling forever into oblivion, with me tumbling close behind.

In this half-haze, snapshots of life outside my skull come in seconds-long clips, stitched in series by some mad editor with nothing in between.

The Polaris climbing a hill I don't recognize, struggling for purchase.

Miranda exiting the vehicle, twice, to clear small-enough branches from the road.

Miranda refilling the gas tank, souring the air with hydrocarbon fumes.

Willa's head and torso leaning through the open passenger door, vomiting until she's dry. Willa's not doing as well as she was at first. Maybe she's losing blood like I am. Maybe it's just the enormous existential stress (being shot, her husband near death, and a corpse at the ravine's bottom, left for the buzzards) that's finally getting to her.

Miranda, driving with a grim expression on her face as if doing duty nobody should ever have to do. She's the only one awake; her mother's finally passed out with her head against the window. Miranda doesn't see me watching her. Watching the hard lines and high-contrast sculpture her face has become in the up-shining light of the dashboard. I guess nobody can say Miranda need controlling anymore. What she's doing now makes her the ultimate adult. *So* adult, she might never glimpse childhood again.

I look at the clock. It's 10:38 p.m. on Saturday. A whole new week to replace this horrible last one will begin in only an hour and twenty-two minutes.

My eyes start to close again.

A whole new week. I wish I could believe I'll be around to see it.

THE NEXT TIME I'M AWAKE, I DON'T REALLY FEEL AWAKE. MY neck hurts. I don't know if the pain is real. If the *situation* is real. I touch my neck and feel the bandage. My fingers come away red and wet.

The Polaris has stopped. There are too many lights outside, but the lights don't make sense. We're still in the middle of nowhere, still surrounded by trees and foot-deep snow. The new lights come from other vehicles. Two of them. The lights on them aren't white, like our headlights. One has the rotating yellow strobe of a utility vehicle. The other is the alternating red and blue of police flashers. In the midst of all of it, people run to and fro. There's activity out there that my tired mind doesn't understand: People in big, matching coats rushing to pull items from a storage box on one of the vehicles.

So this is it. This is how our story ends. I can't make it much longer, Mark might already be dead, and Miranda's outside with uniformed police officers. I can't see if they're questioning her. I can't see if she's already in handcuffs, or at least being escorted from our ride to the back of theirs. I can't see the expression on anyone's faces. Willa's still asleep, or at least unconscious.

I can imagine what the police are saying:

So let me get this straight. You were spending winter break with your parents. You didn't know that your boyfriend showed up, stowed his car, and started exploring the woods. He fell off a cliff. Coyotes ripped off his arm. Meanwhile, unrelated accidents with a pistol and a machete nearly killed you. Is that what happened?

I want to rush out and help Miranda with her cover story, but I'm far too weak for that. Miranda is no good at this kind of thing. She'll screw it up. She can't lie well. She misses details. Why didn't they ask me? I *never* miss details.

In one of my lucid windows back at the cabin, I gave Miranda my best shot at an explanation of what happened that hopefully won't get us all busted. There's one small problem with it: It's more than bullshit. It'll fall apart the minute anyone doubts it even a little.

The way I figure, our story says that Ross was a highly disturbed person. He didn't like that Miranda hadn't told her parents about him because they hated him, so he went to their cabin to confront them. Things devolved quickly. In the tussle, Ross got hold of a gun from the owner's closet and held them captive for days — then held Miranda, too, when she showed up and told him to let her parents go. When I showed up days later, I upset everything. The Wimberlys got free and fought back, but he shot them both. Miranda and I managed to drive Ross away, but he got lost in the storm and fell into the ravine. End of story.

But there are so many problems with that tale. How did my neck get slit? Why was Ross's arm hacked off at the bone? How did I know to come in the first place, and where are Miranda's pleading texts to prove it? The timelines don't work. The motivations don't make sense. The story I've invented is a house of cards: It works ... if nobody touches it, not even a little.

But it's not police who open the doors, carefully removing me, Mark, and Willa one at a time. It's volunteer paramedics, one of whom is still in his pajamas. The vehicle with yellow flashers turns out to be a truck with enormous, knobby wheels and a covered cargo bed: a makeshift mountain ambulance, complete with sutures, morphine, and bags of blood. I tell them I'm type A positive. A man asks if I'm sure. Giving me A positive might kill me if I'm wrong.

I'm staring at the sky, then the inside of the covered truck bed. A broad-shouldered policeman sits with me, probably to make sure I don't try to escape. Our group tortured and killed a guy, after all. They aren't fooled by whatever bullshit Miranda told them, and they know that we're the bad ones.

"What's going on?" I ask the cop.

He might be about to speak when someone new enters the space. Instead he looks at me grimly, then looks at the newcomer in the exact same way. Unspoken knowledge passes between them.

A furry-hooded girl slides into my field of vision. I'm shocked to realize it's Charlie.

"How...?" I start to ask.

"You showed me your map, remember?"

"But..."

"Something kept bugging me after you left," Charlie says. "Bugging and bugging and bugging." Her face scrunches, as if she's a mystery to herself. "That ever happen to you? You just kind of get this feeling that something's not quite right, even if everyone around you says it's fine?"

I'd laugh if I could. She's just described my life.

"I have three older brothers," Charlie goes on. "Country men. The kind you don't dare tell there's trouble unless it's really bad, because they'll break down walls to protect you." She laughs a little. "It gets boring, really."

At that, I almost want to smile. Now she's describing Mark, who's being treated beside me.

Charlie leans closer, in case Mark regains consciousness and hears. "Your name was Aubrey, right?"

I try to nod. It's a mistake. I'm refilling with blood now, but my neck remains cut — not in a nodding mood.

"I told you I once got in trouble," Charlie says. "I told you I knew how it was when nobody's got your back."

Instead of nodding, I wait.

"What I didn't say was that when my dad and brothers found out, they wanted to have my back after it was too late. The asshole who did it to me ... he got away."

The cap door opens. The big cop crawls back inside. I understand the look he and Charlie exchanged earlier. This is one of her brothers. One of the paramedics looked just like him. I can only assume the other two guys out there are her father and her third brother, also a cop.

Charlie introduces us. His name is Nathan.

"Your friend out there has one hell of a story to tell," he says. "She told me and my brother that her boyfriend came up and went psycho on her parents. Held them captive for days, then held *her* captive too after she arrived. She says you came up while all that was going on. Caused a ruckus. Ran the guy off, and he fell down a cliff."

It's hard to look convincing in my lie while I hurt so bad. I try not to blink.

"She also said there were a few accidents. Unrelated." The way he says it, it's clear he's not fooled. "Like the cuts on your neck." We stare at each other for a few minutes. "Hard to believe, isn't it?"

"Look..."

"Hard to believe," he goes on, "but stranger things have happened. I imagine by now the coyotes are getting to him. Might even have ripped off an arm."

"Miranda told us what he did to you," Charlie says. "You, and her sister."

Another quiet beat. Charlie stares at me knowingly, trying to tell me something without having to say it aloud.

"That's what happened," I tell the cop. "It happened just like Miranda said."

"So hard to believe," Officer Nathan says, shaking his head with something like regret, "but who would I be to question the word of multiple witnesses?"

Chapter Forty-Three
MIRANDA

I find Aubrey upright in her hospital bed. The dressing the doctors gave her is tidier than mine: not even a square of gauze so much as an enormous tan-colored Band-Aid. Beneath are a few stitches that cover delicate laser repair to her jugular vein. It's not exactly first aid I could have done at the cabin.

"How do you feel?" I ask.

"Terrible," she says. "It's like someone dragged me through the woods with a machete at my throat."

"Good."

"Good?"

"Last time I was in here, you told me how it'd just occurred to you that maybe joining a cult wouldn't be so bad. The painkillers they had you on really opened your eyes and let you see through the bullshit."

"Oh. Great."

"You also told me I should start wearing pink."

"You?"

"Me," I say.

Aubrey looks pained. "You look terrible in pink. I *must*'ve been high."

I squat down. What looks like a fat black throw rug is within

Aubrey's reach at the side of her bed. When I pet the throw rug, it lifts its head and says *falafel*.

"And how are *you*, Abby?" I ask, scratching behind her ears.

"She's not here; that's how she is," Aubrey answers. "It's so incredibly against regulations to have a pet in the hospital, it's not even funny."

"I told them she was an emotional support animal."

Aubrey frowns. "I thought they started cracking down on that, since anyone can claim that any dog anywhere is an emotional support animal."

I stand back up. "Yeah, well. Turns out the brother of Charlie's who I thought was just a paramedic is actually head of surgery here. I probably could have said Abby was the pope and he'd've said okay."

"He looked like he was thirty."

"Yeah, well. Leightonville is a small town. 'Head of surgery' doesn't take much here."

I walk to the room door, close it, then sit in a chair with Abby at my feet.

"Have you said anything to anyone about what actually happened?" I ask, my voice low.

"No. Not unless it was in the same conversation where I talked about cults," Aubrey says. Then she, too, lowers her voice. "Why haven't the police been by?"

"They will, now that you're awake."

"Well? What's our story? What did you tell Charlie's brother..."

"Nathan," I tell her.

"What did you tell Nathan, up there in the snow?"

"The truth," I say.

Aubrey's quiet, absorbing this. She's probably trying to square it with the fact that neither of us are under arrest.

"At first, I told them what you said to tell them. I said that I was going up to see my parents, but Ross showed up. He went nuts. Held them captive until I arrived, then held me, too. When we got free, he shot them. Tried to shoot me. Dragged you off. I told them he fell off the cliff on his own." I reach down and pet Abby again.

"Although maybe it would have been okay to mention your savior. Dogs don't get arrested for biting rapists in the balls."

"Okay," Aubrey says.

"But then I came clean. I knew it wouldn't hold up. The shed is full of blood and pee and marks where Mom and Dad tied Ross with ropes. The cabin's absolutely covered in blood; I'm taking one of Charlie's dad's rental vehicles up there tomorrow to clean it as best I can. There are bullet holes from the shots I fired before Ross got hold of the gun. There's the machete, and Ross's wounds." I lower my voice to a whisper. "It's not just the arm. I'll bet I fractured his skull when I hit him with the flashlight."

I take a breath.

"The timing doesn't make sense," I continue. "The fact that you came up at all doesn't really work with that version of events, either. I didn't mention the pictures Ross sent, so those are still out there. His phones are up at the cabin somewhere. Both of them. I..." I sigh. "I couldn't live that way, wondering when someone was going to find out. These are police officers. They'd go up to the cabin eventually. All it'd take would be one quick look at the place and they'd know we were lying. I figured telling the truth from the start might get us some leniency.

"So I told them everything. I told them how Dad flipped out because he knew what Ross did to Cassie. I told them how my parents tied him up after it went too far and they didn't know what to do with him — especially since Dad flipped in the first place because he thought Ross might hurt me, too. I even spoke for you, Aub. I hope it wasn't out of turn. I just spilled my guts. I probably could have gotten away with pretending the fall was accidental, but then I thought about the skull fracture and fessed up on that one, too. So it's all out there. Every bit of it."

"What did Charlie's brothers say when you told them?" Aubrey asks.

"They said, 'Sorry, I didn't hear you.'"

"*What?* What's that mean?"

"I think it means we're safe," I tell her. I can finally say those words aloud without double-clutching like I've been doing since we got here last night, because I'm starting to believe them. "Nathan and Carson are the only local police. I got the feeling Leightonville PD would only get involved if they saw reason to — if the local cops flagged anything as suspicious. But something tells me Charlie's brothers won't find anything suspicious. Or *didn't*, because they went up there while we were going back down in the truck. I saw them just a few minutes ago out in the hallway. They wanted to know how everyone was. But it was too weird, to just assume they'd keep our secret, so I pulled them aside and asked if we were okay."

"And what did they say?"

"They said, 'Sorry. We didn't hear you.'"

Aubrey reaches for my hand, which is resting on the bed rail. She grips it tightly.

"I should have told you I was buying Adderall and Xanax from Ross," she says. I'm a little alarmed — and surprised — to see the beginnings of tears in her eyes. "My fucking parents. The insurance wouldn't cover them. I never should have kept it from you. All that time sneaking around..." Her face goes bitter, looking away. "All that time with that son of a bitch, so careful to never let you know. I thought you might think I was after him. I know you don't like secrets. I was ashamed. Ashamed that I was so weak. So needy. So I just crept around and messaged him on his burner whenever I needed a refill. It kept me on his radar. Kept him on *me*. If I hadn't been there in the first place..." She sighs. "It doesn't matter if he drugged me. There was no excuse for being there at all." She squeezes harder. "I can't lose you, Miranda. You're all I have."

When she's finished, I just look back at her.

"Miranda?"

"I'm so sorry," I say with a smile and a squeeze of her hand. "I guess I didn't hear you."

I CIRCLE BACK TO MY FATHER. I PEEKED IN ON HIM EARLIER, BUT he was asleep. He got it worse than Aubrey, but he's going to be all right. Nothing vital hit, thank goodness. They put some blood back into him, put him on IV antibiotics, and made him an appointment with a cosmetic surgeon back home to deal with the burns we made to stop his bleeding. Mom, who's in the adjoining room, already cancelled that appointment. She told me Dad said he likes his scars. They're battle wounds, hard-won from his eldest daughter.

Eldest. God, it's so crazy. Until yesterday, I wouldn't bother with the adjective, because "daughter" was enough. It hasn't settled in that I have a sister, with me "eldest" by just a few months. Unlike so many sisters, we even get along.

I think Dad is still out, but just as I'm about to leave again he speaks my name.

I move to his bedside.

"You're awake."

"Ish," says Dad.

"Do you want me to come back later?"

He takes my hand just as Aubrey did. "I want you to stay."

I consider telling him what I just told Aubrey — about how everything might actually be okay for all of us — but the topic feels too heavy for the moment. Truth is, the bullshit version of our story only falls apart if anyone asks questions, and Charlie's brothers won't ask them. It's karmic repayment they feel they owe for the time they couldn't help Charlie. They weren't there in time for their own sister's time of crisis, so they came in force for mine.

I hear Charlie's voice from yesterday, low and gravestone-serious: *There's law, and there's what's right ... and if there's one thing we understand around here, it's that blood is blood, and family is family.*

Nobody will wonder. Ross's dad's been MIA his entire life, and his mother's a basket case. News has already made it back to the college that Ross had an accident. I don't think he'll be missed. When I called the dean's office, they told me that Ross was under campus investigation for sexual misconduct. When everything settles, I don't think Cassie and Aubrey will turn out to be his only victims.

Poor dumb monster, falling to his death. And yet the karmic wheel keeps right on turning.

"Miranda, I'm s—"

I cut him off. I'm tired of sorries.

"No. Stop. If I'm not sorry, you don't get to be sorry."

"It's not that simple."

"It's exactly that simple. I'm telling you I'm good. Insisting on apologizing is just you trying to make yourself feel better. I don't want the drama. So stop being selfish, you selfish prick."

He smiles. Then he says sarcastically: "Miranda. *Language.*"

I reach into my bag, hanging at my side. The paper thing inside is collapsed, so I pop it back into its proper cone shape. I put it on my father's head, using the elastic string on its base.

"Did you just put a party hat on me?"

"Absolutely not," I say. Then I use my phone to take a picture of Dad looking ridiculous, wearing his party hat in the hospital.

"Why?"

"Because this is a celebration."

He laughs. It turns to coughing.

"I'm serious," I say. "Don't tell me you forgot."

"Forgot what?"

"It's Sunday."

"So?"

"*Sunday*, Dad. *Sunday.*"

"I get it. But what does Sunday..." He stops, understanding. "My anniversary."

"One year sober." I've got a noisemaker in my bag too, so I push it between his lips.

"Kind of a weird thing for my daughter to celebrate." But then he realizes why that is and sighs. "We never talked about it, did we? It was our family's dirty little secret."

"About sobriety?"

"About alcoholism."

Neither of us says anything. It's true. Dad's disease was like a bulldozer in the middle of every family gathering, and we all pretended it wasn't there.

"It's okay," I say. "We're talking about it now."

"I didn't want to burden you with it. You were a child."

"I'm not a child anymore."

He thinks on that. When he looks back up at me, I know he's

finally accepted it: *I'm not a child anymore.* If our past few days have proven anything, that's it. I saw the same realization in Mom earlier today. Their habits of micromanaging and henpecking me will take time to go away, but at least I finally believe that both of my parents — at conscious levels, at least — have shown those things the door.

"Cassie," I say.

It's out of the blue. "What about her?"

"When are you going to tell her that you're her father?"

He looks away and shrugs.

"You *are* going to tell her, right?"

"I don't know. I'm the monster next door, Miranda."

"She doesn't see it that way. Frank was beating her. She told me you did her a favor."

"But she was just..."

"...a child?"

Dad says nothing.

"Cassie's not a child anymore either, Dad."

"All I ever wanted was to protect you," Dad says. "Not just from the Franks and Rosses of the world, but from all its ugliness. I didn't mean to keep secrets. Not from you, not from her, not from anyone I love. It was a rough time. I did what seemed best. That way, Cassie had her family, and you had yours."

His eyes water, but he's a hard man and won't let himself cry.

"I did what I thought was best," he finishes, "and look what it got both of you."

"I'm okay, Dad." I squeeze his hand. "I need you to believe me when I say that."

"But what about Cassie? I abandoned her. She grew up with an abusive stepfather, then *no* father. After her mother died, she had nobody at all. When I saw the ring, the one Ross stole from her," he adds, and his eyes grow dark, "it brought everything crashing back. I didn't want to leave her, you know. I had to, but I didn't want to. I gave her mother that ring to give to her as a gesture. I didn't know if she'd believe it, but I needed her to know that her father would always love her ... from wherever he was, even if it was just across the driveway."

"She believed it."

"You think so?"

I nod. "I know so."

"So you really think I should do it, huh?"

"I do. She'll have a dad. She'll have a sister. Mom didn't have to help you, you know. I talked to her this morning. Mom was as protective of Cassie as you were. She'll inherit a whole new family if you can just get over yourself enough to say something. She won't have to be alone anymore."

Dad still looks doubtful. "Minds don't change that easily. It's still true that I walked out on her. She might not forgive me for it."

"Come on," I say, goading now. "If I understood about Frank, Cassie will understand this ... and my father always told me there are two sides to every story."

Abby

REAL LIFE SUPERDOG

Author's Note

This book is more personal than any book I've written before.

As I write this Author's Note, I'm sitting in an Austin-area coffee shop drinking a chestnut latte. It's not Mozart's, if you know Austin and its coffee shops. It's a chain called Summer Moon, and all I can think now that I've written what I've written is that I *should* have gone to Mozart's. Mozart's is rad. It's right on the lake. You can sit, hang out, and watch the ducks.

In the chair beside me is my 16-year-old daughter Sydney, who's doing her homework. I'm lucky as a dad. Not only do I have two great kids (my eldest is a sophomore at UT, but he's not relevant to this particular story); both of them still like hanging out with me even as teens and beyond. Syd and I even have a regular coffee shop day. I read or work while she does her thing. Sometimes, when the load is light, we play card games.

Laying beside Sydney in her big poofy chair — waiting for when she finishes her homework — is a paperback copy of this book.

It's an early copy, dog-eared and worn. It doesn't have the little chapter heading images that are in the version you're holding, and the cover is a little different. There's no front matter or back matter; the pages contain story and nothing more. That's because when I finished *Winter Break,* I didn't want to take the time to bother with any of that for my first reader. Instead, I uploaded the original, stripped-down copy of the manuscript so I could order a paperback as soon as possible: a single proof copy for Syd because she doesn't read e-books.

Come back in time with me a bit, will you?

Not long ago, when the two of us were camping (my wife hates sleeping anywhere but her bed and my son isn't a big fan of nature), I sat down with my book and Sydney sat down with hers: a young adult thriller called *Five Total Strangers*. In the past, I'd seen her reading *A Good Girl's Guide to Murder* and *The Inheritance Games*. But as we sat and read in the open air that day, something hit me. I realized: *I have a kid who's a reader. I'm a writer. Maybe I should do something about that.*

We started talking about books, and what kinds grabbed her attention. After warming to the topic, I pitched the idea of writing a book for her, but I positioned it as a quasi-collaboration: She wouldn't have anything to do with writing it, but she'd guide it over-all: What were the things she liked and didn't like in the books she read? What would make for an interesting story — one she'd like to read, and one she'd tell her friends about? One, I hoped selfishly, that she'd take pride in sharing: *My dad wrote this,* I imagined her bragging.

So we talked. And I did my research. In addition to Sydney's input, I also wanted to understand the type of book I'd need to write. I wasn't sure I could do it. I tend to write complex stories, for instance, so I needed to make sure the target books weren't too simple. And while I can write clean, I prefer to get gritty ... so I wanted to see, too, what indiscretions the "young adult" genre got away with. I also wasn't sure I'd get the teen voices right, so I ran early chapters by Syd. I told her to be honest. Did I write like her peers talk, or did my characters talk like they were written by a 48-year-old poseur?

I wrote this book for my daughter. As I write this to you, she's finished her homework and is now curled up in the big coffee shop chair, reading it. Yesterday, I showed her the chapter icons I've added but that aren't in her early copy. And so, just now, she asked me: *Dad — if Miranda is the house and Aubrey is the dog, what's* Ross's *image?*

And I said, *It's a rope.*

Such a simple answer. And yet, oh so amazing to be fortunate enough to give it.

There's nothing quite like including the people you love in your art. I've included my son, a visual artist, in the past as well; he's drawn illustrations for a special edition of *Fat Vampire* I'll publish in 2025. I've always felt fortunate to be able to create for a living, but this is the first time it's been this one-to-one. This *direct*. This *unambiguously, deliriously connected to the life I live every day.*

Once I knew that Sydney would be my primary reader, I started including all sorts of little Easter eggs in the book that only she'd recognize. No, I'm not going to tell you what they are. They're for us, and us alone. That's what makes them special. It's a very cool feeling, knowing there's a private connection hidden in a story that so many others will read. I hope you have a chance to experience something like it, because nothing remotely compares.

One thing I will share is that the dog in *Winter Break* is my real dog. Her name is Abby. That's her picture at the top of all of the Aubrey chapters, as well as at the end of the story, wearing her Supergirl outfit. I don't remember for sure, but I think I added Abby to the story just to be ridiculous, not because the story required a dog.

Not long before I wrote *Winter Break*, Abby arbitrarily started making complex sounds that we lumped under the all-encompassing header of "dog noises." It sounded like she was saying words, like *burlap* and *Albuquerque*. So because that was funny in my household, it ended up in Sydney's book. I knew who'd be reading it first, after all, and how amused she'd be. The way I figured it, if I was going to write a love letter to my family, I might as well pull out all the stops.

(Side note: The decision for Abby to save the day by biting Ross in the crotch was more for my wife than Sydney. She's pretty lowbrow, appreciating complex humor like the toilet scenes in *American Pie* and *White Chicks* ... and, of course, whenever someone gets hit in the nuts with a ball on *AFV*. You're welcome, darling.)

The story itself was a joy to write, above and beyond its personal meaning. I never know where a plot will go when I begin, so I only learned the story's many twists moments before writing them. I didn't know that Aubrey would get a point of view, for instance, until she needed one. Originally, I figured the entire book would be told from Miranda's perspective. But then I reached the scene where Miranda finally discovers what her parents have been hiding and I thought to myself, "Well, *this* clearly requires a reset." That's when I knew I needed to back away and leave Miranda's story on a cliffhanger, and the only other place to go was to restart, in a way, with Aubrey.

And of course once I did that much, the door swung wide open. Ross and Cassie got a POV, as did Mark — whoever I needed to tell that part of the story. Layer upon surprising layer, the story took shape. It became much more intricate and satisfying than I'd ever hoped.

When Aubrey started worrying and headed out to reach Miranda, that too surprised me. At that point, the story stopped feeling like a straightforward thriller and took on a claustrophobic vibe full of dark and cold. When it happened, it made me think of my all-time favorite read: *The Shining*. And so — sometimes consciously and sometimes without realizing it — I began paying homage to King's novel in mine. There's even a moment where the similarity became *so* apparent that I decided to lean into it: In *The Shining*, when Dick Halloran is rushing through the snow to save the Torrence family from the ghost-ridden Overlook Hotel, there's a chapter called "Halloran Laid Low." At that point I remember wishing that *Winter Break* had chapter names, because if it did, there'd have been one there called "Aubrey Laid Low."

What was it Picasso said? "Good artists borrow. Great artists steal." *Look, Ma! Look how great I am!*

Apparently.

I'm excited to see how the world likes *Winter Break,* but if I'm being honest, it doesn't really matter. The only reader whose opinion I truly care about — the reader for whom I wrote it — already likes it. I'm fast and I'm prolific; I have words to spare and more than enough to go around ... and so in the big picture, it wouldn't have bothered me if I'd never published this book. It served its purpose the second my girl cracked the spine.

But now that the world has it, I hope the world enjoys it.

And I wish you happiness as abundant as writing this book has made me.

Johnny B. Truant
Austin, Texas
November 21, 2024

What Next?

This where I suggest the book you should read next to spare you hours of searching, right? Cool. I can do that.

All of my MANY books (and their suggested reading order) are at JohnnyBTruantBooks.com, but personally I'd suggest:

PRETTY KILLER: A neo-noir dinner party mystery dripping with feminine revenge.

Twelve strangers follow a mysterious invitation to an elite restaurant only to learn they're not actually strangers at all. Each attendee hides a deadly secret, but one knows the biggest secret of all: *What happened to Casey Davis?*

You can get *Pretty Killer* from the usual bookstores, or you can get it cheaper at JohnnyBTruantBooks.com

Enter the Truantverse

When it comes to stories and the worlds they live in, books are only the beginning.

Visit JohnnyBTruant.com/join to get my best books sooner and cheaper than the other stores.

My list doesn't suck like so many author email lists. Seriously. It has unicorns.

Also by Johnny B. Truant

Winter Break

Pattern Black

Pretty Killer

Cursed

The Bialy Pimps

Namaste

The Target

La Fleur de Blanc

Axis of Aaron

Devil May Care

Screenplay

The Island

Burnout

Sick and Wired

UNICORN WESTERN:

Unicorn Western

The Wanderers

A Fistful of Magic

Shimmer to Yuma

The Man Who Shot Alan Whitney

The Spectacular Seven

Open Meadows

The Unforgotten

The Magic Bunch

Unicorn Genesis

FAT VAMPIRE:

Fat Vampire

Fat Vampire 2: Tastes Like Chicken

Fat Vampire 3: All You Can Eat

Fat Vampire 4: Harder Better Fatter Stronger

Fat Vampire 5: Fatpocalypse

Fat Vampire 6: Survival of the Fattest

The Vampire Maurice

Anarchy and Blood

Vampires in the White City

Fangs and Fame

Game of Fangs

INVASION:

Invasion

Contact

Colonization

Annihilation

Judgment

Extinction

Resurrection

Save the City

Save the Girl

Save the World

Longshot

THE INEVITABLE:

Robot Proletariat

The Infinite Loop

The Hard Reset

Cascade Failure

Reboot

En3my

DEAD CITY:

Dead City

Dead Nation

Dead Planet

Dead Zero

Empty Nest

THE DREAM ENGINE:

The Dream Engine

The Nightmare Factory

The Ruby Room

The Pandora Core

The Engine Convergence

The Tinkerer's Mainspring

GORE POINT:

Gore Point

City of Fire

THE BEAM:

The Beam: Season One

The Beam: Season Two

The Beam: Season Three

The Beam Season Four

The Beam Season Five

Future Proof

Plugged

The Future of Sex

THE TOMORROW GENE:

The Tomorrow Gene

The Eden Experiment

The Tomorrow Clone

Null Identity

COMEDIES:

Everyone Gets Divorced

Greens

Fiends

Decoy Wallet

NONFICTION:

The Fiction Formula

Fiction Unboxed

Iterate & Optimize

The Story Solution

Write. Publish. Repeat.

The One With All the Writing Advice